THE PACT

Hilary Norman's most recent novel is *Susanna*:

'Norman is at the top of her form here. Part thriller, part psychological character study, *Susanna* is an unusually satisfying read.' *Chicago Tribune*

'This searing novel showcases Ms Norman's impressive ability to build poignant drama filled with deep and intricate characterizations.' *Romantic Times*

* * *

'Hilary Norman is in the Rosamunde Pilcher class.' *Sunday Telegraph*

'An internationally acclaimed author of darkly passionate romantic sagas.' *Publishing News*

'An honest-to-goodness storyteller. Her integrity is rare.' *Jewish Chronicle*

'One of the best saga writers.' *Bookseller*

'An accomplished novelist.' *New York Times Book Review*

Also by Hilary Norman and available from Coronet Books

In Love and Friendship
Chateau Ella
Shattered Stars
Fascination
Spellbound
Laura
Susanna

Writing as Alexandra Henry

If I Should Die

About the Author

Hilary Norman was born and educated in London. After working as an actress, she had careers in the fashion and broadcasting industries. She travelled extensively throughout Europe and lived for a time in the United States before writing her international bestseller, *In Love and Friendship*, which has now been translated into ten languages. She still lives in London, where she is now writing her ninth novel.

The Pact

Hilary Norman

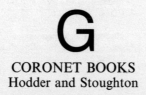

CORONET BOOKS
Hodder and Stoughton

Copyright © 1997 by Hilary Norman

The right of Hilary Norman to be identified as the Author
of the Work has been asserted by her in accordance with the
Copyright, Designs and Patents Act 1988.

First published in Great Britain in 1997 by Hodder and Stoughton
A division of Hodder Headline PLC
First published in paperback in 1997 by Hodder and Stoughton
A Coronet Paperback

10 9 8 7 6 5 4 3 2 1

A CIP catalogue record for this title
is available from the British Library

ISBN 0 340 68880 7

Typeset by Hewer Text Composition Services, Edinburgh
Printed and bound in Great Britain by
Clays Ltd, St Ives PLC

Hodder and Stoughton
A division of Hodder Headline PLC
338 Euston Road
London NW1 3BH

For my mother, Herta Norman,
still my first reader and critic

Acknowledgements

Grateful thanks are due, as always, to many people, old and new friends, and as usual, I list them in alphabetical order:

Staff at The American School, London; the concierge at the Hotel Amigo in Brussels for answering my many strange and unusual questions; Dorothy and David W. Balfour, for going out of their way (literally) to help me, yet again; Howard M. Barmad; Carolyn Caughey; my cat, Charlotte, for helping me understand Cleo; the public relations department of Eurostar; Sara Fisher; Jim Gilles of the *Newport Daily News*; John Hawkins; Jonathan Kern, my husband, for many things (including knowing when I'm a no-go area); Audrey LaFehr; special, sincere gratitude to Mr Nicholas Parkhouse, D.M., M.Ch., F.R.C.S., for his expertise, valuable time and kindness; Mr Robert Purdy at St Mary's Church in Newport, Rhode Island; Helen Rose, my sister, who always helps, and Neal Rose, who seriously helped this time; Lynne Sacks for her British advertising know-how; Dr Jonathan Tarlow, who always guides me through the medical mire, but who really came through in a major way for this one; Michael Thomas; Norman Waterman for his US advertising knowledge and experience; and the staff of the Westminster and Wiener Libraries for their guidance.

Greek mythology tells us that when Pandora, overcome by curiosity, opened the box that she had been forbidden to open, she released from it all the evils and ills that would beset man, leaving only hope within.

1

PROLOGUE

Brussels: July 26th, 1995

Olivia Segal sat, with Cleo, her little tortoiseshell cat, on her lap, on the faded Kashan silk prayer rug and looked up at the clock.

Seven minutes past five in the afternoon in Brussels. Seven past eleven in the morning in New York.

She picked up her little black Ericsson phone, ready finally to make her last resort call. The Belgian police had been courteous and kind enough, she supposed, but she knew they hadn't really believed her story, knew they thought she was crazy, and she had tried and failed again to reach Jamie, and now there was no one left to try but Annie.

Jamie and Annie. Her two dearest friends in the world. Olivia wished, more than anything, that she could have spared them both this – she had tried so hard to handle it alone. But now she was too afraid. She had never considered herself a coward – Annie was always telling her how tough she was – but at that moment, with her left arm broken and the mass of still-darkening bruises flowering over her rib cage and legs, Olivia, all alone in her beautiful but suddenly vulnerable home – about to use a cellular telephone in case her land line had been bugged, for God's sake – was more than afraid. She was terrified. And not just for herself. For all she knew, Jamie – darling, blissfully unaware Jamie – might already be in danger. And from the moment Olivia took Annie into her confidence, from the instant she shared the long-hidden, dark, *monstrous* secrets of the box she had opened, Pandora-like, Annie too might be equally at risk.

Olivia considered, for at least the hundredth time, leaving it all alone, trying to push the ugly truths to the back of her mind. Maybe if she stopped now, kept silent now, they might leave her alone, let her try to forget. Let her live. But Olivia knew that was no longer really a possibility. For one thing, her conscience would not allow her to forget; she owed it to the ghosts, to the long-dead victims, to let the truth be told. To give justice a fighting chance.

And besides, she knew they would not let her live.

It was eight minutes past five.

Olivia made the call.

Annie Aldrich Thomas put down the phone, still sitting on the edge of the king-sized bed, and stared around at the lovely room she was sharing with her husband Edward at the St Regis Hotel. It all looked so normal, just as it had a few minutes earlier, before Olivia's call. Yet nothing, Annie knew, was really the same, not for her. Not any more.

She stood up and walked mechanically into the bathroom, got into the shower and tried to gather her wild, racing thoughts. For one thing, she was due to meet Edward for lunch at twelve-thirty, and now she would have to call and leave word, make an excuse, and she knew that Edward wouldn't mind too much, but Annie hated lying to him, had told too many lies in her own troubled past. Though this time she had no alternative, because it was Olivia who was in trouble and there were things that Olivia needed Annie to do for her. And Annie knew that Olivia would never have made that call if she hadn't been desperate, because even though eight years had passed since her own problems, Olivia and Jamie both still had a tendency to protect Annie from bad things.

They didn't come any worse than this.

She got out of the shower and started drying her hair. In the twenty-something years she had known Olivia, Annie could not remember her ever being really frightened of anything. Calm Olivia. Clever, independent Olivia. The coolest, the most self-sufficient, the boldest of them all. But just now, on the telephone, Annie had recognized actual terror in her friend's voice.

'I wanted to keep it from you,' Olivia had said, breathless and low. 'But I can't seem to find Jamie, and there *is* no one else I can trust, and I can't go on alone.'

'It's all right,' Annie had said, gently. 'You don't have to.'

So Olivia had told her. And now nothing, Annie realized with a sick, awful chill, would ever be the same again.

In his suite at his family's twenty-five room Ocean Drive 'cottage' in Newport, Rhode Island, Jamie Arias was sitting in a comfortable old armchair beneath a Vuillard original of which he had always been fond, re-reading a dog-eared edition of *War and Peace*, and putting off going downstairs to join the others. He had come for his cousin Michael's fifty-second birthday celebrations, but Jamie planned on spending no more time at the Arias compound than he had to because it was hard these days – as the others all realized – for him to be around Peter, his older brother, for too long.

3

Jamie did not intend to allow Michael's birthday to be ruined by family sniping. He had nothing but respect for his cousin, always had, for Michael Arias had been the head of their family for almost twenty years now, since Jamie's and Peter's father had died, and Michael had returned that respect by leaving Jamie to get on with his own life. Yet still, respect aside, they had little in common except blood, and Jamie would be frankly relieved when it was time to get away from the too-large, art and antique laden Newport house, glad to get back to his own place in Boston, back to work at the agency. His own life – modest beside the Arias wealth – but his own.

Sitting now in the comfort of his sitting room, immersed yet again in Tolstoy, Jamie was quite unaware that Olivia had been trying to reach him. Had no idea that she was in danger. If he had known that, he would have been out of Newport and on the first flight to Brussels, family celebrations or not. No matter what.

Anna and Olivia in trouble – especially Olivia, if he allowed himself to be honest – came first with Jamie. Before family. Before everything. They had done for the last nineteen years.

The small black phone on the floor beside her, still wishing she could have reached Jamie but comforted nevertheless by the sound of Annie's reassuring voice, Olivia remained painfully huddled on the rug on the parquet floor of her Brussels living room. Staying away from the windows, wishing for the very first time that she had chosen a less intimate high-rise instead of her characterful, ground-floor apartment, Olivia was aware that some of the trembling and just a little of the sick, clenched feeling in her stomach had eased.

She had known since leaving London that all she had to do was make two calls and Annie and Jamie would drop everything and come to her. It was one of the unwritten rules of their pact, made so many years before when they had all sworn to be there for each other, no matter how far apart they were living – no matter how heavily committed they might be, to family or to work, to *anything*.

She and Jamie had been there for Annie eight years ago during her troubles, and three years after that she and Annie had been there for Jamie when he had needed them. Being there for each other was what they were all about, and now that Annie knew what was going on, she was sure to follow Olivia's instructions, and then she would find Jamie, and they would come to her.

The real question, the truly frightening question, was, would they get there in time?

2

Olivia's Box

The story had lain inside the thick cardboard box, sealed shut with shiny brown tape and locked into the black, airless vault beneath Leadenhall Street in the City of London, for almost twenty years. Its author had been a young man named Anton Rothenburg; its guardian for all those years, one Paul Walter Osterman of Philadelphia. A seeker after justice, Osterman had carried the weight of the Family Rothenburg's tale of evil for a quarter of a century until, close to death, he had passed the burden to another man who – understanding the enormity of what Osterman had given him – had, in turn, placed it for safekeeping inside the vault.

I never knew Anton Rothenburg [Osterman had written] nor his parents or his two sisters. Their tale was passed on to me by a total stranger, a man taken into confidence by seventeen-year-old Anton when they were both nearing their lowest ebb. It was a tale I never asked or wished to hear, but once the horror had burned its scars into my mind, into my soul, I knew they could never be eradicated.

The story changed me – I can't say exactly why. I'd heard many other tales, of course, worse tales, of that nightmare period, and was always appalled by them, but the feelings of sorrow and rage had always moved on after a time, had shifted sufficiently – as such things must – to enable me to go on with my own life. Yet when I learned what had happened to that particular family in Nazi Germany, I became so profoundly affected that my own everyday existence seemed to fade into insignificance and never returned into its formerly sharp, clear-cut focus.

I did not know Emanuel Rothenburg, Anton's father, yet I suppose he reminded me, in some ways, of my own father. He, too, was born in the town of Baden-Baden – though unlike Emanuel Rothenburg he came to live, peacefully, and to die, in the United States. My father, too, loved fine art. I remember, at an early age, watching him standing for the longest time before a beautiful painting in the Philadelphia Museum of Art, remember the look on his face, the passion in his eyes, as he gazed at it. I think maybe I understand just a little of the depth of emotion that a wonderful piece of art can stir in a human soul. My father died many years ago, of natural causes, with his wife and son at his deathbed, loving him, bringing him comfort. Emanuel Rothenburg died when a bullet pierced his brain. After he had already lost much of what had been precious to him.

Once I had heard and read the story of the Rothenburgs, I knew that I was changed forever. Once I'd learned about that tale of evil deeds, I felt that I had been somehow charged with trying to avenge their memory.

I have failed to do that, and now my own time is almost up. Yet the torch still burns fiercely in my mind, and hope still surges. And so I'm doing the only thing I still can.

Passing on the torch.

3

The Pact 1976–1986

They stood together, about halfway up Dukesfield Fell, twenty or so rugged miles south-west of Newcastle-upon-Tyne and ten miles south of Hadrian's Wall, where it had happened a decade earlier to that very day. It was a little after noon on July 4th, 1986, and they had climbed a long way to reach the spot, yet Olivia, Jamie and Annie all felt chilled to the bone. They said it was the wind, blowing from the east off the North Sea, cold enough, they said, to rip the warmth from the hottest day; but they all knew that the chill came from within, from remembering.

'Maybe this was a mistake,' Olivia said.

She looked at Annie's white face and felt a sharp pang of guilt because she had organized the day, had pushed and harried and prodded them, the way she always did when she believed in something, *wanted* something to happen, and now Annie looked as if she might pass out and Jamie just looked so sad, so bleak. And it could all have been so much easier, they could all have met up in London and had lunch someplace civilized – the Connaught maybe, eating roast beef and drinking something red and wonderful –

and they'd have been warm and ten years past the grief, instead of standing on this lovely, terrible hill and seeing it all again in their minds – and when would she ever *learn*?

'I don't think it was a mistake,' Annie said, softly, kindly.

'Nor do I,' Jamie echoed on her other side.

Olivia felt gratitude and love pass through her, felt a little of the ice inside her melt away along with the guilt. She never felt guilty for long; it was not in her nature, she supposed. 'I guess maybe we did have to come,' she said. 'No other place we could really be today.'

They linked arms, stood still and silent for a while, eyes closed, letting themselves rerun the old images in their minds. They had not been allowed to see the wreckage at first hand back in '76, but the pictures on television had been graphic enough. The debris had been strewn over a considerable distance, but the main part of the cabin had lain here, beneath their feet. With the bodies.

'Anyone want to say anything?' Olivia asked, after a while.

'I don't think so,' Jamie answered.

'I think we've said it all,' Annie said. 'They know what we think.'

No one spoke for a time. The wind blew harder, nipped at their ears, tore at the roots of their hair, drove the gentle, summery scents of grass and soil and wild flowers into their faces, brought back again the ugly discordance of that dreadful remembered time when fire and death had scorched savage scars into the hillside.

'Shall we?' Jamie said, at last.

'I'm ready,' Annie said.

They both looked at Olivia.

'Livvy?' Annie said.

Olivia nodded. 'Yes.'

They walked away slowly, arms still linked until the narrowness of the path forced them to separate, and then they reached the road and the hired car waiting to take them back to Riverdale Hall, a country house hotel near Hexham where Olivia had booked rooms. Restored by hot showers, changes of clothes, one shot of malt whisky apiece – even for Annie, who seldom drank wine and never touched spirits – and a fine lunch of freshly caught wild salmon, the three friends felt themselves coming slowly back to the present, felt the memories slipping and sliding away again, for the original rawness had long since gone, the jagged edges smoothed over by time and life.

'Ten years,' Olivia said later, after lunch, as they walked near the river. 'Who would have thought it possible ten years ago that we could ever be happy again? Ever be normal again.'

'Yet here we are,' Jamie said. 'Annie a mother of three – me an old married man—'

'Even if it is to Carrie,' Olivia said wryly.

'Livvy, don't,' Annie scolded.

'We both know what Olivia thinks of Carrie,' Jamie said lightly. 'And you too, Annie, even if you are too nice a person to say it out loud.'

'Meaning I'm not a nice person?' Olivia enquired.

'You're a very honest person,' Jamie said, and smiled.

'I know.' Olivia kicked at a clod of earth. The sun had broken through the clouds, and it was warm now, the wind just a gentle breeze. Dukesfield Fell seemed a million miles away. 'I guess I'll never be as nice as either of you two, which is probably why I'll stay an old maid.'

'You enjoy sex too much to qualify as an old maid,' Jamie said.

'So now I'm not nice *and* a slut. And I'm pushy too.'

'True,' Jamie said. 'But we love you anyway.'

'What you are,' Annie said reflectively, 'is a natural leader.'

'No, I'm not.'

'Sure you are,' Annie said.

'You're our motivating force,' Jamie agreed. 'You keep us together, no matter how many thousands of miles we drift apart.' He stopped walking and looked around. 'This'd be a good spot for some photos.'

The bringing of cameras to each of their reunions was one of their rituals, the updating of the records they had all kept of one another for so long. Whenever and wherever they came together, it always seemed to them as if nothing had changed; they *felt* the same, their friendship was the same. Only the photographs, pored over later, would record that petite, golden-haired, blue-eyed, exquisitely-turned-out Annie had grown perhaps a little too thin; or that sleek, elegant, worldly looking Jamie's dark eyes had new care lines around them or that his almost black hair had one or two silvery threads; or that within the frame of Olivia's dark-brown, bouncing mass of hair, her mobile, expressive, strong face with its not quite perfect nose, its slightly Slavic cheekbones and striking green eyes, a little of the youthfulness – of the carefree, sometimes careless, spark that had always been her trademark – had been rubbed away by passing years.

'When you say I'm your leader,' Olivia said later, photographs snapped, 'what you really mean is that I bully you.'

'True,' Jamie said.

'I prod you, I nag at you. I drive you both nuts until we find a way of getting back together again.'

'Every time,' Annie said.

'And we love you for it,' Jamie added, warmly.

'It's why we're here today,' Annie said. 'You're why we're here.'

'That's not true,' Olivia said. 'We're here because of what today is.'

'Not entirely.' Jamie shook his head. 'Perhaps not at all. If it hadn't been for you, Annie and I would probably have let the day go by – oh, we'd have called each other, and I guess we'd have raised a glass or two to them, but we wouldn't have climbed up to Dukesfield Fell. And, more importantly, we would have been apart.' He paused. 'Mostly because we'd have chosen not to face up to it. We're not as brave as you are, Olivia.'

She flushed. 'That's nonsense.'

'It isn't, Livvy,' Annie argued. 'I'm a dreadful coward.'

'You've had three babies,' Olivia reminded her.

'Having babies is the easy part of life,' Annie said.

'You and Jamie have both had the courage to make commitments.'

'You've had the strength to stay alone,' Jamie told her.

'I'm not alone,' Olivia said, softly. 'I have you two.'

Other people, outsiders – like Edward Thomas who had married Annie in 1981, and, a few years later, Caroline Beaumont, who had become Jamie's wife – tended to assume at first that the pact between the three friends had been sealed during their schooldays. It was a natural enough assumption for them to reach, for it seemed the kind of passionate covenant usually entered into by emotional adolescents and, after all, Olivia, Jamie and Annie had attended that enclave of the United States in Britain: the American School in London's leafy St John's Wood, a coeducational day school committed to helping young Americans away from their homeland ease into and grow in their new environment.

It was certainly true that Jamie, Annie and Olivia had developed a fairly close friendship at the school and that their parents, too, were acquainted with each other, but there had been nothing overly intense about the friendship back then. They had shared classes and outings and gossip; Olivia and Jamie had played basketball and watched Annie play violin in the chamber orchestra; they had gone on field trips together and had liked each other very well, but they'd all had other friendships too. Thanks to their good fortune, none of them had ever felt like insecure foreigners tossed into an alien or hostile environment. Like many of their contemporaries, Olivia, Jamie and Annie all hailed from secure family backgrounds, their lives, either temporarily or permanently, being lived in England instead of back home in the United States. Annie's father, Franklin Aldrich, was a partner in an old and trusted international law practice and, at that time, heading the London office, and their English home was a splendid mews house near Belgrave Square immaculately organized by Grace Aldrich, Annie's mother. Jamie's father, Carlos Arias – a widower of distinguished Spanish descent left with two sons of his own and the care of the son of his late brother and sister-in-law – headed the venerable Arias shipping empire from their Pall Mall offices and ruled, with gentle command, their sumptuous Regent's Park apartment. And Olivia's mother, Emily Segal, was a cardiac consultant at Great Ormond Street Hospital for Sick Children, while her father, Arthur Segal, worked from their house near Kenwood in Hampstead collecting art and antiques and raising funds for numerous charities that encompassed Simon Wiesenthal's Nazi-hunting centre in Vienna and other Jewish charities, as well as UNICEF and whichever current, needy appeal captured his sympathetic eye.

At eighteen, just graduated from the High School, Olivia Segal, Jamie Arias and Annie Aldrich had been secure, confident, successful and contented young people. With the exception of Jamie's mother's sudden death from cancer nine years earlier, nothing grievous had ever befallen any of them.

Until the Fourth of July that year, 1976.

Years later, they all remembered where they were and what they had been doing immediately before they heard the news. That was, of course, what people always said about President Kennedy's assassination, but Olivia, Jamie and Annie had been just five years old at that time and had, therefore, no true memories of their own, just the awareness, passed through to them later, of a vast, daunting, adult, collective grief. What happened to them on Independence Day of 1976 was so entirely personal, so infinitely and intimately shattering, that their memories of that day were etched, and would be forever, like deep, sharp, painful carvings, upon each of their minds.

They had all just arrived at David Orbach's party in Dulwich. The Orbachs had a big house in several acres of garden with a swimming pool and tennis courts, and their Fourth of July parties were famous both for their lavishness and for the shenanigans reported by all those fortunate enough to attend them. Jamie had gone the previous year and had come back to school to tell Annie – whose parents had not let her go – that contrary to popular myth no one had swum nude, but any number had dived into the pool with their clothes still on; and he'd told Olivia – who hadn't been able to go either because her parents wanted her at their own party at home – that he'd seen not a single sign of a real-live orgy, though he'd seldom seen so much unabashed necking in an arena where parents were present.

This year they were all going partly because they were eighteen, but mostly because all their parents were flying up to Scotland for an Independence Day celebration in aid of one of Olivia's father's charities. That, of course, meant there would be no arguments about what they decided to wear, no curfew that night and no repercussions next morning if they showed up long after breakfast and with hangovers.

'What are you wearing?' Olivia asked Annie on the phone at five o'clock that afternoon.

'A dress my mother bought me in New York last month.'

'What's it like?'

'White crepe, with a halter neck.'

'Long?'

'Yes.' Annie sounded suddenly uncertain. 'Is that all right, do you think?'

'It sounds gorgeous. You always look lovely,' Olivia said, meaning it.

'What about you?' Annie asked.

'I've been shopping. You'll hate it,' Olivia added with relish.

'Why should I hate it?'

'I waited for Mom and Dad to leave,' Olivia said, 'and then I went right over to this little boutique off Heath Street – I'd already asked them to hold everything for me.'

'What did you buy?' Annie was intrigued. Olivia Segal came from a family not quite, but almost as conventional as her own, yet Annie thought Olivia the most exciting person she knew.

'I've gone punk – well, kind of punk, anyway.'

'You haven't.'

'Would you believe black Bermudas and a black silk camisole?'

'You're kidding.' Annie was half aghast, half impressed.

'And I found this really wild studded belt *and* a pair of those wrap-around sunglasses we saw in *Vogue*. And a dog chain necklace.' Olivia stopped short of telling Annie that she'd had scarlet streaks sprayed into her dark hair.

'It sounds – lovely.' Annie hesitated.

'But?'

'Isn't it black tie tonight?'

'I forgot to buy a tie.'

'I didn't mean that, Livvy.'

'I know you didn't, Annie.' Olivia liked teasing Annie.

'What if they don't let you in?'

'They will. Jamie said that some people were dressed pretty wildly last year.'

'Still, a *dog* chain—' Annie was lost for words.

'David Orbach has a German shepherd,' Olivia said confidently. 'I can always take it off and pretend it was a present for him.'

The party was due to begin at eight-thirty, and Annie had told Olivia that she and Jamie had arranged to get a lift with Jenny Lee Barnsworth, another student from the American School, and there was plenty of room in Jenny's car if Olivia wanted to join them; but Olivia had already made plans to go with Bill Murray, who lived in Highgate, much closer to the Segals than either the Aldriches or the Ariases, and she and Bill were probably going to have a drink somewhere en route to Dulwich, and no, she and Bill were not an item, but he was an okay guy, and it was a long drive, so she might as well enjoy it.

By the time Olivia and Bill got to the party, the driveway and the street were jammed with cars, and Bill, a gentleman, let Olivia out at the house while he went off to hunt for a parking space. Her gift for David Orbach in her right hand, her small black bag swinging from her left shoulder, Olivia headed jauntily across the big gravel drive towards the brilliantly lit house.

She saw Jamie almost immediately, standing in the entrance hall, saw that his face was ashen and that he seemed to have been weeping, and that David Orbach, close by, was looking at her strangely.

'What's wrong?' Her voice caught in her throat. 'Jamie, what's happened?'

He looked so strange, so perfectly, immaculately dressed in his tuxedo and black tie – Jamie was always such a lovely mix of slenderness and strength – yet at the same time he looked somehow, Olivia thought with a sudden and terrible fear, destroyed.

'Our parents,' he said, in a whisper.

'What about them?' Olivia found she still had David Orbach's gift in her hand, and she pushed it at David and reached out to seize Jamie's left arm. 'What's happened, Jamie?'

He shook his head.

'Jamie, what? *Tell* me.'

Behind her, Bill Murray came through the door, laughing at first, then going very quiet as someone hushed him, drew him away, pulled him and another pair of late arrivals out of the entrance hall and into the first of the music-filled rooms.

'They're dead,' Jamie said, tonelessly, his dark eyes beseeching Olivia's, as if he hoped that she might put him straight, tell him that he was wrong, that he was crazy.

For a long moment, Olivia said nothing.

'What did you say?' she asked, very quietly, at last.

'All killed,' he said.

Someone put a hand on Olivia's arm and she jumped as if they'd burned her.

'It's true, my dear.' Mrs Orbach, David's mother, stood beside her. 'I'm so very sorry.' Magnificent in black Chanel, she looked compassionate and afraid and deeply uncomfortable all at the same time, and Olivia realized in a flash of instinct that, as shocked and sympathetic as their hostess clearly was, she wanted, more than anything, to get her and Jamie out of her entrance hall – if possible out of the house and away from her party.

'Your friend's waiting upstairs,' Mrs Orbach said, gently.

'Friend?' Olivia felt confused, disorientated, almost dizzy.

'She means Annie,' Jamie told her.

'Why?' Olivia stared up at him. 'What's happened to Annie?'

'It's all of them,' Jamie said. 'On the way to Scotland.'

And finally, Olivia understood.

'The helicopter,' she said.

Annie was in a bedroom on the first floor, away from the noise. She was sitting on the floor, on a white rug, all curled up, partly camouflaged by her white crepe dress. She, too, had been crying, but now her eyes were dry and she looked shocked, almost absent. A moth, drawn by the light through the open window, fluttered close to her blonde hair, but she made no move to brush it away.

Olivia and Jamie came into the room. Jamie got down on the floor beside Annie, put one arm around her, and Olivia, her legs suddenly weak, sat on the edge of the big bed.

There was a cheval mirror facing her from across the room. She saw her reflection, saw the black Bermudas and the silk camisole that had seemed so daring and sexy, saw the crazy, idiotic wrap-around sunglasses pushed up into her scarlet-streaked hair, saw the bizarre dog chain around her neck – and abruptly that seemed so offensive, so *revolting*, that she tried to pull it off, but it was too tightly fastened and she was hurting herself, didn't know that she was making small, choking, whimpering sounds until Jamie's hands were on hers, stopping her from dragging at the thing around her neck.

'Let me,' he told her, gently. 'Let me, Olivia.'

She let him, watched the chain hang loose from his hands, watched him lay it on the bedspread. She stared at him.

'Are they really all dead?' She sounded incredulous, like a child.

'Yes,' he said.

Annie still sat curled up on the floor, saying nothing. The moth was resting on the skirt of her dress now. Jamie took Olivia's hand and drew her off the bed and down onto the rug, and they were all three in a row, him in the middle.

'It happened this afternoon,' he said, very softly. 'Somewhere near Newcastle.'

'How?' Olivia asked.

'They crashed. That's all we know.' Jamie paused. 'There's a man downstairs, waiting. My cousin, Michael, sent him. To take us all home.' He paused again. 'We wanted to wait for you.'

'I'm sorry,' Olivia said. 'I was late, wasn't I?'

'It doesn't matter,' Jamie said. 'There's no hurry.'

'No,' Olivia said. 'I guess there isn't.'

The wheels of death ground into motion. They were none of them young children, to be protected from reality or shielded from harsh formalities. Postmortems were conducted, funerals were arranged, inquests were held in conjunction with the main accident enquiry which found, in due course, that the helicopter had crashed because of a mechanical failure. No human error, no suspicious circumstances, no violent storm. Just some hunks of steel and electrical circuits failing to keep the machine in the air. Olivia, Annie and Jamie flew to their respective family homes in the United States for the funerals, fumbled their way numbly through the interments and various rites – the Segals' Jewish service in New York, the Aldriches' Protestant burial in San Francisco and the Ariases' Roman Catholic Mass in Rhode Island – and then returned to Britain for what seemed, to each of them, the most harrowing, the most inescapably tangible part of the ritual, the clearing up of their parents' homes.

There was plenty of help available for the packing up and removal of the large objects, but as with all deaths there were wardrobes to be gone through, and dressing tables, and cabinets and desk drawers. In Jamie's case, there was his older brother, Peter, to help, and Michael, their cousin – the son of Carlos Arias's late brother, Juan Luis – came through for them magnificently well. Michael was, as he pointed out to Jamie, almost twice his age, and as the new head of the Arias family it was his duty to take over the dismal tasks involved with closing down the Pall Mall office and Regent's Park house and transferring their belongings to the main family residence in Newport and the

New York offices, from where Michael intended to rule. Annie, still seeming less able to cope than the others, began the process of trying to sift through Franklin's and Grace's personal files by herself, but all too swiftly crumbled and gave up, asking Richard Tyson, her father's London-based partner, if he would mind having all the papers in the mews house - unsorted for the moment, perhaps forever – packaged up and laid to rest in the archives of her father's London office.

Olivia tackled her own task head on, the only way she could, the only way she wanted to. In her mother's case it was, in a sense, straightforward. Grief and loss, both accentuated by the sight and touch and smell of Emily's belongings. But Emily Segal had been orderly and not over-burdened by sentiment, a thousand miles away from the average Jewish mother. Arthur, on the other hand, had been both disorderly and an unabashed nostalgia collector. Immersed as he had been in so many diverse fields, with his art collection and his numerous charities – which would from now on be administered by the Arthur Segal Foundation – proud as any archetypal Jewish husband and papa of his beloved wife and only daughter, fervent as he had been to hold on to his past and to as many shreds of his heritage as possible – Arthur's wardrobes and drawers and filing cabinets, once opened, seemed almost to seethe with scrapbooks and photograph albums and diaries and other keepsakes.

And the correspondence! Once released from the cabinets and boxes that had until now held them in check, Olivia found a veritable mountain of her father's letters. Much of it was commonplace, dull business communications that could now, without question, be consigned to black rubbish bags, and old postcards from friends, including three from

Max Wildenbruch, the art dealer, on holidays in Tuscany and France; but hidden amongst all these were other things of infinite value. The skullcap Arthur had worn for his bar mitzvah, neatly labelled by his mother. Every birthday card Olivia had ever sent her father. Ancient school reports: Arthur's own, describing a boy to whom friendship had clearly always mattered more than studies. Emily's, the kind to make any parent glow with pride; and Olivia's, every single comment from first grade upward, good or bad or someplace between, preserved. And love letters, simple but intensely moving, that Olivia read unashamedly and wept over, then carefully folded again, keeping to each original crease, feeling she had drawn a little closer to Arthur and Emily with every word.

On the third day of her delvings and sortings, Olivia found in her father's study an old battered pigskin briefcase he had continued using from time to time in preference to the more handsome black calf attaché case that Emily had bought him from Asprey for his birthday two years before. Like just about every single container in the house used by Arthur, it seemed to contain papers, but it was locked and Olivia could find no key. She looked for a while at the tiny gold lock, and thought it would be an easy matter to force it open, but the idea of breaking into something her father had locked seemed somehow offensive to her. *Which makes no real sense at all*, she thought, *when I've just spent the last few days reading his private mail.*

Olivia wondered abruptly, guiltily, why people assumed that death made them privy to everything about those who had died. She had told herself that her own invasion of her parents' privacy was a means of bringing them closer again, of drawing them back, temporarily, from the void. She thought, on reflection, that she had truly felt that, and it was done now, anyway, their intimate words had bled into her mind, were part of her now, and there was no going back and no point in feeling guilty. Jewish though she was, Olivia had never been big on guilt.

She fetched a small, sharp, black-handled knife from the kitchen, returned to Arthur's study and worked at the lock until the pigskin case was open. It was enjoyable work, had a rather satisfying edge of petty villainy to it, and she wondered idly if that, perhaps, was one of the attractions of burglary, the small battle to pick the door lock or quietly break the window, all the while anticipating the opportunity of trespass into another person's private world.

More letters. One from Coutts, the bankers. Two from a firm of insurance brokers. An invitation, on thick white card, to a dinner at the Israeli Embassy, the date already past; another, to the opening of an exhibition at the Hamilton Gallery. And a strange, brief note from Jamie's father, dated June 4th, one month before the helicopter crash, hand-written with a fountain pen and curiously worded in a hurried, uncomfortable, almost telegraphic style.

> Dear Arthur,
> Deeply shocked and dismayed to learn that your suspicions are not, after all, unfounded.
> We must meet soon.
> Carlos Arias.

Olivia told Annie about the note on the telephone later that evening.

'It sounds important. Do you suppose it is?'

'You mean, should you ask Jamie about it?' Annie was calm tonight, partly, perhaps, because she'd taken one of the tranquillizers a cousin had given her before the funeral, but then again she thought that she had been feeling a little better, a little easier, ever since Richard Tyson had agreed to house all the Aldrich papers in their office archives.

'Should I?'

Annie paused. 'I wouldn't.'

'Why not?'

'Because it could mean anything at all, and there's nothing Jamie can do about it now, and it might just worry him.'

'You're right,' Olivia said. 'I guess.'

'But you're not sure,' Annie said.

'Not quite,' Olivia admitted. 'There I was prying into my own parents' private affairs, and suddenly there was Jamie's dad, and I'm not sure I have the right to keep it from him.'

'Keep what, Livvy? It's just a note. It's nothing.'

'It doesn't sound like nothing.'

'Not when it was written, maybe,' Annie said softly. 'But it is nothing now.'

Olivia had said nothing to Jamie, and the note was long forgotten by the time the three friends next saw each other at the communal, non-denominational memorial service held at the end of August at All Souls Church in London, a thanksgiving for the lives of all those who had died in the helicopter crash: the pilot, an Edinburgh man named John Wilkes; Carlos Arias; Arthur and Emily Segal; and Franklin and Grace Aldrich.

There were colleagues, business partners, cousins, uncles and aunts, but both Olivia and Annie were only-children, and the only close blood relatives present were Peter and Michael Arias.

'I've never seen them before, have you?' Olivia said

25

to Annie, as they were preparing to file out after the service.

Annie shook her head. 'They're both very handsome, aren't they?'

Olivia studied the two men as they stood either side of Jamie. 'Michael's very distinguished, isn't he, in a piercing kind of way?'

'Peter's even better looking than Jamie,' Annie whispered, a moment of foolish gossip infinitely welcome after the sorrow of the service. 'A bit like Alan Alda, don't you think?'

'He's too smooth,' Olivia said. 'Look, they're both putting their sunglasses on while they're still inside.' She quelled a sudden, inappropriate urge to laugh. 'They look like Spanish Mafia.'

'Yes, they do.' Annie gave her black cloche hat a little pat in a gesture of tidiness inherited, unconsciously, from Grace Aldrich. 'Jamie doesn't though, does he?'

Olivia shook her head. 'Jamie's more elegant. More like Carlos.' She'd thought, for a while now, that she might be attracted to Jamie Arias, but he was such a warm, easy-going, friendly guy, was that way with just about everyone he came into contact with, that it was impossible to tell if he felt the same way about her. Now, she supposed, with all the brightness and normality gone, and with all of them going their separate ways, she would never find out.

They walked a little further towards the exit, were spoken to by a number of people, had their hands shaken, their cheeks kissed, and Jamie came and walked out with them into Portland Place, into the shock of sunlight and traffic and the rest of the world going about its business.

'I felt so sorry for Mrs Wilkes,' Jamie said, suddenly.

'Who?' Olivia asked, stupidly, confused.

'The pilot's wife,' Annie said.

'Oh, yes. Of course.'

'She looked so sad,' Jamie said, 'and so guilty.'

'No one's blamed him, have they?' Annie asked.

'Not at all,' Olivia said. 'Mechanical failure. Not his fault.'

'But still,' Annie said. 'Poor lady.'

Olivia glanced at her, realized how extremely white her face was, remembered how she had been that night at the Orbach party, how utterly silent and remote.

'Annie, are you okay?' she asked, softly.

'Not really.' Annie's voice was flat. 'Are you?'

'No,' Olivia said. 'I guess not.'

'How can we be?' Jamie said.

Olivia hesitated for a moment.

'Are you both free the day after tomorrow?'

'I am,' Jamie said. 'I don't leave till next Monday.'

'Annie?'

'I have nothing special,' Annie said.

'I think we should go up there,' Olivia said.

'Up where?' Jamie asked, though he thought he knew.

'To where it happened.' Olivia paused. 'Just us. I want to be there. I want to say goodbye.' She paused again. 'I think it might do us all some good.'

'I don't know if I could bear it,' Annie said, slowly.

'It would be a fair climb,' Olivia said.

'We'd need boots and hiking gear,' Jamie added. 'It's quite a way up.'

'You don't have to come, Annie.' Olivia said. 'It's just an idea.'

'Can I think about it, please?' Annie asked.

*   *   *

They all travelled north two days later, having extricated themselves from well-meaning relatives and acquaintances. They took an Intercity train to Newcastle, rented a car, picked up a local road map, drove as far as they were able and then hiked the rest of the way up to Dukesfield Fell. Both Jamie and Olivia kept a watchful eye on Annie, conscious that of the three of them she was the most obviously fragile emotionally, but she seemed perfectly in control today, as prepared for whatever awaited them as they were.

There was very little and yet there was everything. Of the wreckage and debris, not the tiniest scrap remained; if blood had been scattered, it had been washed away, either by officialdom or by nature. But the crater made by the body of the helicopter falling from the sky was there, roped off for safety, and there, too, was the wounded earth, scorched and gouged and ripped.

It was August, the height of summer and a clear day, yet up there it seemed to Olivia and Jamie and Annie that no birds sang, that it was cold and bleak as November, and their losses weighed down on them more heavily there, were suddenly rendered far more real than they had been. For when they had seen the pictures on their television screens, and when they had listened at the inquests and sat at the memorial service – even when they had stood at the gravesides and watched the coffins lowered into the ground – the harsh, unrelenting truth of their parents' deaths had never quite come home to them. But here was where they had fallen, here was where the life had been crushed out of them, where the fire had half-consumed their bodies before the Northumbrian rain had put out the flames.

'I'd like to go down soon,' Annie said, after a while.

'All right,' Olivia said.

'I can go by myself, if you and Jamie want to stay.'

28

'No, you can't,' Jamie said quickly. 'We have to stick together. I'm ready to leave, too.' He looked at Olivia. 'How about you?'

'I wouldn't mind another minute or two. You two go ahead.'

'Just a little way,' Jamie said. 'Will you be okay?'

'Of course,' she said.

Olivia waited until they were some distance away, and then she sat down on the ground. She was glad they had come with her, but now she was glad to have been left alone. It had felt too much like the memorial service with them beside her, that sense of having to stand still and behave well for the sake of others, when what she really wanted to do was to get down on the ground, get as close as possible to where her mother and father had died, and say goodbye to them properly.

She put her hands, palms down, on the cool earth, and shut her eyes. She thought about her parents: about Emily Segal, doctor, wife, mother and individual; about Arthur Segal, philanthropist, husband, father, collector of memories and beautiful things. They had always been such busy people, their lives had been so full, yet they had always found time for each other and for their daughter, had given her so much, all that she'd needed and more, all the love, comfort, sound advice and friendship. It was cruel, Olivia supposed, that they had died so young, when they still had so much to do, so much to give, and yet, she realized suddenly, there at the place where they had died, at least they had had little time to be afraid, and at least they had gone together.

They stayed at an old hotel in the village of Blanchland in the Derwent Valley that night, in no rush to return to London, for they would all be leaving England for the foreseeable future within the week. Jamie and Olivia had both always planned to leave before September in any event, though Annie had intended to remain with her family a while longer. Now there was no longer any alternative. The process of closing down their London homes was almost complete and their lives, as they had formerly known them, were at an end. Jamie was to go to Harvard Business School, where he would be within about sixty miles of the magnificent, art-filled Arias family estate in Newport; Olivia was to go to Paris to study French at the Sorbonne; and Annie, at a complete loss, was going home to lick her wounds at the Aldrich house in San Francisco. This, they suddenly realized with an unexpectedly acute sense of fresh loss, would be their last chance to be together for a long time.

They had dinner in the restaurant, drank a lot of wine – even Annie had a glass – and adjourned to Olivia's bedroom, the biggest, where Olivia and Jamie drank some cognac too, to which they were unaccustomed, and began to talk, honestly and openly, about their feelings and their fears. Nothing, they had all become aware, would ever be the same again. Their frames of reference had been irrevocably distorted; the bedrock on which their personalities had been formed was all broken up; the very people who would, they all knew, have done anything in the world for love of them, had disappeared.

'We had a fight,' Annie said, suddenly, from her chair.

'Who?' Olivia asked, startled.

'My father and I.'

Annie's chin came up, abruptly, and they saw that her blue eyes were filled with anguished tears, and Olivia realized then that Annie was the only one of them who had, until then, said hardly anything at all about her personal feelings.

'The last time I saw my father,' she said, 'we had a terrible fight.'

Neither Jamie, on the bed, nor Olivia, sitting on the floor, said anything, both sensing that this was not a moment to interrupt her, that Annie needed time.

'It started about the party,' she went on. 'Just a silly argument, really. He didn't want me to go, but I told him I was eighteen and he couldn't stop me, and he gave way and I was so glad, because Daddy and I never fought, or hardly ever, but then he started making all kinds of rules, about what I should wear and how I should get there and when and how I should get home.'

'All fathers do that,' Olivia said, putting down her cognac glass on the carpet.

'I know,' Annie said. 'I knew it then, too – and I'd never really minded before, and I don't know what was wrong with me that day, but it just seemed to get to me, and I couldn't seem to stop arguing with him. Even when he said things that I knew made perfect sense, I argued.'

'I expect he understood,' Jamie said.

'No,' Annie said, and the tears were really flowing now. 'He didn't understand at all. I saw it in his face. He looked so hurt, and I knew I'd hurt him, but I just told myself it was my fault for always having given in to him about everything – for having always been such a good little girl – and it would do us both good if I made a stand once in a while.'

They waited for her to go on.

'And you didn't get a chance to make up with him,' Olivia said, at last.

Annie shook her head. 'My mother came home from the

hairdresser's, and she heard what we'd been arguing about, and she smoothed things over a little because she could see it was all a storm in a teacup, nothing we wouldn't both get over.'

'She was right,' Jamie said. 'You would have.'

'But we didn't,' Annie whispered. 'He still looked so hurt, and I just left the room, and my mother asked him to go and help her with their packing, and when it was time for them to leave for Scotland I was in the bath – and I could have gotten out and gone to kiss him goodbye, but I didn't. My mother stuck her head around the door and blew me a kiss and told me to enjoy myself, and that was that.'

Olivia looked up at Jamie, then back over at Annie.

'And you've been tormenting yourself about that all these weeks.'

'Yes.' Annie took the handkerchief Jamie reached across to offer her, and wiped her eyes. 'Of course.'

'Then you're a bit of a goose, Annie Aldrich. I guarantee your dad forgave you – probably forgot all about it – before they even got into the helicopter.' Olivia paused. 'He knew you loved him, didn't he?'

'I guess so.'

'You know so.'

'Olivia's right,' Jamie said. 'Your dad would hate to think you were making yourself crazy – that's the kind of fight all kids have with their fathers.'

'I know,' Annie said.

'Your lips say that,' Olivia said, gently, 'but your eyes don't look so sure.'

Annie bit back the tears that were threatening again. 'I'm just so sad, you know?'

'We all are,' Jamie said. 'I guess we'll all be sad for a long time.'

'At least,' Olivia said, 'we have each other.'

'Not for much longer,' Annie said, miserably. 'You'll be in Paris, Jamie'll be at Harvard. I'll be thousands of miles from you both.'

'That's just distance.' Olivia got up from the floor, bent to pick up her glass and poured a little more cognac for herself and Jamie. 'We can write letters and phone and visit each other. We're none of us short of funds – we can get on a plane pretty much whenever we want to.'

'It's not the same as being in the same city, though,' Jamie said. 'I know I'm going to miss you both like hell.'

'It's strange, in a way.' Olivia joined him on the bed, glass in hand. 'We were friends in school, but we weren't all that close, yet now I feel this really strong bond with both of you.'

'It's not so surprising,' Jamie said, 'given the circumstances.'

'Grief, you mean,' Annie said.

Olivia shook her head. 'It's more than grief, Annie. I think it's that we all realize that no one else in the whole world will ever be able to comprehend better than us what we've been through – the way the crash has changed our lives, has already started to change us.'

'I know what you mean,' Jamie agreed. 'This afternoon, standing up on Dukesfield Fell, there was such a strong connection between us – I felt it, I mean I *really* felt it, tangibly. I knew – or I thought I knew – what you were both thinking – I don't mean I was reading your minds, but—' He shrugged, unable exactly to express what he wanted to say.

'I think I understand, too,' Annie said, quietly. 'Though I'd be lying if I said I'd felt it up on that place – I was too wrapped up in my own misery, I don't think I was paying much attention to either of you.'

'We were all pretty wrapped up,' Olivia said. 'That was why I wanted to stay behind on my own for a few moments.' She paused. 'But I still knew that you were both there for me, and it helped a lot.'

They all fell silent for a time.

'Do you think we will all write regularly?' Jamie asked. 'I mean, when we all get hooked up in our new lives – I'm not saying we won't intend to write, or that we won't want to, but—'

'But you're just being a realist,' Annie said.

'It doesn't matter if we write letters or not,' Olivia said. 'What matters is just that we keep in touch somehow. Knowing me, I'll pick up the phone more often than a pen, or I might send tapes—'

'Good idea,' Jamie said.

'And Livvy's right about paying visits once in a while,' Annie said.

Olivia took one more sip, then put down her glass. 'But none of those things,' she said slowly, thoughtfully, 'are what really matters when the chips are down.'

'What do you mean?' Annie asked.

'I mean that what really counts is what we're going to need the most.' She paused. 'And that's being there for each other. When things get rough – *really* rough, I mean – for any one of us. Which they will, some time. By the law of averages.'

'So what are you saying?' Jamie asked her.

Olivia stood up. The mix of cognac and wine was buzzing in her veins, yet her mind felt curiously clear and resolute. 'I'm saying that we all take a vow – make a pact, I guess – to always be there for each other when we're needed.'

Annie, still in her chair, took a breath. 'Yes,' she said. 'I'd like to do that very much.'

'Jamie?' Olivia looked down at him.

'Sure.' He smiled at her. 'You want to do this properly? Swear to stay in touch, swear to do all we can for each other?'

'No.' Olivia shook her head. 'Not just "all we can". People always say that – it's like having a get-out clause all neat and ready in case we have something better on. I'm talking about a real pact, a solemn promise that if any of us gets in any kind of a serious jam, and needs help, then the other two will drop everything and be there to see them through.'

Annie stood up. 'Like family, you mean.'

'Just like family,' Jamie said, getting up, too. 'The way our parents would have been there for us if we really needed them.'

'*In loco parentis.*' Annie smiled. 'My father would have liked the sound of that.'

'They all would,' Olivia said, softly. She felt a new warmth that had little to do with liquor coursing through her, a renewed strength and sense of hope.

'We need our glasses,' Jamie said. 'One more toast to our pact.'

They found them, came to stand close together, and raised them.

'To always being there,' Jamie said.

'No matter what,' Annie added.

'Come hell or high water,' Olivia said, and drained her glass.

For the next ten years, as they grew and worked and lived their separate lives, the friends exchanged letters and phone calls and got together mostly for the odd vacation. They reunited, too, for Annie's wedding, in London in 1981, to a banker named Edward Thomas, and the following year

Annie and Jamie went to New York, where Olivia was living, to celebrate her engagement; five months later, they returned to commiserate with her on her split from her fiancé – only to find that she felt she'd had the luckiest of escapes and needed no commiserations. In 1985 – by which time Jamie and Olivia had attended the christenings of Sophie, William and Liza, Annie's and Edward's children – they were all together again in Boston for Jamie's marriage to Caroline Beaumont, a rising star in the advertising world. And on the Fourth of July, 1986, they all climbed Dukesfield Fell again to commemorate the tenth anniversary of the helicopter disaster.

None of those reunions – not even the last, they all agreed – came under the category of 'being there' for each other; they were simply moments of importance, of substance in their lives, snapshots in time when good friends wanted to be together. They had been lucky in those ten years, had had no real need to call for help.

But those times would come. They had all gone on with their lives determinedly, courageously and successfully, yet those grievous losses, that massive body blow to normality, could not be sustained without some damage. They were all strong in their own ways, yet like the rest of the human race they all had their Achilles' heels too, and it was, perhaps, to be expected that the violent, untimely deaths of their parents would exacerbate those weaknesses.

In Annie's case, it was her fear of admitting that she was not always able to cope perfectly with everything life threw at her. With Jamie, it was his need to live up to the memory of the father he had lost. And for Olivia, it was, more than anything, her compulsive passion for truth.

Three times in the next decade, still stirred by the distant but unfailingly dark backwash of the helicopter crash, those vulnerabilities would threaten each of them, and on each occasion, the strength of their pact of friendship would be tested to the limit.

The first call for help would come from Annie.

4

Olivia's Box

My name is Anton Rothenburg. By the second half of the nineteen-twenties, when I was still just a young child, my family had lived in our large grey stone mansion on the outskirts of Baden-Baden for two generations. We – my father, Emanuel Rothenburg, my mother, Hedi, and my two younger sisters, Lili and Trude – were, I now realize, an archetypically successful, contented, comparatively wealthy and assimilated German Jewish family. Our religious practices were liberal; we went to synagogue on the High Holydays, on Jarhzeits – the anniversaries of the deaths of our grandparents – and when we were invited to weddings or bar mitzvahs. My parents had a wide circle of acquaintances in which they were respected and popular, and my sisters and I had good friends and were happy inside and outside school. Mama loved throwing parties, played bridge and canasta twice a week and went shopping on Sophienstrasse and, at least twice each month, in either Stuttgart or Frankfurt. Papa cherished us all and went about his business of dealing in fine art with a joy that he readily transmitted to us, often telling us how conscious he was of his great good fortune in having some of life's loveliest and often precious creations pass through his hands, and, above all, in being in a position, from time to time, to add to his personal collection of late nineteenth-century Symbolist paintings. As a small boy, of course, I understood and appreciated little of these things – I only came to understanding later, when, from the time of my own bar mitzvah, my father began to share confidences with me, to talk to me almost as if I were a man. But in those early years, before the troubles began to touch us, all I really knew, all I really understood, was that we were happy.

By the beginning of the thirties, the Rothenburg Symbolist Collection had become moderately well known in Baden-Württemburg and beyond, and our mansion was something of a lovingly protected treasure trove that encompassed works by Bonnard, Gauguin, Emile Bernard, Vuillard, Redon, Munch, Hodler and more. Well before January of 1933, when I was almost twelve and when Adolf Hitler became Chancellor, my sisters and I became used to hearing our parents discussing whether or not they should be making plans to move us and the collection from Germany to America.

'There's no great rush,' Papa would tell our mother regularly when she raised the question. 'No need to panic. We can make our arrangements carefully, take our time.'

The stranger had come to call for the first time almost a year earlier, in the second week of February 1932. I still remember that day quite clearly. It was a Sunday, after lunch, and we were all in the salon, with Mama playing Chopin at the piano, when Maria, our housekeeper, brought in his visiting card. The card announced him as Georg Brauner, but Papa said later that he thought it might not be his real name. The man spoke fluent German, but with a foreign accent that Papa said he was unable to place. Not that either his name or his accent especially mattered to my father.

Georg Brauner said that he had come to help.

'What makes you think that I am in need of your help, Herr Brauner?'

Emanuel was forty-two years old, with light brown hair that had lately begun to grey and recede a little, and a waistline that was not as slim as it had once been. He was an easy-going, placid man, and until recently he had also been gregarious and outgoing, the kind of man who enjoyed welcoming strangers into his lovely home, but the times were growing increasingly troubled, and these days Emanuel tended towards caution. That February afternoon, sitting opposite the elegant, composed, dark-haired stranger – whom he estimated to be at least ten, or maybe even fifteen years younger than himself – in the tranquil, familiar and secure setting of his own library, surrounded by fine leather editions of Goethe, Dumas, Scott and the like, Emanuel felt curiously and uncharacteristically uncomfortable.

'I'm aware, Herr Rothenburg, that you wish to leave Germany.' Brauner, having come directly to the point, did not wait for Emanuel either to confirm or to deny what he had said. 'I'm also aware – as you must be – that it's likely to prove extremely difficult, perhaps even impossible, for you to take your collection with you to the United States.'

Emanuel sat perfectly still. He was unsure which aspect of Georg Brauner's statement had upset him most: the man's presumptuousness or the sudden, discomfiting knowledge that a stranger knew his private business. He regarded his cigar box on the rosewood and leather table, his urge to light a cigar only controlled by the awareness that he would have to offer Brauner one out of common courtesy, and Emanuel wanted Georg Brauner out of his library, out of his house, far more than he wanted the cigar.

'I can't imagine,' Emanuel said, slowly, 'where you have

obtained your information, Herr Brauner, but I have to tell
you that it is inaccurate.'

'Which part of it?' Brauner asked.

'I beg your pardon?'

'Which part of my information is inaccurate, Herr
Rothenburg? That you plan to leave Germany for the
United States, or that you will encounter problems if you
try to remove your paintings?'

'As I said,' Emanuel replied, irritated but still picking his
words carefully, 'I cannot imagine how or where you could
have learned anything about my plans, but I can assure you
that it is all entirely inaccurate.' He paused. 'Now, if there's
nothing else—' He prepared to stand up.

'Please, Herr Rothenburg . . .' The younger man's voice
was softer now and clearly conciliatory. 'I can see I have
annoyed you.'

'Not at all,' Emanuel said. 'I'm simply a busy man who
doesn't want to waste your time any more than my own.'

'Just a few minutes more,' Brauner went on, 'and I assure
you that neither of us will be wasting our time.'

He wore a beautifully cut, dark grey three-piece suit,
a lighter grey silk tie and immaculate black shoes. As
Emanuel watched him reaching into an inside pocket for
a slim gold cigarette case which he opened and offered to
his host before taking a lighter, also gold, from his right
outside pocket, Emanuel thought that there was something
suave and altogether too smooth about Brauner that might
perhaps, in another man, have spelled confidence trickster;
and yet it was patently clear to Emanuel that neither the
expensive suit nor any of the accessories were a sham. The
outer skin matched up to the inner man; something about
Georg Brauner, in spite of his youth and his instantly
dislikable slickness and sharpness, spelled old European

money, inherited elegance and innate sophistication. All of which warned Emanuel that he might be sensible to swallow his irritation, at least for the few moments more that Brauner had asked for.

'Very well.'

Brauner, legs crossed and relaxed, leaned forward, his manner suddenly conspiratorial. 'I really can help you, Herr Rothenburg. I have a great deal of cash at my disposal, but more relevantly to you, I have a most useful network of contacts both inside and outside Germany.'

Emanuel made a small, slightly dismissive gesture with his hands, but said nothing.

'Your personal collection is a great tribute to you,' Brauner went on. 'I, too, am a lover and something of a collector of art – though I don't, of course, have either your experience or expertise, but you have my utmost admiration for what you have achieved.'

'Thank you.' Emanuel waited for more.

Brauner gave a small nod. 'To business then.' He paused. 'I believe that I can assist you in moving your entire collection to America.' He noted the fresh flicker of annoyance in the other man's eyes and went on swiftly. 'Please don't trouble to tell me again that I'm wrong. Even if I am – even if this whole conversation is purely hypothetical – it surely can't do any harm just to let me finish what I have to say.'

Emanuel sighed. 'If you insist.'

'As I said, I can help. Believe me, I can.'

'Why?' Emanuel asked.

'Why would I help?' Brauner smiled. 'What's in it for me, you mean?' There was no response. 'Payment in kind,' he said, and again he paused. 'A Bonnard for a Hodler, perhaps, theoretically and, of course, hypothetically; a Munch for a Redon. All negotiable, naturally.'

'Naturally,' Emanuel said, almost amused for the first time.

'That's it.' Brauner gave a little shrug. 'All very simple, on the surface. Much more complicated beneath, of course.'

'Of course.' Emanuel's voice was tinged with soft irony.

'So.' Brauner leaned back again. 'What's your first reaction to my proposition?'

'First and last,' Emanuel said, and the irony and amusement were both gone. 'I thank you, Herr Brauner, most sincerely, but the fact remains that I do not need your help.'

'Because you have your own contacts in the United States?' Brauner's question was gentle. 'Fellow art lovers and friends?' He paused. 'Your colleague, Max Wildenbruch, in Manhattan, for example.'

For the second time, Emanuel felt a frisson of unease. 'I'm sure you'll understand if I don't choose to discuss my personal acquaintances with you,' he said stiffly.

'Of course,' Brauner said. 'After all, you don't know too much about me.'

'I know nothing about you, sir.'

Again, Brauner smiled. 'Except one thing. That I am in a position to help you. And that I am willing to help you. At a price.'

'And I say to you again, and for the last time, that I don't need your help.' Emanuel rose from his chair and waited while the other man, left with no real alternative, stood up too. He put out his right hand. 'Thank you for coming, Herr Brauner. I'm sorry it's been a wasted journey.'

Brauner shook his hand. 'Not wasted at all.'

They walked out of the library along a corridor into the high-ceilinged, wood-panelled entrance hall. The

Rothenburgs' two Great Danes, lying on either side of one of Hedi's favourite Hodlers, stirred and wagged their tails but did not get up.

'I shall be staying at Brenner's Park,' Brauner said at the front door, 'if you change your mind.'

'Will you be in town long?' Emanuel was still cordial.

'A few days,' Brauner said.

'I hope you enjoy them.' Emanuel opened the door. A blast of cold winter air blew in from the driveway.

'I shall,' Brauner said. 'Though I'd prefer it if the Casino were open. I hear there'll be roulette again next year.' He paused one last time. 'Are you a gambler, Herr Rothenburg?'

'Occasionally, on my travels. I'm not a true gambler.'

'A pity,' Brauner said. 'Had you been, I might have suggested a wager on how long it would take you to change your mind about my offer.'

Emanuel almost admired the man's persistence.

'And I would have advised you not to waste your money,' he said.

Georg Brauner did not return to our house for fifteen months, but once inside Papa's library for the second time, he became morbidly insistent upon reminding my father of the many injustices being heaped upon the Jews in our country. Papa hardly needed reminding that the Gestapo had, for almost a month, had powers to arrest, interrogate and intern without due process of law; or that Jewish artists were being excluded from exhibitions; or that books by Jewish writers were being burned; or that Jews were not only being discriminated against but humiliated and, in a growing number of cases, murdered. When he pointed out that Brauner had told him nothing he had not already known, Brauner asked him why, in that case, when so many of his people were leaving, and if he had such wonderful contacts abroad, we were still in Baden-Baden.

Because, in our case, my father replied, honestly – as he had so often told our mother – there was no urgency. No attempt was being made to halt the mass emigration, which was, after all, the Nazis' main aim: to rid Germany of what Brauner called 'his people'. Papa said that he had never achieved anything fine in his life by being hurried, and he did not plan to start now.

'So,' said Brauner, 'you still believe you don't need my help.'

Papa looked him straight in the eye.

'I know that I don't,' he said.

My father meant what he had told Brauner. Ours was not an ordinary position; we were, he firmly believed, less vulnerable – at least for the time being – than many German Jews because of Papa's status in the local community and because of our family's wealth. My father had often told us that money itself meant little, and that love, good health and contentment were of infinitely greater importance. Yet as the rumours and increasingly hard evidence of growing brutality and shocking discrimination around the country began to bite more regularly into my parents' peace of mind, Papa said that he had begun to appreciate the true value of his riches. His money and his respected position were, after all, enabling us to continue our lives in an almost unaltered manner. Even if there were difficulties for some local Jews in the shopping streets of Baden-Baden or Stuttgart or Frankfurt, Mama could always send Maria, our housekeeper, or Rudi, the chauffeur, to do the shopping and avoid unpleasantness or embarrassment. At the earliest hint of anti-semitism at our school, Papa had arranged special tutoring for Lili, Trude and myself at home, and I, for one, was happy about that plan since my best friend and neighbour Leo Landau's father, Samuel, who agreed with Papa, had arranged for Leo to share lessons with us. Our tutor, Professor Eichinger, was younger and less stuffy than many of the teachers at school had been, but while our lessons were certainly less formal and more enjoyable, he kept discipline and made sure that we worked harder than we might otherwise have done. And as for Papa himself, as he pointed out, he still dealt, as he always had, with artists, and the vast majority of artists were, by nature and design, liberal human beings, above and beyond the baseness of racism and thuggery. In other words, we were luckier than most.

Still, my father was neither foolish nor complacent. Month after month was passing with no sign of any improvement in the general situation. Any lingering hopes he might have been harbouring that our family could simply continue to ride out the storm and remain in our lovely home were crumbling. But worse than that, it was becoming increasingly clear to Papa that if he wanted to remove us to America before things grew any uglier, then he might, after all, have to consider losing perhaps the greatest part of the Rothenburg Symbolist Collection. Lately, I heard him say to Mama, the country seemed to be overflowing with so-called dealers claiming to be prepared to 'take care of' Jewish-owned art works, but Papa said he had no faith in the promises of double-dealing opportunists. At least Georg Brauner, he remembered wryly, had been frank enough, even at the outset, about his plans to gain from helping them, and at least Brauner had claimed – even on his second visit – that he would be able to spirit at least fifty per cent of the collection over the Atlantic.

'Perhaps I was wrong not to have listened to him,' Papa confided to Mama.

'I don't think so,' Mama reassured him gently. 'I think you were right not to trust him.'

'Maybe.' Papa sighed. 'But right or not, if he were to return again now, I can tell you I might almost be glad to do business with him.'

Brauner did come back on the afternoon of September 30th, 1935, fifteen days after the passing of the Nuremberg Laws. Fifteen days for Emanuel to have fully absorbed the new laws that meant that Jews were no longer eligible as German citizens, that marriage and physical relations between Germans and Jews were forbidden, that any remaining hope of normalization was gone. Fifteen days for Emanuel to finally extract his head from his rich native soil and try to complete the travel arrangements for himself and his family irrespective of the losses he now knew their departure would entail.

Brauner looked fit and suntanned.

'You look well,' Emanuel told him, cordially.

Hedi and the children were all at home, the two young girls and fourteen-year-old Anton and Leo Landau being tutored in the library, and so Emanuel had brought Brauner into their salon, the family's favourite room, cosier and less intimidating than the large lounge in which they had so often, in happier times, entertained many of the top families in Baden-Baden. This room contained the wireless and gramophone, a well-stocked bar, the baby grand piano that Hedi and Anton liked to play, the most comfortable, well-used furniture in the house, and three paintings, a de Chavannes, a Denis and, in pride of place, a Bonnard.

'I've had a good holiday this year,' Brauner replied.

Emanuel had used the moments in which Hedi had organized coffee for them to compose himself, to try to quieten the almost violent surge of relief that had overcome him when he had learned that Brauner was at the front door. To show eagerness would be not only undignified but counter-productive, he warned himself as his guest settled himself into an armchair facing him. He wanted Brauner to be in no doubt of his own change of heart; he wanted him to know that there was business to be done between them; but he wanted, also, desperately, to try to maintain control over the bargaining.

'Am I correct in thinking,' Brauner asked, 'that you are, at last, beginning to come to terms with reality?'

'You mean am I planning to leave Germany?' Emanuel knew they were beyond game-playing, was conscious that this might be his last chance with Brauner.

'That is what I mean.'

'When we last met,' Emanuel said, at last, 'you made an offer of help.'

'The last time,' Brauner said, 'and the first, too.'

'For which I was grateful,' Emanuel said. 'But which I rejected.'

'I can't say I noticed the gratitude,' Brauner said.

'In which case, I apologize.'

'No need.'

'That's kind.' Emanuel felt a knot of sickness in his stomach, but forced himself to continue. 'I realize now, with hindsight, that I was perhaps too hasty in my response.'

'Really?' Brauner picked up his cup and saucer and drank some coffee.

'I need to know' – Emanuel saw there was no point delaying, that it was better to get it over and done with – 'I need to know, Herr Brauner, if your offer of assistance is still available.'

Brauner set down his cup and saucer. 'It is,' he said.

'Then perhaps' – Emanuel prided himself that his relief did not show – 'we could discuss some business in a little more detail.' He paused. 'The terms you originally mentioned were, as you yourself said, purely hypothetical. Not realistic.'

'Not at all realistic,' Brauner agreed. 'I believe I suggested something to the effect of a Bonnard for a Hodler, and a Munch for a Redon.'

'Exactly.' Emanuel smiled. 'Perhaps you might be ready to make a more workable suggestion.'

'With pleasure,' Brauner said.

'Some more coffee?' Emanuel asked.

'No, thank you.' Brauner paused. 'The price for my help, given the worsening of your situation, has, of course, grown higher. Considerably higher.'

'How much higher?' The knot in Emanuel's stomach grew tighter, though he had tried to prepare himself for this moment, had realized that old money and influence notwithstanding, Georg Brauner – whoever he really was – was still, of course, not much better than most of the other opportunists he had lately encountered.

'You agree that there is little time to waste,' Brauner said.

'I do.'

'You understand, also, that though I am a far freer agent than you, able to travel where I wish and with any of my possessions I see fit to take, a private arrangement to remove items belonging to you could still be risky for me.'

'Yes,' Emanuel said, 'I understand.'

'Good.' Brauner paused. 'Can we see the works right away?'

'We can.'

'And do you agree that, subject to our agreeing terms, I may also select and extract certain items right away?'

Emanuel's stomach fluttered again. 'Subject to agreement, yes.'

'Very well. Let's begin.' Brauner looked directly, piercingly, at him. 'You are in possession of two Gauguins. Am I correct?'

'You are.'

'And a number of sketches by Munch.'

'Correct.'

'I shall take both the Gauguins and all the sketches, and in return, I shall see to it that one of the paintings in this room – the Denis, I think – begins its journey to New York within one week.'

Emanuel stood up. His face was very pale. 'It's out of the question.'

'Which part?'

'All of it. You know it's impossible.'

'On the contrary,' Brauner said, pleasantly, looking up at him, 'it's perfectly possible. And it's the kind of bargain I intend for the whole collection.'

'But it's ludicrous – derisory. It's no bargain at all.' Outraged, Emanuel struggled to find the words. 'It's like comparing the *Kurhaus* and the Casino with this house – it's quite out of proportion.'

'Of course it is.' Brauner shrugged. 'Nevertheless, that is my offer.'

'Then with respect, sir, I cannot deal with you.'

'Are you quite certain of that?' Brauner was perfectly calm and mild.

'Absolutely certain. You could surely not have expected me to agree?' Emanuel stood up, rage beginning to boil inside him. 'I think, sir, that it's time for you to leave.'

'Sit down, Herr Rothenburg.'

Emanuel stared down at Brauner.

'I asked you to sit down,' Brauner said. 'Please.'

Slowly, Emanuel sat. Perhaps, he thought, the man was toying with him – maybe his offer had simply been a bad joke and now they would start again seriously. He could take a joke with the best of them, had always been known around Baden-Baden for his fine sense of humour.

'You still don't understand,' Brauner said. 'You still don't fully comprehend the gravity of your situation.'

'On the contrary,' Emanuel said.

'No,' Brauner said. 'You don't.' He paused. 'Nor do you understand the extent of my influence, both inside and outside Germany.'

Emanuel said nothing, just stared at him. There had been no joke. And there was worse to come, he knew that now, too, as surely as he knew his own name.

'Max Wildenbruch has sworn an affidavit in your favour in New York,' Brauner said. 'He, above all others, has been a most generous friend, and instrumental in helping you obtain the necessary papers for you and your family. Has he not?'

Emanuel still said nothing, his mind whirling.

'Has he *not*?' For the first time, an ugly tone coloured Brauner's voice.

'Yes. He has.'

'Wildenbruch asks no payment for himself,' Brauner went on. 'But the oiling of the system's wheels and the greasing of essential palms has already cost him dearly, has it not? For which you have agreed to pay, have you not?'

For the very first time, Emanuel felt fear, real fear of actual danger, clutch at his heart. This man, this smooth, impeccable stranger, was dangerous to him and to Hedi and the children. He knew that now.

Brauner leaned forward again. 'Listen to me now, and listen carefully, because this is your last chance, Emanuel Rothenburg. Are you listening?'

'I'm listening.' Emanuel's voice was very soft.

'Those same contacts who would make it possible for me

to arrange safe shipment of your works of art to New York could just as easily be persuaded to prevent you, your wife and your children, from ever leaving Germany.'

Emanuel's pallor had increased and his heart was pounding.

'Don't you believe me, Rothenburg?' The last pretence of courtesy had vanished. 'I think perhaps you do.'

'Yes.' Emanuel nodded very slowly. 'I believe you.'

'Good,' Brauner said. 'Very good.' He sat back again. 'I think some fresh coffee would be a fine idea now. Perhaps your wife would be kind enough to arrange it.'

'Yes.' Emanuel got to his feet carefully, feeling ten years older. 'I'll ask her.'

'Thank you,' Brauner said. 'And then, if you agree, we can begin our negotiations in earnest. If you do agree.'

At the door, still dazed, Emanuel looked back at the younger man.

'I agree,' he said. 'Of course, I agree.'

The 'negotiations' went on into the evening. Papa escorted Brauner down to the vast converted cellars beneath our house, into the high-ceilinged rooms kept at the perfect temperature and the perfect humidity to safely maintain the valuable canvases and aged papers of the Rothenburg collection. Papa told Mama later that he had watched Brauner as he had viewed the works, had watched his expression, his dark eyes, his mouth, and he thought he had seen real passion on his face, true lust; and Papa saw that the man wanted these works not solely for their value, but for themselves, and whether his yearning was for their beauty or for the prestige with which their ownership might endow him, my father sensed too that Brauner's desire was powerful enough to give him almost anything he wanted.

At eight o'clock, we all sat down to the dinner that Brauner had requested. Brauner sat between Mama and Lili, and though at the time, of course, I could not fully understand the situation, I think I can now imagine all too well how my father must have felt during that meal. And how that emotion must have grown later, when Papa himself stood on a ladder in the cellar and took down the Gauguins and the Munch sketches; and when he wrapped them, with love and with real pain; and when he stood at the front door and watched Georg Brauner climb into the back of the black Mercedes that had waited for him for more than seven hours.

Knowing that it would not be long before he came again. Knowing that the blackmail had begun. Not knowing where it might, if ever, end.

5

For Annie

In the spring of 1987, the three friends were living separate lives in three different countries. Olivia, single, free as a bird and a skilled linguist – whose preference it had become to travel widely, enjoy life to the hilt and to interpret, whenever possible, for travelling authors, journalists and film and television companies – was living in Switzerland, running the Segal Translation Agency out of an office in Geneva. Jamie – free-spirited, gentle, gregarious Jamie – was in Boston, less than sixty miles from the Arias family mansion in Rhode Island, doing what he both loved and excelled at: being an advertising man and running his own agency in partnership with his less than gentle or free-spirited wife, Carrie Beaumont Arias. And Annie, married to Edward Thomas, an English banker fifteen years her senior, with three children, was living an archetypically British, ostensibly joyous life in an Oxfordshire village.

Annie's call for help came at two minutes after ten in the morning, Geneva time, just before Olivia was due to leave her office for a meeting at Gilles-Breque Pharmaceuticals, a corporation for which she had done a number of public relations interpreting jobs. It was only nine o'clock in Britain, and as Olivia picked up the receiver and heard Annie's voice, she registered a brief instant of surprise because Annie was usually much too busy, as a mother of three little ones, to call during the day.

'Livvy?' Annie's tension came over loud and clear.

'Annie, hi. What's up?' Olivia picked up her briefcase, laid it down on the top of her desk and began stacking papers into it.

'Nothing.' Annie paused. 'Everything.'

'Tell me.'

'I can't. Not like this. Not on the phone, I mean.'

'The phone's all we have right now, Annie.' Olivia stopped filling the case and sat back down behind her desk. 'Has something happened? Are you okay? Are the kids okay?'

'Fine. The children are fine.' Annie paused again. 'So far.'

'What do you mean?' Olivia glanced at her watch. 'Annie, you've obviously called to tell me something.'

'Yes.'

Olivia gave it three whole seconds. It was not an aspect of her character that she especially liked, but she had never been overburdened with patience. 'Annie, for crying out loud, tell me.'

'I need you, Livvy,' Annie said, very softly. 'I know you're probably much too busy, but I was thinking, remembering the promise we made to each other back in '76.'

Olivia felt a sudden chill. If Annie was thinking about their pact after all these years, that had to mean she was in major trouble.

'Do you remember, Livvy?'

'Of course I remember.'

As if it were yesterday, the three of them in the room at the hotel near Dukesfield Fell, drinking cognac and trying to decide how they were going to cope with their futures, without each other. *If any of us gets into any kind of a serious jam, and needs help, the other two will drop everything and be there to see them through.*

'I didn't know who else to turn to. I'm sorry.'

'Don't be a dope. That was the whole point of the pact.' Olivia's mind ticked over. She didn't need to check her diary to know how busy she was. If Annie needed her to fly over right now, it would be tough trying to find another interpreter for all her clients, but that, after all, had been part of the deal they'd all agreed to. *Come hell or high water*, she remembered.

'What about Jamie?' she asked. 'Have you called him?'

'Not yet. I thought you might.'

'Of course I will, if you want me to.'

'It's all my own fault.' Annie was close to tears. 'I'm so weak, I'm such an awful coward—'

'What are you talking about, Annie?' Olivia could hardly believe her ears. 'You're amazing, the wonderful life you've made for yourself, the way you are with your children—'

'I'm not amazing at all, Livvy.'

Suddenly, Olivia thought, Annie didn't sound like Annie. The woman she knew was a confident, capable person, but right now Annie didn't only sound distraught or depressed – she sounded diminished.

'I'm a mess,' Annie went on. 'You just wouldn't believe how much of a mess I've made of everything.'

Olivia stopped checking the time, stopped even thinking about her meeting. 'Is it Edward? Is your marriage in trouble?'

'Not really. Not yet.'

She'd said 'so far' when Olivia had asked her if the children were okay – Olivia didn't like the way the conversation was going.

'Okay,' she said, positively. 'You want me now, right? I'm not sure if I can actually get over there today – I will, if I can, but—'

'No,' Annie said abruptly. 'You can't come here.'

'So what do you want, Annie? Do you want to meet in London? Or do you want to come here. I'd love it,' Olivia added quickly. 'You haven't stayed with me in an age.' She paused again. 'Annie, sweetheart, this is no good – you have to tell me what this is about. If I'm going to be able to help you at all, you're going to have to tell me *something*.'

'I'm scared to tell you.'

'That's just crazy.'

'I'm scared because when I tell you, you'll never feel the same way about me again. Nor will Jamie.' Annie sounded close to tears again. 'I hate myself so much, Livvy, and I'm afraid you'll hate me, too, when you know.'

'Nothing could ever make me hate you, Annie.'

'Maybe. Maybe not.'

Olivia was growing more alarmed by the second. 'Annie, tell me now, right now. Do it real fast, like pulling off a Band-Aid.'

Annie was silent.

'Come on, Annie.'

'I'm a junkie,' Annie said.

Olivia, in shock, said nothing.

'Valium,' Annie went on. 'Diazepam. They call it being dependent, but that doesn't describe it at all.' She paused one more time. 'I'm addicted to tranquillizers, Livvy, and if I don't do something soon – if you don't help me do something – I think they're going to destroy me.'

*   *   *

Olivia realized a while later, after she'd called Jamie in Boston and enlisted his help, that until now she had pretty much fallen for the image that Annie Aldrich Thomas had wanted her friends to have of her life in England. Namely, that it was just about as perfect as anything could be.

Married to Edward Thomas, a man she loved, with three children – Sophie, aged five, William, aged four, and Liza, aged three – a golden retriever named Bella, two cats named Leo and Boots, and a stable of horses, living in Banbury Farm House (a three-hundred-year-old house in the village of Stone Bridge, Oxfordshire, with a thatched roof, oak beams and a glorious back garden), Annie had long since become accepted into English village life. She was, of course, an American, but she had received part of her education in England, and she had, from the beginning, made valiant efforts to fit in. She had no apparent arrogance, she was strong, plucky and patient, yet she also displayed sufficient humility to her neighbours to encourage them to offer first their help and, later, their friendship. Edward, fifteen years older than his wife, thought the world of her, was consummately proud of Annie's ladylike beauty and calm, of the impeccable way she cared for their home and brought up their children; of the manner in which she had fitted, so seamlessly, into his world.

Olivia and Jamie had observed Annie's new life mostly from a distance through the regular correspondence that Annie had scrupulously maintained, but they had both visited the Thomases from time to time, had even stayed in the pretty guest suite at Banbury Farm House, and though Olivia thought of herself as reasonably intuitive, she knew now that she, like Jamie, had utterly failed to notice that Annie was unhappy. Had utterly failed Annie.

*   *   *

It was an accident – the third in a trilogy of minor disasters one year earlier, in the autumn of 1986, that had first made Annie wonder if she might, perhaps, have a problem. First, in the second week of September, she had forgotten to tell Edward that it was four-year-old Sophie's first open day at Stone Bridge Primary School, and so Edward had been unable to attend; and Annie had had to bear the looks of generously reined-in disappointment on both father's and daughter's faces and to explain to Sophie's teachers and the other parents why her husband was not present. Second, just a fortnight later, on the morning when Annie had been supposed to catch the eight-eleven train to London to meet Edward for an important solicitor's meeting and luncheon, she had overslept and missed the train and had not arrived until the meeting was over and the luncheon well under way.

And then there was the accident.

To begin with that morning, Annie had woken up with all the symptoms of premenstrual syndrome: tension head-ache, sore breasts and a sense of gloom and irritability. She'd taken a two milligram Valium – as she did on more mornings these days than in the past – showered, applied her make-up and dressed, feeling a little better; but then at the breakfast table first Sophie, then William and, finally, inevitably, little Liza had begun acting up – Annie's children's bouts of naughtiness always started with the oldest and then rolled inexorably down towards the baby like a snowball.

'Sophie, go fetch your blazer, please.' Annie stood and picked up her coffee cup and cereal bowl to put them in the sink.

Sophie shook her blonde curls, cast her blue eyes

downwards and played with the remainder of the toast on her plate.

'Sophie, stop that and go on, please.' Tension gripped Annie's stomach.

'I don't want to.'

'Don't be silly, sweetheart.'

'I don't want to go to school today, Mummy.'

Annie stopped clearing the big pine kitchen table. 'Why?' she asked, instantly anxious, alert as she always was to the slightest hint of illness in any of her family. 'Don't you feel good, sweetheart?'

'No,' Sophie said.

Annie came right over and laid a hand on her forehead. 'You're cool enough. How don't you feel good?'

'I feel sick.'

'You do?'

'Sick and tired,' Sophie said and then grinned hugely. She had begun adopting expressions her parents used all too frequently, thought it wonderfully amusing.

'Sophie, you're a naughty girl,' Annie said, good-humouredly. 'You know you should never tell fibs about feeling ill.'

Sophie threw her bit of toast at William.

'Hey!' William, three years old but big for his age, threw it back and hit Sophie on the cheek.

'William, stop that.' Annie retrieved the toast and wiped Sophie's buttery cheek. Sophie wriggled and pushed her away. 'You, too, miss.'

In her high chair, little Liza began crying and Bella whined. Annie ignored them both and went on removing dishes from the table and placing them in the sink. The tension that had vanished the instant she'd believed her older daughter unwell, returned, and with Edward away in

London all this week and Marie-Louise, their Swiss–French mother's help, already on her way to Oxford for her day off, Annie knew from past experience that the whole package was a recipe for a really bad day. She'd probably be better off taking a second pill to prevent things getting out of hand, before she let it get to her. Annie believed in preventative medicine; Grace Aldrich, her mother, had taught her that vitamin C kept colds away. Annie had learned for herself that diazepam kept panic attacks away.

Upstairs in her bathroom – with Sophie in her blazer and William ready for nursery school, both minding little Liza, all downstairs waiting for the off – Annie took the small plastic bottle from her mirror-fronted cabinet, shook out a little white pill and swallowed it. ('May make you sleepy. If persists next day do not drive.')

She wondered sometimes about that caution, yet Peter Cary – Edward's old family doctor – had told her that it was all right to take the odd pill when she needed it, and he knew that wasn't necessarily at night, and the white printed label on the bottle said 'To be taken when required' and nothing about taking only at night. And in any case, the pills never seemed to make her sleepy during the day, just soothed her, smoothed away those knots in her stomach and made her better able to cope.

She had delivered both Sophie and William safely and was on her way to collect some groceries from Tryon's, their general store, when it happened. An ancient Morris Minor stopped just ahead of Annie's Range Rover at the crossroads, waiting to turn into Stone Bridge Road. A large gap opened up, but still the Morris Minor waited, its right indicator sticking out like a yellow popsicle.

'Go on, Mummy,' Liza said from her safety seat behind Annie.

'We can't go yet, Liza,' Annie said, glad she'd taken the extra Valium, which was so much better than allowing herself to get edgy and impatient behind the wheel.

'Want to go pooh-pooh, Mummy,' Liza said – she was always saying she wanted to go pooh-pooh when she wanted things to move faster.

The Morris Minor started to edge out, then stalled.

'Mummy, go!' Liza said, the first note of genuine desperation lengthening the second word.

'Take it easy, sweetheart.'

Annie took her foot off the brake and pulled smoothly out, preparing to bypass the Morris in order to get to Tryon's before Liza really kept her promise and poohed in her pants. The traffic to the right was way off, held up by a Royal Mail van while the pillar box outside Dolins Bakery was emptied. She began to turn right, driving smoothly and sweetly, making a perfect, textbook turn—

'Pooh-pooh!' Liza shrieked.

Reflex made Annie look up into the rear-view mirror to see if Liza's round cheeks had gone bright red as they always did when she was really about to go – and the Range Rover's nearside front wing crunched hard into the United Dairies milk float that had come out of nowhere.

'Oh, my God,' Annie said.

Liza shrieked again, much more piercingly than before.

'Oh, my *God*!' Annie pulled up the handbrake and turned around. 'Liza, are you okay?' Frantically, she unfastened her seatbelt and wriggled herself right around. 'Sweetheart, *speak* to me!'

Liza's cheeks were scarlet.

'Pooh-pooh, Mummy,' she said disgustedly.

Having exchanged details with the milkman and no longer able to contemplate groceries or Tryon's, Annie headed for home. What she needed most right now was to get Liza bathed and changed and then to phone Edward straightaway and confess about the car. Not that he'd mind; he wasn't that kind of a husband, thank God, he'd only care about her and Liza. But still, if she didn't tell him this morning, Annie knew she'd get a bad case of the guilts, which would get worse as the day progressed, and there was always the possibility that if she waited until evening when Edward phoned from London, she might forget to tell him, and then he'd get home and see the damage and he might think she'd deliberately tried to keep it from him.

For heaven's sake, Annie, she told herself as she turned the Range Rover into their nice, broad, obstacle-free driveway, *Edward isn't like that – it wouldn't occur to him to think you'd deliberately hide anything from him.* But he might, she reasoned as she freed her smelly, tear-stained daughter from her safety harness, if she didn't call him right away, if she did other things first and maybe forgot. If Edward got home and found the dents and she'd said nothing, it would be only natural for him to think just exactly that.

'Are you and Liza all right?' was all Edward wanted to know when she reached him at his office in the City.

'We're fine, Edward. Not a scratch, not even a bruise.'

'And the milkman?'

'He was fine, too – and he was really nice about it.'

'So he should have been.'

'The car's a bit damaged though,' Annie confessed, 'and the milk float had a real dent in it.'

'That's just metal, darling,' Edward said. 'Nothing to get upset about.' It was such a relief to hear his gentle, wise voice that Annie felt much better for a while. But then later on the tension came back and she started seeing pictures in her mind of how much worse the accident might have been – and before long it would be lunchtime and she'd have to go and pick up William, and she really wasn't sure she was in a fit state – she wasn't calm enough, and she'd thought that the second pill would have soothed her sufficiently, but clearly it hadn't, so she'd better be sure to have another before she got back into the car again.

That night Liza, who had appeared till then quite unfazed by the whole incident, woke up screaming, and Annie, dragged horribly from her own heavy sleep by the piercing, terrifying sound of her daughter's distress, was only able with difficulty to glean from the two-year-old's garbled account that she had dreamed they were all in the car and Mummy had made a big bang and everyone was dead – Mummy and Daddy and Sophie and William and Liza, too.

At that moment Annie knew that it was time to get a prescription for a higher dosage of tranquillizers from the doctor, because, after all, her children were her responsibility, and she'd only driven into the back of that milk float because her nerves had allowed Liza to distract her, and she needed to be perfectly calm to drive properly, safely.

To function well, sensibly, *normally*, as she'd been brought up. To keep up appearances. To keep Edward's household running properly. To be a good wife to him. And a good, safe mother. The way her own mother had been.

6

She had swallowed her first tranquillizer the day Franklin
and Grace had been buried. Susan Aldrich, a cousin, had
handed her a few tiny white pills and had told Annie they
would make things a little easier. 'Trust me,' Susan had said
– and Annie had swallowed one obediently, and her cousin
had been right; the pain had still been there, but the pill
had dulled the edges a little. She'd taken an occasional one
up until the memorial service, but once that, too, had been
endured, Annie hadn't even thought about taking another
tranquillizer for several months, until a prolonged bout of
insomnia had sent her to a doctor in San Francisco who
had immediately written her a prescription for a handful
of two milligram Valium.

'Just to relax you,' he'd said.

'Tranquillizers?' Annie had been dubious.

'Better than sleeping pills,' the doctor had told her.
'And certainly better than not sleeping.' He'd looked at
her anxious expression and smiled. 'Now don't look so
worried. This is just to get your sleeping pattern back
on track.'

The tablets had done their work, and Annie had been careful not to abuse them, had stopped after a few nights' good rest and had stuck the bottle, still two-thirds full, in the back of her night table drawer, not taking it out again for several months, when another period of insomnia had threatened to become debilitating. And that was all. A prescription drug, as safe and respectable and useful as any antibiotic, used for a specific problem and then forgotten.

Meeting Edward, generous, successful, attractive, older Edward, whom she accepted was probably as close a figure to Franklin Aldrich as she'd been able to find, had seemed the greatest blessing to Annie. Edward Thomas, with his intelligent grey eyes, fine, strong bone structure and silver-templed hair, had turned out to be precisely what he had promised to be; apart from a fondness for pheasant and grouse shooting, which Annie loathed, there was no dark side to him, no hidden agenda, no nasty surprises. He was a kind and decent man, a splendid husband and father, and married life for Annie Aldrich Thomas had, in most ways, worked out just as Edward had vowed it would when he had proposed to her.

And yet as lucky as she now accepted she was, some things still seemed to have taken their toll on Annie. The loss of her parents, her roots and her safety net. The moving from place to place, the jolting back and forth by circumstances and fate. The anchoring in what had been decreed by her marriage as her new, permanent home, the place in which Edward Thomas's wife was expected to thrive, grow old and, ultimately, be buried. The pressures that her foreignness exerted on Annie, the strain of concealing those pressures from both Edward and their children and their neighbours and friends. Annie coped well enough with the basics, with learning the rules of cricket and rounders and rugby football, and she became adept at making jam roly-poly, which William adored, and Yorkshire pudding, which Edward liked on Sundays. But the really tiny, yet crucial things, the subtle differences in British manners and etiquette and basic thought processes, made Annie – strictly in private – desperately afraid of doing the wrong thing.

Edward and their friends all seemed to think that she was a perfect wife and mother – and Olivia told her more than once how super-competent she was – but Annie looked at their neighbours and acquaintances and at the wives of Edward's three brothers, all living in Oxfordshire or Gloucestershire, and found herself wanting. She thought that she felt, perhaps, something like the way an American tree sparrow might feel, living in the midst of a flock of indigenous English birds; her feathers looked ordinary enough – to most people, she probably did look like a regular sparrow – but Annie knew that she neither was, nor ever would be, and instead of rejoicing in her originality, she fretted over it.

Yet she would not, could not even contemplate sharing her problems with her husband or with anyone else. Annie came from the kind of stock who got on with life, who put on a brave face, who acted when necessary, and Annie acted with such excellence that she often believed in her own performance. But increasingly the act had come to require a little more help than before, and where some people might have downed a glass of wine or a vodka martini, Annie, who hated the idea of drinking alcohol around her children, reached for her crutch, the Valium bottle, instead.

*　　*　　*

Little things had started going wrong long before the car accident. In the past, Annie had had such a good, sharp memory, but over a period of time she realized she was forgetting things, so she began making lists and sticking little memory joggers where she knew she'd be sure to see them: on the fridge, on mirrors, on the windscreen. But still things went wrong – the odd arrangement, here and there. Edward once told Annie that she had become known in the village for being well organized, but one week she forgot first that it was her turn to do the church flowers, and then she got the time of Sophie's dentist appointment wrong. And once, she dragged William and Liza up and down Stone Bridge Road looking for the car, and William kept trying to tell her something, but she'd gotten too distracted to listen to him, and it turned out she'd parked it in the car park instead. No one seemed troubled by the little things – no one else ever really seemed to even notice them – but Annie did, Annie noticed them, and when she did, she took another pill. It was incumbent on her, she told herself, to be happy, calm and organized for her family's sake. Her wonderful life was far too precious for her to take risks with. And there was certainly nothing risky about taking the odd tablet given to her by Dr Cary; she had, after all, started out with two milligram tablets back in 1976, and even if, these days, she sometimes took three tablets in a day whereas in the beginning she'd only ever taken one, the prescribed dosage on the bottle was up to three daily, so she knew she was perfectly safe.

It was the accident with the Range Rover and Liza's nightmare that sent her to Peter Cary, in early October of 1986, for a supply of five milligram tablets.

'I don't think I'd be happy to do that,' he told her.

Annie sat on the bumpy, horsehair-stuffed chair she'd sat on so many times in the past, in the doctor's cosy, over-warm, comfortingly old-fashioned surgery, and looked at him in surprise.

'Why not?' she asked.

Peter Cary scratched his white head and looked back at her with eyes that seemed more intent and alert than they had ever been before. Annie had often privately thought that while she was perfectly happy to entrust all the normal family influenzas and childhood diseases to this ruddy-faced old man, she would be inclined to take anything more potentially serious to Andrew Miller, her private general physician in London. Yet suddenly here she was, asking for a slightly higher dosage of what Dr Cary had unquestioningly been giving her for years, and he was looking at her with these new, curious, watchful eyes.

'Why do you think you need five milligram tablets, Annie?'

Annie felt flustered. 'I just thought—' She stopped, feeling as if she was on trial, as if saying the wrong thing, giving the wrong answer to the doctor's trick question, might result in her being sentenced to no pills at all.

'How many pills do you find you take in a day?' Cary asked.

'It varies,' Annie said.

'One? Two?'

'Two, sometimes,' Annie said.

'Three?'

'Occasionally.'

'How occasionally?'

Annie knew she was floundering. If she told Peter Cary the truth, the real truth, if she told him that she felt she had to have stronger tablets because she was afraid she couldn't go on functioning as a good, safe mother without them, he was bound to want to tell Edward, and Edward knowing about her needing tranquillizers was the last thing on earth she wanted.

She decided to back off.

'Just once in a while,' she said. 'Mostly it's still just one, or two maximum, but now and again I just can't seem to get to sleep properly with the one at night, and then I end up having to get up and take another pill a couple of hours later, and so I just thought if I took one five milligram it might help me get a really good night's sleep.' She paused. 'I guess maybe it's not such a great idea after all.'

'I think not,' the doctor agreed, gently.

'So shall we just leave it as the usual?' Annie asked.

Peter Cary leaned forward over his desk. 'Any other problems you want to tell me about, Annie?'

'No,' she said brightly. 'No problems. It's just me – you know – I've always been a little nervy now and again.'

'And you're sure there's nothing else?'

'Nothing at all.'

Three days later, on her next visit to London, Annie went to see Andrew Miller, and this time she was more prepared than she had been with Dr Cary.

'I'm nervous of flying,' she told him. 'I mean, really scared. And the thing is I have a couple of long-distance trips coming up, and this is the only way I can face them.'

'You say that diazepam agrees with you?' Dr Miller asked.

'Pretty well.' Annie smiled at him. He was everything Peter Cary was not: good-looking, young – in his early forties, she guessed – and as slick as his state of the art surgery.

He nodded. 'I can prescribe a few two milligram tablets for you.' He reached for his prescription pad.

'I don't think they'd be strong enough,' Annie said quickly. 'I really get scared, Dr Miller, and I'm afraid of panicking on board.' She paused. 'I lost my parents in a helicopter crash, you know.'

The doctor took that in. 'You want five milligram tablets,' he said.

'I'd feel happier just knowing I had them,' Annie said.

'Don't you have a doctor closer to home, Mrs Thomas?'

Annie fought to stay cool. 'I'm not too happy with him,' she said. 'And I knew I was coming to London, and you looked after me so well when I had the stomach problem—'

Andrew Miller smiled. 'I'm glad I could help.' He reached for the prescription pad again. 'Would you say ten tablets would be enough?'

'I may have a few flights to get through.' Annie made a show of working it out. 'Maybe fifteen would be better? It would save me bothering you again.'

The doctor nodded. 'I'll make it twenty.' He started to write. 'But I'd suggest you break them in half, take one half an hour or so before take-off, and see how you go. You may not need the second half.'

'That sounds sensible,' Annie said.

For a while, just knowing she had them, in addition to her regular two milligram prescription, made her feel strong enough to tuck them away in the back of her dressing-table drawer. Until the end of October, when Edward asked her to help him host a house party – and there were so few things he asked of her that she told him it would be fine, but the planning got on top of her and she began to dread getting the details wrong. And by the weekend of the party, she was gulping down pills like M&Ms, and on the first day she made a mistake over the seating plan, and then later that same evening, the main course was badly undercooked and she hadn't noticed. And Annie looked at Edward, just after he'd taken his first bite, and she saw the dismay on his face, and then she saw him cover it up, and he was just as much a gentleman as he always had been.

But before the next week was over, Annie was taking ten milligrams at a time.

'I'm flying into London for three days' work with a Swiss feature writer,' Olivia told Annie on the phone a few weeks later, 'and a meeting at the Arthur Segal Foundation, but I could snatch about three hours or so on Friday afternoon. Can you meet me in Harrods? We could do some shopping and have lunch.'

'I'm not sure,' Annie floundered.

'Come on, Annie, I'm longing to see you.'

Given more warning, in her current jittery state, Annie would have thought up a decent excuse, but as it was, with Olivia's warm, energetic voice practically dragging her out of the house, Annie simply caved in.

'What time?'

'Twelve-thirty okay for you?'

'Fine,' Annie said.

She was already terrified by the prospect.

Apart from a short bout of panic in the crush of people on the ground floor, she was doing okay until they sat down at their table in the Georgian Restaurant. It was something about the change in atmosphere, about the old-fashioned serenity of the long, endless dining room. Annie felt a strange sensation almost immediately, an alarming, inexplicable detachment from everyone and everything in the room, as if her mind was made of cotton wool, her body of lead. She looked across the table at Olivia to see if she'd noticed, but Olivia, thank God, was engrossed in the menu. Annie wondered if she could manage to reach for her bag, to get to her pills, take one more . . .

'I guess I'll go for the buffet,' Olivia said. 'How about you?'

Annie had the terrifying sensation of sudden paralysis. Maybe her vocal cords were paralysed, too? Maybe if she tried to open her mouth to answer, no words would emerge . . .

'Annie?' Olivia put down her menu. 'Are you okay?'

Annie felt the panic rising, felt a new urge either to scream or to run or maybe both, but instead, somehow, she dug the nails of her right hand into her own thigh, and, mercifully, she felt the pain, and if she felt that, then maybe she could at least speak, could find a way to escape from this place, from this moment, without Olivia finding out the truth.

'Annie?' Curiosity gave way to concern. 'What's wrong?'

'I don't feel too well.' There. Words, real words. She dug her nails into her other leg. 'I'm really sorry, Livvy, but I think I'm going to have to leave.'

'You feel nauseous?' Olivia began immediately to respond. 'Hold on while I get these parcels together—'

'Our drinks,' Annie said. 'We have to pay.'

'Yes.' Olivia looked around for a waiter. 'I'll take care of that. You get to the ladies' room and I'll meet you there.'

Annie stood, not knowing if her new, leaden legs would hold her up, but they did. She felt a little relief, wondered fleetingly if she might, after all, be able to sit out lunch. *No*, her mind told her, *get out while you can.*

'Do you know where it is?' she asked.

Olivia smiled up at her, warm and gentle and calming. 'I'll find you.'

Annie sat, her head in her hands, in the privacy of the lavatory, and gave in, for a moment, to tears. She knew what she wanted, more than anything. She wanted – she *longed* – to tell Olivia everything. Livvy would be shocked, would probably think her utterly weak and foolish, but she would still know what to do, would take over and help her deal with it. Except that the first thing she would insist on was taking her home and making sure she told Edward everything, and Annie could not bear that.

And so instead of telling Olivia the truth, Annie got another pill out of her handbag and swallowed it there, inside the stall, without water, and when she heard Olivia's voice calling her name, she called back that she was all right now, and then she dried her eyes and checked her face in her compact mirror; and even if Livvy did see she'd been crying, it was natural enough to be upset when you were sick.

'I think I must be coming down with something,' she said outside, by the basins. 'Sophie wasn't feeling too good earlier in the week.'

'Guess we'd better cut things short,' Olivia said.

'I'm so sorry, Livvy.'

Olivia put a hand on her arm. 'Don't be a goose. You can't help being ill, can you?'

'No.' Annie said, deeply ashamed, 'I suppose not.'

Olivia tucked an arm firmly through hers. 'Think you can make it out to the street?'

'I hope so.'

'I'll get you out. Just hold on to me.'

Annie felt better, almost normal, the instant they were

outside the store in the fresh air. There were plenty of black taxis, all waiting in line.

'I'll be okay now,' she said. 'You go back inside, go on shopping.'

'I'm taking you to the station,' Olivia said.

'No, you're not. There's no need.'

'Maybe not, but I still am.'

All the way to Paddington, Annie sat quietly, knowing that Olivia would take her silence for queasiness or weakness, but her thoughts were hammering in her head. She ought to tell her now. *But what about Edward?* This was the perfect moment to tell her. *But what about the children?*

She told her nothing.

With Olivia safely back in Switzerland, Annie began to consider the possibility that perhaps she ought, after all, to speak to Edward about the tranquillizers; not making too big a deal, just a mention, perhaps, she thought, of the tensions that had led her to start down that road. The more she thought about it, the more sensible an idea it seemed to her. Edward would not condemn her. She hadn't wanted to tell him before because she'd hated to upset him, but if she went on much longer, she knew she would end up upsetting him far more grievously, because she had a pretty good idea by now that she was addicted to Valium. Or at least, whereas in the past she had believed she could have stopped taking her pills and survived, now the very notion of existing without them was inconceivable.

She decided to broach the subject that coming weekend. They would be at the London flat together, away from the children, and they were going to a birthday dinner at the Savoy, and it ought to be an easy-going affair, and with a bit of luck and the usual help of her yellow pills, she ought to manage the party well enough, and then she would tell Edward on Sunday morning.

If it hadn't been for Ludovic Brandt, the man whose birthday they were helping celebrate, Annie thought she might have gone through with her plan, but as it was, a few chance words by Ludo, thrown into the conversational ring so casually, so innocently, ruined everything.

'I'm bloody tired, as a matter of fact,' he replied to Babs Standish's comment that he was looking marvellous. 'Haven't had a decent night's sleep in weeks.' He swigged down a generous mouthful of Château Croizet-Bages. 'Think I'll ask the quack for some sleeping pills.'

'Personally, I'd rather stick to claret,' Babs said.

'Anything's better than pills,' Edward said.

Annie, seated on Ludo's left, tried not to freeze.

'I don't know about that,' Charles Standish said. 'Those pills the doc gave me for my blood pressure just about saved my life.'

'That's different,' Edward said. 'I'm talking about the dope kind – sleeping pills, tranquillizers, that kind of rubbish.'

Annie thought about the contents of her handbag, the pretty little round porcelain box in which her Valium nestled, their very presence a comfort to her. 'Surely they can be very useful,' she said to her husband, 'to those who need them?'

'People who need such things,' Edward answered, with a sharpness that startled her, 'are either fools or weaklings.' He softened a little. 'I think – I hope – I'm a reasonably tolerant man on the whole, but I quite frankly despise people who can't cope with life without resorting to drugs.'

*   *   *

Later, alone with him at the flat, Annie found him in his study going through papers at his desk.

'Thought you might like a little nightcap.' She held out a cognac snifter.

'Thank you, my love.' He took it from her. 'Nothing for you?'

'No. You know me.' She paused. 'Mind if I join you for a few minutes?'

'I wish you would.' He sipped at his drink. 'Good evening, wasn't it?'

'Lovely.' Annie sat down on the chesterfield. The question she wanted yet feared to ask was burning a hole in her tongue. 'Edward?'

'What, darling?'

She began carefully. 'You seemed so upset tonight.'

'Did I? When?'

'When Ludo mentioned sleeping pills.'

'Yes,' he said.

Annie waited a moment, but he said nothing further. 'Why?' she asked.

'Why did that upset me?'

'Yes.' She looked at his face, saw an unfamiliar dark look in his eyes. 'If you'd rather not tell me, I don't mind,' she said quickly. 'It's just that things don't usually get to you that way.'

'And you were concerned.'

'Yes. A little.' Annie waited again.

Edward drank a larger swallow of cognac, then set the glass down on his leather-topped desk. 'I suppose it's never come up before, has it? Not between us, I mean.'

'Sleeping pills, you mean?' Annie said, still very careful. 'No reason why it should have, I guess.'

'Not just sleeping pills,' Edward said, not quite looking at

79

her. 'Other things, too, as I said in the restaurant. Painkillers. Tranquillizers. Pills to dull you, then get you going. Pills to help you survive.'

Annie leaned forward, her hands on her knees. Her heart was pounding too fast. 'Edward, you sound as if you're talking about yourself.'

'No,' he said. 'Not myself. Not exactly.'

Her palms were suddenly damp. He knew, she thought, in terror. Oh, Lord, he *knew*.

Edward's voice was very soft. 'My mother,' he said.

It had been the one dark secret of his life, he told her; the only thing of significance he had not shared with her. He had not exactly lied to her about his mother. Sophia Thomas had died of bone cancer, but what Edward had not told Annie was that his mother had also been a morphine addict. The drug had not only destroyed her, but it had also ruined his father's life and wrecked his and his brothers' childhoods.

'We saw our mother euphoric when she'd had enough, and we saw her when she tried to stop – and she did try, I'm sure of that,' Edward told Annie, and she'd never heard his voice so laden with sorrow. 'She'd shake and sweat, and she'd have such awful pains – pains just from the withdrawal, not even related to the cancer. That came later, and by then it was impossible to tell which was which, not that it mattered, not that it helped her or us. Our mother was in agony, more kinds of agony than you can ever begin to imagine.'

'Oh, Edward,' Annie said, her voice little more than a whisper. 'I'm so sorry. So terribly sorry,'

'No need,' he said. 'Not any more.' He smiled at her anxious face. 'I have you now, and the children, and my brothers have good, decent families, too, and I'm a very,

very lucky man.' He paused. 'But you see now why I feel as I do about drugs.'

'Yes,' Annie said. 'Of course.'

She saw how he felt – oh, how clearly she saw that. And she knew just as clearly that any hope she might have had of telling him about her problem was gone. That she could never, ever confide in him about that, of all things.

And more than that – worse than that – she had a brand-new fear after that night in London. Her husband had told her that his childhood had been destroyed because of drugs, and so Annie was afraid now – she was *terrified* – that if Edward ever learned the truth about her, she might be responsible for ruining the rest of his adulthood as well. Perhaps even the lives of their own children.

So instead of telling Edward, she went on.

And instead of getting help, she took more.

She survived Christmas and New Year by keeping herself so madly busy that the sheer discipline, mixed with adrenalin and, as always, her pills, dragged her through. But with the festive season over, reality stepped in with renewed vengeance. Edward was back in London for at least five days of most weeks; Marie-Louise was visiting her family in Switzerland; Sophie, William and Liza were constantly seeking ways to fill their school-free days. And worst of all, however much Valium Annie took during those post-Christmas days and nights, it never seemed to be enough. She trembled too much, she felt her heart racing, sometimes missing beats altogether, she perspired; her mind wandered, she made her lists, scribbled down her memory joggers but forgot to look at them, forgot she'd even made them, let people down, most often the children; her legs and arms felt strange, her words, once in a while, slurred, and she dropped things all the time.

'I'm sorry' – Jane Reece-Smith, the mother of one of William's friends, told her one morning outside school on a day when it was Annie's turn on the rota to pick up both boys and take them home – 'but I've decided I'd rather collect Michael myself today.'

'Oh,' Annie said, vaguely. 'I don't mind fetching him at all.'

'I'm sure,' Mrs Reece-Smith said. 'But still, I'd rather do it myself.'

The unmistakably chilly quality in the other woman's tone cut through Annie's morning fog. 'Is something wrong?' she asked.

Mrs Reece-Smith looked her in the eye. 'Frankly, Mrs Thomas, you don't look up to it.'

'I'm fine,' Annie said, defensively.

'No,' Mrs Reece-Smith said firmly, 'I don't think you are. If you don't mind my saying so, Mrs Thomas, you seem a little woolly to me. A little wobbly, perhaps.' She paused. 'Are you unwell?'

'No.' The other woman's steady gaze unnerved Annie. 'That is, I think I may be coming down with something.'

'A touch of flu, perhaps,' Mrs Reece-Smith suggested.

'Perhaps.'

Nothing more was said, but Annie knew now that her deficiencies were being observed. And if Jane Reece-Smith considered her unsafe to drive her son – which was, more or less, what she had said – then perhaps she was right.

Within twelve hours, Annie had called every other mother on the school driving rota and withdrawn her services.

'I've been getting bad migraines lately,' she told them all. 'I never seem to get warnings any more – and I don't want to take any risks with the children.'

None of the mothers argued. No one was anything but polite, even kind, but Annie felt that she'd jumped just before someone else had pushed her. She was running out of time. The drug that she had always believed had been her helper, was wrecking her life. The way morphine had wrecked Edward's mother's.

She had to quit. Before someone told Edward, or before Sophie or William heard a rumour at school. Before something awful happened. Before it was too late.

She made up her mind to quit, no matter how hard it was. She worked out a plan. Mrs Reece-Smith had suggested the flu, so that was what Annie told her friends and neighbours she had – just a mild case, and she needed no help, just a little peace and quiet. She told Olivia and Jamie she was going out of town, so that they wouldn't call, and she got the children away on sleep-overs for a whole week because she thought she might start climbing the walls or getting sick or having the D.T.s or something, and if the house was empty there would be no one to see.

For the first few days, apart from the tension of waiting for something to happen and the fear that her will might not be strong enough to stop her reaching for her pills – she had locked them up, but she hadn't thrown them out; she hadn't been able to bring herself to do that – it wasn't too bad. She felt almost smart, almost vindicated. *See*, she told herself, *it's okay, I'm okay, I can give them up, I'm not an addict*.

But then it started.

It was a nightmare. A real, honest-to-God waking night-mare, a thousand times worse than she had anticipated. She felt physically sick, as if she were getting the flu, but worse. She shook and felt so dizzy that it seemed as if the floor was moving. But the worst thing of all was the despair, so awful, so intense that she wanted to die, and the knowledge that there was only one other way of ending it, and that was getting to her pills. Except that she couldn't find the key to the cabinet she'd locked them into, and afterwards she didn't remember doing it, but later – hours later, days later, she wasn't sure – when she was starting to come out of it, she found that she'd torn off the door.

Respectable, neat, clean, golden-haired, blue-eyed little Annie Aldrich Thomas had ripped off the hinges with her bare hands, and she had the cut fingers and broken glass everywhere to prove it.

She thought she might go mad. For a long while now, she had been obtaining her tablets simply by telephoning her two doctors – Peter Cary in Stone Bridge and Andrew Miller in London – alternately, and asking for repeat prescriptions. Suddenly, her supply system had begun to fail her. Both physicians were displaying growing reluctance to go on prescribing for her. Both had suggested, independently, that it was time for Annie to seek psychiatric counselling. And then, just a fortnight after her own, secret, futile attempt at withdrawal, Peter Cary threatened to stop the Valium completely unless Annie agreed to see a specialist or to let him talk to Edward, and Andrew Miller told her that he wanted to reduce both the strength and quantity of her prescription.

'To see how you manage,' Miller said, in his calm, gentle manner.

'I won't manage,' Annie told him, desperately.

'Then diazepam on its own isn't enough for you.'

'It has to be,' Annie said.

'Why? Why won't you talk to a specialist, Mrs Thomas?'

'You know why.'

Andrew Miller remained very patient. 'And you know, because I've told you repeatedly, that there is no more reason for your husband to learn of an appointment with a psychiatrist than for him to find out you've seen me. We're all equally bound, Mrs Thomas, by patient confidentiality.'

'I know that.'

'Then why won't you at least give it a try?'

Annie stared at him across his big desk in total frustration. She'd told him and told him. 'Because it would mean lying to Edward, and I've never done that, not really.'

'You haven't told him you come here, have you?'

'I don't, often,' she said. 'They're only pills,' she added, trying to explain, to make him understand how she felt. 'Like aspirin or antibiotics. Going to see someone would be different.'

'Diazepam is nothing like aspirin, Mrs Thomas. And you don't come here often because you telephone my assistant instead, and she sends you an automatic repeat prescription.' Dr Miller shook his fair, handsome head. 'And it's been very remiss of me to permit that to go on for so long.'

He did let her get away with it that time, gave her, because of her obvious distress, the five milligram prescription that she had begged for, but he reduced the quantity and made it clear that she would have to return in person when her supply ran out and that he could not guarantee to go on treating her if she continued to ignore his advice.

* * *

She went shopping that afternoon. She went to Fortnum & Mason for Edward's favourite mustard, and then she went to Hatchards in Piccadilly to buy the latest Jeffrey Archer novel for Edward and some books for the children, and from there she walked up to Piccadilly Circus and went into Boots to have her new prescription filled. She had succeeded until then in blocking the new fears that Dr Miller's warning had aroused in her, but handing over the piece of paper with his familiar, overly large scrawl to the pharmacist, Annie was assailed by a sudden attack of panic. What if this was the last time? What if he did refuse to give her any more? She was even less likely to be able to talk Peter Cary round than Andrew Miller, which meant she'd have to find another doctor, and of course London, and even Oxford, were both filled with doctors, but she didn't think you could just walk in out of nowhere and add yourself to a strange doctor's list. And what if she couldn't? What if she ran out of pills?

She was trembling when she left Boots, and a part of her – the old Annie Aldrich Thomas part – hoped it wasn't visible to anyone else, but another part of her didn't care about that any more, cared only about where she was going to get another slip of white paper with her recipe for comparative calm, for a semblance of normality, of sanity, if it came to it.

The man was right in front of her before she saw him, practically touching her. He was brown-haired and very pale skinned, clean shaven and wearing sunglasses, even though it was almost dark.

'Need some help?' he asked her.

Annie was startled enough to stop walking.

'No.' She shook her head. 'No, thank you.' She moved away, looking for a taxi.

The man moved with her. 'You don't look too good.'

Annie tried to ignore him, stepped to the kerb and looked decisively to her right, searching for an empty taxi.

'I said you don't look very well,' the man said.

She turned her head just a little to look at him, then looked quickly away again back into the traffic. She felt ill with shock, knew now for certain that her inner terrors were on show to the whole world. She longed to get the little Boots paper bag out of her handbag and open the new bottle of pills, felt she needed to swallow one down instantly if she was going to be able to make it to the station, let alone home.

'I can help you,' the man said, very close to her ear.

Annie turned and started walking away. The trembling became shaking, the feeling of nausea threatened to become actual sickness. It was a cold, damp afternoon, but she felt perspiration on her forehead and upper lip. She abandoned the kerb, afraid she might keel over into the path of the buses and cars, got closer to the shops, to the walls, preferring a solid wall beside her just in case, to stop her from falling.

'I know what you need,' the man said.

'Go away,' Annie said, through gritted teeth.

'I can get you anything,' he said, right behind her. 'No prescription, no quacks, no questions.'

'Go *away*,' Annie said, furiously, and anger and fear pushed some of the sickness temporarily out of her system, pumping sanity-saving adrenalin into her blood. 'Get away from me or I'll call a policeman.'

The man was beside her, walking at exactly her pace, and smiling. 'Now why would you do that?' he asked confidently. 'I'm just offering to help you, that's all. You need help. I can see that.'

Annie stopped walking, right outside a pizza parlour.

'Please,' she said, and tears filled her eyes. 'Please, leave me alone.'

'Okay,' he said, easily. 'If you're sure.'

'Yes,' she said. An awful smell of onion, cheese and cheap beef swam around her head. She thought again that she might faint.

He smiled again. 'Last chance,' he said. 'Sure?'

'I'm *sure*,' Annie said, a sob in her voice.

He nodded. 'Right, then.'

Annie felt the glass wall of the pizza parlour behind her, felt the weight of her two Hatchards bags anchoring her. About fifty yards away, she spotted a For Hire taxi, wondered if she could make it if she ran.

'If you change your mind, I'll be around,' he said, and walked away.

For a moment, Annie closed her eyes. Then, opening them again, she saw that the taxi was still there, stuck in traffic. A man was walking towards it from the other direction, a man in a navy blue coat, carrying a briefcase and an umbrella.

A respectable man, Annie thought. *Not a drug addict.*

Home came into her head then, Banbury Farm House, with its thatched roof, so solid and safe. And Edward. And the children.

Annie opened her mouth.

'*Taxi!*' It was almost a scream. People around her stared as she launched herself, like a demented diver, towards the street. She reached the cab at the same instant as the man with the briefcase. She saw his hand reaching for the door handle and flung herself in front of him, felt the bag with the Jeffrey Archer book strike him on the shin, saw his startled, pained expression but experienced no guilt, no shame, only desperation.

She got the door open, threw her bags inside, clambered in and slammed the door shut again.

'Paddington Station,' she said, panting, and lay back against the seat.

The shame, she knew, would come later.

The Valium lasted her for one month. She called Dr Miller's rooms, tried to persuade his assistant to post a repeat prescription to her, but the doctor had either alerted the woman or placed a note on her file, and Annie was given no alternative but to make another appointment. She was in his surgery two days later, clammy-handed and full of foreboding.

'No more,' Andrew Miller told her, as he had said he would. 'Not unless you agree to see a psychiatrist.'

Annie looked at him, saw that he meant what he said.

'All right,' she said. 'I will.'

'Good.' The doctor opened his black leather address book. 'I'll call her now, set up an appointment for you.'

'Can't I do it myself?' Annie asked.

'No. I have to make the introduction.'

'You mean you don't trust me.'

Miller looked right at her. 'Probably not, in these circumstances.'

'Okay,' Annie said. 'You call.'

'When for?'

'I don't have my diary with me.'

'That's a pity,' Dr Miller said lightly.

'I don't. I really don't.' Annie reached down to the floor for her handbag. 'Look for yourself.' She opened it and put it on the desk. 'Please look. I didn't bring my diary with me.'

Andrew Miller's smile was kind. 'I believe you, Mrs

Thomas. But it doesn't alter my decision. No appointment, no prescription.'

Annie sagged. 'Tomorrow,' she said.

'Fine.' The doctor nodded and picked up the telephone. 'Though I'd be surprised if she had a free appointment that soon.' He looked at Annie's tightly drawn face, into her despairing eyes. 'I'll try my best.'

His best was not good enough. Annie was not certain, as she left Miller's rooms, stepped out into Wimpole Street, whether she was more, or less, distraught because the psychiatrist had been unable to find her a space for another three days. She had seventy-two more hours to fret over how she was going to handle the appointment, what lies she would spin to Edward if she had to, how honest she would be with the psychiatrist. Whether or not she would attend the appointment at all, and if she did, what the outcome would be. Would she come away with the only thing she wanted, needed – her precious yellow pills? Or would she be forced to endure a torture that could only be infinitely worse than the few days of attempted withdrawal she had put herself through in January?

She was not certain, later, much later, how she had reached Piccadilly Circus, whether she had taken a taxi or got on a bus or walked all the way. She could not even remember the final thought that had pushed her into that ultimate, irrevocable decision; that one flash of insanity that had risen and flickered above all the other rambling, incoherent craziness.

Once there, in that hubbub of traffic and rushing flow of people, Annie knew why she was there, what she had come for. She was looking for the man. For him or another like him. For a drug dealer.

'If you change your mind,' he'd said, 'I'll be around.'

Annie waited outside Boots for over an hour. From time to time, self-consciously, she checked her watch, to make it seem to most people as if she was waiting for a friend. Most people. Not the ones who would see through the façade of respectability, past the Aquascutum coat and the carefully applied, not-overdone make-up, to the naked desperation beneath.

'Need any help?'

Annie looked at the man. Not the same one. This one was younger, with close-cropped fair hair, a neat beard and no sunglasses to conceal his green, sharp eyes. A shudder passed through her, making every hair stand on end, giving her goose bumps, making even her nipples rigid beneath her Rigby and Peller handmade bra.

The man's eyes were on her face, focused hard on her.

'I said, need any help?' he asked again.

Annie became very calm. She and Edward had sailed to New York a few years ago on the *QE2*, and they'd passed through a violent storm from which they had emerged, it had seemed to them at the time, from one moment to the next. Out of surging, tumultuous waves into a peaceful, mirror-like ocean. That was how she felt at that moment.

'Yes,' she answered. 'Yes, please.'

They walked into Leicester Square, turned a corner into an alley, and Annie told him what she wanted, and he told her that would cost her fifty pounds, but she only had forty-seven pounds on her, plus her return ticket to Oxford, and she calculated – still marooned in that sea of temporary calm – that she needed to keep at least twelve pounds in order to get safely to Paddington Station and then from Oxford back to Stone Bridge. For thirty-five pounds she only got half of what he had been going to give her for fifty. That was the name of the game, he told her.

'Seller's market,' he said, not unpleasantly.

Annie did not argue.

She vomited twice, once in the lavatory on the train, once back home in her own bathroom, and then she stood under the shower for a long time, the way she understood victims of rape often did. When she swallowed the first of her new yellow pills, she felt suddenly terrified that they might be poisonous, that they might make her ill or even kill her. But the pill just did what it always did, dulled her nerve ends, took the spikes off her feelings, made her tolerably comfortable; and after a while, she became almost happy, because she knew now that she didn't have to go to see the psychiatrist at all, that she could cancel that appointment, and that she could voluntarily cut down on what Peter Cary and Andrew Miller prescribed for her, and they would be pleased with her, and Edward would never have to know.

And in the meantime, she could have as much Valium as she wanted.

7

Edward thought she was ill.

'I'm worried about you,' he said one rare weekday lunch-time in March – rare in that he was at home – over Marie-Louise's vegetable soup and potato cheese, served at the big pine table in their kitchen. 'You look very tired, darling.'

'I am a little tired,' Annie admitted. It was the first time in a long while that she had been forced to keep up appearances with Edward for so many hours on end, and the strain was proving almost unbearable.

'Could you be coming down with something?'

'No, I don't think so.'

'You really don't look well at all.' Edward peered at her pale face and shadowed eyes more closely, leaned forward a little across the table, eyeing her over the salad bowl. 'In fact you look quite dreadfully tired. Perhaps you should see Peter Cary?'

'I'm not ill, Edward.'

'Just for a check-up.'

'I don't need a check-up,' Annie said sharply. 'Please don't stare at me like that.'

'All right,' Edward said, surprised. 'Nothing for you to get het up about.' Unpersuaded, he leaned back again. 'It isn't like you to get so upset about little things.'

'I guess not,' Annie said, quietly. 'I'm sorry.'

'No need to apologize, darling.'

'Yes,' Annie said, 'there is.' She felt a great urge to cry, to let it all go, to unburden herself. But the memory was still there, like a warning beacon standing in her way, of Edward describing his mother's morphine addiction and the ruination of his boyhood. She could not unburden herself to Edward. Not now. Not ever.

'Annie, love.' Edward reached tenderly for her hand. 'What is it?'

'It's nothing,' she said, tightly. 'I'm just over-tired, as I said.'

'Which was why I suggested you see the doctor.' Seeing her expression, he held up his left hand. 'It's all right, I know you don't want to, though I don't quite understand why. I thought most Americans believed in check-ups.'

'I haven't been an American for years.' Annie forced a smile. 'Not a real one anyway. More of a stiff-upper-lip Brit these days.'

'What about a holiday?' The suggestion came carefully.

The dropping, at least for the moment, of Edward's threat to speak to Peter Cary about her flooded Annie with relief. 'That might be wonderful,' she said. The thought of escape flew like a scrap of heaven across her mind's eye. Blue skies, white beaches, no responsibilities, just time alone with Edward might heal her.

'Good,' he said, pleased. 'Where would you like to go?'

'I don't know.' *Anywhere*. 'How about you?'

'I couldn't go, my darling,' Edward said ruefully. 'I wish

to God I could, but there's no time, not for a few months at least.'

Heaven vanished. 'Then I can't go either.'

'Of course you can.' Edward let go of her hand and helped himself to a second serving of potato cheese. 'I expect it would do you the world of good.'

Annie put her knife and fork together and stood up. 'If we can't go away together, Edward,' she said coolly, 'then I don't want to go at all.'

'Can't you sit with me till I've finished?' he asked, mildly.

'No. I have things to do before Marie-Louise gets back with Liza.'

'What things?'

Annie felt cornered. 'All kinds of things,' she said with a touch of aggression. She longed to get upstairs into the privacy of the bathroom and take a pill. She picked up her plate and the fork slithered off onto the tiled floor with a clang. 'Damn,' she said, harshly, and bent to pick it up.

'Take it easy, darling,' Edward said, looking surprised.

'I would,' Annie responded, 'if you'd leave me alone.'

'I do,' Edward said, stung. 'Most of the time.'

'Yes.' Annie, at the sink, stared down at the globs of half-eaten potato cheese on her plate and felt sick and ashamed and yearning to cry or to go to sleep or to scream. Or to take two pills.

In silence, Edward stood up and brought his own plate over to the draining board and set it down. He looked at her, touched her right arm with one hand, but she wouldn't look back, didn't move a muscle, just went on staring down into the sink.

'I'll leave you, then,' he said, quietly. 'Go upstairs and do some work.'

Annie nodded, not trusting herself to speak.

'You're sure you're all right?' he asked, one more time.

'Mm,' she said, her voice stiff from the effort of holding it all in.

'See you later, then.'

'Later.'

When Marie-Louise brought Liza home, Annie was deeply asleep on top of their bed, and Edward, who had covered her carefully with an eiderdown, cautioned them not to disturb her. She was quite worn out, he said, and Marie-Louise – who had known for a very long time that Annie took too many tranquillizers, but who had been reminded by her parents in Switzerland at Christmas that so long as the children were being well looked after, it was not her place to interfere – kept silent. Though even Marie-Louise had not the least idea that Annie was heavily asleep because she had taken fifteen milligrams of Valium after lunch, which would in itself have knocked out a normal person for the best part of a day. Except that Annie had already swallowed ten milligrams first thing that morning, not to mention the ten she'd taken before bedtime the previous night.

Early the following Monday morning, Edward drove Annie, who had told him she wanted to go shopping, into London. She had woken up with a head and limbs so heavy that it had taken a long ice-cold shower to allow her to fix herself up sufficiently to pass muster, and what she wanted more than anything was to crawl back into bed and sleep forever. But the outing was necessary, even vital, for her tablet supply was low, and because Edward had been home for the past week this was the first opportunity she'd had to get to Piccadilly Circus and her lifeline.

'We could have lunch,' Edward said as he dropped her off outside Harvey Nichols. 'I won't see you till Friday otherwise.'

'Oh, Edward, I'd love to,' Annie lied. Playing for time, trying to think up an instant excuse, she juggled her handbag and umbrella and the carrier bag that contained a sweater she'd told Edward she needed to exchange. 'But there are so many things I have to do.' Her mind was too fuzzy to come up with anything better. 'Maybe I could call you later?'

'I'll be in meetings all morning.' He heard hooting and glanced up into the rear-view mirror. 'Darling, we're blocking the traffic, I must move.' He blew her a kiss as she got out of the car.

'I love you,' Annie said.

She wondered, as Edward smiled and drove off into Sloane Street, why she had said that; thought it was probably guilt. She told the children that she loved them every night at bedtime and often when she was parting from them, even for an hour or two, but it was not a custom of hers or Edward's to exchange loving remarks unless they were making love or engaged in a serious, intimate conversation. *And when did we last do either of those things?* Annie tried to remember as she forced herself into the department store, feeling hemmed in on all sides by tall, slender, daunting, confident young women, knowing that even if she managed no more legitimate shopping that day, she still had to exchange the sweater or risk having to explain to Edward why she had not.

She reached Piccadilly Circus before noon, took up her accustomed position outside Boots, made all the usual gestures that she felt lent respectability to her pathetic waiting: shifting impatiently from foot to foot, hugging her shoulder bag close in case of snatchers and checking her wristwatch periodically to indicate that the person she was expecting to meet was late.

When she was at last approached, it was by a young woman she had done business with twice previously. It was hypocritical and quite absurd, Annie realized, yet she remembered feeling a sense of shock and disgust the first time the woman had spoken to her because she had felt so sure that drug-peddling had to be a male pursuit. She knew now that was nonsense, and the woman knew precisely what Annie wanted, and Annie knew the price, and all that needed to happen was for the cash and the black market diazepam to change hands.

They were in an alley between Piccadilly Circus and Leicester Square, and Annie was opening her bag, preparing to take out the cash she had brought with her, when the girl glanced up and her expression turned from disinterest to iron.

'Drop me in it, lady,' she said, softly but violently, 'and you're dead.'

And then she fled, ran like the wind, pushing past two men standing near the corner, and disappearing into Leicester Square. And Annie, utterly bewildered, just stood there, not knowing what had happened, or what to do, and then she saw one of the men turning to follow the fleeing woman. Saw the second man coming towards her.

'Excuse me, madam,' he said.

Annie knew, right away, that he was a policeman.

'I'd like a word.'

Annie watched him put his hand into a pocket, knew that he was pulling out identification, and there was nothing she could do but watch the hand, watch the wallet thing with the badge and photograph, and she was numb – she was almost always numb these days, but this was different, this was worse. And as the next moments passed and the police officer spoke to her and the other man returned, without the young woman, as they asked her to come with them to the station to answer some questions, even the drug-pusher's threat of murder had ceased to reverberate in her mind. One thought and one thought only rolled around and around in Annie's bleak, befuddled brain.

Edward. Edward, who still loved her, would find out the truth about her now. Poor, trusting Edward.

She began to weep soon after they got to the police station, and they were utterly genuine tears, and yet she found herself realizing with sudden and surprising clarity that the crying might just be helping her, for the officer talking to her was gentle and courteous, seemed almost sympathetic. The more incoherent she was, the more incapable of answering the policeman's questions intelligently, the clearer it became to Annie that they weren't really interested in her at all. She was just a pathetic woman with more money than sense, getting what they referred to as her Class C drugs through illegal means. But it wasn't as if she was taking heroin or cocaine or even marijuana, and even through Annie's semi-permanent fog of Valium and fear she could see that what they wanted was the woman who had been going to sell it to her. And suddenly Annie Aldrich Thomas, impeccably brought up, educated, honest-as-the-day-was-long Annie, was finding the strength to lie to a British policeman, to tell him that this was a first, that she had never done it before. And she knew even then he didn't believe her, she thought they might even have watched her before, but she kept to her barely coherent story, kept on sobbing, pleading with the officer not to tell her husband, and she had the sense that she might – just *might* – be going to get away with it.

She ought to have felt relieved. She ought to have felt the luckiest woman on earth to have escaped with just an unofficial warning. Yet what occupied Annie's mind most as she sat, red-eyed and still shaking, in her First Class seat on the train back to Oxford, was the fact that she was returning to Banbury Farm House without her envelope of pills. All her thoughts of Edward, her fears for Edward and for their marriage, had been pushed right out of her mind now by that one fact, that single, overriding, overwhelming terror. She was going to run out of Valium.

She was going to run out of Valium, and Peter Cary wasn't going to write her a prescription just like that, and she couldn't face having to beg him, to lie to him, and she couldn't get back to London to try to talk Andrew Miller around, or, heaven forbid, to venture back into Piccadilly Circus where the woman might just be waiting for her with a knife instead of an envelope of black-market drugs. And Annie remembered the agony of withdrawal, and she couldn't face that either, not with Marie-Louise and the children in the house.

She was going to run out of pills.

She thought, perhaps, that she could face anything rather than that.

She was standing in little Liza's nursery at four o'clock that morning, gazing almost unseeing down at her youngest child, when it came to her. She had not yet slept at all, had forced herself to take only half her usual night-time dose, all too conscious that from now until her next prescription, every precious milligram counted; and so

Annie was comparatively calm, not sufficiently doped to be able to rest, but the jagged, fiery edges of the worst of her panic had at least been a little smoothed, dampened down.

The words, spoken eleven years before in the hotel room near the hillside where her parents, their parents, had died, came back to her.

'*To always being there*,' Jamie had said, and she had responded: '*No matter what.*' And Olivia, the strongest of them, had drained her cognac in one and added: '*Come hell or high water.*'

They had reminded each other of their pact last summer, at their reunion up on Dukesfield Fell and, later, at Riverdale Hall, but they had spoken mostly of good things, of their achievements, of their separate lives but continuing, constant friendship in spite of their separation. Annie had been taking Valium for years by then, but that reunion had taken place only a matter of weeks before she had driven the Range Rover into the milk float in Stone Bridge Road, the day before she had made the decision to start increasing the dosage of her tranquillizers.

On the seventeenth night of March in 1987, Annie stared down at her little girl's golden head, at her beautiful dark lashes, at the round, soft cheeks that puffed just a little with her smooth, regular, sleeping breaths, and made another decision.

'There's no place else left for me to go,' Annie said, very softly, and a single tear, of self-pity and shame and love and regret, ran down her left cheek and fell onto her daughter's soft, pink blanket. 'I think – I really think, my beloved – this is my very last chance.'

She bent down low and kissed Liza, very gently and carefully, on the top of her head, and then she went just as quietly into Sophie's and William's room, and kissed them both too, and neither of them woke either, for which she was grateful.

And then she went back into her own, Edward-less bedroom, picked up the white telephone and lay down with it on top of their quilt, on her side, her eyes on the digital alarm clock on her bedside table.

She waited, not sleeping or moving, even when she heard Marie-Louise getting the children up and ready for breakfast and school, and Edward had asked Marie-Louise not to disturb Annie in the mornings until she was feeling better. Most mornings, Annie liked going into her children's rooms and helping them dress, and then sitting with them at the breakfast table. But this morning, she stayed where she was, still watching the clock.

She waited until one minute past nine.

And then she called Olivia.

8

'So,' Olivia said, when Annie had, at last, told them everything, 'how are we going to tackle this?'

It was a little after ten o'clock at night, and the three friends were sitting in Olivia's living room: Annie, superficially neat as always in a navy cashmere two piece, but leaning back, exhausted and drained, in an armchair; Jamie on the settee, his body language relaxed enough in jeans, sneakers and an old Harvard sweatshirt, only the furrow between his dark eyes and the tautness of his mouth betraying his anxiety; Olivia, cross-legged on the carpet in her favourite old Norma Kamali tracksuit, the most focused and determined of them.

Annie had been in Geneva for three days.

'One thing's clear,' Jamie said. 'It can't be tackled overnight.'

'It has to be,' Annie said. 'Well, not overnight, of course, but in a short time. I don't have any longer.' She looked at their perplexed expressions. 'I can't stay away too long without Edward finding out.'

'Would it really be so terrible if he did?' Olivia asked.
'Yes.'

They were in the large, comfortable apartment on the rue
du Marché that Olivia had chosen on her move to Geneva,
as much for its location at the heart of the city as anything.
Life in Switzerland was pretty heavenly so far as she was
concerned. At home, she had all the comforts and luxuries
of a prosperous cosmopolitan city, yet in no time at all
she could be sailing on Lac Léman or skiing at Gstaad or
Verbier or crossing the frontiers into France or Italy.

It had taken three days after Annie's cry for help to
make their plans and postpone their arrangements. Olivia
had found it relatively easy, with the wealth of translation
agencies in Geneva, to track down a satisfactory replace-
ment for her clients. Jamie, rather less easily, had talked
Carrie, his wife, into taking over two presentations and a
host of meetings and lunches at Beaumont-Arias back in
Boston. And Annie, racked with guilt, had lied her head off
to Edward, telling him the story they'd all agreed on before
she'd left home: that Olivia had some major problems of
a private nature and needed support – and kind, generous
Edward had volunteered to see that everything at home
ran smoothly in her absence, making it possible for Annie
to gather her Valium and a suitcase of belongings and get
herself on a flight to Geneva.

Once Annie had begun to talk that first day, to unburden
herself, it had seemed an unstoppable torrent. She'd kept it
all inside her for so many years, knew now that secretly she
had *longed* to talk about it, had sometimes even, on those
rare occasions when no human being had been in the house,
talked to Bella, the dog, and Leo and Boots, the two cats.

'The cats always lost interest pretty quickly,' she had

told Olivia and Jamie in the soft pinkish light of Olivia's cosy, comfortingly untidy sitting room, 'but Bella used to make me feel better, she used to sit at my feet and listen while I scratched her chest, and if I cried she put her head on my knee.'

'Talking to animals is good,' Olivia had said, 'but a little limited.'

'Better than nothing,' Jamie had pointed out. 'Or no one.'

'Except that Annie did have someone,' Olivia said.

They'd all agreed on two rules of play straight off. Here, within these safe walls, while they were all together, there was to be absolute honesty. Annie was going to tell them everything, no matter how long it took and no matter how ugly it was, and Olivia and Jamie were going to talk back whichever way they saw fit. And then somehow, whatever it took, they were going to see to it that Annie's problem was dealt with. Even if the unburdening made her feel better momentarily, there would be no returning to life as it had been. Annie had come this far, and, however painful, neither Olivia nor Jamie intended to allow her to slip backward.

'Why would it be so terrible if Edward did find out?' Olivia looked up at Annie from the floor, her expressive face even stronger than usual, her green eyes more penetrating. 'What do you think might happen?'

Annie flushed. 'He couldn't take it.'

'Are you sure?' Jamie asked. 'Edward's always seemed a particularly strong, stable man to me.'

'And me,' Olivia added.

'You're both forgetting his mother.'

'Not at all,' Olivia said. 'But you're not his mother, Annie, you're his wife. His partner.'

'He couldn't take it,' Annie said, obstinately. 'Trust me.'

'He wouldn't like it.' Olivia uncrossed her legs, changed to a kneeling position. 'He'd hate it – he'd be horribly upset, of course he would be. But mostly, I think, he'd be concerned for you, about you. About getting you right, having you happy and well again.'

'Maybe,' Annie admitted, 'if it were just me and him. But I'm supposed to be the mother of his children.'

'You're a wonderful mother,' Jamie told her.

'I'm a drug addict. A junkie.'

'No, you're not,' Jamie argued. 'You're dependent on tranquillizers. You've been *made* dependent on drugs by doctors who should know better.'

'I'm out of control,' Annie said.

'You've never harmed the children,' Jamie said.

'I've risked harming them.'

'How?' Jamie asked. 'From what you've told us, you've taken a thousand precautions – or you did when you realized there might be a risk.'

'I've still been taking care of them under the influence of drugs.'

'That's true,' Olivia said. 'But now you want to stop. You do want to stop, don't you, Annie?'

'Yes.'

'How much?'

'More than anything.'

Olivia wasn't letting her off the hook. 'What about withdrawal? You couldn't take it last time. Can you bear it now, do you think?'

'No, probably not,' Annie said, softly. 'But maybe if I'm not alone, I may stand a better chance.'

Jamie stood up and walked over to the window. He

pushed back one of the curtains and looked out into the rainy night. It was quiet except for the low sound of car tyres swishing over the wet streets.

'We have to get professional help,' he said. 'We can't handle this alone.'

Annie looked frightened. 'What kind of help do you mean?'

'What do you think he means?' Olivia said. 'We need a doctor.'

'A doctor will say I should withdraw slowly,' Annie said. 'Go home and see a specialist in England. Let my family help me. That's what a doctor's going to say.'

'And you don't want that,' Olivia said.

'I can't risk it,' Annie said. 'I won't risk it.'

Olivia went next morning, Annie's fourth morning, to visit her own doctor. Dr Diana Brünli had originally trained in her native England, before marrying a Swiss dermatologist and resettling in Geneva. Olivia had seen the doctor only once as a patient, but they had met again at a seminar which Olivia had attended as Gilles-Breque Pharmaceuticals' interpreter. The two women had sat together at lunch and got on famously, and had since then met at least once each month for pleasure.

'If your friend insists on doing this the hard way,' Diana Brünli told Olivia in her spick and span blue and white surgery on the rue de Lausanne, 'then it really has to happen in a hospital or clinic.'

'I don't think Annie wants to go to a clinic,' Olivia said. 'I know it doesn't make any sense, but she seems to feel that would be a greater betrayal of her husband. She knows she's been lying to Edward for so long, but she feels there are degrees of lies. Actually spending time in a hospital without telling him is too much for her.'

'And she won't consider telling him?'

'Absolutely not.'

'You say the husband is a decent type?' Dr Brünli asked.

'So far as I know, Edward's a pussycat.' Olivia shrugged. 'But then, of course, I've believed for years that Annie was perfectly happy, so for all I know, Edward might be a sadist in private.'

'But you don't really believe that.'

'Not for a minute.'

'Which doesn't help us get over the fact,' Diana Brünli said, 'that your friend seems to be willing to do almost anything to stop him finding out about her dependency problem.'

'Or about her withdrawal.' Olivia shook her head. 'Annie seems to think that with our help, she can go cold turkey and then go straight back home and carry on as if nothing ever happened. I told her – and Jamie told me I was being incredibly tactless and I guess I wasn't exactly diplomatic – that she was talking about this as if it were a back-street abortion in the bad old days. But this isn't that simple, is it?'

'Not simple at all,' the doctor agreed. 'Even if Annie can make it successfully through the worst symptoms of rapid withdrawal, that won't be the end of it, not in such a long-term case. Withdrawal could go on for months. She might not feel good for a long, long time. She may never feel as good as she would like to feel. She'll need help.'

'So what can you suggest?' Olivia asked. 'I don't know who else to go to, Diana.'

'To a specialist,' Dr Brünli replied, 'who will tell

you the same thing as I am – that Annie has two alternatives. Either she goes home to confide in her husband and then begins a carefully monitored long-term withdrawal with his help, or she runs the risk of crashing hard and fast in a clinic.' She smiled wryly. 'I don't think I have to tell you which alternative I'd recommend.'

Olivia was silent for a moment.

'Could it be done at home? In my apartment?'

'The rapid withdrawal?' The doctor shook her head. 'Not without risk.'

'When you say risk, what do you mean? To Annie's physical health, or her sanity?'

'Both, potentially. Anything could happen; she could suffer a convulsion – it doesn't happen that often, but it does happen, and unsupervised, that can be dangerous. She could try to kill herself—'

'She wouldn't be left alone.'

'She could still try, Olivia. You have a kitchen full of sharp objects. You have windows she could jump out of.' Dr Brünli saw Olivia's shocked expression. 'I don't say it's likely, but it isn't out of the question either. She could even attack one of you – aggression can be a symptom of withdrawal.'

'I don't think Annie has an aggressive bone in her body,' Olivia said.

Diana Brünli's smile was gentle. 'But Annie in rapid withdrawal may not be much like the Annie you know.'

Olivia went home and told Annie and Jamie what Diana had said.

'I don't want to go to a clinic,' Annie said, anxiously, as they had known she would.

'It's the only way,' Olivia said, 'if you want to try and do it the fast way.'

'No.' Annie's face was very pale, and her palms were perspiring. 'I can't do that. I'd have to give Edward as my next-of-kin, and they might contact him.'

'They wouldn't,' Jamie said. 'Not if you told them not to.'

'You can't be sure of that.' Annie shook her head violently. 'I want to do it here,' she said. 'With you two. I know it's an awful lot to ask, but that's why I came to you.' Her voice was rising with a touch of hysteria. 'If I was going to go into a clinic, I could have done that in England. If Edward finds out that I ran away from him, that I came to Switzerland and lied to him, that'll be the end. I'll lose him and the children. I know it.' She paused, and her eyes filled with tears. 'I'd rather go home and carry on.'

'You'd rather carry on drugging yourself to the eyeballs and lying to him that way,' Olivia said, bluntly.

'Yes,' Annie said.

'I thought you wanted to stop,' Jamie said. 'More than anything.'

'I do.'

'Then check into a clinic,' Olivia said.

'I can't,' Annie said.

She took a pill and rested for a while that afternoon, and Jamie and Olivia sat in the kitchen, where they knew she couldn't hear them talking about her, and racked their brains for the solution.

'There is only one,' Olivia said, at last.

'Tell me,' Jamie said.

'We do it here.'

'But your friend said it could be dangerous.'

'Not with proper supervision,' Olivia said. 'If we get the apartment set up carefully enough – if we find a doctor—'

'You don't think Dr Brünli would go for it?' Jamie asked.

'I don't know. She might, or she might tell us we're nuts, or she might simply have too many commitments. Or she might help to persuade a specialist to help us.'

'In other words,' Jamie said, 'if Annie won't go to the clinic, we bring the clinic here.'

'Exactly,' Olivia said.

'Oh, yes,' Annie said, when they told her after she'd woken up. 'Oh, yes, please – oh, thank you, Livvy, thank you.'

'It might not work out,' Olivia warned her.

'But you're going to try, aren't you?' She sat up on her bed.

'We'll try,' Jamie said.

'How long do we have?' Olivia asked Annie. 'I mean, how long before Edward starts to get restless?'

Annie swung her feet down onto the floor. 'Another week. Maybe longer.' She looked at them both, and her eyes were filled with new hope. 'Oh, God, do you think we stand a chance?'

'I'm not sure,' Olivia said.

'A week's pretty tight,' Jamie pointed out. 'It might take that long to fix it up. If it can be fixed up.'

'It can,' Annie said. 'Livvy's the greatest organizer in the world, we both know that.'

'I'm not so hot,' Olivia said. 'Just because I manage to get the three of us together every now and then doesn't mean I can set up a makeshift clinic in my home in a day or two.'

'The three of us live in different countries,' Annie pointed out, still with her new-found optimism. 'The people you want to get here are probably all in the same city.'

'Well, doesn't that make it nice and easy?' Olivia said ironically.

'You probably can do it,' Jamie said. 'Annie's right. If anyone can, it's you.'

'Me and my big ideas,' Olivia said.

It took some doing, but Diana Brünli came through for them, providing them with a doctor and two nurses 'on loan' for the duration by the chief professor of a suburban clinic specializing in the rehabilitation of drug dependent patients. Because the treatment would be carried out on uninsured private property, both Annie, as the patient, and Olivia, as the apartment's lessee, were asked to sign legal documents releasing all concerned from liability.

'It's going to cost a fortune, isn't it?' Annie asked, the evening before Dr Gianni Dressler and his team were due to arrive. Jamie was in the kitchen cooking them dinner. He'd been in there for a couple of hours, ever since he'd had a fight with Carrie, his wife, when she'd telephoned to demand to know what was taking him so long in Geneva. Jamie hated fighting with anyone, Carrie most of all, but he found cooking therapeutic, and the kitchen at home in Boston was where he regularly disappeared to when he and his wife fell out, which they did increasingly often.

'That's all covered,' Olivia told her.

'I'm going to pay the bill,' Annie said, anxiously. 'Don't you even think about paying for it, Livvy.'

'You can't pay it,' Olivia said. 'Not unless you've changed your mind about Edward finding out. Consider it a gift from Jamie and me – you know we can afford it.'

'That's not the point.' Annie was sitting in an armchair in her room, twisting a paper tissue in her hands, shredding it into her lap. She'd destroyed an entire box of Kleenex in a single afternoon.

'Don't worry about the bill, Annie.' Olivia, growing edgy too, was sitting on the side of Annie's bed. 'You have more important things to think about.'

Annie's small smile was bitter. 'You know what I need right now, don't you?'

'If you were me,' Olivia smiled back, 'it would be a double scotch. As it's you, I guess it's a Valium.' She'd got a prescription from Diana Brünli for some pills to tide Annie over till the controlled withdrawal could begin. 'Do you want a glass of water?'

'I shouldn't.' Annie's longing was almost palpably obvious.

Olivia shrugged. 'If you were giving up cigarettes or alcohol from tomorrow, you'd be entitled to just one more.'

'And it would be lovely to think I might sleep at least a little tonight.'

Olivia stood up. 'When are you calling Edward?'

'Later.' Annie flushed darkly. 'More lies.'

'All in a good cause.' Olivia had given up, for the moment, trying to talk Annie into coming clean with Edward. Maybe after the worst was over, she and Jamie had decided, they might be able to talk some sense into her, but right now there seemed little point. At the door, she looked back at Annie. 'He still thinks you guys are looking after me, doesn't he?'

'Yes.' Annie's voice was very soft. 'I'm so sorry.'

'I don't mind, Annie.' Olivia was gentle. 'So long as it helps in the long run. That's all that matters now.'

'It has to help,' Annie said, shredding the last of the tissues. 'It *has* to.'

Olivia opened the door. 'I guess,' she said, 'in the last analysis, that's up to you.'

Dr Dressler – young, arrogant and handsome, with curling black hair and violet eyes – and his nurses took over completely. It was not in Olivia's nature to take so many orders amiably, especially when a strange man was directing her to move furniture in her own apartment, to remove and lock up every pill and potion, every bottle of wine and every remotely or potentially sharp object – even glasses – to go shopping for each and every item he'd written on a list and to be sure to bring *exactly* what he'd asked for. But Jamie was with her, and Jamie knew Olivia well enough to recognize when she was starting to get mad, and twice that first morning he thought it best to get her out of the way before she erupted, and Olivia was grateful for his help, because the last thing she really wanted was to upset Gianni Dressler when it was likely he might be Annie's last chance.

It was a little like getting ready for a small war to break out, Jamie commented apprehensively to Olivia at one point as her windows were closed and locked, but Olivia pointed out wryly that if that were the case this was one war they'd be sure to lose, since Dressler clearly agreed with what Diana Brünli had said about Annie's unpredictability in the grip of rapid withdrawal and had ordered every knife and fork, every pair of scissors, every hammer and screwdriver – even the needles in Olivia's seldom-used sewing kit – to be locked out of reach.

When all the preparations were complete, Dr Dressler

sat them all down together around the table in Olivia's dining room. In keeping with the precision of his other arrangements, there was nothing casual or relaxed about this piece of planning; it had all the charm and bedside manner, Olivia thought privately, of a corporate rationalization meeting.

'All right,' he began, in the almost unaccented American English he had perfected during his time at Harvard Medical School. 'Since we're all going to be in this together, I'm going to run through the kind of thing that may happen to Annie over the next week.'

'I think Dr Brünli already told us most of what to expect,' Olivia said.

'Please' – Dressler flashed Olivia a sharp-eyed look of disapproval – 'do me the courtesy of allowing me at least to begin before you interrupt.'

'I'm sorry,' Olivia said, trying to sound as if she meant it. 'I was just trying to save time – because we have so little, I mean.'

'Preparation,' Gianni Dressler told her, still crisply but less harshly, 'is all-important in cases like this. The more Annie understands about the symptoms that may affect her, the more easily she may find it to cope with them.'

'Forgive me, Dr Dressler,' Jamie ventured, 'but isn't there a likelihood of Annie expecting more symptoms just because you've told her to?'

'Perhaps,' Dressler replied. 'Nonetheless, experience has shown us that ignorance is far from helpful.' He turned his face away from Jamie, away from Olivia, and deliberately focused all his attention on Annie. 'Forgive us,' he said, with sudden and considerable courtesy, 'for discussing you as if you were not here.'

'I don't mind,' Annie said, softly. 'I really don't mind.

It's a relief, in a way, to listen to other people talking about it, about my problems.' Her face was pale, but her cheeks were a little flushed. 'I've been so secretive about it for so long.'

'And how do you feel about my telling you what you may possibly expect?'

'I want to know,' Annie said, instantly. 'Everything. Please.' She glanced at Olivia and Jamie, then looked back at the doctor. 'Tell me. I need to know everything that's going to help me get through this.'

The smile Gianni Dressler bestowed on Annie, Olivia thought, was very gentle and, startlingly, for such an arrogantly efficient man, almost sweet.

'Good,' he said. 'Now, Annie, you're not – I repeat, not – to be overly alarmed by this list of symptoms. It's extremely unlikely that you will experience all of them. We already know, of course, a little of what to expect from your previous attempt—'

'When I ended up breaking open a locked cabinet with my bare hands' – Annie tried to smile, but her mouth and voice quivered – 'just to get at my pills.'

'This time,' Dr Dressler said, 'there will be no pills to get at.' He paused. 'Adrenalin can give a person unusual strength,' he explained, and leaned forward in his chair. 'Think about what your tranquillizers do to your system, Annie. You use them to control your anxiety, to relax yourself, physically and emotionally, to help you sleep, get you through difficult situations. Everything slows down: your heart rate, your thought processes, your movements, your breathing. They dull your senses, they calm you, and your adrenalin levels become low.'

'And when you stop taking them—' Olivia, who had

started to speak without thought, broke off abruptly. 'Sorry,' she said. 'I'll be quiet.'

'It's all right, Olivia,' Dressler said, politer now. 'I imagine you were going to say that when you stop taking tranquillizers, the opposite happens, and that's exactly right.' He returned his attention to Annie. 'The big problem we face in your case is that we all know you're going to try to come off your drug much too quickly, which means amongst other things that your heart and breathing will speed right up, your whole system will start to race and your senses will no longer be dulled. As a consequence of that, unfortunately, you'll be having to face up to real fear, real emotion, real pain; your adrenalin levels will soar, and you'll probably think you're going out of your mind.'

'And will I be?' Annie asked, softly.

'No.' Dressler shook his head. 'Absolutely, categorically, no.'

He ran through the list of potential withdrawal symptoms, studied Annie's changing expressions as he described the more acceptable, more easily tolerable discomforts ranging from nausea and flu-like symptoms to palpitations and chest pains, moving downhill to the more horrifying possibilities that might include hallucinations, aggressive outbursts, suicidal feelings and convulsions.

When he was finished, the room was silent and Annie's face was only minimally paler than Jamie's or Olivia's.

'Any questions?' Dressler asked.

No one spoke.

'Nothing?'

'I have one,' Olivia said, and her wide mouth was tightly drawn.

'Go ahead,' Dressler said.

'How the hell did a drug that can do this much harm ever get to be prescribed like goddamned aspirin?'

Dressler made a small grimace. 'Olivia, I'm afraid we just don't have the time to really get started on that conversation, but if we ever do have a spare few hours I'll be glad to speak with you at length on the subject. The bottom line is that, used correctly, preferably in the short term, diazepam is a useful, safe drug.'

'And if I'd thrown away that very first bottle,' Annie said, slowly, unhappily, 'instead of stashing it in the back of my drawer, I'd be okay.'

'Possibly,' Dressler said. 'Though you might, instead, have turned to an alternative. Drink, perhaps. Which leads me to probably the most important thing I have to tell you.' He paused again, his eyes fixed hard on Annie's. 'Whatever happens here in the next few days – however successful we are in getting you through the first traumatic stage – withdrawal from a long-term addiction is a long-term, ongoing problem.'

'Dr Brünli told Olivia it might go on for months,' Annie said.

'There's no *might* about it,' Dressler said grimly. 'You know I'm not in favour of this kind of crash programme, Annie, but I was persuaded it was, for the time being, the best option on offer and I'm determined that we will make it work for you. If I didn't believe we could be successful, I wouldn't be here.' He stopped again, loading his next words heavily. 'But in order for it to keep on working – in order for you to start to put your life back in shape – you're going to have to be very strong for the long haul.'

'That's the real problem then, isn't it?' Annie said, and fear shone out of her blue eyes. 'I'm not strong. I never have been. If I had been, I wouldn't have gotten myself into this mess.'

'That's not true, Annie,' Olivia told her.

'Of course it is.'

'No,' Olivia insisted, then glanced at Dressler. 'May I?'

'Be my guest.' He sat back.

'I think,' Olivia said, carefully, 'and Annie, you know it's true because you've told us yourself – that your real problem is not lack of strength, but that you expect too much from yourself. You're just as strong – maybe stronger – than either Jamie or I. The difference is that we both accept that we make mistakes, that we screw up, that there are things we're no good at or things that we hate to do or just *can't* do, period—'

'You can do almost everything, Livvy,' Annie said.

'Me?' Olivia smiled wryly. 'Don't kid yourself.' She paused. 'The point is that while I don't enjoy failing – who does? – I can admit to failure, I can even laugh about it, whereas you really beat yourself up about those things, refuse to let yourself off the hook.' She shook her head. 'For God's sake, Annie, you thought that screwing up a seating plan at one of Edward's dinner parties was a catastrophe, and we all know that Edward probably didn't give a damn and that even if he did, he adores you far too much for it to have mattered for more than a passing minute.'

Dressler looked back at Annie. 'Does that sound a fair assessment to you?'

Annie nodded, a small, weak nod of her head. 'I guess so.'

'Do you believe what Olivia says about you being as strong as she and Jamie are?'

'No. Not really.'

'I do,' Jamie said, quietly.

'And so do I.' Gianni Dressler smiled at Annie again, one of his rare, infinitely charming smiles. 'I'm not pretending for one instant that your years of deception at home have been either wise or kind. But you have been going through a sickness, Annie, for a very long time, and you have succeeded, for the most part, in continuing about your business in spite of that sickness. You have also succeeded in keeping your secret from your husband. All this you achieved by sheer determination, by a particular kind of strength.'

'All you have to do now' – Olivia leaned across the table and reached for Annie's hand – 'is channel that strength, that determination, into this fight.'

'You can do it,' Jamie said. 'I know you can, Annie.'

Annie was close to tears again. 'I hope so.'

'Do more than hope,' Olivia said, gripping her hand more tightly. 'This is your big chance, Annie, and I, for one, am not going to let you blow it.'

Gianni Dressler rose from his chair.

'Your friends have said it for me. So, shall we begin?'

Jamie looked up at the doctor. 'How do we begin?'

'By waiting,' Dressler answered.

9

As it had been for Annie the first time she had tried to stop, for the first forty-eight hours, apart from the apprehension she felt and they all shared, nothing much of consequence happened to her.

'The diazepam is still in your body tissue,' Dressler explained to Annie. 'You've been taking such large doses for so long, and it's still working in your system. We have to wait for it to be gone, for the reaction to start.'

'Maybe it won't,' Jamie said.

'It will,' Dressler said.

'Ever the optimist,' Olivia commented.

'You're the linguist,' Dressler said, unruffled. 'I'm the doctor.'

Until that day, Annie had called Edward each evening to let him know that she was well and to find out about him and the children. Tactfully, always diplomatic, Edward had asked after Olivia's invented problems, and Annie had kept her answers noncommittal, as if Olivia were in the room and might hear her. Each time he asked her those gentle, concerned questions, Annie's face grew hot with shame and guilt, and when she put down the receiver her hands were trembling and her palms sticky with perspiration.

'I'm such a liar,' she had said to Jamie after one of the calls. 'I'm such a terrible *liar*.'

'Only because you don't want to hurt him.' Jamie had tried to reassure her. 'That doesn't count – it's more of a white lie.'

'You don't believe that any more than I do,' Annie had said.

'Sure I do,' Jamie had said, but they had both known he was lying too.

'I think it's time we switched on the answering machine,' Dressler said to Olivia on the third morning. 'Once Annie's symptoms start in earnest, she won't be able to handle a normal conversation with her husband.'

'All right,' Olivia said, her stomach sinking, and went to turn it on. They had all agreed in advance that when the time came, Jamie would field all telephone calls, would cover for Annie, explain to Edward that his wife was off somewhere outside the apartment, taking care of Olivia.

Annie became restless before lunch that day, complained of a headache, paced a good deal, asked for windows to be opened more than once so that she could breathe properly, went to the bathroom over and over again, fretful and acutely embarrassed that the key to the door had been removed, wanting privacy and solitude one moment, needing company and reassurance the next.

Edward telephoned at nine o'clock that evening, Annie not having rung him. They all heard his voice taping, calm, deep and English, and right after the click that signalled his replacing the receiver at his end, Annie had her first full-blown anxiety attack during which she shook so hard and for so long, her teeth chattering violently all the while, that Olivia and Jamie both silently feared that she might never stop.

'Can't you do something for her?' Jamie asked Dressler.

'It will pass,' the doctor answered.

'But she's so distressed,' he whispered.

'There's nothing he can do,' Olivia said softly, taking Jamie's arm and leading him out of the room, leaving Annie with Dressler and one of the two nurses he had now called in to assist.

For the next twenty-four hours they had their work cut out for them. The symptoms hit Annie one after the other, sometimes more than one at a time, buffeting her physically and emotionally like a kind of internal tornado. It was the way Olivia imagined it might be watching a loved one taking a beating from a gang of thugs with one's arms tied behind one's back. Annie gasped for breath. Her speech became garbled. She ran back and forth to the bathroom, needing to pee again almost as soon as she'd gone, then suffering bout after bout of diarrhoea. She paced faster and faster, grew frustrated and angry, struck at walls with her fists, kicked at a wardrobe door, splintering the corner and badly bruising her toes, yet unable to sit still long enough to allow Dressler or the nurses to look at her foot. Assailed by despair, she went into the bedroom and flung herself down on the bed, face down, sobbing quietly for a while, and neither of the nurses seemed able to console her so Olivia and Jamie went in, ignoring Dressler's words of caution, and sat down on either side of her. Olivia held her hands, Jamie put his arms around her, and they saw that they weren't quite reaching Annie, could still do nothing to help her, yet

123

they thought, they hoped, in spite of her desperation, that she felt their love.

'Which might make us feel a little better,' Olivia said afterwards, outside the bedroom, 'but does her damn-all good.'

'It may be what makes all the difference in the long run,' Jamie said quietly. 'It's love she's going to need more than anything.'

'Annie's never been short of love,' Olivia said, 'but it didn't stop her getting into the state she's in now.'

'I know.' Jamie shared her wretchedness. 'God, don't I know.'

The telephone rang again, and this time it was Carrie, her voice extra cool and clipped because Jamie hadn't called her all day and she still didn't know when the hell he was coming back to Boston, and perhaps if his *friends* – she underlined the word with sarcasm – could spare him five minutes, he might find time to call her at the office?

'Maybe you should call her right back,' Olivia suggested, seeing Jamie's anxious face.

Jamie shook his head. 'She's in the mood to fight,' he said. 'I'm not.'

'Things not so great with you two.' It was not a question.

'Things aren't easy,' he admitted.

'Have they ever been?'

'No.' Jamie mustered a smile. 'But I still love her.'

'Then she's a lucky woman,' Olivia said.

'I'm not sure she'd agree with you.'

'Then she's also a fool.'

Annie slept for a while that night, fitfully waking up each time escaping from the clutches of some black, not quite identifiable nightmare. Alternately she shivered and begged for blankets, then sweated, drenching her nightdress and pleading for the windows to be opened. Olivia and Jamie took it in turns to sit with one of the nurses, while Dressler slept on the couch in the living room.

A little after five in the morning, she got out of bed, heading for the bathroom, but the walls seemed to close in on her and the floor was tilting, and she cried out and stumbled to the floor, and Olivia and the nurse helped her back to the bed, and Annie started to weep, and Olivia realized, with the most intense pity, that she had wet herself, and she was thankful beyond words for the nurse's calm presence, because though she would not have minded one scrap changing Annie's nightdress and bed linen, she knew that Annie could not have borne it.

'She seems more comfortable this morning,' Jamie said to one of the nurses, a young Swiss woman named Ruth with blonde hair and blue eyes who reminded him a little of how Annie had looked in her late teens. 'Or is that just wishful thinking?'

'I know you wish it,' Ruth said, gently. 'And it's true, at least for now.'

'But that doesn't mean it's over.'

'No,' she answered. 'I'm sorry.' She paused. 'Martina, my colleague, told me it was not a good night for Annie.'

'No,' said Jamie. 'It wasn't too good.'

'Annie has very fine friends,' Ruth said, and smiled at him.

'Thank you,' Jamie said.

Twenty minutes later, Annie walked into the kitchen where Olivia was drinking a cup of coffee.

'Hi,' Olivia said, looking up at her.

Annie didn't answer. If she had been pale before, now she was almost as white as chalk. Even her lips seemed bleached to cream. Her eyes stared at Olivia, but Olivia felt she was not seeing her.

'Annie, what's wrong?' She put her cup down on the table and stood up, moving slowly, sensing she needed to be very careful. 'Annie, what is it?'

Annie went over to the sink, put out her right hand and touched the stainless steel with her index finger. Then she took away the hand and gazed at the finger.

'Annie?' Olivia felt uncertain what to do. Gianni Dressler was on the telephone in her bedroom and she hadn't seen either Ruth or Martina for a while. She had believed one of them had been with Annie.

'It doesn't feel like me.' Annie spoke at last in a hushed, scared voice.

'What doesn't?'

'This.' Annie held out her hand. 'Or this.' She reached up and touched her own cheek. 'Nothing feels like me.'

'You mean you're numb?' Olivia asked gently, trying not to let her own fear show. 'What do you mean, Annie?'

'I don't know.' Annie was still staring the same vacant stare. 'I don't *know*.' Her eyes wandered round the kitchen, then seemed to fix on the wall facing her. 'I was sitting down, and I think I was asleep for a while. And then I woke up and I wasn't me. I wasn't inside myself any more.'

'Okay,' Olivia said. 'It's okay, Annie.' Still moving slowly, she went over to her friend and took her arm. There was no response. 'I know what this is, and so do you.' Gently, she pushed Annie over to the table and down onto one of the chairs, meeting no resistance. 'You remember when Dressler told us the things that might happen – you remember, Annie?'

Annie shook her head.

'There was something called depersonalization – I think that's what it was called.' Relief flooded Olivia as she remembered what the doctor had said. 'It's very common when your anxiety level goes too high. It'll stop, it'll go away when you calm down again.'

'I'll go away,' Annie said, softly, but the fear was still there. 'That's how it feels, like I've gone away.'

'No, Annie,' Olivia said more firmly. 'That's not what I mean.' She looked over at the door, wondered if she should call for help, decided that would only panic Annie more. An idea struck her. 'Give me your hand.' Annie did not budge, so Olivia took the hand herself. 'You feel me touching you?'

Annie gave a tiny shrug.

Olivia pinched the skin on the back of the hand. 'You feel that?'

Annie blinked. 'I think so.'

Olivia put down the hand again, then reached up and suddenly, quite hard, pinched Annie's cheek instead.

'Ouch,' Annie said.

Olivia smiled.

'See?' she said. 'You're still here.'

'I thought I was going crazy,' Annie said to Dressler a little later. 'I've had similar things happen to me before, but never nearly as frightening.' She looked weakly at Olivia. 'A long time ago, when you and I were having lunch in Harrods, I had a panic attack that was a little like that – remember, I told you I was ill?'

'Sure, I remember,' Olivia said. 'I only wish I'd known what you were really going through.'

'It's a normal effect of withdrawal,' Dressler told Annie. 'It's unpleasant, as I warned you it might be, but you have to try to remind yourself that it is perfectly normal under the circumstances, and you are not going crazy.'

'Maybe I shouldn't have pinched her,' Olivia said.

'Why not?' Dressler asked, easily. 'It didn't really hurt her, and it worked, didn't it?' He gave a small smile. 'I shouldn't make a habit of it, though.'

The telephone rang, but Olivia, having grown accustomed to not answering it, stayed where she was.

'It's Edward,' Annie said, even though they couldn't hear the machine from the kitchen, where they still were.

'Could be anyone,' Olivia said. 'Could even be for me.'

'It's Edward,' Annie said, positively.

'He won't call again till this evening, will he?' Olivia asked.

Annie stood up. 'I want to talk to him.'

'If it was him,' Dressler said, 'it'll be too late.'

'I want to talk to Edward.' The despair was back in her tone. 'I want to see Edward.'

'Are you certain about that?' the doctor asked her, quietly. 'If you are, I'm all for it.'

Annie sat down again. 'I miss him,' she said. 'I miss my children.'

'I know,' Olivia said.

Annie stood up again. 'I'm going to call him.'

Olivia was startled. 'You're going to tell him?'

Annie stared down at her, and her eyes were suddenly cold. 'I want to talk to my husband. Why don't you want me to do that?'

'I do.' Olivia glanced uncertainly at Dressler, who gave

her the smallest, hardly perceptible, shake of his head. She thought he was reassuring her, but she wasn't sure. 'Of course I want you to talk to Edward, Annie. It was you who wanted him kept in the dark.'

'I don't know what you're talking about, Olivia.' Still, the same coldness. 'I only know I want to speak to him.' She began to walk out of the room.

'Annie?' Olivia stood up, looked down at Dressler for help.

'Let her go,' he said.

'But what if she calls him? This isn't really Annie, is it? It's part of the withdrawal, isn't it? If she calls him, it'll all be for nothing.'

'It's certainly another part of withdrawal,' Dressler agreed. 'But if she calls him, I'd say it was the best thing in the world, for her and for him. For the whole family.'

Olivia sat down again. 'You're right, of course.'

Annie did not call Edward. Halfway to the telephone, she experienced another attack of dizziness, felt as if she were choking, felt violently nauseous and had to be helped to the bathroom by Ruth and Jamie. By the time she had recovered again, not only had the desire to speak to her husband left her, but she was utterly appalled that she could even have thought about calling him.

'Please,' she begged Olivia, clutching at her arm, 'please don't let me call him. You mustn't let me talk to him – I don't care if you have to lock me up.'

'Okay,' Olivia soothed her. 'We won't let you call, not if you don't want to. You don't have to worry about Edward – he's fine, and the children are all fine, too. Jamie spoke to him last night, remember?'

'He didn't tell him anything, did he?' The naked fear was still in Annie's eyes. 'Oh, God, he mustn't tell him.'

'Jamie knows that. He hasn't told him anything except what we arranged. Stop worrying about Edward, Annie. There's nothing to worry about.'

'I just love him so much,' Annie said.

'I know you do,' Olivia said.

Just before three o'clock that morning, Annie woke up out of a shallow, restless sleep and saw a large coiled snake, dark brown and gleaming, lying on the big square pillow beside her face. She screamed so loudly that not only Martina and Jamie, who were with her in the bedroom, but also Olivia and Dressler, both camped out in the living room, came running.

'Take it away!' she pleaded piteously, on her knees over by the window, cowering, covering her eyes. 'Oh, God, please take it *away*!'

Jamie, beside her on the rug, tried to put an arm around her shoulders, but she shrieked again and flung his arm away as if it had burned her. 'Annie, sweetheart, what is it? What did you see?'

'The *snake*!' Her hands still covered her face. 'On the pillow – get it away from me, please!'

'It's gone, Annie.' Dressler, grim-faced but calm, spoke loudly and firmly. 'Annie, uncover your eyes and look.' He waited. 'Annie, uncover your eyes right *now*.'

It was the first time any of them had heard him raise his voice, but it worked. Annie took her hands away from her face, and her eyes were as huge and saucer-like as a small, terrified child's as she stared disbelievingly at the bed and saw that there was, indeed, nothing there.

'Where is it?' she whispered.

'There was no snake,' Dressler told her.

'There was.' Annie's breathing was rapid, painful sounding. 'It was right beside me, there on the pillow.'

Dressler went over to her, indicating with a small nod to Jamie that he should leave her side. 'There was no snake, Annie,' he said again. 'It wasn't real. It was just a hallucination.' He sat down on the floor beside her, cross-legged and easy, like an old companion. 'Remember I told you you might get hallucinations.'

Annie looked at him. 'But it was so real.'

'I'm sure it was.' The doctor smiled at her. 'With some people, it's spiders, with some it's monsters. Many people just see weird faces hovering over them while they're lying in bed.' He paused. 'Want to talk about it?'

She shook her head and shuddered.

'How about some warm milk then?'

Annie looked back towards the bed, became more conscious of the others in the room, saw Olivia's pale, concerned face. 'Has it really gone, Livvy?' she asked, still childlike, needing more reassurance from someone she knew better than the doctor.

Olivia went to the bed, picked up the two white pillows, held them up for Annie to see, turned them over, then drew the quilt back so that she could see the clean white sheets beneath.

'Okay?' she said. 'Nothing there.'

Annie nodded slowly. 'Okay.'

Dressler got up, helped her to her feet, and she stumbled and almost fell down again because her legs were so weak, so like jelly, and her stomach was churning and the relief at knowing there was no snake was already gone, and in its place was the most intense shame.

'Don't do that,' Dressler told her, quietly.

131

'Do what?' Annie asked.

'Feel embarrassed or ashamed,' he said.

She looked at him. 'How can I not?'

'Feel proud instead,' he said, simply.

'Proud?' She was incredulous.

'That snake was a symptom of withdrawal. You're in withdrawal because you've quit, because you've stopped taking the drug. That's good reason for pride.'

Annie considered being proud of herself for about ten seconds. And then she made a dash for the bathroom and threw up instead.

'What next?' Olivia asked Dressler later, after Annie had been persuaded back to bed and had, at last, fallen asleep.

'Couldn't say.'

'More snakes?' She ran a hand abstractedly through her thick dark hair.

'Maybe. Or not.'

'Might the worst be over?'

'I doubt that very much.'

Olivia found herself mentally rerunning the symptoms list Dressler had gone through six, or was it seven, days ago? It seemed to her that Annie had already endured far more than her fair share of what had been on that list, yet suddenly she realized there might, after all, be a lot more to come.

'Tell me again, Doctor,' she said. 'Annie doesn't have to go through everything you described, does she?'

'Of course not.' Dressler looked tired. 'And I think, if you don't mind, that you could call me Gianni.'

'Okay,' she said. 'You look tired, Gianni.'

'So do you.'

'Do you think it would be okay if we slept for a while now?'

Dressler glanced at his wristwatch. 'I'd say that was a good idea. Jamie and Martina are still in there with Annie, so she's perfectly safe.' He paused. 'He should get some rest, too.'

'The snake thing really freaked Jamie,' Olivia said, and gave a small smile. 'He hates them, you know. I think it made him even more protective of Annie, which was why he refused to give up his shift.'

'He's a very good friend,' Dressler remarked. 'He's obviously intelligent and articulate, yet he knows when to be silent and lend support.' He glanced at her. 'Is there something going on between you two?'

'Between Jamie and me?' Olivia was startled. 'Of course not.'

Dressler shrugged. 'Why not? You're both very attractive people, and you seem unusually close.'

'He's married, for one thing.'

'Not especially happily, though,' Dressler said.

'Not all the time, maybe,' Olivia said, 'but he still loves Carrie.'

Dressler was right, of course, in a way. She had always, all the way back to their school days, found Jamie attractive, but she hadn't thought about him in that sense for years. Jamie had fallen hard for Carrie, and Olivia had never suffered from a shortage of available or eager male companionship, but even if Jamie had remained single and free, she had long since resolved that the closeness of their particular friendship was too precious to take risks with.

'Do you think we are doing the right thing for Annie?' Olivia asked Dressler, her thoughts returning to the grim situation they were all enduring, fresh doubts and weariness suddenly threatening to overwhelm her. 'I mean, I know you and Diana both said this isn't the ideal way—'

'It's a lousy way,' Dressler said bluntly. 'But the only one there was.'

'What really scares me—' Olivia stopped.

'Yes?'

Olivia looked at him. 'What's going to happen when Edward finds out? I mean, he will find out somehow, some time. They do have a close bond. At least I always thought they did – Annie says they still do.'

'You're afraid he might not forgive her?' Dressler asked.

'Of course.' Olivia shook her head. 'If it were me – if it were my marriage, and if I found out that my partner hadn't had enough faith in me, hadn't trusted me enough to share something so – so *crucial* – I don't think I could forgive. Or maybe I could forgive, but I'd certainly never forget.'

'You're not Annie's husband,' Dressler said.

Olivia looked at him curiously. 'What about you? If it were your wife.'

'I'm not married,' he said.

'But if you were.'

'I'm not sure.' Dressler took a moment. 'I know more about this kind of problem than most men, so I should have greater understanding. Yet if I'm candid with you, Olivia, if I were in a relationship I believed entirely honest and open, I think I would find it hard to get over.'

'And you're a doctor.' Olivia's heart sank. 'Edward's just a man.'

'And an Englishman at that,' Dressler said.

* * *

Through the daylight and twilight hours of the seventh day, Annie saw no more snakes, faced no specially traumatic assaults on her sanity. She had a bad pain in her jaw which Gianni Dressler explained was a commonly experienced kind of neuralgia severe enough sometimes to have patients begging dentists to extract all their teeth; if it became unbearable, he told Annie, he could give her something to relieve it, but Annie told him no, partly because having got this far she wanted no more drugs, and partly because the pain, at least, was real, not imagined, was something tangibly bad for her to focus on, for her to fight.

'It's the first symptom I've had that hasn't made me feel as if swallowing a Valium might take it away,' she explained, holding the left side of her face with the lightest possible touch, since anything firmer made it worse. 'I know it's happening because of the withdrawal, because you tell me it is, but it doesn't feel that way. Does that make sense?'

'Perfect sense,' Dressler said. 'And it's a good, healthy response, Annie. More reason to be proud of yourself.'

Annie managed a tiny smile, then winced as the pain bored through her jaw again. 'How long does it usually last?' she asked. 'I wouldn't want you to think I'm that brave, or some kind of masochist.'

'It shouldn't last too long, hopefully.'

'This isn't the most exact of sciences, is it?' Annie said ruefully.

They might all have preferred it if the pain had gone on. But instead, just after nine-thirty that evening, Annie had a convulsion. They were all in the sitting room – Annie with her feet up on the bigger of the two sofas, Jamie and Ruth on the other, Dressler in the armchair closest to

Annie, Olivia on the rug – watching CNN Headline News. Annie had found some relief for a while from the neuralgia by applying an ice pack to her jaw, but then she'd become shivery and complained of the cold, so Ruth had covered her with a blanket. There was a sense of comparative peace in the room for the first time. They all felt it, were all tentatively optimistic, even Dressler.

'I'm so hot,' Annie said, suddenly, and kicked the blanket away.

Ruth started to stand up, but Dressler stopped her with a gesture.

'You okay, Annie?' he asked her from where he sat, his tone easy, calm.

'No.' Her voice was fretful, like a sick child's.

'What's up?' Olivia asked her, gently, taking her cue from the doctor, trying not to over-react despite the warning prickle on her spine.

'How about some water?' Jamie asked.

It happened so swiftly. Annie gave a single sharp cry, then tumbled from the sofa onto the floor, twitching and jerking. Jamie and Olivia both leapt to their feet in alarm, but Dressler and Ruth were already at her side.

'It's all right,' Dressler told them. 'Nobody panic.'

'She isn't breathing.' Jamie stared down at Annie's chest, saw that it wasn't moving. 'Doc, she isn't *breathing*.'

Olivia got down on her knees, trying to reach Annie, but Dressler pushed her away.

'Keep clear.' It was an order. 'She'll be fine.'

'Do something!' Olivia felt her own heart pounding. 'Her mouth – shouldn't you stop her biting her tongue?' Dressler ignored her. 'For God's sake, Gianni, why don't you *do* something?'

The jerking stopped. Annie's whole body seemed to slump into relaxation, and Olivia and Jamie watched a stain forming on the back of her dressing gown as she urinated involuntarily.

'Oh, God,' Olivia said, softly, and Jamie turned away.

Dressler pronounced Annie safe and well, and aside from a feeling of confusion and disorientation and a slight headache, she did seem to have suffered no serious ill-effects. But less than three hours later, she had a second convulsion in the bedroom, no longer, no more superficially harmful, but this time, when Dressler emerged from the room to speak to Jamie and Olivia, they could see that his expression had altered.

'I'm concerned about her.'

'Why? What's wrong?' Olivia asked.

'Two seizures in such a short space of time. I don't like it.'

'But you told us she might have convulsions,' Jamie said, anxiously. 'What's worrying you?'

'I told you that convulsions can happen in rapid withdrawal,' Dressler agreed, 'and neither of these were prolonged.' He paused. 'I've decided to admit Annie to my clinic.'

'You can't,' Olivia said. 'She doesn't want that.'

Dressler's violet eyes were keen and clear and decisive. 'If Annie were to have a more prolonged seizure, without prompt emergency treatment,' he said, 'it could be fatal.'

'Shit,' Jamie said, and looked at Olivia.

Olivia thought about Annie and her greatest fears of all, of Edward finding out, of losing his confidence, his trust, his love. Of losing him and even her children. And then she looked at Gianni Dressler and his last four words jangled in her head. *It could be fatal.*

No contest, she thought.

'What are we waiting for?' she said.

10

Edward arrived the following evening.

No one had told him. The admission to Dressler's clinic had gone smoothly, Annie's insistence that her husband not be informed had been respected. But in all the panic, Jamie, whose role it had been to see that all Edward's calls were returned and the sham continued, had forgotten to phone England, and shortly before ten that morning Edward had rung again. The trouble was that Olivia, fresh from the relief of knowing that Annie was safely tucked up in a hospital bed and of having her apartment to herself again, had picked up the telephone without waiting for the machine to take over.

'Olivia?' The man's voice had sounded surprised.

'Yes.' It had taken her a full two seconds to realize who it was. Her right hand flew to her mouth and she screwed her eyes shut in anguish at her stupidity and carelessness.

'Olivia, it's Edward Thomas speaking.'

Olivia took her hand away from her mouth. 'Hello, Edward.' She knew her voice sounded strained. 'How are you?'

'I'm very well, thank you. How are *you*, more to the point?'

'I'm fine.' *Oh, Lord*, she thought. She was supposed to be the one with problems, the reason Annie was in Geneva. Her mind raced. 'Actually, I'm not that great, really.'

'So I gathered from Annie.'

Olivia waited for the next, the obvious question.

'Is Annie there, please, Olivia?' Edward asked.

'No, Edward.' *Shit*, she thought. 'Not at the moment.'

'Only I haven't spoken to her in days, as you know.'

'Yes.' Her brain, usually reasonably agile, seemed to have turned to mush. Guilt, she decided. She had never been much good at telling lies.

'In fact, the only person I've spoken to has been James Arias.'

Olivia knew he was on to them, on to something, anyway. 'Jamie's been the only one here, Edward.' She paused. 'You know, because of the problems I've been having.'

'So Annie has been with you, has she?'

'Yes. Of course. She's been great.'

'Annie's very fond of you, Olivia,' Edward said. 'I hope she's been having a bit of a break, too. She was exceptionally tired before she left, you know.'

'I know.' At last, here was something to latch on to. 'That's why she's not here this morning,' she said, quickly. 'She's having some time to herself.'

'Good. Shopping, I imagine.'

'I expect so. Probably buying presents for you and the children. How are they?'

'They're wonderful,' Edward replied, then paused. 'I'm glad to hear you sounding so well, Olivia. I rather had the impression from Annie that you were quite under par.'

'I was.' Olivia thought about Annie in the clinic. She

140

had not the slightest idea yet how long she might be there, whether she would be coming back to the apartment with Dressler and his nurses, or whether that was all over now for keeps. 'I still am, a little,' she added, for good measure.

'Anyway,' Edward said, rounding the call up, 'will you ask Annie to call me as soon as she gets back? I'm in London.'

'I will,' Olivia said.

'Tell her I miss her,' Edward said. 'I mean, I want her to take the time she needs, but I do miss her very much. So do the children, especially Liza – well, all of them, really.'

'I'll tell her,' Olivia said, guilt making her feel slightly sick.

'Thank you, Olivia.' He paused again. 'You'll make sure she calls me, won't you, please?'

'Of course. When I see her.'

'Good talking to you again. I wish you well.'

'Thank you, Edward.'

Olivia hung up. *Hell*, she thought. *Bloody, bloody hell*. He was already suspicious. If he didn't hear from Annie by lunchtime, he'd know that something was up. Christ, she felt so *ashamed* – of lying to Edward, of not lying well enough. Most of all she felt ashamed of letting Annie down so badly.

She looked down at the telephone, thought about the nice, caring, sensible, clever man at the other end. *If it were me*, she thought, *I know what I would do*.

He came after leaving two more messages on the machine and receiving no response, either from his wife or from Jamie or Olivia. Instinct drove him to organize his plane reservation, to leave one final message in a strong, clear voice, telling whoever might be listening that he would be flying to Geneva that evening; instinct and sudden fear, though he was uncertain exactly what he was frightened of. Something was wrong with Annie, he knew that much, though what he did not know. She might be ill. She might be having an affair. She might be wanting to leave him and be working out – with her two old friends and, perhaps, some Swiss lawyer – the best way of going about it. She might simply be sick of living with him. Edward didn't really believe that was it – for all the strain he had noticed in her face recently, for all the weariness one of his sisters-in-law and some of their neighbours and friends had remarked on, he had continued always to observe the love in Annie's eyes. Not just for Sophie and William and little Liza. It was still there for him, too, he was certain. Almost certain. He suspected, somehow, that his first fear was the right one. And the worst.

Annie, his beloved Annie, was ill.

'How could you?' he asked Olivia at the airport, when she had told him, as gently and carefully as possible, that Annie was in a clinic but that she was in no danger. 'How could you even *dream* of not telling me my own wife was ill?'

He was walking fast, sweeping towards the exit, desperately upset but crisp and determined that nothing and nobody was going to keep him from Annie for a single moment more than was absolutely necessary.

'Edward, please listen.' Olivia strode beside him, tried to take his arm, to slow him down, but he shook her off. 'Edward, there's more you don't know – things you have to know before you see her.'

'More?' He ground to a halt, his eyes filled with new fear. 'What more?'

'Can we sit down somewhere? Have a cup of coffee?'

'Coffee?' Edward laughed harshly. 'If you think I'm going to waste time drinking coffee while my wife's lying in some hospital bed, you must be mad.' He started walking again, then stopped abruptly and took hold, quite roughly, of Olivia's left arm. 'How ill is she?' His grey eyes bored into hers. 'Tell me the truth, Olivia. I need to know the absolute truth.'

'I agree,' Olivia said softly. 'But we have to go somewhere and sit down quietly so that I can tell you everything. It can't be done in the back of a taxi on the way to the clinic.' She paused. 'And I swear to you, Edward, on everything that's ever been important to me, Annie is not in danger – not in the way that you think, anyhow.' She saw the confusion, the fresh alarm in his face. 'Come on,' she said, very gently, 'and I'll tell you.'

'Oh, God,' he said when she'd finished. 'Oh, my God.'

Olivia said nothing, just sat back against the vinyl seat and watched his devastated expression in the dim light of the bar. Edward had downed a malt whisky while she had been speaking, and she was pretty sure he needed another, but she thought she should keep silent now, knew that she had said enough. More than enough.

'I don't know what to say,' he said, very softly. He looked at Olivia directly for an instant, and she saw that there were tears in his eyes, and then he looked away again. 'If it's any help to you—' He stopped and cleared his throat, blinked hard and began again. 'If it's any help to you, I don't blame you or Jamie – I accept – I think I can accept – that you thought you were doing the right thing by Annie.'

'No,' Olivia said. 'We didn't think we were doing the

right thing at all. We just came to see that it was the only possibility she would consider. All the others were even worse, even more dangerous.'

'Like telling me, you mean.' Bitterness arrived in Edward's tone.

'No, Edward. That was never a possibility. Not in Annie's eyes.'

'Because she thought she might lose me.'

'Yes.'

'How could she think that?' He shook his head, still dazed. 'How could she think such a thing about me?'

'I don't know,' Olivia said. 'But I'm afraid she did.' She hesitated. 'I think—'

Edward looked piercingly at her. 'Yes?'

'Nothing.'

'Olivia, what do you think? Tell me. Please.'

She took a breath. 'I think it might have had something to do with your mother.'

They went together to the clinic. Edward saw Gianni Dressler first, spent ten minutes with him, then went to Annie's room. Jamie was sitting in a chair between the bed and the window. He rose as Edward walked in, put out his right hand with automatic courtesy, then dropped it back to his side as the other man gave him the briefest of nods and passed him.

Olivia, at the open door, caught Jamie's eye, gestured to him to come out into the corridor. And then she saw Annie's face. It was almost ghostly white with shock, and her blue eyes, catching Olivia's for a second, were loaded with condemnation.

Jamie came out, and they closed the door. Dressler was a few feet away, watching them.

'It's the best thing,' he said to them both. 'You know that, don't you?'

'You didn't see her face just now,' Olivia told him.

'It's still the best thing,' Dressler insisted. 'Believe me.'

'I thought she knew,' Jamie said. 'I've been sitting with her for more than two hours, and she never asked where Olivia was, never asked after Edward, and she never really slept, hardly even dozed. I was convinced she realized he was on his way. But then, when he walked in—'

'Annie's been keeping this secret from him for virtually their entire marriage,' Dressler said, 'and now she's been found out. This has been her greatest nightmare, along with what may or may not happen next.' He paused and gave them a smile of great warmth. 'Whichever way it goes, you two good friends, you two very nice people, it's still Annie's only realistic way forward.'

'I guess we knew that anyway,' Olivia said.

'That doesn't make it any easier for Annie though, does it?' Jamie said.

'How are you feeling?' Edward asked Annie, sitting on the side of the high hospital bed, holding her icy right hand in both his.

'Not too bad.' Annie's voice was so quiet it was almost inaudible.

'Dr Dressler tells me you're doing very well.'

'He tells me the same thing.'

'He seems a good man.'

'He is.' Annie swallowed hard. 'You mustn't blame him. He wanted you to know. I wouldn't let him tell you. I wouldn't let Olivia or Jamie tell you either.'

'No. I know.' Edward paused. 'I don't blame any of them.'

'Just me,' Annie said.

'Just myself,' Edward said.

She was appalled. A tinge of colour crept back into her cheeks. 'You can't, Edward. You can't possibly think that you have anything to blame yourself for.'

'I'm your husband,' he said simply. 'We've been married for six years. We have three children. Yet you've felt unable to share your pain with me. I'd say that means I have rather a lot to blame myself for.'

'No.' Annie took her cold hand from his, saw its tremor, tucked it, ashamed, beneath the covers. 'Please, Edward, don't do this to me. Not on top of everything else.'

'Do what?' He was newly confused. 'What do you mean?'

'Don't try taking my guilt away from me.'

'But you have no reason to feel guilty.'

'Edward, please.' Her eyes filled with tears. 'Please let me.'

'Let you what, darling?' he asked. 'I don't understand what you want.'

'I want—' She broke off, her mouth trembling, swallowed down the sob building in her throat, tried again. 'I've waited too long for this moment. I need it.'

'What do you need, Annie?'

'I need you to blame me, Edward. I need you to blame *me*. Not yourself. I'm the guilty party here – *me*. This is all my fault. All my doing. My weakness brought me here, my pathetic weakness and my deceit.' She gathered a little strength. 'Suppose I'd been hiding a lover all these years instead of bottles of pills. Imagine I'd finally plucked up the courage to try to dump him for the sake of our marriage—'

'There's no comparison—'

'Edward, please, let me,' she pleaded. 'It isn't so very different – well, of course it is, because there's never been anyone else, I've never *wanted* anyone else and I never will. But, still, try and listen to what I'm saying.'

'I'll try.'

She gritted her teeth despite the nausea that was threatening to overwhelm her again. 'Imagine that I'd come here to ask Livvy and Jamie to help me get over my lover, and let's take it a step further: imagine I'd found it too hard, too unbearable and maybe I'd done something really stupid – taken an overdose or something – and you'd come and found me here in this clinic now.' She paused. 'Would you still feel you were to blame?'

'No, of course not.' Edward shook his head. 'But Annie, darling, you can't – you really, honestly, can't compare taking too many tranquillizers with taking a lover.'

'I don't just take too many tranquillizers, Edward,' Annie said, quite brutally. 'I'm an addict.'

'Valium's not exactly heroin, Annie.'

'I've bought it from pushers on the street,' she said. 'I've even been arrested for it.' She saw the horror on his face. 'I was never charged – they weren't all that interested in me really. But still.'

They were both silent for a few minutes. Annie stared down at the white hospital quilt covering most of her body. Edward looked at the wall, seeing nothing, isolated with his thoughts.

'Can I ask you something?' he said at last.

'I wish you would. Ask me anything you want.'

'Did my telling you about my mother make a difference?' He paused. 'You were going to tell me about the pills, weren't you? Before I told you about her morphine addiction.'

Annie could not look at him. 'I might have. I was planning to.'

'And I made you afraid to,' Edward said, quietly. 'Oh, dear God.'

He stood up and walked over to the window. The curtains were drawn, and he lifted one back a little way and stared out into the night. His thoughts, Annie's words, seemed to be roaring in his mind, filling his brain, overloading it. He was, had always been, a controlled man, but suddenly he felt as if he wanted to weep, even to scream.

'Edward?'

He heard her voice, weaker suddenly, desperately afraid, but he did not, could not seem to, turn around.

'Edward, what is it?' She was newly frightened. 'What have I said?'

'Nothing,' he said, with an effort, then turned back to face her. 'Nothing at all, Annie.'

'Yes, I have.' She was staring up at him, curiously, fearfully. 'I've upset you somehow. Talking about your mother. You don't want to talk about her, obviously, otherwise you would have done years ago. I'm sorry, Edward, I just wanted to try to explain. I need to at least *try*—'

'I know.' He came and sat down on the bed again. 'But you're very tired now, darling. I can see it, hear it. You have to rest – you have to sleep. The doctor told me not to exhaust you and I'm afraid I have.'

'No,' Annie said. 'I mean, yes, I am tired, but I don't care about that.' Her eyes sparkled with tears. 'I've missed you so much. I thought I had to do this without you – you have to believe I thought I had no choice.'

'I do believe that.' He stood up again. 'You have to sleep now, Annie.'

'I will.' The fear was still there. 'Where will you be?'

'At the Des Bergues.'

'And you'll come tomorrow?'

'Of course I'll come.' His face was full of reassurance as he bent to kiss her, first on her forehead, then on her mouth. 'Try not to fret too much, my darling. Tomorrow we'll speak to Dr Dressler together, and he'll tell us exactly what we have to do to get through this, how to get you completely well again.'

'It might take some time,' Annie said.

'I imagine it might,' Edward said. 'But we have the time.'

She lay back against the pillows, tried desperately to muster a smile for him, but failed. 'I'm sorry, Edward,' she said, very quiet again. 'I'm so very sorry for everything.'

'Me too,' he said.

Olivia slipped back in to see Annie after Edward had left. Jamie had offered to go with him to the hotel, and Edward had thanked him but told him a little stiffly that he could manage very well on his own, so Olivia had asked Jamie to go back to her apartment and rustle up something simple to eat because she didn't think she could face a restaurant that night.

Annie was still awake, and though she told Olivia that Edward had been wonderful, Olivia could see that she was still fretting about something.

'I'm not leaving until you tell me.'

'Oh, Livvy, there's nothing to tell. Nothing real, at least. Just more of my imaginings.'

'Share them with me anyway,' Olivia encouraged, gently.

Annie sighed. 'We were talking about it, or trying to, and then—'

'Then?'

'We talked about his mother.'

'And?'

'And it was all right, for a moment or two anyway. And then suddenly he got up and walked away, over to the window, and he seemed to shut down. It was as if he couldn't bear to talk any more, not just about her or his childhood, but about anything.'

'He was probably exhausted,' Olivia said.

Annie smiled wryly. 'That's why he said we should stop, because I was too tired to go on.'

'He had a point. You look wrecked.'

'I guess I am.'

'And Edward's had a tough day.' Olivia looked at Annie's frightened eyes. 'Oh, Annie, sweetheart, don't give yourself such a hard time.' Olivia felt a stab of the greatest pity for her friend. 'Edward's right about you being exhausted. You're still in the midst of early withdrawal and you've had to confront what you were most frightened of. What you need right now is to go to sleep, and I mean real sleep, not just lying there with your eyes closed.'

'Olivia's absolutely right,' Gianni Dressler said, from the doorway.

'I don't think I can sleep,' Annie said.

'Then we'll do something to help you,' Dressler told her.

'I thought you said no drugs,' Olivia said.

'I don't want to go backward,' Annie said, anxiously.

'And I don't intend to let you,' the doctor reassured her.

'You really do need some proper rest,' Olivia said to Annie, standing up.

'Leave that to me,' Dressler told her, then turned to

Annie. 'And you can trust me not to set you back. All right?'

'Yes,' Annie said, softly. 'Thank you.'

'Olivia?' Dressler looked back at her. 'With the greatest respect' – he smiled at her – 'please get out of here.'

Olivia smiled back at him. 'I'm leaving.'

'Now.'

Olivia blew Annie a kiss and opened the door. 'Call us in the morning when you're awake.'

'Go,' Dressler said.

'I've gone.'

Olivia set her alarm clock for seven-thirty and called Edward at the Des Bergues, asking if she might meet him for breakfast before he went back to the clinic. They met in the Pavillon restaurant and ordered coffee and croissants.

'What can I do for you, Olivia?' Edward asked her.

'I wondered if there was anything more I could tell you, that might help you take care of Annie.' Olivia paused, trying harder than usual to be tactful, still well aware that she and Jamie had overstepped the bounds of friendship, had usurped Edward's own role. 'Anything, I mean, that might have gone on in the last week that perhaps you ought to know about.'

'Other than the fact that my wife has been trying to withdraw from a serious drug addiction, you mean?' Edward's words were cutting, despite the lightness of his tone.

Olivia put down her coffee cup and looked at him candidly. 'Edward, we've been through the apologies, and I honestly don't think it's going to help Annie or you or your family for us to start all over again. You know why we did it, right or wrong.'

'Yes.' Edward was softer. 'I'm sorry.'

'No need.' Olivia hesitated only briefly, then plunged back in. 'I went in to say goodnight to Annie last night after you'd gone. She seemed upset about the way your conversation had ended.'

'Olivia' – Edward leaned in towards the table – 'I know you mean well, believe me, I really do know that, but there are certain things—'

'I know' – Olivia interrupted – 'I know. They're none of my business, and Annie didn't say much – believe me, Edward, she's much too discreet to say too much. But she used the words "shut down" when she mentioned the way your talk last night had ended, and that worried me.'

'I'm sorry you've been worried—'

'Oh, Edward, don't be so stuffy,' Olivia jumped back in. 'It doesn't matter a bit whether I'm worried or not. I just thought you might want to know that it had worried Annie. Upset her. Because anything right this minute that upsets Annie is important. And that doesn't mean,' she added, quickly, 'that she isn't to be upset, because that's not real life.'

'I know what you mean,' Edward said, relenting. 'You mean that things that upset her need to be dealt with, not pushed under the carpet.'

'Yes,' Olivia said, 'that is what I mean.'

'And what you're skirting around' – he managed a smile at her – 'which is rather unlike you, if I may say so—'

'I know it is.' Olivia smiled back at him.

'What you're skirting around, is the subject of my mother.'

Olivia said nothing.

Edward's eyes were darkening again, but he kept going. 'Olivia,' he said, quietly, 'I've coped with that particular subject all my adult life by doing what I did last night with my wife. By shutting it off.' He paused. 'I'd had a bit of a shock yesterday, one way and another, and I suppose there came a point when I couldn't take any more.' He paused again. 'I told myself that nothing was going to make me dredge it all up again. There was nothing to be gained by it. I'd proved that, after all, hadn't I? I'd bottled it up the way they claim these days is so bad for you. I walled up all those awful memories, entombed them, if you like, and I went on with my life and did pretty well in spite of them.'

'Yes, you did,' Olivia said. 'Clearly, you have dealt beautifully with your life. You're a very successful man with a lovely family.'

'And a deeply unhappy, drug-addicted wife.'

'Yes,' Olivia said, softly.

'In other words, what was good for me may not have been so good for Annie.' Edward picked up the coffee pot, poured some more into both their cups. 'And my sealing off the darker side of my own life made it harder for Annie to approach me about her own troubles.'

'It certainly contributed,' Olivia agreed. 'I sincerely doubt that it's been all that's kept Annie silent.'

'No,' Edward said, 'I expect that's true.' He took a breath. 'I have a question. Though it's one I don't think you'll be able to answer.'

'Shoot,' Olivia said.

'How could I not have known what was wrong with Annie? How in God's name could I not have seen how much my wife was suffering?'

Olivia looked at him, saw how tortured he was, how genuinely wretched, and her heart went out to him. Yet in order to most effectively answer his question, to give

Edward and Annie their best chance of repairing the damage, she knew she had to be honest, to tell it how she saw it.

'No one's blaming you, Edward,' she said. 'Least of all, Annie.'

'But . . . ?' Edward's mouth quirked again. 'Surely there's a but.'

Olivia nodded. 'But there is something you have to realize. You've always believed that Annie was doing fine. You saw what she wanted you to see, but I also think you might have seen what *you* wanted to see – and by the way, so did I, so did Jamie.'

'You weren't living with her,' Edward said, sombrely.

'That's true, but Annie's a good actress – I never realized that before, but I do now. And she's also very brave, even if she sees herself as a coward and a liar.'

'So what do I do now, to help put things right?'

'You're going to have to stop accepting Annie at face value,' Olivia answered. 'You're going to have to take a sledgehammer to that outer shell of hers – you're going to have to break through and keep on breaking through to the *real* Annie.'

'I'm not sure,' Edward said, 'that I'm much of a sledge-hammer type.'

'No,' Olivia agreed, 'I'm sure you're not. But I expect you'll find a more tender, gentle way of cracking Annie's shell, if you really try. And let's face it, Edward, the only chance you have of helping her – of helping you all – get through this mess, is by facing it together. Dealing with it together.'

Annie stayed at the clinic for another week, with Edward coming in every day to see her and to participate in some of the counselling sessions that Gianni Dressler recommended they take together.

She was already looking better. She accepted that she had a long way to go, that it might be several months before she was entirely over withdrawal, that perhaps she might never feel as good, as invincible, as she might choose to feel. But she would, ultimately, be taking control of herself and of her body and mind. She would need help, had to learn, now that she had begun, to keep on asking for that help. She would need to keep busy, to feel useful and productive and to be patient with herself. Exercise was highly recommended, together with work, general activity, and love.

'What can we do now? Jamie and I?' Olivia asked Dressler at Au Fin Bec, a popular and friendly restaurant on the right bank.

They'd planned dinner for three on Jamie's penultimate evening in Switzerland, but Jamie had backed out at the last minute, with urgent business to take care of.

'About Annie, you mean?' Dressler asked.

'Of course.'

'Nothing,' Dressler said. 'You do nothing.'

'But they're going home the day after tomorrow.'

'Don't you think they should?'

'Of course I think they should,' Olivia said impatiently. 'But Jamie and I are both anxious about abandoning Annie back in England where all her troubles started.'

'You're not abandoning her. She'll be with Edward and their children.'

'You know what I mean, Gianni.'

'Of course I do.' His eyes were warm. 'You have to leave them to it, Olivia. You'll stay in touch, naturally, let Annie know you're there for her, just as you've always been.'

'But she waited six years before she told us anything was wrong.'

'That was before. This is now.' Gianni paused. 'I know it's a hard thing for you to walk away from Annie while she's still so vulnerable.'

'You admit she is still vulnerable.'

'And will be for a long time. Perhaps always. But Annie's no fool, Olivia. The toughest thing for her was her dark secret, the hole she'd dug herself into. Now that she's on her way up out of that particular hole, I'll be surprised if she lets herself fall back in without giving a good, loud yell first.' He smiled. 'Annie knows you and Jamie are a telephone call away. But you have to let her tackle this next stage by herself.'

'So?' Annie was the first to ask the following evening at Olivia's apartment. They were dining alone, Edward having understood that he was simply not invited, that this was a special occasion for the three friends. 'How was last night with Gianni?'

'Good,' Olivia answered.

'What do you mean, good?'

'Not bad.'

'You're aggravating Annie,' Jamie chided her. 'She's not supposed to get aggravated, remember?'

'Gianni never said that,' Olivia said. 'He prescribed "real life". Being aggravated by me has always been part of real life for Annie and you.'

'Don't we know it,' Jamie remarked.

'I want to know about last night,' Annie insisted.

'Pleasant,' Olivia said. 'Enjoyable, in fact.'

'Livvy, that won't do,' Annie said. 'I need details. Romance is good for my soul – my drop-dead-gorgeous doctor says so.'

She knew she was babbling a little, that the euphoria of being released from the clinic and of feeling almost well would not, could not, last; but tonight, at that very moment at least, she did not care.

'So go get some romance,' Olivia told her.

'I'm an old married lady,' Annie said.

'So get some with your husband.'

Annie looked at Jamie. 'She's not going to give anything away, is she?'

'Doesn't look like it.'

'You know they're going to have an affair, don't you?'

Jamie made no comment.

'Enough.' Olivia poured wine into Jamie's glass and refilled her own.

'Olivia Segal' – Annie wasn't ready to give up – 'this man is every red-blooded woman's fantasy.'

'He's arrogant,' Olivia said. 'A successful, handsome doctor, and Swiss-Italian – I'm surprised his ego made it through my front door.'

'Olivia has a point,' Jamie grinned. 'Two egos that size might be a tight squeeze, especially in this little apartment.'

'So you do think he's handsome,' Annie said.

'I'm not blind,' Olivia said drily, ignoring Jamie's crack.

'So you are going to have an affair with him?'

'Nothing's impossible.'

The pause that followed was long and awkward.

'I'm scared,' Annie said abruptly.

'Of going home?' Olivia asked, gently.

157

'Yes.' Annie shook her head, angry with herself. 'I want to go back more than anything – I feel I'll go crazy if I don't see Sophie and William and Liza for one more *day*.' She paused again. 'But it's where it all began, isn't it?'

'That's not really true,' Jamie said. 'I'd say it began eleven years ago when that helicopter crashed.'

'Jamie's right, Annie,' Olivia agreed.

'But it all came to a head in Stone Bridge,' Annie maintained. 'And it's all still there, waiting for me. The house to run, the children to look after, the community to fit into.'

'But one important thing has changed, Annie,' Olivia said. 'The two most important things of all, I should say.'

'Edward knowing, you mean,' Annie said.

'Yes,' Olivia said. 'You have Edward to share your problems with now. And you don't have to fight them all by yourself any more.'

Annie was smiling. 'I'm going to miss you both so much,' she said softly, and felt tears beginning to threaten.

'We're going to miss you too,' Jamie told her, and reached for her hand.

'We'll be calling you a lot,' Olivia said. 'We're probably going to drive you crazy, checking up on you.'

'Feel free,' Annie said. 'And come whenever you can.'

'I'd come now,' Jamie said, 'if I thought it would help.'

'We both would,' Olivia agreed. 'But Gianni says you have to deal with the next bit yourselves – you and Edward, not you alone.'

'I know,' Annie said. 'And you've done more than enough for me, both of you.'

'We failed you, Annie,' Jamie said.

'You've never failed me.' Annie was vehement.

'We ought to have known,' Jamie insisted.

'That's how Edward feels,' Annie said. 'But I know he's wrong, that you're all wrong about that. I know what a great liar I've been—' She held up one hand, fending off protests. 'You can call it acting, putting up a façade, whatever you like. But if part of getting myself straight again is acknowledging the truth about myself, then let me at least be honest about what I know.' She paused. 'I lied. To myself, and to everyone who loved me. And I almost let it go too far.'

'Thank God you didn't,' Olivia said.

'Thank God I had you two,' Annie said.

Olivia spent a long time at the airport next day; first, with Jamie, seeing off Annie and Edward on their British Airways flight to London, and then, a little later, seeing Jamie off back to Boston.

'Give my love to Carrie,' Olivia said, then grinned. 'If she can stand it.'

'Carrie doesn't hate you, Olivia,' Jamie said earnestly.

'I'm not exactly her Woman of the Decade.'

'She's jealous of you.'

'I know she is,' Olivia agreed. 'What I've never understood is why.'

'She must have her reasons.'

'She does know we've never been anything more than friends, doesn't she?' Olivia looked at Jamie, at his beautiful soft dark eyes and sleek hair. 'Though maybe, if I were Carrie I might feel that way too about an unattached female who got too close to you.'

'I doubt that,' Jamie said.

They strolled slowly towards Passport Control, taking their time, making the most of every remaining minute they could share.

'Be safe,' Olivia said, when they got there.

'You too.'

'And be happy. Don't let Carrie get you down.'

'She doesn't, Olivia.' Jamie paused. 'I wish you two got along better.'

'It's not just me though, is it? She doesn't like Annie much more.'

'You're not being quite fair, are you?' Jamie wasn't being critical, just frank. This was old territory; they'd trodden it before, and would do again. 'Carrie's always known neither of you liked her, right from the start.'

'I guess that's true,' Olivia admitted. 'And I am sorry for that, Jamie. I do wish I could have loved your wife. I meant to.'

'I know you did.' He picked up his travel bag, then hesitated and put it down again. 'If you do get involved with Dressler,' he said, 'watch yourself, won't you?'

'Sure I will,' she said lightly. 'You know me. Easy come, easy go.'

'Like hell.' Jamie took her hand. 'That's just your front, Olivia – we all have façades, not just Annie.'

'Don't worry about me,' Olivia told him.

'I can't help worrying about you. I always have.'

'I know. Me too.'

They embraced. Olivia felt his slender strength, smelled his old familiar fragrance and thought how important he was to her, how fundamental his and Annie's friendship had become to her whole life.

'Love you,' Jamie said, softly, against her ear.

'Love you back,' Olivia said.

And then he was on his way, stopping for just one more instant to look back and wave at her and blow her a kiss, and then he was gone, out of sight. And Olivia turned, when she was sure he wasn't coming back, and began to walk towards the exit, heading for the garage where she'd left her car. And she had the strangest feeling, reflecting bemusedly on those parting words of love, words they'd spoken to each other almost every time they'd said their farewells over the years, that this time, for her – she knew and accepted that it had only been for her, not for Jamie – there had been a curious difference.

She thought – she was not certain, she didn't think she *wanted* to be certain, because not only was it wrong, it was also out of the question, utterly and entirely impossible – but she thought perhaps that she had meant it.

And not just as a friend.

11

Olivia's Box

By the summer of 1938, fifty-five thousand Jews from Germany and Austria had escaped to the United States of America, but not a single member of our family was amongst that number. My father, who had once been so confident that his high standing, wealth and contacts would mean that he could, if sorely pressed, arrange safe passage for us all at comparatively short notice, now knew better. The emigration paperwork that his old friend Max Wildenbruch's affidavit ought to have ensured had mysteriously failed to materialize; the essential arrangements taken care of by Max's lawyers that ought to have enabled us to travel to America had repeatedly and inexplicably fallen apart. Papa, after one call to New York, said that Max had sounded perplexed and upset; he had done the same for Ferdy Steiner from Nuremberg, and the Steiner family were now safely ensconced in an apartment on Seventy-third Street in Manhattan. It made no sense, Max Wildenbruch said, when all they heard was that the Nazis were encouraging Jews to get the hell out of Germany.

It made perfect sense to Papa, Mama and to me, though we all kept our fears from Lili and Trude. As time had passed and the Nazi terror had gathered strength and savagery, Brauner's blackmail had grown ever more systematic and brutal. Mama and Papa had seen him at the outset as nothing worse than an opportunistic collector; now we knew he was an unscrupulous thief. With deadly efficiency, Brauner had ransacked our cellars and by now the bones of Papa's cherished Symbolist Collection had been picked almost clean. What had begun, seemingly, as a rather one-sided business deal to make it possible for us to leave Germany with at least a small percentage of our pride and possessions intact, had become a bargain for far higher stakes. If Papa continued to cooperate, Brauner had told him in the early months, he would use his influence to allow us to remain, unmolested, in our home. If Papa went on quietly handing over his treasures, Brauner had said a few months later, he would see to it that we were allowed, eventually, to leave Germany for America. But all that had long since changed. Brauner no longer bothered dangling carrots of help; now he simply used his personal power to threaten us all. Brauner had friends in high places, he reminded my father repeatedly; all he had to do was to inform on Papa, implicating him in anything from race defilement to some fictitious anti-Nazi plot, and then Papa would at the very least be sent to the concentration camp at Dachau, near Munich, or, more probably, be executed.

It had taken three years. Since the autumn of 1935, Brauner had come and gone eleven times, his visits irregular and unpredictable, and we all suspected that Baden-Baden might be only one of his ports of call, that he might be trawling around Germany, cold-bloodedly reaping his once-in-a-lifetime artistic harvest.

All that remained in our cellars by September 1938, were a small group of works by Hodler, Redon and Ibels. Out of the one hundred and thirteen paintings that had left the house, my father had learned from Max Wildenbruch that only nine had reached him: six during the first year of their arrangement, just three in the second, when Papa had still clung to the vain belief that Brauner was to some paltry degree – because it suited him – keeping his word.

'What happens when the cellar is empty?' Anton asked Emanuel late one September evening as they walked together in the garden.

'Who knows?' Emanuel said, softly.

Emanuel knew better by now than actively to lie to his son. Anton was seventeen now, and infinitely more mature than a young man his age ought to be. There was little purpose in lying, for the boy knew as much as his parents did about the ever-growing dangers facing the Jews of Germany and – since March that year – of Austria.

'I suppose Brauner will skulk back to wherever he came from, and never come back again,' Anton said quietly, as they walked in the dark.

'I suppose so,' Emanuel said.

'What will happen when they've taken the house and find the whole collection gone?'

'They may not take the house,' Emanuel said.

'They will, Papa. You know they will. The laws have all been passed. Everyone knows it's only a matter of time before they throw us out.'

'Perhaps.'

They walked on in silence for a while, thinking. About what had befallen the Viennese Jews almost overnight after the *Anschluss*; all rights immediately taken away, physical assaults and humiliation. About the burning down of the main synagogue in Munich in June, and in Nuremberg in August. About the arrests that had begun in the summer all over Germany and were still going on. About the rumours that kept filtering through, slowly and terrifyingly, of the fate that had befallen those arrested.

'And after they've thrown us out' – Anton was unable to leave it – 'what will they do to us then, Papa? When they open up the cellars. Everyone knows about the collection, they won't be able to pretend it never existed.' He paused. 'What if they say we plotted with Brauner to rob them?'

Emanuel patted his son's shoulder. 'You mustn't worry so much about things that may never happen,' he said gently. 'Things we can do nothing about.'

'But he's made so many threats, Papa.'

'Only to keep us doing his bidding,' Emanuel said with an ease he did not feel. 'Once he has all the paintings, he won't need us any more. He'll simply be finished with us.'

They walked a little further. The gardener had mown the back lawn that afternoon, and the scent was sweet.

'Surely,' Anton said, after a while, 'he might see us as witnesses.'

'Witnesses?'

'He's a criminal, isn't he?' Anton paused. 'A foreigner, smuggling art treasures out of the country. And we know what he's done.'

'I don't think we need worry about that,' Emanuel said tightly. 'Brauner has friends in high places. He's told us that often enough.'

'Mama says that just means he's bribed a few Nazi officials here in Baden-Baden.'

'And I say we don't have to worry about his crimes,' Emanuel insisted. 'When he's finished with us, our papers will come.'

Anton stopped and stood very still.

'Do you really believe that, Papa?'

Emanuel went on walking. 'I have to believe it,' he said.

Papa did not, of course, believe it. He knew as well as Mama and I did that his small, blissful empire of beauty and peace was gone forever. He would go on scrabbling around his swiftly dwindling network of contacts day after day, trying desperately to find a means – *any* means – of safe exit, at least for Mama, Lili and Trude and myself, if not for himself. But I don't think he any longer had any real faith that he would succeed.

Our family had been taken in, taken over, and then betrayed by the man who called himself Georg Brauner. We had been at his mercy for three years, and before much longer, our usefulness to him ended, he would, we realized – looking at it in the best of lights – abandon us completely. Though if my fear was right, and if Brauner did see us as witnesses – if he did regard our presence as some kind of personal threat – there was, of course, no telling what he might do.

We heard that Dachau and the newer concentration camps were filling up with every passing week. We and countless other families much like us who had waited too long to leave our homeland were now waiting like helpless chickens in a broken coop, to be devoured by the Nazi fox. And with all possible exits continuing to be blocked to us, Mama, Papa and I knew that we and the girls were, to all intents and purposes, trapped. We did our best to wear our bravest faces for Lili's and Trude's sakes, and even at night, after they had gone to sleep, we seldom voiced our true feelings. Mama and Papa were doubtless keen to spare me what little they could.

But I think – I know – they were as terrified as I was.

12

For Jamie

'It's crazy,' Annie said, after Olivia had outlined her plan for getting back at Carrie Beaumont Arias. 'I mean I love it, in a way, but it's completely, absolutely crazy, and it scares me.'

'Why?'

'Because it's so off-the-wall.'

'It's perfect,' Olivia said.

'But it seems so – immoral.'

'We're dealing with an amoral person, Annie. It's the only way to really get to her. To hit her where it hurts.'

'You really hate Carrie, don't you, Livvy?'

Olivia thought about that for a moment. 'I wouldn't say I hate her. I don't think I've ever hated anyone – actually *hated* anyone – in my life. But I do most certainly despise her.'

'We could never pull it off,' Annie said.

'If I didn't think we could,' Olivia answered, 'I wouldn't be suggesting you got involved.'

It was January 1990. They were sitting at Annie's kitchen table at Banbury Farm House. Almost three years had

169

passed since Annie had swallowed her last Valium, and she often felt like a completely different woman, as if that whole nightmare had happened to someone else. That was one of the aspects, if she was totally honest, that she appreciated most about the plan Olivia had just shared with her. As recently as a year ago, Annie doubted if Livvy would have considered her strong enough or tough enough to participate in anything like this. It was, she realized, a tribute to her recovery that they were sitting there today, working out ways to help Jamie.

'But are you sure it isn't wrong not to tell Jamie?' Annie asked Olivia. 'After all, we'd be doing it for him. Doesn't he have a right to know?'

'No.' Olivia shook her head definitely. 'For one thing, knowing Jamie, he'd never agree to go along with it.' She looked down at the notes she'd made, and her green eyes glittered at the thought of what was to come. 'And for another, this whole thing is only going to work – really work – if Jamie doesn't know a damned thing about it.'

If Olivia's parents, she sometimes thought, had lived to see their daughter become an adult, they might, she hoped, have been proud of her, but they were also bound, she was certain, to have been perplexed because she was so unlike either of them. Arthur Segal, her father, had been born in Berlin in 1933 to Jewish parents who had made it to the United States one year after his birth, aided in their quest for a peaceful, safe existence by Arthur's mother's affluent brother, already living in Manhattan. Arthur had become a well-respected art dealer and philanthropist, his own collection of paintings – much of it directed to him by old Max Wildenbruch in New York and including some of the great French Impressionists at the top end and a large number of works by young, up and coming artists at the other – both admired and envied. His collection had, in his lifetime, spent more time out on loan to public galleries than hanging on its owner's own walls. Arthur firmly believed that art was created to be seen and enjoyed, to be shared, not hidden away. That had also been his general philosophy on life, which was why he had become something of a slave to his fund-raising activities, and why he had regularly given substantial sums of money to so many charities.

Arthur had often claimed to have been shamed into doing his good works because of Emily, his wife and the driving force in his life. Emily Segal was a paediatric heart surgeon, and no man could have been prouder of his wife than her husband. Emily, a truly selfless person, loved her family and respected her Jewish heritage, but it had always been understood that her work often had to come first – before birthdays, before regular Friday night dinners, before even the High Holydays – if a child was sick and needed her help. She was fortunate in that she was naturally pretty and slender, but unlike most of the other wives in the Segals' social circle, Emily had no time or patience for shopping or beauty parlours. Where was the sense, after all, Emily asked, in buying great clothes or hairstyles when she spent most of her life in white coats or sterile overalls with her hair scraped off her face and covered?

Unlike Olivia – who skied regularly to downhill racing standards and who had, over the past decade, also gone scuba diving, backpacking, hang-gliding and horse riding in the Grand Canyon – neither Arthur nor Emily had been especially physical folk. Their vacations, at the rare times when Emily could get away, had been restful affairs, usually in France or Israel or occasionally in Italy, with unadventurous swimming and gentle strolls their only exercise. They had shared an abiding passion for each other's bodies, but neither would have claimed to have unusually powerful sexual appetites. They were two immensely successful, worthy people, yet they were also highly conventional. Emily, the child of two doctors, had grown up believing fervently in the liberation of women, yet she had wanted marriage and children as much as Arthur, though a ruptured uterus had forced them to stop at one daughter.

Olivia sometimes thought she might be a throwback to some forgotten relative, some irresponsible, unbridled Jewess – probably on Arthur's side, she mused, some Russian girl who had not toed the conventional line, a fellow spirit. Not that Olivia was particularly bold compared to some young women she had encountered on her travels; she only seemed adventurous when she compared herself to her mother or father. Perhaps, she reflected in the odd, rare, guilty moment, she was trying to compensate for being such an unworthy successor to the Segals, was trying to make up for her undoubted inadequacies by making her life as action-packed as possible. She worked hard and played hard, she tried to be decent, was not an unhelpful or particularly unkind person, was certainly not a bad all-round human being, but compared to her parents, Olivia did sometimes feel useless. She wondered if she might have taken a completely different road if Arthur and Emily had lived, thought she probably would have done. They had known about her plans to go to the Sorbonne in the fall of 1976 and they had not expressed disapproval, yet Olivia suspected they might have urged her on to higher things if time had allowed. As it was, she had her qualifications – was, she supposed, a comparatively distinguished linguist –

and her business, and she also knew how to have fun better than most people she met.

Olivia's affair with Gianni Dressler, which had begun in earnest within a week of Jamie's and Annie's departure from Geneva in the spring of 1987 and had continued with considerable passion into the summer, had run its course by autumn of the same year. There had been, since then, a number of other men. It was not in Olivia's nature to be alone for long. Not that she minded being alone; in fact, she cherished her independence, enjoyed her own company and greatly valued her women friends. But Annie had once told Olivia that there was a spark in her green eyes that ignited in the presence of attractive or interesting men.

'It isn't deliberate, I know that,' Annie had said. 'But I've watched it drawing them to you, and then they seem to find it impossible to pull away again.'

'God, Annie,' Olivia had said, 'you make me sound like a vamp.'

'Not at all,' Annie had said. 'But you do have that spark.'

'And how on earth' – Olivia had laughed at the notion – 'would you describe this so-called spark?'

Annie had thought for a few moments.

'It's a promise,' she'd said, 'of fun, adventure, and warmth.'

Later, on reflection, Olivia had thought it was not a description she found either unflattering or displeasing.

The men drawn in and out of her life since the violet-eyed, dynamic Dressler had all been interesting, intelligent and attractive in one way or another, but only Gianni had pointed out to Olivia, more than once, one of the very few things she had ever, if she was honest with herself, tried to bury in her mind.

'You realize, of course,' he had said on the evening they had agreed, mutually, though not without a degree of regret, to end their relationship, 'that whatever you say and however much you deny it, you're in love with Arias.'

'Don't be absurd,' Olivia had said. 'Jamie's one of my best friends, I've told you.'

'Friendship doesn't rule out love,' Gianni said.

'It does in this case.' She was adamant. 'As does marriage.'

'To a woman you dislike.'

'What does my dislike have to do with it?'

Gianni smiled. 'That depends on why you dislike her.'

'I dislike Carrie for reasons that are none of your damned business,' Olivia said irritably. 'And just because I never fell in love with you, Gianni Dressler—'

'Nor I with you,' he countered charmingly.

'—does not mean I must be in love with anyone else.' She shook her head impatiently. 'Honestly, Gianni, I thought you were above this kind of chauvinistic crap.'

'Surely not.' He grinned again. 'How could a Swiss-Italian male surgeon possibly not be a chauvinist?'

'That's true.' Olivia softened slightly. 'I guess you can't help it.'

'Just as you can't help being in love with your Jamie,' Gianni said. 'You're forgetting I've seen you together many times.'

'You've seen two old friends. Dear friends.'

'And I repeat, since when does friendship preclude love?'

Olivia sighed. 'You really are full of shit, aren't you?' she said, more good-naturedly now, aware that he was deliberately goading her to get a reaction.

'If you say so.' Gianni paused. 'Why do you dislike Jamie's wife?'

'And I repeat,' Olivia said, 'none of your business.'

For all that it was true that Olivia had instinctively disliked Caroline Beaumont from the first time they had been introduced – and if she and Annie were perfectly honest, they had certainly been guilty of mistrusting her even before they had met her – she had quickly enough grown to see that Jamie's happiness with Carrie in the early days of their marriage was genuine.

Whatever life had thrown at Jamie Arias, he had remained the same charming, gentle man, in private and in public; and even in his working world of advertising, an industry populated by any number of cut-throat types, Jamie had become known as much for his old-fashioned courtesy and innate empathy as for his considerable talent for copywriting.

Jamie was permanently, guiltily aware that his late father, Carlos Arias, had anticipated that he, like his older brother Peter and their cousin Michael, would automatically enter the family's shipping business. Had Carlos lived, Jamie, who had adored his father, suspected that he might have felt compelled to do just that. As things were, he had prepared himself, when the moment of truth came, for a battle royal with Michael, the head of Arias Shipping, but to his great relief his cousin – who had elected to rule from their New York offices, an easy flight in a private jet from the Arias family compound at Newport – had given way gracefully, had said that he thought that what Carlos would have wanted, more than anything, was for his sons to be contented men.

'If you prefer the plebeian buzz of advertising,' Michael

said, grinning at his young cousin, 'to the splendour and power of your own shipping company – and I have to tell you that neither Peter nor I even begin to understand why – it's your decision to make.'

After all, Michael pointed out, Jamie's personal share of the family fortune was his, safe and sound, with no strings or conditions attached. Jamie, however he might choose to spend his time, was an immensely wealthy young man. He might just as well be a happy one too, Michael Arias reasoned.

Jamie chose advertising. His swift, creative, agile brain, his hunger to learn at least *something* about almost everything he happened upon in his daily life, his eager, still boyish fascination with other people's lives and businesses – what they did, what they liked, what made them tick – made him an ideal candidate for the industry. He had told Olivia once that though his education had been a fine one, he believed his real schooling had come via television; he claimed he had been far more stimulated over the years by what he had watched on that small, much-maligned box of tricks – from news and documentaries through feature films right down to cartoons and even children's programming – than by most of his teachers or tutors.

'I can watch *Dallas*,' he told Olivia, 'and I know I'm watching grade-A junk, but I'll catch a snippet of conversation between J.R. and another oil baron, and in a second I'll be reaching for a reference book or searching for a database on my computer – you can really get quite an education watching soaps.'

Jamie Arias could be told one afternoon about a new merchandising campaign up for grabs, and by next morning he was likely to know more than anyone in any other agency about the new product, how it had been created and why and for whom, and then his real talent, his natural gift for writing hard, sharp, incisive, witty and, above all, unforgettable copy, would come to the fore. Since leaving Harvard in 1980, he had worked for eighteen months at Ogilvy & Mather as a copywriter – a period he had loved with a passion; for Leo Burnett first as an account supervisor, then as an account executive – two of the most frustrating years of his life; and then, given an opportunity by a man named Norman J. Kane for which he would be forever grateful, as a creative director for the small, high-flying Kane Agency. Kane, a middle-aged, rough, gruff, Brooklyn-born New Yorker, had started calling Jamie his pet whiz even before he'd won the agency its first Clio, and when Jamie showed no signs of offence at being referred to that way, Kane told people gleefully that was because Arias was a true gentleman. And though he'd been born and raised an American and denied being descended from the Spanish aristocracy, Kane knew that class was what gave him his edge.

'I'm forever telling him it isn't true,' Jamie told Annie one day on the phone, 'but he doesn't want to know, so I've stopped arguing.'

'Maybe you are an aristocrat compared with him,' Annie suggested.

'As far as I'm concerned,' Jamie said, 'they don't come any more aristocratic than Kane.'

One of the things that Norman J. Kane loved so much about Jamie Arias was his seemingly limitless capacity and desire for learning. Kane was tickled to death when his beloved agency won its Clio for Jamie's innovative dog food campaign, but what pleased him infinitely more was the fact that the pet food manufacturers reported that their sales curve was moving steadily upward. Jamie understood that Clios and Andy Awards were great ego trips but did not necessarily equate with long-term success for the client, the creative team involved in the campaign, or the agency. Jamie accepted that sheer hard work on the basics, getting the bedrock of a proposed campaign as solid and immaculately researched as humanly possible, looking way beyond the high of a big award – flattering as it certainly was – was just as fundamental to success as the near-orgasmic joy of hitting the occasional, inspirational big idea.

It was while he was working for Kane at the end of 1984 that Jamie first met Caroline Beaumont at a party thrown by his boss, who wanted to get a closer look at Beaumont with a view to asking her to join the agency. It was, on Jamie's part, adoration at first sight. Carrie Beaumont was everything he was not: she was tough, intensely ambitious and too fiercely focused to even know what being free-spirited was. But she was also the loveliest woman Jamie had ever met, and from the first moment on he pretty much threw himself at her feet, blown away by the sparkle of brilliance in her cool blue eyes, by her smooth, pale skin and natural spun-gold hair and by the low, crisp snap of her Bostonian voice.

The luck of it [Jamie wrote to Olivia] *is that Carrie seems to have fallen in love with me too.*

I don't see anything lucky about it [Olivia wrote back to Jamie] *since falling in love with you can't be exactly hard to do, given that you're probably one of the most eligible bachelors living in Manhattan.*

Not relevant [Jamie wrote back, joyfully] *since if anyone's the catch in this relationship, it's Carrie. The Beaumonts have just as much money as the Ariases, and*

Carrie's a lot shrewder than I am, more sophisticated and practical than I am – definitely a lot more desirable than I am – and a real whiz in advertising.

Carrie, who was also five years older than Jamie, turned down Norman Kane's offer flat and, instead, snatched her brand-new fiancé straight out of Kane's arms. She had plans, and she'd been coasting along in New York for a while now, gathering experience and contacts and biding her time until she could have exactly what she wanted. What she wanted was her own small but perfectly formed agency, based in her home town, Boston.

'I know you'd probably rather stay in New York, darling James,' she told him, pre-empting any arguments, 'but your family does live in New England, after all, so you must understand why Boston really is the only city I feel truly, entirely comfortable living in.' She took a short, efficient, aerobics-trained breath and swept on. 'And I know I'm a bit of a spoiled bitch in that I do tend to go after what I want, and I apologize for that, James, I honestly do, but I know what I want now, *really* want, for the first time in my life.' The wide blue eyes passed lovingly, lingeringly over his still shell-shocked but delighted face. 'I want you for my partner. In business, in marriage, in life.'

She got no arguments from Jamie.

'I think she really does love him,' Annie told Olivia during a telephone call in the early spring of 1985.

'Well, why wouldn't she?' Olivia said acidly. 'As I told Jamie, he's handsome, he's clever – he is richer than she is, whatever he might prefer to believe – and I'm beginning to think he's hers to command.'

'Why don't you like her?' Annie asked her, then instantly

corrected herself. 'Why do we both dislike her when we haven't even met her?'

'I talked to her once,' Olivia said. 'When they were both at Jamie's place and I asked him to put her on so I could say hi.'

'And?'

'And she was cool. She was polite enough, and she said the right kind of things about looking forward to meeting me, and how much James – you know she calls him James, for Christ's sake—'

'That's not so bad, surely?' Annie said, mildly.

'No, it's not *so* bad, but it isn't Jamie, is it? Anyway, she said all the usual stuff about how much James had told her about us, and what wonderful friends we sounded.'

'But you didn't think she meant it?'

'I *knew* she didn't mean a word of it.'

'Still,' Annie said carefully, 'maybe we ought to suspend final judgement until after we've actually met Carrie – it might be fairer.'

'I dare say it would be,' Olivia said.

Annie smiled into the telephone receiver. 'But you just don't like her.'

'She was cool, Annie. Too cool. Jamie Arias is not a cool person.'

'No,' Annie agreed. 'He isn't.'

Olivia and Annie flew together from London to Boston in the first week of June, five days before the wedding. Jamie came to Logan Airport to meet them. He looked fit, relaxed and undeniably happy.

'I have to admit,' Olivia said without delay, 'I don't think I've ever seen you looking better.'

'You, too,' he said, hugging her, then embracing Annie on

his other side. 'And you look just wonderful. Motherhood certainly agrees with you.'

'Think so?' Annie grimaced. 'I think it makes me fat and tired.'

'Well, if it does, it doesn't show.' He picked up both their travel bags and began walking them towards the exit.

Olivia looked around. 'So where is she?'

'Carrie couldn't make it,' Jamie said. 'She sends her apologies, but with less than a week to go she just has so much to do.'

'Of course she has,' Annie agreed. 'I didn't really expect her to come.'

'When are we meeting her?' Olivia wanted to know.

'This evening,' Jamie said. 'If you're up to it, not too jet-lagged.'

'We'll be up to it,' Olivia said definitely. 'Or I will, anyway.'

'I wouldn't miss it,' Annie said.

'Where are we eating?' Olivia asked.

'It'll just be drinks, I'm afraid, at the Ritz Carlton.' Jamie looked apologetic. 'Carrie and I have to go to a dinner with a potential client tonight.'

'Sure you can manage drinks?' Olivia didn't bother concealing her irony.

'Come on, Livvy,' Annie said. 'I remember how impossible it was managing my time when it got close to our wedding.'

'I'm really sorry,' Jamie told them both. 'And so's Carrie.'

'I'm sure she is,' Olivia said.

'She can't wait to meet you.'

*   *   *

If they'd disliked her unfairly before they'd met Carrie, they positively loathed her when they did come face-to-face. She was beautiful, she was charming, she was welcoming and, as she had on the telephone, she said all the right things, but Olivia felt Carrie's own distaste for her and for Annie lapping over her like sour waves.

'She's jealous of us,' Olivia said to Annie later at Durgin-Park as they waited hungrily for their broiled lobsters.

'Don't be silly.'

'It may be silly but I'll bet the rent I'm right.'

'You don't mean jealous because we're women.' Annie grinned. 'She certainly couldn't be jealous of me.'

'Why not?' Olivia said. 'You look fantastic.'

'But I'm married with three children.'

'And still beautiful, and Jamie loves you.' Olivia paused. 'Seriously, Annie, Carrie's definitely pissed that we're here. She's certainly jealous of our closeness to Jamie.'

Annie drank some Perrier. 'Maybe,' she said thoughtfully, 'I would be too if I were her.'

'I doubt it.'

'No, honestly,' Annie insisted. 'I do remember that before Edward and I got married, he had a couple of good women friends. They used to lunch together, had the odd dinner, but that began to peter out when we got engaged, and after the wedding it stopped completely.'

'Because you wanted it to stop?'

Annie shook her head. 'No, I never said a word. But I do think I'd have minded if it had gone on.'

'Even if they were just friends?' Olivia looked surprised.

'I'm afraid so, yes.' Annie grinned ruefully. 'I guess it's not the way we're meant to be these days – I guess I should know better – but that is how I felt.' She paused. 'So if Carrie is jealous, I think I can understand her a little, especially in your case.'

'Because I'm single.'

'Single and beautiful and smart, and yet the absolute antithesis of her. And sharing more past history with Jamie than she ever will.'

'I guess,' Olivia said.

'So maybe we should go easy on her.'

'Play things her way, you mean?'

'Maybe.'

'Playing things Carrie's way,' Olivia said, 'would probably mean us going home. You want to go home, Annie?'

'No.'

'Nor do I.' Olivia spotted their lobsters heading their way, and raised her glass of Chardonnay. 'Here's to our darling Jamie,' she said, warmly. 'May Carrie make him as happy as he deserves to be.'

The marriage had been okay to begin with – better than okay, because they were in love and sex was good – sensational, sometimes, if Carrie was in the mood to let herself go. And they were both thriving on building a new home – the charming townhouse in Beacon Hill that Carrie had found while Jamie was still in New York, and a new business – Beaumont-Arias Advertising on Newbury Street – together. And they still, most important of all, respected each other. But that was the element that went first, and after that it was the start of a long downhill slide to hell on wheels.

The trouble was, whereas Jamie had recognized Carrie's greatest character flaw long before they had married (he knew that she was a little compulsive about being in control of herself, of business, of the people she surrounded herself with, and especially of a prospective husband), and had realized that he loved her enough to put up with it, Carrie, who had zeroed in on Jamie's faults just as swiftly, had decided, instead, to eradicate them. Jamie's faults, as Carrie saw them, began as dear little blemishes that she, with her accustomed efficiency, would soon wipe away. But the gentleness that she had assumed would make him a most biddable husband, was of a genuinely moral kind more deeply rooted than she had at first suspected. Jamie was a truly tender-hearted man, yet he was not a docile one. Though modest, he was neither self-effacing nor unaware of his assets or his talents. He was far from egocentric, but he did like himself, was happy in himself, and so once he recognized Carrie's intention of changing him, the same strength of will that had allowed Jamie to draw away from the Arias family's might begin to manifest itself in this new situation as a mild-mannered, light-hearted obstinacy.

Carrie liked her way in most things.

'James, darling, you can't wear that tie tonight,' she said when they were getting ready for dinner with her family at the beginning of the second year of their marriage.

'What's wrong with it?' He glanced at the mirror over the fireplace in their bedroom. It was a perfectly nice tie, pure Italian navy silk with neatly designed flecks of vivid pink enlivening it. 'I bought it this afternoon.'

'Did you?' Carrie peered carefully at her face and gave it a final fine-touched brushing of translucent powder. She was, she realized, a borderline obsessive about her own physical perfection. There was no question that natural born beauty was a trial, almost as much of a curse as it was a blessing. After all, she reasoned, a plain woman had lower expectations of herself and aroused far fewer in others; a beautiful woman had to be constantly on the alert for imperfections. Which was why Carrie, however busy her schedule – and she was a workaholic – always made time, and bullied others into making time for her, for her facials and workouts and massages and other treatments. She still remembered the instant when Jamie had first seen and fallen in love with her, and she was under no illusions that he, or any of the other men who'd ever been in love with her – and there'd been a few – would have felt even remotely the same way had she been homely. Jamie was, of course, hers now, and she knew that he really didn't mind, scarcely even noticed, if her hair was less gleaming than usual or if she had even the slightest *trace* – heaven forbid – of a zit; but Carrie's standards regarding her appearance were as rigorous as they were about most things in her private or professional life.

'Where did you get it?' She returned to the subject of Jamie's tie, touching Chanel No. 5 to her wrists and behind her ears. Carrie had strict rules about perfume. She had no objection to wearing more recent creations like Chanel No. 19 or perhaps the new Givenchy perfume, or even, at a pinch and at the *right* kind of gathering, Giorgio, but when they were seeing her parents or other bona-fide Bostonians, only the true classics like No. 5 or Houbigant would do.

'A little place down the street.' He was deliberately obtuse.

'Which place?' Carrie stood up. 'If you tell me, I can change it for you.'

'Why would you want to do that?'

'Because it's awful.' She smiled at him fondly. 'You know your taste isn't always quite what it might be.'

Jamie looked back in the mirror again. 'I like it.'

Carrie sighed. 'Oh, well, if you like it that much—'

He knew she'd left the last sentence up in the air in the hope that he would cave in and tell her that she was probably right, and that anyway, if she didn't like it there wasn't much point in wearing it. He knew that six months ago he most likely would have said exactly that, and if it came to it now, he didn't actually give a damn about the tie itself – he liked it well enough, but it was just a tie, after all – but there were principles at stake here, so he said nothing more and kept the tie on.

Carrie liked having things her own way at Beaumont-Arias as well as at home or when they were travelling together. Usually light-heartedly, Jamie tried to point out to her that he had never regarded marriage as an end, for either of them, to personal choice; to make her see that the differences in their tastes and in their characters were a bonus, that different attitudes were positive and healthy, would keep them both on their toes and stop their relationship from becoming dull. But as time went on, Carrie's desire to control all the decision-making in their partnership grew more intense; she wanted to approve everything Jamie wore, drove and did, inside and outside the house, and when Jamie was less than pliable, she stamped her beautifully shod feet and created hell.

Not in public, of course. Carrie Beaumont Arias's public face was of the contented, serene woman who had been fortunate enough to find a way to keep her brilliant career and discover the most wonderful husband and partner in the universe. To friends and acquaintances and colleagues, she and Jamie were an idyllic blend, a marriage created in heaven and staying there. But when they were alone, the face became increasingly ugly, for Carrie was more than spoiled, more than obsessive about perfection, more even than simply manipulative – Carrie was a full-blown control freak. And once she began to see clearly, after about a year of marriage, that Jamie was still not hers to control, Carrie began to do what she had always done with people who crossed her and with whom she could not immediately or easily dispense. She put him down.

'You know you made yourself look absurd this afternoon, don't you?' she told him in the spring of 1986.

They had just sat down in their cream and chintz, soothingly decorated and furnished drawing room with a couple of dry martinis. Jamie had removed his jacket, loosened his tie and unfastened the top button of his shirt, and was just contemplating kicking off his shoes.

'Which particular part of this afternoon?' he asked, staying amiable.

'At the presentation, obviously.'

'Which particular part of the presentation?'

'Every part that followed the opening niceties,' Carrie said.

'Ah.' Jamie sipped his martini. 'So that bit went okay.'

Carrie set her own glass on the side table next to her armchair. 'You just refuse to learn, don't you, James? You really don't want to know.'

'Know what, Carrie?'

Jamie was tired, he knew that much. He'd slept fitfully the previous night, and then the pitch to Ralston's for their new light beer account had begun badly because big Fred Ralston had started the proceedings by declaring that he'd never really liked their mainstream Ralston Beer campaign in any of its subtly evolving forms, and if their sales curves were still healthy it had everything to do with their beer and fuck-all to do with Beaumont-Arias's work. Jamie and Carrie had taken what Ralston had thrown at them in their stride, had done what Jamie had regarded as a fine job of smoothing big Fred's ruffled feathers so that Maggie

Carmichael and David Baum, their top creative team, had been able to begin their new pitch from a position of reasonable strength. The Ralston jury was out, but Jamie was cautiously optimistic. He was also in no mood for one of Carrie's viper sessions.

'I'm very tired,' he said.

'And you think I'm not?'

'No, I'm sure you are.'

Carrie returned to the subject of the Ralston presentation.

'I said that you made yourself look absurd this afternoon because of the idiotic way you built up Baum and Carmichael to Fred Ralston.'

'What would you have had me do?' Jamie took a bigger swallow of his drink.

'Obviously,' Carrie said, 'you should have sacrificed them on the spot.' She looked at his startled expression. 'For goodness' sake, James, Ralston as good as demanded their heads – he said he had no confidence in them—'

'In our campaigns,' Jamie corrected her. 'Not in Maggie and David. In any case, you knew he was only bitching because he likes throwing people off-balance.'

'What Ralston wanted,' Carrie went on crisply, ignoring him, 'was for the two of us to take over and give his ego a good stroking. He knows perfectly well that we're still the real number one creative team at Beaumont-Arias.'

'I didn't think that was what he wanted at all,' Jamie argued, going on eating. 'And given the terrific job Maggie and David did today—'

'Baum and Carmichael did an okay job today,' Carrie insisted, 'and nothing more. I'm not too sure about you right now – not with your attitude – but I know that I could have taken those same ideas and left Fred Ralston thinking he'd been dealing with geniuses instead of mere adequates.'

'You know I won't play that kind of game, Carrie,' Jamie said. 'It's immoral and ruthless and rather short-sighted.'

'Are you accusing me of immorality, James?' Carrie's eyes flashed a sudden cold lightning blue. 'Because I'm more capable than you of recognizing what a client needs, or of admitting when a team is on the wane?'

'Carmichael and Baum aren't on the wane, Carrie. You've just decided you don't like Maggie any more, though I'm not quite sure why.'

'You're the last person to cast that particular stone, since you know very well that you insist on running your whole life – our business included – by surrounding yourself with only the people *you* like.'

'Trust,' Jamie said, calmly. 'Not necessarily like.' He met her eyes.

'Meaning what precisely? That you don't like me?'

'Not very much. Not at times like this.'

'I'm not sure if I care whether you like me or not,' Carrie said softly. 'What I find much more disappointing is the fact that I find myself not respecting you any more.' She paused. 'And what, frankly, worries me even more than that is that I've noticed I'm not alone in that.'

'Ah, Carrie,' Jamie said.

'What does that mean?'

'It means, what are you trying to do? Pick another fight?'

'I can't see the point in fighting, unless it's for the pleasure of making up, and I have no desire for that tonight.'

'So it's just malice,' he said, hating the thought.

'If you say so. I'd prefer to call it honesty. A few home truths.' Carrie paused. 'I'm sorry if they hurt you.'

'They don't, on the whole,' Jamie said, quietly. 'I don't, on the whole, believe they have much to do with truth.'

'That's a pity,' Carrie said. 'But then again, not accepting what others think of you is part of what's wrong with you.'

He tried, for a long time, to laugh it off. He was a modest man but he still knew his own worth, and so he tried to make Carrie see that he thought her accusations ridiculous, and then, as she became more aggressive, to let her know that it did both upset and anger him. But Carrie was becoming masterly at the arts of spite, mockery, insinuation and sneering. She could be subtle when she wished, tiny pinpricks of hurtful banter, or she could be barbaric, locating a nerve and drilling it over and over again till her victim – whether a new secretary or a salaries clerk or a copywriter like Maggie Carmichael – was about ready to scream. But with Jamie, her greatest challenge was in finding a suitable nerve. When Carrie wanted to get at her husband, she criticized everything about him: his lovemaking, his decisions, the way he looked, his softness, his creativity. But nothing rang true, because Jamie just went on being Jamie, working successfully, being popular, being so goddamned fine at whatever he liked doing – and that was the worst of it from Carrie's point of view. Her husband *did* like what he did, and he liked himself, had no deep-seated dark shames or angsts. The only two abiding guilts he'd ever suffered from were the sense that he'd let down his late father first by choosing advertising over shipping and then, even though Jamie had long since lapsed, by marrying a non-Catholic.

It was love that provided Carrie with her greatest weapon. Jamie did still love her. In spite of her. He had thought, when her attempts to denigrate him had first begun, that he could see through her hardness to a softer interior, had fancied that if he could only find a way to penetrate the steel, he might uncover a nicer, gentler person. But then he had realized that he was playing Carrie's own game – wanting to change her – and so he had forced himself to stop thinking that way. If he loved her, Jamie rationalized, he had to love her as she was, even if it was tough to do.

It became tougher. In the late spring of 1987 – shortly after Jamie had answered Olivia's call and flown to Geneva to help Annie with her addiction nightmare – Carrie fell pregnant and insisted on a termination. Displaying real vulnerability for the first time in a long while, she begged Jamie to understand, told him it was simply too soon for her to think of having a baby, that continuing to build up their business was just too important to her. And in spite of a startlingly deep stab of Catholic guilt, Jamie did almost understand that, though he also suspected that her decision had been made because pregnancy would make her fat and imperfect and out of control; but he thought he could understand that too, and it was, after all, her body, and mostly therefore her decision to make, and they were both still young and there was plenty of time. Six months later the same thing happened, with the same result, but this time Carrie laid all the blame for the unwanted pregnancy on Jamie.

'You're a careless, callous, selfish fool,' she ranted at him in the clinic, and then she lay back in the high white hospital bed and began to weep bitterly, and Jamie's heart went out to her because whatever she said, he thought that in spite of her reasons for aborting the pregnancy she was still mourning the loss of her child.

*　　*　　*

But then, less than two months later, Carrie went, without consulting him, without ever raising the subject, to be sterilized. The first Jamie knew about it was when she called him from the clinic after waking up from the anaesthetic.

He waited for two hours, trying to clear his head, to calm himself, before he went to see her.

'How could you do this?' He asked the question quietly, almost gently, though he knew as he spoke that finally, at that moment at least, he hated her. 'Tell me, please, if you can.'

Carrie was pale but composed. 'Oh, I can,' she said.

He waited. 'Go on.'

'Are you sure you can take the truth?'

'Yes,' Jamie said. 'I can take it.'

'All right.' Her eyes were on his face. 'The truth is that I found I couldn't contemplate having your child, James.' She paused. 'That if you had been less of a disappointment to me – as my husband and as my partner – I might have gotten over my own fears and gone through with it.'

He got up from his chair and walked out of the room and went down in the elevator and out into the street, and he took a cab and went home to Beacon Hill and packed a suitcase and went to the Meridien Hotel on Franklin Street, the site of the old Federal Reserve Building.

He stayed for two nights, going into the office as usual, knowing that even Carrie was likely to be out of action for at least a day or two. He was, for the very first time in his life, desperately lonely. He wanted, very badly, to talk to Olivia, but each time he reached for the telephone something – pride, he thought, with a kick of shame – stayed his hand.

Carrie called him early on the second morning and asked him to come home.

'I don't think so,' Jamie said.

'Please,' she said, her voice soft and unfamiliar, 'come back.'

'I can't.'

'I need you to.'

'Why?'

'I need my husband,' she said, simply.

Jamie looked around the empty, lonely hotel room. 'I wanted babies,' he told her. 'I wanted children.'

'I know,' she said, and there was real sorrow in her voice. 'Me too.'

'Then why?' Jamie shook his head. 'For God's sake, Carrie, why did you do this? Just to spite me? To punish me? *Why?* I need to understand this.'

'No, you don't,' Carrie said.

'Yes, I do.' He paused. 'If there's ever to be anything between us again, I do need to understand why you did this thing.'

Carrie sighed. 'Of course,' she said. 'You're always the same. The ever-understanding, long-suffering Jamie.'

He frowned. 'You never call me that.'

'No.'

'So why now? And why make it sound like a term of abuse?'

'Because I married a man named James Arias, not a boy called Jamie,' Carrie replied. 'Olivia's and Annie's friend.'

She came to the Meridien that night and asked if he would have dinner with her. They stayed inside the hotel, went to Julien – a grand vaulted affair of a French restaurant that had, in the days of the Federal Reserve Building, been the board room – and sat in wing-back chairs, both pecking disinterestedly at their food to the chagrin of the maître d'hôtel and waiters.

Jamie asked Carrie how she felt, and she said she felt fine, and he had to admit that she had seldom looked more beautiful, or softer, or more vulnerable. All through the meal she was quiet and distant, yet it was not, he felt, a deliberate, calculated remoteness, but a distance created by depression and, he thought, fear. Jamie could not remember ever having seen Carrie really afraid before.

She asked, near the end, for a very fine Armagnac.

'I'm going to do something now,' she said when the waiter had brought it to her, 'that I've never done before in my whole life.' She paused. 'I'm going to beg.'

'Don't,' Jamie said, appalled.

'I have no choice,' Carrie said. 'So I'm begging you, James, to come back to me.'

'Why? What for?'

'Because I need you. I'm alone, and I feel as if I've lost you, and I suppose I deserve to lose you. And I know what an eighteen-carat bitch I've been, will probably go on being —'

Jamie almost smiled then, admiring her, in spite of everything, for her honesty.

' – but I do need you, James. I find – and it does surprise me a little, I have to say it does – but I find that I really do need you.'

Jamie thought about his father again then. Carlos had never questioned the faith handed down to him by his own father; he would have found the terminations hard enough to accept, and the sterilization almost impossible. And yet, at the end of it all, Jamie knew that Carlos would still have held to his marriage vows, would never have contemplated divorce.

Jamie was not like his father, nor was Peter. Cousin Michael, who strongly resembled his own late father, Juan Luis Arias, was the one who had taken on the mantle as head of the family and Arias Shipping, and who, though sadly childless, had remained a good, staunch, unquestioning Catholic. If Jamie did stay with Carrie, he would not lie to himself and pretend it was because of his faith; but it might perhaps, in part, be because of the guilt he had always felt about having failed Carlos in the past. He did not want to fail him in this, too.

He looked into the eyes that had so often lately looked at him with such disdain, such diamond-coldness, but that seemed suddenly to reflect a naked, raw insecurity torn from its hiding place deep inside her. And he sighed, and he knew that he would go back to her because, Carlos aside and despite all she had done to hurt him, he still saw in her now what he had once loved.

And because he thought that, despite her hardness and callousness and the bravado that would, almost certainly, return within days, perhaps even hours, Carrie was probably, deep down, like most people, genuinely afraid of some things: of being left alone against her will, of losing her perfect beauty, of growing old – or maybe even, though Jamie doubted that, of losing him.

And he felt pity for her.

13

In March of 1988, Olivia, on a visit to Boston before relocating from Geneva to Strasbourg (her restless, nomadic nature had drawn her to Alsace and the attractive old city, which buzzed these days with international activity, making it a perfect base, at least for a while, for the Segal Translation Agency), was disturbed by the changes in Jamie. He seemed tired and, she thought, not exactly depressed, but his *joie de vivre* had vanished along with the natural, easy-going contentment that had always been such an essential part of him.

It was not difficult to see the cause of the changes. A few of Carrie's digs at Jamie were public these days, though with other people around, her fault-finding took on a more indulgent, patronizing face. But in Olivia's company – a woman Carrie had never liked, who she knew had never liked her, and for whom, in a crisis, Jamie was maddeningly likely to drop anything at a moment's notice – Carrie hardly bothered to put on an act at all. After all, she reasoned, the more unpleasantly she behaved towards Jamie in his old pal's company, the more uncomfortable she was likely to feel. And so far as Carrie was concerned, the sooner Olivia Segal left Boston, the better.

'Why are you putting up with this?' Olivia demanded one day over lunch in the sushi bar at Agatha on Berkeley Street. 'It's not as if you're blind to it – you've told me you hate the way she behaves. Why don't you leave her, for Christ's sake?'

Jamie drank some saki and smiled wryly. 'You make it sound so simple, but then I guess you always do.'

'It seems pretty simple to me.' She paused. 'It's not some deep-seated Catholic guilt, is it?'

'No,' he said, and smiled again. 'Not entirely, at least.'

'Carrie doesn't love you, Jamie,' Olivia said, bluntly. 'If she did, she couldn't treat you the way she does. She's using you – your talent, your good nature, your wealth. Let's face it, you're still a beautifully presentable and useful husband.'

'Carrie's just as talented as I am – perhaps more,' Jamie answered quietly, 'and she doesn't need my money.'

'Because she has enough of her own?' Olivia was scathing. 'Everyone knows that two fortunes are better than one.' She had listened to Carrie's sniping and observed her attempts to undermine Jamie for six days now, and she'd started out with a degree of diplomacy, just a smidgeon of delicacy, but now she was growing desperate to get through to him. 'She's hurting you, Jamie. She's *damaging* you – can't you see that? Of course you can, you're not a fool, or you never used to be.'

'I'm not a fool,' Jamie said.

'So why not leave her?' Olivia looked into his eyes, saw how wounded he was, and wanted to weep for him, wanted to wring Carrie's slender neck. 'Don't you know how much better you are than her?' she asked more gently. 'How much better you deserve than this?'

'Maybe,' Jamie said.

Their sushi was laid out before them, and more hot saki. It all looked wonderful but neither of them moved to touch it.

'I'm not ready to leave Carrie,' Jamie said a moment or two later. 'I know it seems strange to you, I know that if you were in my place you might walk out—'

'If I were in a marriage where my partner put me down every time he opened his mouth, you bet I'd walk out.'

'It isn't always like that.'

'You mean she behaves like a halfway decent human being occasionally?' Olivia couldn't keep her sarcasm down. 'I'm impressed. Let's give her the Humanitarian of the Year award.'

'Shut up, Olivia.'

Olivia blinked at the harshness of his tone.

'If I tell you that Carrie doesn't always act the way she has this past week, then it's up to you whether or not you believe me.'

'Of course I believe you.'

'Then please' – Jamie smiled at her – 'try and stop interrupting me every time I try to tell you how it is for me.' He paused. 'For me, not you, okay?'

Olivia nodded. 'Okay. Of course.'

'As I said, it may seem strange to you, but I have this thing about marriage vows – not just because I was born a Catholic. But my parents did feel the same way.'

'Your parents *were* good Catholics, and they had a good marriage.'

'Olivia, shut up,' Jamie said pleasantly.

'I'm sorry.'

'You're right, of course, up to a point. My parents were both religious, and they did have a good marriage in the long run, but my father once told me that it was pretty rocky for a while. They could have separated without divorcing, but my father said it never occurred to either of them to do that.'

Olivia waited a second. 'I expect they still loved each other.'

'And maybe Carrie and I don't any more,' Jamie said softly. 'I don't deny that. As you said, I'm not a fool. But I do still care for her, about her, and I do happen to think, hard as it may be for you to believe it, that she still needs me.'

Olivia looked at him for a long moment.

'As a matter of fact,' she said, very gently, 'it isn't so hard for me to believe that Carrie needs you.' She waited another instant. 'But I do find myself hoping – and I'm sorry if this hurts you – you know the last thing in the world I want to do is hurt you, Jamie—'

'I know.'

'But I do find myself hoping that the time will come when you realize – without too much pain, and without any guilt – that you don't need her.'

Everything changed the following autumn. Until now, despite their differences, both husband and wife had remained faithful: Jamie because he had no wish to stray; Carrie partly because infidelity, if discovered, would have tarnished her image, and partly because Jamie, whatever his failings, had seemed a safe haven of sorts in this new era of AIDS and herpes and God knew what other inhibiting horrors.

Suddenly, though, Carrie had found someone else.

Someone even more suitable than James Arias. Wealthier, older, worldlier, tougher – arguably even more attractive. Certainly more ruthless, more like herself. And the supreme irony was that Jamie had brought them together, had invited the other man into their home, had believed that, of all men in the world, this had been one of the two he could trust with his life, certainly with his wife. Except that Jamie had forgotten Carrie's powers of seduction and persuasion, those same powers she had used to ensnare him just a few years before. And now Peter Arias – Jamie's older brother, recently separated from Daisy, his wife, somewhat ashamed of himself but just as crazily in love with Carrie as Jamie had been in those early, heady days of 1984 – was set to replace him.

Michael Arias, as head of the family, came to Boston to see Jamie. He was forty-five years old and an impressive man to be around, distinguished and handsome, less gentle perhaps than his uncle had been, but proving himself a clever, measured and effective leader.

'Is she here?' Michael asked when he arrived at the house one Sunday morning in late October.

'No.'

Jamie walked ahead of his cousin into the library. It had always been one of his preferred rooms, but now he favoured it especially because Carrie had spent less time in there than any other part of the house, and so now it reminded him of her less, did not have the faint whiff of her scent that much of their home seemed to be pervaded by.

'Where is she?' Michael asked, sitting in one of the leather armchairs.

Jamie shrugged. 'You tell me.' With Peter based with Michael at Arias Shipping's head office in New York and

Carrie's dedication to Beaumont-Arias undiluted despite the break-up of her marriage, the lovers were tending to spend their weeks apart, sharing alternate weekends in Boston or Manhattan. 'I only know that she's not here. I imagine she's with my brother.'

Jamie did altogether more imagining than was good for him. Images kept flashing through his mind, of his wife and his brother, naked between silk sheets – the kind Carrie liked, the only kind she would have in their house. Peter had sworn to Jamie that they had never made love in the Beacon Hill house. 'What do you take me for, for Christ's sake?' he had asked indignantly, and Jamie had not cared to answer the question truthfully. He took Peter for exactly what he was. A traitor. A stranger whom Jamie would have liked to beat to a pulp. He had always been a gentle man. He did not feel gentle any more.

'I've spoken to Peter, of course,' Michael said.

'Of course.'

'I found it hard,' Michael went on, 'to express my feelings.'

Jamie looked into his cousin's face, searching, he realized, for a point of contact, of familiarity, of sure, solid ground. 'How do you feel?'

Michael's dark eyes, a rich velvety colour like Jamie's own, seemed almost black. 'Deeply angry,' he answered quietly. 'Shocked.' He paused. 'More disappointed, I think, than I can ever remember feeling.'

Jamie experienced a semblance of comfort, of reassurance. 'Thank you,' he said.

'What for?' Michael asked, wryly. 'I didn't stop it from happening.'

'Did you know about it?'

'No, of course not. But perhaps I should have.'

Jamie thought back, suddenly, to his childhood, simpler times spent in the magnificent Arias home on the cliffs at Newport. He remembered a time when he was still just a little boy of around four, a day in summer, not long after Juan Luis Arias, Michael's father, had died, when the whole family had been there in the gardens. Carlos sitting in a white cane chair beside Barbara Arias, Jamie's and Peter's American mother. Jamie recalled her beautiful, pale face and her dark hair, still lustrous then, before the cancer had turned it dull and stolen her away just a few years later, from her sons, from her husband. Jamie remembered Peter, at about ten, teaching him how to kick a ball around, and he remembered being hit by the big ball, full in the stomach, and going down and crying with the shock of it. And he remembered Michael, his big, grown-up cousin – eighteen or nineteen back then, Jamie guessed – picking him up and checking him over and soothing him until the tears had gone.

'Pedro, for God's sake,' he remembered Michael scolding Peter, 'you must be more careful.' At home in those days, Carlos had called them all by their Spanish names – Miguel, Pedro and Jaime – and his sons and nephew, who, like most young people, preferred conformity outside in the real world, were happy enough at home with the sense of individuality – even, the two older boys felt, of exclusiveness – that those private identities seemed to give them.

'Jamie' – Michael's voice broke into his thoughts – 'are you all right?'

Jamie smiled. 'I'm fine. I was just remembering.'

'Carrie?'

'No.' Jamie shook his head. 'Us. As a family.' He looked at his cousin. 'You were always protective of me.'

'You were very young,' Michael said, shrugging it off.

'You were always like a brother to me,' Jamie told him, and smiled again at another memory. 'You know, Olivia once said that when the three of us were all together, we reminded her of the Mafia.'

Michael raised an eyebrow. 'Did she?'

'Olivia's always had a vivid imagination.'

'Has she? I don't really know her all that well.'

'I guess not,' Jamie said. 'Not well enough.' He paused. 'She's my closest friend.'

'Closer than Annie?'

'Sometimes, maybe.' Jamie thought about them. 'Annie's more like my little sister.'

'And Olivia?' Michael asked.

Again Jamie smiled. 'Olivia's different.'

Michael stayed for lunch, cooked by Jamie himself since their housekeeper had the weekend off. It was not the most relaxed of meals. So long as they were talking old memories, reliving the distant past, the conversation went easily and the atmosphere between the two cousins was warm, but whenever the present intruded, the contrasts between them became emphasized. Aside from blood and memories, they had little in common to discuss, especially now that any mention of Peter was a grinding of fresh salt in Jamie's wounds. Michael asked, over coffee, if Jamie wanted to fly back to Newport with him where he and Louise, his wife, had been staying the weekend, but Jamie declined, claiming that he had too much paperwork to get through before Beaumont-Arias reopened in the morning. It was only half true, and he felt that Michael probably knew that, but if he did, he showed no sign of being offended.

'I'll try tackling Peter again this week,' Michael promised before he left. 'Though I get the impression there won't be much I can do to cool things down.' He paused at the door. 'Would you take Carrie back, if she and Peter ended the affair?'

'No,' Jamie said, and found that he meant it. 'Never.'

'Good.' Michael reached out his right hand and laid it on Jamie's shoulder. 'You know I'm with you a hundred per cent on this, don't you, little cousin?'

Jamie nodded. 'I know. And I appreciate it. It does help.'

'You know, too,' Michael went on, a little uncomfortably, 'that that doesn't mean I can turn my back on Peter. Maybe I should be able to do that, to take the ultimate religious or moral high ground, but I find that I can't.' He scanned Jamie's face anxiously. 'I hope you understand.'

'I do.'

'It isn't easy for me,' Michael said. 'Seeing Peter every day at the office, knowing what he's done to you – what he's doing.' His eyes were very dark. 'I'm very angry with him. I try to imagine what your father would have said to him – or my own father, come to that.'

'I'm glad they don't have to know about it,' Jamie said.

'That's something, I guess,' Michael said. 'Not too much though, from where you're standing.'

'No,' Jamie agreed. 'Not too much at all.'

Once Carrie saw that Jamie was not going to ask her and Peter to end their affair, nor, under any circumstances, to beseech her to come back to him, she began, with considerable relish, to rub his nose in the dirt. His brother was the better man, she told Jamie, exhilarated by her newly heightened capacity to wound – Carrie the picador, piercing her husband with the lance of her magnificently ill-chosen infidelity, paving the way for the kill.

'I want a divorce,' she said right after the second Monday morning campaign meeting that November, just after the last account executive had left the boardroom. 'And I intend to have it on my terms.'

'I hardly think you're in a position to lay down conditions,' Jamie said.

'Oh, I disagree.'

'How can you possibly disagree?' Tiredly, Jamie began to stack his folders, getting ready to leave.

Carrie got up from her chair at the opposite end of the oval table and came to Jamie's end, pulling out the chair to his left and sitting down.

'Because morally,' she answered, slowly and carefully, smoothing down the skirt of her new pink Versace suit, confident for the moment in her appearance thanks to forty-eight hours of alternate sweat and pampering at her favourite spa, or 'fat farm', as Peter had teasingly referred to it (which had led to their first really big fight), 'at the end of the day, I doubt if anyone would blame me for going to another man.'

Jamie looked up. 'And how do you figure that?'

'Easily.' She paused. 'Once people knew what had driven me away from my husband, out of our marriage bed.'

'And what exactly did drive you, Carrie?' Jamie found that he felt as calm as he sounded, like a weary nurse calming a delusional patient. Any moment now, Carrie would presumably tell him how patronizing he sounded. He supposed, maybe, that he felt patronizing, amongst other things.

'Your own sick little affair drove me,' Carrie said.

'My affair?' Startled, he stopped sorting his papers.

She smiled at him. 'Not so little, perhaps, on reflection.'

'Just who am I supposed to have had an affair with?'

'With your two friends, of course.'

Jamie grew very still.

'Did you imagine I didn't know?' Carrie asked, looking directly at him, her blue eyes very large and clear.

For a long moment Jamie stared back at her. And then he laughed. He leaned back in his chair and threw back his head and laughed, deep and long. And then, when all the laughter had gone, he sat forward again and his eyes, fixed on her face, were almost black.

'You must be mad,' he said, quietly.

'Must I?' Carrie stood up, returned to her original seat at the far end of the table and picked up her own files. 'I think not, James,' she said. 'I think you would do well to understand that I'm not in the least bit mad. And that if you make any fuss about my divorce terms – if you offer even the slightest resistance to my demands – I will not only smear you with every last glob of mud I can find, but I will also drag both your beloved friends through the dirt with you.'

Jamie watched her turn her back, go to the door, open it and walk through it without glancing back at him, watched the door close behind her. Her words were repeating themselves inside his head, over and over again. In all his thirty years, he was not aware of having ever heard anything more patently absurd, more open to ridicule. More outrageous. Especially when it came to Annie. He could maybe *just* have comprehended a hint of jealousy of a gorgeous single woman like Olivia, though Christ knew there'd never been anything of that nature between them, not even in their school days when he'd thought Olivia the most attractive girl he'd ever known. But Annie – of all people, *Annie*. And Jamie knew that Carrie's accusation had nothing whatever to do with jealousy, it was entirely down to poison, nothing else. And he felt a rage growing within him, greater, more powerful even than the fury he had felt when he had learned about her infidelity with Peter.

'How dare she?' he muttered, unaware that he was speaking aloud. 'How *dare* she?' His fists were so tightly clenched on the arm rests of his chair that even his short, neatly clipped back fingernails cut into his palms. He stayed in the chair, allowed the rage to rise and rise, filling him, consuming him, conscious even in the midst of its heat that it was safest to do that, to let it take him over here, in this room, where there was no one to see him. No temptation to allow it to fire fully, to be directed at the man and woman whom he knew now that he hated, honestly, truly *hated*, with all his soul.

It passed. He had no awareness of how long he sat there, his Jamie Arias, Gieves & Hawke-suited outer shell containing and controlling that inner explosion of loathing.

'Okay,' he said, quietly, to himself. 'Get a grip.'

He closed his eyes, took a deep, composing breath, then opened them again. The white-hot fury had gone and only a dark, bottomless contempt remained. And a great sadness. Carrie had taken the best, perhaps the purest, thing in his life, his friendship with Olivia and Annie, and had tried to soil it, to pollute it with her own special brand of filth.

He would not let her. He could not let her. Even there, in the aftershock of his rage, still seated at his end of the boardroom table, Jamie was clear-headed about that one thing. No matter how he felt, no matter how close to murderous he might feel, no matter how intense his desire for revenge, Jamie knew that it was more important to protect Olivia and Annie. He doubted, when all was said and done, if Carrie would go through with her threats, because that kind of exposure might end up backfiring on her own image, and maybe – just maybe – Peter might have retained enough shreds of decency to make her draw the line somewhere. But Jamie could not be sure of either of those things, could not be certain that Carrie might not be so obsessed with malice that she would wilfully kill Annie's marriage and destroy Olivia's professional life.

He could not risk that. Olivia was probably tough enough to withstand anything that Carrie could throw at her, but Annie was still fragile, still needed to be protected, and Edward had already put up with so much and Jamie was not going to endanger that family's hard-earned happiness.

At least, he reflected wryly as he rose at last, calm enough to put together his folders and leave the boardroom, there were no children for Carrie to use as bargaining chips in their divorce. He sighed. Even if he did ultimately have to give in to most of her financial demands, at the end of the day it was really only money, and Jamie had the rare, privileged consolation of knowing that he would still have more than enough.

He saw Peter just once during the next three months, while their respective lawyers were battling it out. It was an accidental meeting in January 1989, capricious fate leading them both, at the same hour of the same day, into the electric train department of F. A. O. Schwarz in New York.

Jamie was buying some rolling stock to add to the collection he had begun last year for William Thomas, Annie's six-year-old son. He didn't notice Peter until he'd handed over his American Express card and was waiting for his parcels to be wrapped. His brother was standing near one of the big fully operational German electric sets, but he wasn't looking at the distinctive green train just gliding past him; he was looking across at Jamie and it was clear from his expression that he had been debating whether or not he might make his escape before being spotted.

Jamie nodded at him curtly, and Peter began to walk towards him. His face was taut, his handsome mouth a straight, compressed line.

'Hello, Jamie.'

'Peter.'

They had not seen each other since the last of several heated encounters in the period immediately after Carrie had first told Jamie about their affair. The passion and the rage had gone out of Jamie now, squeezed out by the relentless litigious process and the increasing tedium of seeing his adulterous wife every day at the office. Jamie would never have thought it possible to regard Carrie and her savage tongue as tedious, but he found that she had now ceased almost entirely to wound him. He fancied that he had grown a new, protective outer layer, an uncharacteristically thicker skin that carried him through research meetings, campaign strategy meetings, luncheons with clients, presentations and corporate dinners – all those occasions when Jamie accepted that for the sake of Beaumont-Arias and its employees he and Carrie had to perform together as smoothly and effectively as possible.

'Unlikely place to meet,' Peter said.

'Indeed,' Jamie said.

'I was looking for a birthday gift for Andy.'

Peter and his ex-wife, Daisy, had two young sons, Andrew and Paul, and Daisy Arias, James had heard on the ever-fruitful grapevine, was so disgusted with Peter's behaviour that she was talking about trying to cut back on his visitation rights to the boys.

'I've already organized his gift,' Jamie said, quietly.

'So the trains aren't for Andy?'

'No.'

'I only ask because that's what I was thinking of for him.'

'No,' Jamie said again. 'They're not for Andy.'

The sales assistant returned at that moment and handed back Jamie's American Express card. 'Is this zip code correct, sir?'

'It's a British post code,' Jamie said, glancing at the delivery address on the invoice. 'That's fine.'

'And can I just check the name again, sir?' The woman gave Jamie an apologetic smile. 'My pen was fresh out of ink when I wrote it down.' She bent over the counter. 'It looks like William—?'

'It's William Thomas,' Jamie told her.

'Thomas, that's it.' She smiled again. 'Thank you, sir.'

'You're welcome,' Jamie said.

'That must be your friend Annie's boy,' Peter said behind him.

Jamie looked at him. 'It is.'

'Nice for him,' Peter said, 'having such a fond' – he gave a small, amused-looking grin – 'uncle? Does he call you Uncle Jamie?'

'He does not,' Jamie said, and a little of the rage that he had thought all squeezed out or simply under control, came back, tightening his throat. He looked at his brother with distaste. 'Goodbye, Peter,' he said.

Peter smiled again, a knowing, ugly smile. 'Be seeing you.'

'As seldom as possible,' Jamie said.

14

What irked Jamie far more than the financial settlement was the fact that Carrie was insisting not only that he remained her business partner – thus ensuring that Beaumont-Arias held onto the clients won through Jamie's personal talents – but also that he became, in terms of major decisions, a silent and, thereby, impotent partner. It was not that Carrie was trying to ignore the scandal that her brother-swapping exercise might create. On the contrary, she was contriving, with considerable panache, to turn it into an enthralling bonus.

'Peter and I have suppressed our feelings for years, you know,' Carrie was telling people, oh-so-confidentially, oh-so-discreetly. 'It was simply a case of James and I having married too quickly – we found that out pretty early, I'm afraid to say – and we've all tried so very hard, but finally I guess we had to give in. And we're all on such good terms, it's all so civilized, and that must be obvious to everyone because otherwise how could we even *think* of staying in business together?'

*   *   *

Jamie moved out of the Beacon Hill house that March
into a duplex condominium on Rowes Wharf overlooking
the harbour, bought a trim white sailing boat called the
Joie de Vivre – Carrie hated boats – and tried to enjoy his
regained bachelor status. It was good to be an individual
again, wonderful to be free – at least at the start and end
of each working day – of his wife's savage tongue, yet he
was a million miles from being even close to happy. He felt
that he had failed in every way that counted. Before Carrie,
he'd been so confident, his only sense of failure that to his
late father, but here he was, not yet thirty-one, and he'd
screwed up his marriage, as good as lost his brother, all
but abandoned control of his business and put his two
dearest friends in jeopardy. Oh, sure, Olivia and Annie
would both say that it was all down to Carrie, none of
it his fault, but Jamie knew it all came down to two basic
flaws of his own. He was weak, and he was a damned fool.
He had provoked Carrie during the years of their marriage
by seeming to be strong enough to withstand her, strong
enough to keep loving her. Yet at the end of the day he
had capitulated, and now he was left with nothing that he
really valued – except for Olivia and Annie, and Lord knew
Carrie had done her best to taint even that.

Olivia and Annie came to visit him in May, Annie just for
a few days. She was in great shape, hair newly bobbed,
and full of pride and enthusiasm for a new project recently
embarked upon.

'I'm studying reflexology,' she told Jamie and Olivia. 'I
know some people turn up their noses and think it's all
trendy nonsense, but it was one of the alternative therapies
that really helped me with my stress levels after I first
kicked the tranquillizers – and they're doing so much

serious research into using it as a pain management technique.'

'I've done some reading about it,' Jamie said. 'It all seemed to make pretty good sense.'

'Anyway,' Annie went on, 'I'm doing a lot of the written work by correspondence, and I go to evening classes during the week when Edward's in London and Marie-Louise is home with the children.' She was flushed with excitement. 'I've been told that I have quite an aptitude for it, and a couple of our neighbours have said that they'll let me treat them when I qualify, and it would be so great to feel useful outside the house.'

'Did you get that?' Olivia asked Jamie. 'She says *when* she qualifies, not if, or maybe, or she probably won't be good enough and even if she is, the neighbours will back out at the last minute.'

'It's okay to mock.' Annie was laughing.

'Not mocking,' Olivia said, 'just teasing.'

'I think it's fantastic.' Jamie squeezed Annie's hand. 'Edward must be very proud of you.'

'I'm proud of me,' Annie said softly.

'So you should be,' Olivia told her.

Annie went home after four days, but Olivia said she could stay on in Boston for another ten, and Jamie was grateful for that, for already he felt a little more like his old self, felt some of his confusions coming into clearer focus.

'I have some things to say,' Olivia said to him just after breakfast the morning after Annie had flown back to London. 'Things that Annie wasn't sure I ought to say to you just yet, but which I'm going to anyway. Okay?'

'Sounds ominous.'

The remains of their juice, croissants and fresh brewed

coffee were on a low table between them, and they were sitting facing each other on the two soft leather settees that Jamie had installed into the glass-surrounded alcove off his sitting room. The alcove jutted out over the wharf below, giving the sensation of hanging directly above the harbour, blue and sparkling this morning and already alive with gulls and sailing boats and commuter and tourist ferries.

'Right.' Olivia drained her coffee cup and set it down. 'First, I'd like to get one thing straight in your head. You are *not* a failure, and if I ever hear you saying or even feel you starting to *think* that way again, I will fly straight back here from wherever I am and beat the crap out of you. Clear?'

'Clear enough.' He smiled, deciding that her own chic new, shorter, hair emphasized her marvellously mobile face, made her, startlingly, even more feminine than before.

'I think, maybe,' Olivia went on, more slowly, more thoughtfully, 'that Carrie's got you confusing basic decency with weakness.' She looked into his face, saw his vulnerability. 'Don't you realize that your decency and your gentleness and your kindness are your special strengths, Jamie? They're the reason Annie and I both love you so much – part of the reason, at least – and I'm pretty certain they're part of the reason for your success with your colleagues and your clients.'

'For what that's worth,' he said wryly.

'Oh, come *on*,' Olivia said, exasperated. 'You're thinking failure again. Falling in love with a super-class bitch like Carrie wasn't a failure – just the aberration of all time. And getting the hell *out* of your marriage has got to be the best thing you've ever done, whatever it's costing you.'

'If all it was costing me was money—' Jamie stopped.

'You mean the business,' Olivia said.

She and Annie had both asked him about his clearly unsat-
isfactory arrangements with Carrie at Beaumont-Arias, but
Jamie had been reluctant to talk about that and so they had
both withdrawn from the subject.

'I still don't understand,' she went on now, 'what's going
on there. It's the only part of your divorce proceedings
that I think you're crazy to be going along with. I mean,
surely it's insane for you to go on pouring even one
ounce of your talent or effort into Carrie's and Peter's
coffers.'

'Peter doesn't figure in this,' Jamie said.

'The hell he doesn't,' Olivia retorted. 'He's still sleeping
with your wife, isn't he? They're still talking about getting
married, aren't they?'

'They are.'

'So how long do you plan to go on helping Carrie pay
her bills?' Olivia threw up her hands. 'And don't start
telling me again that she doesn't need your money. We
all know she's never really needed it, and you've always
said that she didn't need your talent either, but it hasn't
stopped her using both, has it?'

'Have you finished?' Jamie asked, quietly.

'For the moment.'

'Good.' He paused. 'Do you really think I'm unaware of
what you're telling me?'

'No. Of course not.'

'And do you think I'm enjoying the way things are at
Beaumont-Arias?'

'No, I don't,' Olivia said. 'But that doesn't explain why
you're putting up with it.'

'I have my reasons,' Jamie said.

'Which you won't tell me.'

'That's right.' There was no way on earth that Jamie was

going to tell Olivia about Carrie's threats. He hated the thought of Olivia feeling pushed away or excluded, but he knew he had no choice, because if she found out the truth she would very likely blow sky-high, and then Lord knew what shit would hit the fan and it was probably Annie who would end up suffering, and Jamie was still not prepared to risk that.

'May I ask another question?' Olivia asked.

'Could I stop you?'

'Are you planning to find a way out?'

'Ultimately, of course,' Jamie replied. 'But there's a lot to consider.'

'Losing some of your clients,' Olivia surmised.

'Losing them wouldn't be the biggest issue,' Jamie said. 'But if I left Beaumont-Arias, I might be forced to walk out on them, to abandon them to Carrie. I see that as morally indefensible.'

'If that's true,' Olivia said, slowly, considering, 'then surely what you have to do is find a way to get the best for them and for yourself.'

'Easier said,' Jamie told her.

'Easily done,' Olivia argued. 'If you want it enough.' She paused. 'You're a brilliant man, Jamie. A creative man. Isn't it time you started using those gifts to your own ends? And if that does mean learning how to be a little more devious and a little more selfish, surely it's worthwhile if it's the only way you can really cut loose?'

'And regain my own self-respect, you mean?' Jamie asked softly.

'There's not a single reason on earth for you to have lost that,' Olivia said. 'Believe that, Jamie, even if you believe nothing else.'

*   *   *

It was so good for him, having her there with him, having her strength and audacity and capacity for both luxurious and simple pleasures. Olivia was keen to share some of the energy and satisfaction she was finding in her own life in Strasbourg. Yes, she confessed in a quiet moment, living alone was sometimes lonely, but most of the time she enjoyed her own company, and there were, of course, a couple of new men – one a young Canadian lawyer, the other a French music teacher – neither of them serious relationships, both of them just good, light-hearted company, people with whom to lark about generally and to share all that rich Alsatian food.

'It's what you need,' she told Jamie on her seventh evening in Boston.

'I'm okay as I am,' he said.

'No, you're not. Which is my main reason for being here. To remind you – before it's too late and you fossilize – what it's like to have fun, *real* fun.'

Jamie was wary. 'Am I up to this, I wonder?'

'Take a few days off and find out,' Olivia said. 'I have almost a week left. We could make some real plans.'

'I can't,' he said. 'I'd love to, but it's impossible.' He looked at her face, saw her disapproval. 'Not because of Carrie – or not in the way you're thinking – not because she mightn't like it but because she probably would, and I won't leave town right now because I don't trust her.'

'Okay,' Olivia said. 'That makes sense.' She smiled at him. 'Guess we'll just have to find ways of squeezing some fun into your schedule.'

'Guess we will.'

She made it a week to remember. Tossing aside her guide books and seizing instead upon two or three groups of students and a couple of tutors around Harvard Square, grilling them for Boston know-how, Olivia the organizer set about cramming their days and nights with activities ruthlessly designed to get Jamie back on the road. His heavy commitments at Beaumont-Arias might have dampened a less determined spirit, but having extracted from his secretary a schedule of Jamie's appointments and meetings for the next seven days, Olivia mapped out her own agenda which entailed whipping Jamie in and out of the Newbury Street office several times each day.

She turned him into a tourist, led him by the hand from tavern to tavern, to The Bell in Hand, the oldest in the country, to Clarke's, one of the sportiest in the city, to The Black Rose, the most fervently Irish. She took him to lunches and dinners at The Salty Dog, the Union Oyster House, Locke-Ober's and the Ritz-Carlton Dining Room. She took him to listen to jazz at Saffi's and the Regatta Bar and Ryles, and she took him dancing at Spit and the vast, noisy, neon Metro. During the day, working around meetings, business lunches and cocktails (that week, at least, Jamie had no official dinners to attend), she took him on a Swan Boat ride on the Public Garden's Lagoon and for a picnic on the Common: Carrie's face when she saw Olivia carrying in the wicker hamper she'd filled with everything from cold lobster to chocolate-dipped stem cherries from Bailey's, was a picture both Olivia and Jamie would cherish for years to come.

'You realize you're killing me,' Jamie told Olivia on the day of the picnic, after he'd had to run back to Newbury Street for a presentation rehearsal between courses. 'By the time you go back to Strasbourg, I'll either be on my knees or flat on my back.'

'No, you won't.' Olivia fed him a cherry. 'I've figured out that this is like dragging someone into aerobics classes every day until the endorphin high gets to them and then they just go on and on.'

'Until they drop dead.'

'Until they realize that life is richer and more alive and just plain *better* when it's being lived to the full.'

She took him to the children's petting zoo at Franklin Park, prodded him up the spiral pathway through the huge New England Aquarium. She paid through the nose for tickets for a Celtics game at Boston Garden, bribed someone to let them and a stash of hot dogs into Fenway Park even though neither the Red Sox nor any other team was playing. She got him to jog with her along the Esplanade beside the Charles River. And no less than three times she got him out onto the water in his beloved, barely-baptized, pure white *Joie de Vivre*.

She was due to return to Strasbourg the following Monday.

'Michael called,' Jamie said to her on Friday evening, on their way to dinner. 'Louise suggested we might like to come out to the Newport house for Sunday lunch. Daisy's going to be there with the boys – Michael said that if the weather holds they'll probably be barbecuing.'

'No Peter, I take it,' Olivia said.

'Definitely not.'

'Sounds like fun.'

'Are you sure? I mean, it's going to take over an hour getting out to the cottage, and lunch is bound to take at least the same amount of time – and then there'll be the trip back.' Jamie's eyes were teasing. 'All that for just one ordinary family lunch.'

'I daresay I'll find us something more to do while we're there,' Olivia said, playing it straight.

'As long as it's not jogging,' Jamie said.

*   *   *

Olivia had only been inside the Ocean Drive mansion once before, and had found it attractive from the outside, raised as it was on a small hill, overlooking the ocean: a white, handsome house with a Spanish tile roof and delicate verandas. But once inside, she found it too large and, perhaps, a little too overbearing for her personal taste. Her own early childhood homes, first on Riverside Drive and then on Park Avenue, had been pretty splendid by Manhattan standards, and the Aldriches' family house in San Francisco had been nothing short of exquisite both in style and dimensions; but the Arias mansion had been more than grand enough even before Michael and Louise had added a new wing, and she knew that Jamie had never liked the changes, would have preferred his father's and uncle's fine home to have remained unadulterated.

Still, Olivia had to admit, if the proportions of the house were too grandiose for her liking, the collection of art that hung on the majestic walls was eclectic, impressive and fascinating. On the way to Jamie's suite of rooms alone, she saw a Bonnard, two Picassos, a portrait by Delgado and a large, melancholy painting by Puvis de Chavannes on the staircase, and a Dali in the small dressing room attached to the marble bathroom. She thought about her father then, and how he would have admired and enjoyed many of the works here, remembered what Arthur had once told her about the way great paintings, whether famous or not, could transcend their settings, carry with them other lives, other atmospheres, sometimes even other worlds. Olivia felt that way now, here, inside the mansion which was a part of Jamie's heritage but in which he seemed, to her at least, so out of place, yet she could look at the Picassos and the beautiful little Bonnard and the bizarre Dali and think about Jamie's father and uncle assembling them over the years, and the house itself just melted away, and there was the connection, and any lack of harmony had ceased to matter.

'Anyone want to join us for a bike ride?' Olivia asked later when they'd finished eating. The gardens in which they sat fell away in glorious abundance from the house, shaded by oaks and elms, willows, chestnuts and firs, and, on this warm and sunny late spring afternoon, vivid with all the colours of the rhododendrons.

Jamie groaned. 'I knew it was too good to last.'

'Sounds too energetic for me,' Louise Arias said, 'after all that food.'

'I'm too tired from cooking,' Michael said.

'First time he's done more than switch on the espresso machine since last summer.' Louise looked benevolently at her husband.

'How about you, Daisy?' Olivia asked.

'I haven't cycled since I was fourteen,' Daisy Arias said, 'and found the exercise was overdeveloping my calves.'

'I've always been proud of my muscles.' Olivia smiled sweetly at Daisy. 'Especially my thighs.'

They were sitting in an imperfect semi-circle of white cane chairs on the lawn of what Jamie called their second layer of garden. It was very warm for May, but with a pleasant breeze. Michael wore a British panama hat and, with his eyes shielded by dark glasses, Olivia thought he looked like some impenetrable, old-fashioned spy, though earlier on, at work on the big stone barbecue, he'd been every inch the classic American family man, and she had to admit he'd served up some of the best steaks, ribs and hamburgers she'd ever tasted. Louise, his wife, auburn-haired, hazel-eyed, svelte in slender cream wool pants and perfectly toned sweater, had started out, Olivia thought, a little uptight – which, given the awkward mix of company, was very understandable – but several glasses of Chablis on, she had relaxed into a genuine Sunday afternoon peaceableness. And then there was Daisy, Peter's ex-wife, pretty, blonde and soft-featured, long since over the infidelity that had first split them up and glad to let her boys maintain contact with their uncle and cousins, yet always still just a little uncomfortable in the presence of the Arias family, more so now than ever before in the face of Peter's awful betrayal of Jamie.

'I shouldn't have come,' Jamie had said in a lull before lunch, when he and Olivia had been fleetingly alone. 'I think poor Daisy's embarrassed.'

'I don't see why she should be,' Olivia said. 'She's hardly responsible for what her ex-husband gets up to.' She gave a sudden grin. 'Unless, of course, she's hoping that you two might get together.'

'For God's sake, Olivia—' Jamie looked around, appalled.

'It's not so unusual,' Olivia said. 'The two aggrieved parties. That kind of thing – all that lusty mutual outrage—'

'Olivia, shut up.'

'You're much better looking than Peter, and younger, of course.' She checked him over appraisingly. He was wearing blue jeans, sneakers and a cricket sweater; he looked, she thought, stirred, like a dark-haired Gatsby.

'I hardly think she'd want to go from one brother to the other.'

'It didn't stop Carrie,' Olivia said, and walked away.

*   *   *

'I guess the boys are too young to come biking,' she said now, lunch over and the coals on the barbecue dampened down. She glanced over to where Daisy's and Peter's sons were kicking around a couple of footballs at the foot of a copper beech tree.

'Paul can ride a bicycle,' Daisy said.

'Where were you thinking of riding?' Michael asked Olivia.

'Cliff Walk, I thought,' Olivia said.

'Paul can't ride there,' Daisy said quickly. 'It isn't really meant for cycling, Olivia, just for walking.'

'It is pretty rough in parts,' Louise said. 'And steep.'

'We'll be careful,' Olivia reassured her.

Jamie sighed. 'You really want to go, don't you?'

'I'd love it,' she said. 'I've been starved of the ocean for so long.'

'We've been out on the boat three times in a week,' Jamie said.

'Not enough. I need more.'

He stretched his long legs out lazily in front of him. 'You realize this is the first peaceful hour I've had all week.'

'You realize it's my last day with you,' she countered. 'This way I can have you and my last fix of ocean.'

'See what I'm up against?' he said to his cousin.

Olivia looked at Michael. 'Has Jamie never told you what a pushy broad I am?'

'Not exactly.' Michael smiled at her. 'But we're learning.'

'Would you like to join us?' she asked him.

'I think I'll pass,' Michael said. 'But thank you for the offer.'

It was a gorgeous afternoon. The bicycles that Jamie had unearthed for them in one of the garden sheds were old and rusty and harder to ride than the modern, light-weight bikes that Olivia had ridden for the past several years, and Jamie grouched for the first fifteen minutes about aching legs and no respite and how he was beginning to think he might be glad to see the back of her. But then the rugged splendour of their surroundings and the invigorating quality of the air began to work their magic, and Olivia's intermittent gales of laughter as she veered to avoid bumps and narrowly missed coming off altogether, were too infectious for him to continue belly-aching; and in any case Olivia had taken no notice, so there seemed little point, after all, in complaining about a few aches and pains, and they paused every now and then to look away from the ocean back to the famous Vanderbilt and Astor mansions and, especially, at Rosecliff, Jamie's old favourite, regarded by many as the most romantic of the great Newport houses.

'Makes your place look like a doll's house,' Olivia teased, gazing up at the forty-room mansion, unable to conceive of living with the slightest degree of normality in such vastness.

She looked at Jamie now, astride the old bicycle, one foot on the ground, dark hair blowing a little in the wind, thought suddenly how noble he looked, and it was an odd thought for her to have, for God knew she'd never considered him quite that way before, and there was that pang again – *dammit* – and she'd believed she'd put that behind her, back in its box, and thoughts like that were no good at all, unless she wanted to lose one of her two best friends in the world.

'Peter and Carrie are planning to move into the west wing,' Jamie said suddenly, his eyes black against the sunlight. 'Michael told me, while he was throwing steaks on the barbecue. He's awfully embarrassed – Louise is, too – but we all know it's Peter's house as much as his or mine, so there's not a lot anyone can do about it.'

Olivia was silent for a moment and then she said, very quietly: 'The hell with them both.'

'I guess,' Jamie said.

She looked at him, sharply. 'Don't tell me you've forgiven them.'

He didn't answer right away, kept his eyes focused on Rosecliff for a few seconds more, and then he looked back at her. 'No,' he said. 'But I'm starting to get used to it.'

'Okay,' Olivia said. 'That's good. I guess.'

'As good as it gets, I think.'

She watched him for another moment, and a surge of emotion blew over her like an adrenalin rush.

'Let's race,' she said, suddenly.

'We can't,' Jamie said. 'The walk's too bumpy.'

'You're getting soft on me.'

One of those brief, painful images of his brother and his wife flashed across Jamie's mind.

'Wanna bet?' he said.

'Last one to The Breakers buys dinner tonight,' Olivia said.

'Deal,' Jamie said and straightened out his wheels.

'On three,' Olivia said. 'You count.'

Jamie smiled. 'One—'

They both hunched over.

'Two—'

She was fooling about when it happened. They had both known before the off that racing on those cranky, archaic machines was absurd, and they were pumping the pedals as hard as they could and achieving little in the way of speed but laughing a good deal. Olivia's goal had been to get Jamie's mind off Peter and Carrie and to get her own off Jamie, and if they couldn't get a decent race going, she guessed she'd have to work harder, clown around a little, and so she stopped abruptly and climbed up on the low wall with her bike, and Jamie yelled at her not to be such a damned fool, that it was dangerous up there, but Olivia knew better – she *always* knew better – and she was off, and the wall looked wide enough so long as she kept a straight line, and she was pedalling furiously again, and Jamie, on the path itself, was fighting to keep up with her.

She went over a few hundred yards from The Breakers.

Jamie saw it happen, and yet it was as if he wasn't really seeing it. She veered suddenly to the left, corrected herself, and then her right foot seemed somehow to be stuck. He couldn't tell what had happened, if it was her sneaker or a lace, but she made a sound, gave a kind of low yell, a startled, warning kind of a sound, and then she and the bicycle tipped slowly to the right and disappeared.

He'd seen it, but he couldn't believe it, *refused* to believe it. And then he heard her scream, and he screeched to a halt – it had seemed so slow, yet it had happened in just a few seconds – and his own bike crashed to the ground, and he heard yelling and did not quite grasp that it was his own voice yelling.

'*Olivia!*'

In his mind he saw her as he would when he got to the edge of the wall and looked over, bloodied and unconscious, or broken, or—

He reached the edge and forced himself to look.

She was only eight or ten feet down on an outcrop of rain-smoothed rocks. She was quite still, face down, her right leg drawn up and bent at the knee, the bicycle on top of her, and her left arm was thrown back over her head. She was not moving.

Jamie felt his heart literally stop.

'Olivia.' It came out in a croak. He tried to clear his throat. 'Olivia.'

She still did not move. He could not see her face.

'Olivia!'

'Will – you – get – the – fuck – down – here.'

Her voice was perfectly steady and quite calm, each word clearly separated, as if punctuated by dashes.

Jamie stared down at her, his heart pounding. 'Are you okay?'

Her voice blew up to him again with the wind, its familiar, low huskiness as welcome to him as desert rain or manna from heaven or a sharp fingernail on a long inaccessible itch.

'No, Jamie,' Olivia said, 'I am not okay.' She paused. 'I am not dead, nor do I seem to have broken anything much, but I am definitely not okay.' She paused again. 'Okay?' The question was acidic.

He smiled. 'Okay.'

'So are you coming down, or do we wait till I turn as rusty as this so-called bicycle?'

Carefully, forcing himself to stay slow, knowing that if he fell too, he'd be no use to her at all, Jamie made his way down, using a drainage pipe for support, until he was beside her.

'Can I move the bike?' he asked, afraid he might hurt her.

'No, I really love having it on top of me,' she answered.

'Your right sneaker's hooked on a spoke,' he told her.

'Tell me about it,' she said.

He started to extricate the lace, then stopped.

'Why have you stopped?' she asked.

'So you do want me to help you?'

'Yes, Jamie.'

'Do you recall whose idea it was to go bike riding?'

'Mine, Jamie.'

'And do you recall whose idea it was to have a race?'

'Mine.'

'And do you recall who decided to be a wise-ass and get up on the wall, even when someone else told her not to be such a damn fool?'

A moment or two passed. Somewhere above them on the pathway people walked and talked. Gulls wheeled and called over their heads.

'Jamie?'

'Yes, Olivia.'

'Do you think you could please help me now?' Her voice was sweet now, compliant and gentle and utterly out of character. 'I really would quite like to see if I can get back on my feet.'

'I thought you said you weren't hurt.' He was alarmed again. Quickly, he detached the lace and released the sneaker. 'Where's the pain?' He lifted up the bicycle and set it over to their right.

Slowly, Olivia sat up. She flexed both arms, then both legs, one at a time, then she moved her head, tentatively, first to the right, then to the left.

'Nowhere.' She smiled at him. 'You looked really scared.'

'I was,' he said, sitting down beside her. 'You have dirt on your face.'

'Wipe it off, please,' she said.

* * *

Like the fall itself, he didn't exactly know how it happened. He felt curiously disembodied, as if it were happening to another person. He went to wipe the dirt off her face, as she had bidden him, with his large white handkerchief, and then he saw that she had a scratch on her left cheek, saw that she was bleeding, and something deep inside him seemed to move, to come alive, something that he had not known – something he truly *believed* he had not known – was there. And instead of wiping her cheek or telling her that she was bleeding, or getting her up on her feet and starting to get her back up onto the path, he kissed her. Not on the cheek or forehead or on her hair, the way he had done countless times in the past. On her lips. Right on her wide, soft, surprised mouth.

'Jamie,' she said – nothing else – and kissed him straight back.

It was the most extraordinary kiss. All the first kisses he'd ever had until then had been either hungered for, pleasurably anticipated or, in less passionate encounters, bordering on obligatory. This one, flying into his life, into his body and soul, so abruptly, so entirely unpremeditatedly, seemed simply unavoidable. His mouth and Olivia's mouth were drawn irresistibly together. Their lips had to touch, had to kiss, they had to allow their mouths to open so that they could kiss more deeply; Jamie felt as if he might stop breathing, stop functioning, might literally curl up and *die* if he did not go on kissing that well-known, well-loved, oh-so-familiar mouth, and it wasn't really him kissing Olivia, it couldn't be, because that simply could not, would never happen. And yet their tongues were touching and exploring, and it felt like diving down, down, into some wondrous, fathomless, indescribable place, and Jamie heard a small sound and realized it

231

was a moan, and he was not sure if it was his own or her moan.

And he stopped kissing her and drew back.

Olivia, who felt that perhaps she might have been struck by a bolt of genuine, non-proverbial lightning, looked long and hard into his eyes.

She waited for him to speak, and when he did not, she knew, with an exquisite jolt of joy, that there was nothing to *be* said, and that he felt exactly the same as she did.

'Jamie,' she said at last, and her voice was shakier than it had been right after the fall.

'Yes?'

'Let's go home.'

They went back to the house hardly speaking. In the Arias drawing room, sitting beneath a sinuously, poetically lovely Gauguin original, they explained what had happened, went through the motions, let Louise fuss about how much worse it might have been, let her and Daisy clean Olivia up as well as they could given her refusal to take a bath and stay the night, and thanked them politely for finding her an unripped pair of Calvin Klein jeans and an utterly unOlivia-like flowery silk blouse. They talked Michael out of calling the doctor and out of flying them back to Boston in either the Arias helicopter or the jet, and they bade them all farewell and got back into Jamie's car and drove back to Boston. Back to the apartment on Rowes Wharf.

Their conversation was minimal. They both knew that it was not over, that neither wanted it to be over. Jamie felt out of control, liked feeling that way because he was with Olivia, not with Carrie, and though he was aware that Olivia was taking control, there seemed to him to be no similarity at all between her and his wife. He was safe with Olivia. She was a little crazy, sometimes a lot crazy, but she cared for him as much as he did for her, always had, and so he let her take over, went on feeling as he had since the kiss – slightly remote, slightly absurd, immensely excited, ready to do just about anything she asked him to. A normally responsible, conventional guy going AWOL.

Olivia knew exactly what she was doing – she'd have been a damned liar if she'd tried to deny it – yet in a sense she felt no more in control than Jamie. There was a nagging in her mind like a dull drumbeat, a warning that this was not wise, that it was, of course, not exactly dangerous because Jamie was Jamie, familiar and kind and safe, and Jamie would never hurt her, yet at the same time she knew they might both *be* hurt unless they stopped right there. Yet still she carried on regardless, encouraged him to open the bottle of Krug she'd put in the refrigerator three days before – they were both easy champagne drunks, always had been, just a glass seemed to go straight to its target, relaxing as a hit of pre-med – and then she went right on into his en-suite bathroom and turned on the taps and threw about a third of a bottle of Guerlain foam bath into the water – she wondered, for an instant, why Jamie, a fast shower man, had such a thing in his bathroom, more to the point who had given it to him, and a fierce and idiotic jealousy stabbed at her – and when it was full, she turned the taps off and went to fetch him and their champagne.

'Come on,' she said, after she'd downed half a glass, made him do the same, and refilled them both herself.

'Where?' he asked, dazed.

'Just come.' She knew she had to act fast, in case her courage evaporated with the bubbles in the bath.

Jamie looked at the tub, turned around and saw, in awe and with immeasurable delight, that Olivia was unbuttoning Louise's blouse and unzipping the Calvin Klein jeans. She wore a pale blue, broderie anglaise brassiere and matching panties. Her body was slim and firm and smooth, and she had the most exquisitely perfect navel that he had ever seen.

'Did you fall off that cliff, or did I?' he asked, not knowing if the sudden wild pulsing inside his head was from the Krug or the sight of her.

'I think maybe we both did.' She was a little breathless.

'Yes,' was all he said, all he was capable of saying.

'Come on,' she said again. 'Before we change our minds.'

'Have we made them up then?' he asked, softly.

'Oh, yes,' Olivia said. She smiled. 'I need a bath. Your family all said I should take a bath, so now I'm going to take one.' She looked into his face. 'You need one too,' she told him.

'Definitely,' he agreed, and began, with fingers that had gone half numb, to unbuckle his belt.

'No sense in wasting water, after all,' she said, and, taking off the brassiere and panties, stepped into the tub without another glance at him, lay back in the foamy, delicious water, gave a long sigh and closed her eyes.

He was hard as a rock before he touched her.

'Do you mind if the rug gets wet?' she asked, not moving, eyes still shut.

'No.' His voice was husky. 'Not at all.'

'Good.'

It was a regular-size tub. He tried to settle in, facing her, his back against the cold steel of the taps. Still she didn't move, made no effort to make space for him, but her eyes were wide open now and she was watching him carefully. They were both long-legged, but the tub was large enough for her to be able to stretch out her legs while he had to bend his at the knees. His shins were level with her breasts. Her breasts were paler than the rest of her body, her nipples a dark peach colour and erect. Jamie thought that he might, in a moment or two, have a heart attack.

'What now?' he asked.

'First,' she said, 'we have some more champagne.'

'And then?'

'Then, I guess, we wash.'

'Do I get to wash you?' he asked, almost humbly.

'Well, I should hope so,' she answered fervently, then added, as a polite afterthought: 'If you like.'

'Yes, please,' he said, and reached for a bar of soap. It was Roger & Gallet sandalwood; he was glad it wasn't just Dove, which he often used. 'Where would you like me to begin?'

'Sometimes,' Olivia said, 'I start with my feet, other times with my arms and shoulders and neck.'

Her feet were surprisingly soft, their toenails painted the same shade of pink as her fingernails.

'For someone so active,' Jamie said, contemplating the arch of the left foot, resisting the urge to tickle the sole, 'you're not at all athletic looking.' For the first time in many hours he thought of Carrie, who had gone to the gym like clockwork all through their marriage, and whose body had remained unquestionably splendid but had, he'd sometimes thought, feeling guilty for his sexism, seemed a little too hard, a little too unyielding. Nothing about Olivia's body, he reflected, soaping her ankle, was hard except, of course, her nipples.

'Is this supposed to be therapy for me?' he asked her

suddenly. 'I mean, I don't mind, I don't mind at all, I'm not that crazy, but I'd like to know.'

'Shush,' she said. 'Wash me and don't talk about it and don't think about it.' She smiled at him. 'We fell off a cliff, remember? Things happen after you fall off a cliff. The rules stop.'

He kissed her then, dropped the soap into the water and made no effort to find it, and their bodies were touching now; he felt her breasts against his chest and if he had thought he was hard before, then he'd obviously never known what hard could be. He touched her left breast and felt her shudder, and with his other hand he reached down into the bubbles and parted her thighs a little way, though they were cramped between his own legs in the constraints of the tub, and he felt the soft curls of her pubic hair and looked down, blew away a little foam and saw it, with the most intense jolt of pleasure, like a small dark cloud, tendrils waving in the water like a mermaid's, and he felt it with his fingers and went a little further and heard her moan.

'Am I allowed to say that I don't really believe this is happening?' he whispered.

'You're allowed,' she said. 'Don't stop.'

'I won't stop,' he said, and stopped. 'Are you sure it's okay?' he asked, with difficulty. 'I mean, you can change your mind any time if you want to.'

'Are you nuts?' Olivia asked, huskier than usual, and her own right hand went down into the water and found him, encircled him.

'Jesus,' he said. 'Oh, sweet Jesus.'

It began in earnest then. Everything went to hell, they were so hungry, so starved for each other. Their mouths became fused, and their bodies, and water cascaded over the sides of the tub onto the floor. They both wanted to touch each other everywhere, to feel, to know every part of the other's body, and it was every birthday and Christmas and, for Olivia, every Chanukah, since time immemorial, and if this powerful, overwhelming need to have this man, this beloved, familiar man, inside her, to have him joined with her, was pure lust, or if it was, maybe, pure love, it didn't really matter, not now at least. It was what it was, and she only knew that she had never, in all her life, experienced anything more utterly, ineffably, joyously, perfectly right.

They had to get out of the tub, it was simply too small, and they knocked over the bottle of Krug – though it didn't matter, they were beyond champagne – and they grabbed at towels and half dried each other, but every new touch was inflaming, and the bathroom was snug and warm and they threw the towels down on the floor and pulled each other down. And Olivia had never been so ready, had never felt quite so monumentally wanton, and she flung her arms back over her head and opened her legs, and she saw Jamie hesitate, saw the question in his eyes—

'I'm on the pill,' she answered.

'Thank Christ,' he said—

And he entered her slowly, as slowly as he could bear, and he was bigger than she had imagined – though she hadn't realized till now that she *had* ever imagined – for such a slender man, with such beautiful hands. Oh, God, they were beautiful, they were so clever and deft and giving, and they were on her now, everywhere, and so was his mouth, and he was moving inside her, and she was moving with him, and there was a molten place in her, and she thought she might erupt, knew she would—

'Oh, God,' she said. 'Oh, Jamie—'
And she did. They both did.

They both wept afterwards too. Not for long, but lustily, in each other's arms, still on the pile of wet towels on the bathroom floor.

'Why are you crying?' Jamie asked her gently, kissing her tears.

'Why are you?' she asked back, licking his salty cheek.

'I guess,' he said, slowly, holding her tightly, 'because today we fell off a cliff, and tomorrow we have to get back on real land.'

'Not me,' she said. 'I get to fly.'

'Oh, yes,' he said, and held her even closer.

And now they both knew why they were crying.

Jamie awoke next morning to find Olivia already dressed and packed, sitting waiting for him in the living room.

'Why didn't you wake me?' he asked, seeing the time. 'You know I'm taking you to Logan.' He came over, bent down to kiss her. She accepted his lips but made no real response.

'I'd rather you didn't,' she said. 'Take me, I mean. I was going to wake you to say goodbye.' She looked up into his face, saw confusion, guilt and the start of misery in his eyes. 'Don't look like that, Jamie.'

'Like what?' He sat down beside her on the sofa. He was suddenly, uncomfortably aware of his nakedness beneath his white bathrobe. He tied the belt more tightly. He felt indescribably wretched.

'And don't feel that way, either,' Olivia said.

'What way?'

'You're feeling guilty, aren't you?'

'Why should I feel guilty?'

'Not a single reason in the world. But you are.' She paused briefly. 'You think we acted on impulse, and you're right, we did, and that's me, isn't it? That's typical Olivia, leaping without looking, same way she fell off the damned cliff.'

'Wonderful cliff,' Jamie said.

'Yes. I agree.'

'Well, then.'

'But you're not an impetuous man, Jamie, are you? At least you never have been, not like me, anyway. So now you're bound to start fretting and angsting all over the place, worrying about what I'm feeling, because we know you're not really over Carrie yet and so you're going to start thinking you've taken advantage of me.'

'You ran the bath,' Jamie said.

'I did. Quite. And I got you to open the champagne and get in the bath with me.' Olivia smiled right into his dark eyes. 'So you see, there really is no reason for you to look at last night as anything more or less than what it was.'

'And what was it, Olivia?'

'Friendship,' she answered.

'Uh-huh,' he said, clearly unconvinced.

'It was, Jamie, darling. Friendship and true, true love – but only the kind of love we've always had for each other. And the rest of it was—'

He jumped right into her pause. 'Yes? The rest of it was what?'

'A physical response to a build-up of tension,' she said. 'A wonderful response, and I'm not denying that we were very attracted to each other, but—'

'But?'

'But it was a one-off.' Olivia looked into his eyes again, then looked quickly away. 'We both know that, Jamie, admit it.'

Jamie shook his head. 'I can't. I don't know it. I thought—'

'What did you think? That it was the start of something?' Olivia stood up, walked over to the alcove overlooking the harbour. 'We are what we've always been. Best friends. You've been through hell lately, and we had a great week together, and I pushed you hard, made you do all kinds of things you wouldn't normally want to do.'

Jamie got up, too, joined her by the window but kept a foot of space between them, didn't dare touch her, even brush against her. 'I hope you're not suggesting that I didn't want to make love to you.'

She smiled again. 'No. Not that.'

'That's something.' He looked out over the harbour, towards Logan.

'It was beautiful,' Olivia said. 'It was good, better than good, for both of us, and I know I won't forget it.' She took a breath. 'But I don't think either of us should ever talk about it again, and I know we'll never do it again, and that's fine, too.'

Jamie turned back to face her. 'So we're just good friends, is that it? I mean, is that *it*? Last night never really happened?'

'I didn't say that.'

'It's what you meant.' He heard the tinge of bitterness in his voice and disliked himself for it. He knew, after all, what she was doing, that she was freeing him from an entanglement that she knew would only cause him more pain because she didn't want it.

'I guess,' Olivia said. 'In a way.'

Jamie managed a smile. 'You're right.' At last, he reached out to touch her, lightly, gently, on the arm; it was safe now, the intimacy had gone, the danger had passed. 'It is better this way.'

'I wonder,' Olivia said, with a brightness she did not feel, 'what Annie would have to say to us if she knew.'

'You don't think we should tell her.'

'Maybe not.'

Carrie's accusations and her malice came back into Jamie's mind. *Your own sick little affair with your two friends*. And her outrageous threats. *I'll drag them both through the dirt with you*.

'I guess you're right about that too,' he said.

They were both silent for a moment.

'If we're going,' Jamie said, 'we'd better go or you'll miss your flight.'

'I told you,' she said, 'I don't want you taking me.'

'I always take you.'

'Not this time. I couldn't stand the airport farewell, not this time.'

Jamie shook his head. 'Me neither.'

He called her a cab, pulled on some jeans and a shirt and carried her bags downstairs to the lobby where the doorman took them out to the waiting car. They embraced there, the way they always had, old, dear, trusted friends, and then they walked, arm in arm, out into the street. The traffic on Atlantic Avenue flowed past, thick and loud and fast; Olivia often remarked on the contrasting outlooks of the two faces of Jamie's building, the one inland unremittingly ugly, the other, the ocean, as calming and attractive as any city view could possibly be.

'I'll call you when I get home,' she told him.

'You'd better,' he said. 'Any time, even if you're delayed.'

She got into the cab. 'Just one more thing.'

'What?' He crouched on the sidewalk.

'Only that if Carrie the Kvetch ever tried to cast any doubts about your lovemaking skills – and knowing Carrie I'll bet she did – then I am here to tell you that the woman's a fool as well as a liar.'

At least, she thought, as the cab drew away, she'd left him smiling.

15

Jamie announced the opening of his own agency, JAA, that August. It had been a battle all the way, with Carrie – now married to Peter – blocking his plans wherever and whenever she could, and her new husband doing his darnedest to look the other way – which had greatly aggravated her – but a deal had finally been struck.

'I've left it all behind,' Jamie told Olivia on the telephone. 'All my clients, all my colleagues. I'm continuing to take care of my old accounts under the auspices of Beaumont-Arias – in which I'm still a silent partner – but in the meantime, I'm free to run my own ship with what Carrie calls a free hand.'

'Sounds pretty accurate,' Olivia commented wryly, 'since it seems as if you're going to be trying to function with one hand tied behind your back.'

'Not really,' Jamie said. 'Sure, I've given up a lot, and Carrie is going to be holding a lot of the aces, but where new accounts are concerned, we're going to be rivals on the same turf, and I'll just have to see if I can still cut it. To be honest, I haven't felt so liberated or invigorated in years.'

*   *   *

Three months later, word was out that James Arias's new agency was the place in Boston most likely to spawn original, product-selling, dollar-earning campaigns. Jamie's old skills at reaching into disparate worlds, his still-boyish capacity for excitement when a prospective client showed him a new product or service, his natural communication gifts and, above all, his talent with words and pictures and images, had all soared back up to the surface the way a half-drowned diver might head through murky water back to sunlight. Word was out, and Carrie hated it.

When Maggie Carmichael and David Baum, Jamie's favourite old creative partnership, turned up on JAA's Boylston Street doorstep, his non-poaching agreement with Carrie forced him to resist the temptation to greet them with open arms.

'This wouldn't be poaching,' Maggie pointed out over a cappuccino in the café next door to Jamie's office. 'You know we left Beaumont-Arias five months back for Steinfeld-Nicholson in New York—'

'Where we were miserable as sin,' David continued, 'and pining for home.'

'Except we both knew that home wasn't just Boston,' Maggie went on, 'and God forbid we should sound like we're brown-nosing—'

'God forbid,' David echoed.

' – but home to us is any agency you're running, Jamie.'

'And with all due respect to Carrie Beaumont Arias Arias—'

'Or whatever you're meant to call a woman who marries a succession of brothers,' Maggie chimed in.

' – she has no right to dictate to us where we work,' David finished.

Jamie drank some more cappuccino. They looked at him.

'So?' Maggie said.

'So?' David said.

Jamie put down his cup.

'So let me talk to my lawyer.'

'It's not exactly kosher,' Bob Jacobson, his lawyer, told him.

'But would I be in breach of contract?' Jamie asked.

'Strictly speaking, no.'

'But?'

'But we might be wise to think about the spirit of the agreement.'

'The spirit of the agreement was to stop me taking away Beaumont-Arias employees—'

'And recently departed employees,' Jacobson emphasized.

'Baum and Carmichael left five months ago. They went to New York, to another agency. Now they're back and they want to work for JAA.' Jamie paused. 'Can I hire them or not?'

'You might be inviting aggravation,' the lawyer said.

'I'm used to aggravation from Carrie,' Jamie replied.

'Then hire them.'

There were no signs of retaliation for more than a month, and then, out of the blue, in the *Boston Daily News* of December 23rd – extracted, with due caution, in the next edition of *Advertising Life* – Carrie showed her claws again.

A man by the name of Silas Gilbert, whom Jamie recalled slightly as having worked unspectacularly in Beaumont-Arias's accounts department, gave an interview in which he talked about his personal impression of the dreadful years Mrs Arias – a lady Gilbert said he both admired and respected – must have endured with her first husband, and how supportive and loyal she had remained to him in spite of her love for his brother.

Jamie read Gilbert's words in the *Daily News*, headlined in yellow, with swiftly mounting disbelief and rage.

I heard them one day at the office. They were talking in the boardroom after some big meeting – I say talking, but really it got pretty heated and their voices were loud enough for anyone outside the room to hear.

Mrs Arias told Mr Arias that once people knew the truth, no one would blame her for going to another man – not morally, anyhow – I remember she used that word, 'morally'. She asked him if he imagined she didn't know about the sick little affair he'd been having with his two friends. I could hardly believe my ears, but I'll tell you, I couldn't drag myself away – I mean, sure it's not nice to listen at keyholes, but it wasn't too hard to hear, and who wouldn't have stayed to listen, I ask you?

I mean, a lady can only take so much, after all. Mrs Arias knew her husband had been screwing around with two other women – one of them married with kids, if you listen to gossip – and some kind of a junkie, too, apparently. I'd say Mrs Arias was right. You could hardly blame her for leaving him for another man.

'How could you do this?' Jamie asked Carrie two days after *Advertising Life* had landed on his desk. He had been trying to confront her ever since he'd seen the piece in the *Daily News*, but she had been out of town until this morning, when he'd marched right into her office without giving Mark Reiss, her fresh-faced young P.A., a chance to buzz her first.

'How could I do what, James?' Carrie was sitting calmly at her desk, a single folder of paper in front of her. The rest of the surface was, as usual, gleamingly polished and almost bare, aside from one photograph of her with Peter on their wedding day. 'And I'd appreciate it if you would not come bursting into my office without the courtesy of calling first.'

Jamie slammed *Advertising Life* down on the desk. 'I've known for years that you were a bitch, Carrie, but I honestly never dreamed you could sink this low.'

She raised a beautifully plucked brow. 'What can I have done to upset you so, James? Do tell me, please.'

'How much did you pay Gilbert? I gather he left a while back. Is he out of work? Did you take time searching for the right man for the job? How much *did* you pay him?'

'Wouldn't you prefer to sit down?' Carrie asked politely. 'You look as if you need to.'

'I intend to do my utmost to avoid ever having to sit down anywhere in your company again,' Jamie said, coldly. 'Unless, of course, it's in a courtroom.'

'Is that a threat?'

'Did you honestly imagine I'd let you get away with defaming a friend of mine?'

Carrie shook her head, her blue eyes wide with mocking innocence. 'James, James, which friend can you be talking about?' She looked down at *Advertising Life*. 'You surely can't be referring to that little interview with Silas Gilbert. What does that have to do with me?' She scarcely paused to draw breath. 'And which friend of yours has been defamed by it? I've been longing to know – everyone's been longing to know – please do tell.'

Jamie stared down at her, his expression pure disgust. 'How do you sleep at night, Carrie?'

'Very well, thank you,' she answered. 'That is, of course, when your brother lets me.' She smiled up at him, quite serenely. 'How are Olivia and Annie, by the way? I do miss hearing your little stories about them, you know.'

'So you make them up yourself instead,' Jamie said.

'Hardly,' Carrie said, dismissively. 'It's so unnecessary when the truth is so much more fun.'

'So you admit you were referring to Annie,' Jamie said.

'You mean Silas Gilbert was referring to her, don't you?' Carrie paused. 'Would you like me to admit that, James? Would you like Mr Gilbert to name both your friends in another interview?'

'Do that, and you'll regret it for the rest of your life.'

'Try bringing an action,' Carrie countered, 'and just see what I'll do.'

'I want to sue for libel,' he told Bob Jacobson, 'and I want a court order to have her stopped from saying another word.'

'I don't see how you can do either,' the lawyer said, 'since you tell me you and Carrie did have the conversation Gilbert's quoted – and the rest of it was gossip, which he admitted.'

'But there's no way he or anyone could have heard us in the boardroom,' Jamie said. 'The walls are well insulated, the two doors are thick and they were both closed. And

248

neither of us was shouting. I'm telling you, Carrie put him up to this.'

'I don't doubt it,' Jacobson said, 'but it'd be hard to prove – and pointless, too.' He paused. 'Bottom line, Jamie: you can't sue a man for telling the truth, and I repeat, you did have the conversation he says you did.'

'It isn't the man I want to sue,' Jamie said frustratedly. 'Carrie paid for that story, we both know that.'

'We'll never prove it, and even if we could we still couldn't bring a case.'

Jamie shook his head. 'So she's allowed to call a friend of mine – and I stress a *friend*, Bob – a junkie, and get away with it.'

'The women weren't named, Jamie,' Jacobson said gently. 'Be grateful for that.'

'Grateful?' Jamie repeated bitterly.

'From what you tell me, if you let the whole thing drop now, it's likely to die a not-too-ugly, natural death. If you try to fight Carrie, other people may get hurt.'

Jamie knew Jacobson was right, that he had no choice but to sit back and grit his teeth and let it go. The attorney had made it plain enough: if he allowed this scurrilous but relatively minor piece of scandalmongering to fade away, it was unlikely ever to permeate either Annie's or Olivia's European circles.

He thought about Olivia that evening at home, after his meeting with Jacobson, thought about her long and hard. He had seldom permitted himself either the luxury or the pain of thinking about what had happened between them the previous spring. He knew that it had meant nothing more to her than what she had told him. Friendship. Olivia had always been scrupulously, sometimes uncomfortably, honest. *Friendship and true, true love, but only the kind of love we've always had for each other*. He'd thought, with a leap of hope, that he'd seen something else in her eyes that morning, something more, but she'd been so adamant, and ever since then it had been business as usual between them. Friendship.

Bob Jacobson had not asked for the identity of the women Silas Gilbert had talked to the *Daily News* about, and Jamie had not volunteered their names. With nothing to be done, there would have been no purpose served. As it was, he could only hope and pray that no real harm had been done, especially to Annie. At least, thank God, he reflected, there were few, if any, people in Boston or in the agency business who knew about the close bond between the three of them.

A sudden chill went through him. What if Carrie had somehow learned about what had happened between Olivia and himself, if one of the family – Louise or Daisy, perhaps, or even Michael – had talked about his bringing her to the Newport house? Michael would, after all, have seen no special reason not to mention that to Peter in passing, but Jamie could imagine Peter and Carrie discussing it, remembered Peter's unpleasant innuendo when they'd met last January in F. A. O. Schwarz, could easily envisage them building something out of nothing.

Except that it had not been nothing. And supposing, just supposing, Carrie had been having him watched. He poured himself a stiff drink and shook himself out of it. Nothing had happened until he and Olivia had got back to the apartment. No one could have seen them here. There were no bugs in his home, no hidden cameras; this wasn't some sick, paranoid movie. This was normal, not especially happy, Jamie Arias, doing precisely what he had just been mentally accusing his ex-wife and brother of doing, building something out of nothing.

He took his drink over to the window, took a swallow and looked out over the harbour. There was, as Bob Jacobson had said, only one sensible course of action he could take. Carrie had thrown a nasty little jagged rock into the pool they both swam in. Now all Jamie could do was to stand on his dignity and wait for the ripples to disappear.

Olivia saw a lot of US trade magazines and papers in the course of her working life, wherever she was, and she always scanned *Advertising Life* for any mention of JAA or Jamie himself. Reading the reprinting of the Silas Gilbert interview in the second week of January had her out of her chair and about halfway to the ceiling, spitting with fury.

She called Jamie.

'What are you doing about this?' she asked.

'Apparently, there's nothing I can do.'

'What do you mean?' She was incredulous. 'You have to sue, Jamie.'

'I can't.'

Olivia listened as he gave her Bob Jacobson's outlook and told her that, on reflection, he had to agree with the attorney. He sounded so calm, so *resigned*, even when he told her about his confrontation with Carrie, that Olivia felt like flying across the Atlantic to shake him.

'We *have* to do something,' she said. 'I mean, she's still making threats, Jamie – there's no telling what lies she could tell any time she gets it into her head to start with you.'

'Then I'll have to deal with that if it happens,' Jamie said.

'But what about Annie?'

'What about her?' He was alarmed. 'You haven't told her about this?'

'Not yet.'

'You mustn't tell her, Olivia.'

'Why not? Annie's pretty strong these days, and she and Edward are in great shape.'

'Which is why I don't intend to rock the boat for them,' Jamie insisted. 'Or for you.'

'For God's sake, Jamie.' Olivia had never felt so exasperated with him. A realization struck her. 'Are you concerned Carrie might know about us, about what happened after Newport? Because if you are, you can stop worrying – I don't give a damn what Carrie knows or says, okay?'

There was a brief silence.

'I don't want you to tell Annie about any of this,' Jamie said at last.

'Don't you think she has a right to know?'

'She probably does,' Jamie acknowledged, 'but I honestly don't see there's anything to be gained by telling her, other than that Edward might go nuts and take Carrie on and for all that Edward's a smart guy, he doesn't know Carrie as well as I do.'

'I can't stand the idea of Carrie getting away with it,' Olivia said.

'How do you think I feel?' Jamie asked.

'I can imagine.'

'Can you, really?'

'Of course,' Olivia said, more gently.

'Promise you won't tell Annie,' he said again.

Olivia knew she wasn't going to change his mind.

'Okay,' she said, giving what she felt was a reasonable portrayal of someone giving in gracefully.

'Promise me, Olivia.'

Olivia crossed her fingers. 'I promise.'

And then she called Annie.

'I'm coming to see you,' she said.

'How lovely,' Annie said. 'When?'

'Tomorrow.'

'Couldn't you wait till the weekend?' Annie thought of her jam-packed diary, full of study plans, arrangements for the children and dinners with Edward.

'No,' Olivia said.

'Oh. Okay.'

'I have something you need to see,' Olivia offered by way of explanation. 'It's important.' She paused. 'But Annie, if you happen to talk to Jamie, don't tell him I called. If he finds out I'm coming to England, tell him you think I must be coming for a meeting with my father's Foundation. Whatever you do, don't tell him about this conversation.'

Annie was as outraged as Olivia had known she would be. It was the evening of the following day, and they were sitting at the kitchen table in Banbury Farm House, the clippings from *Advertising Life* and the *Boston Daily News* spread before them. Edward was in London, Sophie, William and Liza were all in bed, Marie-Louise was out with her boyfriend – a cattle farmer who wanted to marry her – the two cats, Leo and Boots, were curled up asleep by the Aga, and Bella, the golden retriever, was under the table, replete from the remains of the roast lamb she had just finished.

'I don't know what Edward's going to say,' Annie said.

'Do you have to tell him?'

'Oh, yes,' Annie said, definitely. 'I don't let myself keep secrets these days. Too much trouble.'

'You're right.' Olivia remembered the awful, painful days

and nights in Geneva with Gianni Dressler and his team, and then she thought about her own secret, her night with Jamie. She wished, sometimes, she had confided in Annie about that; it might have been a comfort. Too late now.

'At least we're not mentioned by name,' Annie said.

'I wouldn't care if I was.'

'I'm afraid I would,' Annie said. 'Very much.'

'Of course you would. It's different for you, obviously.'

Annie looked at the clippings again, at the photograph of Jamie with Carrie. 'She really is a dangerous bitch, isn't she?'

'She sure is.'

'Why did she do this now? Do you know?'

'Apparently she and Jamie had some kind of problem a month back, something to do with the agencies. He said he was expecting some kind of retaliation after that and he was only just starting to relax. He's mad as hell, of course – especially about you – but he believes there's nothing he can do about it because Carrie did once accuse him of having an affair with us both, and no one can prove this Gilbert character didn't overhear them.'

Annie's eyes were very wide and blue. 'But how could Carrie dream up such a thing? About *us*, for God's sake? I mean, forgetting the junkie reference, which is horrible enough—' Her cheeks were flushed with anger. It was one thing acknowledging her problems within the small therapy group she still regularly attended; this was quite another.

'I know,' Olivia said, gently. 'I know.'

'I mean, it's *unthinkable*,' Annie went on.

'Absolutely,' Olivia agreed.

'Jamie's more like our brother – Carrie knows that.'

'Carrie has a dirty mind.' Olivia smoothed down both

clippings on the table, using the flat palms of her hands. 'Carrie has to be stopped.'

Annie looked alarmed. 'You really think there may be more?'

'Whether there is or not, I have no intention of letting her get away with this.' Olivia paused. 'You realize she's been using this accusation against Jamie all along, don't you? It has to be why he let her have the divorce all her own way.'

'Did Jamie tell you that?'

'Not exactly. He didn't have to. Once he let slip that this sleazebag, Gilbert, could have heard them talking about us, I knew that Carrie must have been holding this over him.'

'But there's nothing to *hold*,' Annie said, anguished.

'You know Jamie,' Olivia said. 'He'd never take that kind of risk with us. He'd have been afraid of creating problems for you with Edward, for one thing.'

'You're right. Of course you're right.'

More appalled than ever, Annie stood up and walked over to the sink. She ran the cold tap for a moment, turned it on so full that the spray hit a spoon and spurted up at her. She turned it off again, forgetting why she'd run the water in the first place.

'My God, Livvy,' she said. 'What are we going to do about this?'

'Good,' Olivia said, with some satisfaction.

'Good what?' Annie came back to the table and sat down again. 'What's good? I don't see anything good.'

'You agree we have to do something.'

'Yes, of course.' Annie was growing angrier by the minute and found, to her surprise, that the anger felt stimulating in a strong, positive way. 'Yes, of course I agree we do. But what?'

Olivia smiled at her. 'As a matter of fact, I have had an idea.' She paused. 'I made notes on the flight over. It's going to take a lot of working out, and we're going to need a little help. But I do seem to have a plan.'

Annie smiled back. 'Surprise, surprise,' she said wryly. 'Go on then,' she added. 'Tell me.'

'Okay,' Olivia said. 'Here it is. We know certain things about Carrie, about what makes her run, don't we? We know that she's a selfish, narcissistic tyrant, that both success and her self-image are all-important to her, and that it follows that the best way to teach her a lesson would be to rip a good-size hole in that image.'

'Go on,' Annie said again, riveted.

'We know, too, that the lady is a whole lot more than just a giant ego. She's also mega-smart, with eyes and ears everywhere. Which is why we need to plan this little revenge plot very, very carefully.'

Annie frowned for the first time. 'I take it we're only planning on teaching Carrie a lesson. We're not going to do her any real harm.'

'Certainly not,' Olivia said crisply. 'But we are going to play dirty.' She gave Annie one of her cool, challenging looks. 'Wouldn't you say that Carrie deserves dirty?'

'Oh, yes,' Annie said, thinking about Jamie, kind, easy-going, brilliant Jamie. 'Oh, definitely yes.'

'It's insane, and I still don't see how we can possibly pull it off,' Annie said later.

'We can pull it off,' Olivia said. 'I know we can. It'll take a lot of work, and I'm going to need you with me a lot of the time, so we're going to have to talk to Edward – that is, of course, if you agree.'

'I don't know,' Annie said, and shook her head. 'I mean,

I can see that it really might be the perfect way to hit Carrie where it hurts. 'But I still don't quite understand why you've come up with something so – so extreme.'

'What's to understand?' Olivia asked bluntly. 'We both agreed she deserves dirty pool, didn't we? Don't we?'

'Definitely,' Annie said. 'That's not what I mean, Livvy.' She looked intently at her friend. 'I mean you've always been the most headstrong of us, the most daring, but you still lead a conventional, normal kind of a life – you work hard, you play hard – you love life.'

'Yes, I do,' Olivia agreed.

'So how come you're willing to drop everything and run real risks with someone as nasty as Carrie? I mean, for heaven's sake, Livvy, if she catches you out' – Annie paused – 'if she catches *us* out, she could make life hell.'

Olivia shrugged. 'I think it's worth the risk. For me, at least.'

'But why? That's what I don't entirely understand.' Annie was still perplexed. 'I mean, is there something I don't know about? Has Carrie done something to you that you haven't told me?'

'No, of course not,' Olivia said quickly. 'Don't you think what she's done to Jamie in the past, and what she's threatening to do to us – to you, mostly – is enough?'

'Yes. I think.' Annie was still unconvinced, still had the gnawing sense that Olivia was keeping something from her. 'You realize how much money a plan like this could swallow up?'

'I have more money than I can easily spend,' Olivia said steadily. 'I'd like to spend some of it on giving Carrie what she deserves.'

'Me, too,' Annie said. 'I guess it's not the money that bothers me.'

'So what does?'

Annie shook her head again. 'It's just so extreme.'

'You said that already.'

'I know.' Annie paused. 'So there's nothing else? Nothing I should know about?'

The Newport cliff flashed back into Olivia's mind and, following on after it, the way it always did, Jamie's bathroom, the two of them in the tub.

'Nothing,' she said, firmly, finally.

'Okay,' Annie said.

'Okay, what?'

'Okay, I'm in.'

'How come?' Olivia looked at her shrewdly. 'I mean, if you think it's so wild, and so risky, which I guess it is.'

'To help you help Jamie, of course,' Annie said. 'Our pact, partly. The fact that Carrie should be stopped in her tracks, and I agree that if we can pull it off, it would be a sensational way to stop her.' She smiled. 'A little because I'm so glad you think I'm strong enough again to join you in this.' She paused. 'Mostly because I can't conceive of deserting you – especially when I think you've flipped a little.'

'But are you sure?' Olivia asked. 'I don't want to force you into doing anything you don't want to, Annie.'

'I'm sure,' Annie said, decisively. 'But I'm still not quite sure about not telling Jamie. Doesn't he have a right to know?'

'No.' Olivia shook her head definitely. 'For one thing, knowing Jamie, he'd never agree to go along with it.' She looked down at the notes she'd made, and her green eyes sparkled at the thought of what was to come. 'And for another, this whole thing is only going to work – really work – if Jamie doesn't know a damned thing about it.'

Annie was silent for a while, and then she said: 'How much of this do we have to tell Edward?'

'I thought you didn't like keeping secrets these days.'

'I don't. And I can see that we have to give him some idea of what we're planning.'

'Just not quite all of it,' Olivia said.

Annie smiled ruefully. 'No. Not quite. I mean, Edward wouldn't dream of trying to tell me I couldn't do something I really wanted to do, but he might try to talk me out of it, so don't you think it would be best to keep the details to ourselves?'

'Absolutely best,' Olivia agreed. 'As the old saying goes, what he doesn't know won't hurt him.'

'So long as we don't get caught,' Annie said.

16

The first approach arrived forty-two days later, on Monday, February 26th, a letter in a grey envelope marked for Carrie's eyes only and brought directly into her office by her personal assistant. Carrie, on a call, indicated to Mark Reiss that he should leave the envelope on her blotter. It was another forty minutes before she opened it.

Dear Mrs Arias,

I have been asked by the president of a Swiss corporation renowned in its field to approach you directly with regard to a dramatic breakthrough on their part which they will shortly be ready to share with the citizens of the United States of America.

Though I am not empowered, at this early stage, to disclose to you any further details, I have been authorized to assure you that the new product concerned will bring new confidence and renewed mental health to a large sector of the American nation, and vast, unprecedented revenue to its creators and those concerned with its introduction and distribution.

261

You will, I am certain, understand that something of such potential enormity will require exquisite handling for its launch into the public domain. In other words, Mrs Arias, the perfect campaign. No other agencies are being approached at this point because of the necessity for maximum confidentiality, and your company has been selected for a number of reasons.

Beaumont-Arias is a compact agency, but substantial and experienced enough to handle such a campaign. It encompasses the necessary talent in all required areas. It has, to our knowledge, no pre-existing accounts that might throw up an undesirable conflict of interests; and it has a Chief Executive who has already passed certain essential security checks.

I shall be in touch with you again in forty-eight hours. If you are interested in learning more about the product concerned, I would ask you to indicate accordingly at that time.

Sincerely yours,
G. Schnabel

Carrie read the letter twice, glanced at the letterhead – G. Schnabel, AG, and a post office box number in Bern, no actual address, no telephone or fax numbers – and laid it to one side. She pressed a key on her intercom.

'Mark, how was that letter delivered? The one marked my eyes only?'

'By messenger, Mrs Arias.'

'Which firm?'

'FedEx, Mrs Arias.'

She let the key snap up and gave the letter one more look.

'Bullshit,' she said. Probably nothing, she decided, and

even if one of the pharmaceutical majors had come up with the new Prozac or whatever, she was almost certain that every other chief executive of every other agency in the country had been sent the same letter.

The second letter arrived while Carrie was in a meeting. This time a telephone number was given. If Mrs Arias was seriously interested in this unique opportunity, then Herr Schnabel would be available to speak to her between 9 a.m. and noon, Eastern Standard Time.

Carrie made the call to the Bern number at five minutes to twelve.

'Herr Schnabel, please.'

'Who is speaking, please?'

'Carrie Beaumont-Arias.' Carrie spoke reasonable French, but almost no German; there had seldom been a necessity to learn, since most Germans and Swiss had a fine command of English.

She was put through almost immediately.

'Mrs Arias, this is Gerhard Schnabel speaking. I'm so glad to hear from you.' His voice was pleasant, with the lilting quality of most Swiss-Germans.

'Your letters intrigued me,' Carrie said. 'A little cloak-and-dagger for my tastes, but I was prepared to make one call.'

'And I thank you for that,' Schnabel answered courteously.

'So what is this product?' Carrie looked at the new Cartier watch that Peter had given her for Christmas. She had a lunch meeting at half past. 'I must tell you I have an appointment in fifteen minutes, so I can only give you two.'

'Of course,' Schnabel said. 'Mrs Arias, if you believe that

your agency might be interested in preparing a presentation for my clients—'

'Who exactly are your clients, Herr Schnabel?'

'That I am not at liberty to tell you at this stage, Mrs Arias.'

'What are you at liberty to tell me?' Carrie was irritated.

'Very little, I'm afraid.'

'Then why ask me to call?' Her irritation magnified.

'To establish a point of contact, firstly,' Schnabel replied. 'And to explain to you that my clients are adamant that there can be no direct meetings or even telephone conversations with them, and no in-depth details about their product can be discussed unless you have first signed a legally binding document to guarantee their confidentiality.'

'This is absurd,' Carrie snapped. 'I'm a busy woman, and if your clients have done the research you claim they have, then they'll know my agency has handled a great many highly sensitive accounts.'

'Mrs Arias' – Schnabel sounded pacifying – 'I can assure you they realize that, but nevertheless they are insistent that any agency who wishes to know more must first sign such a document.'

'I thought Beaumont-Arias was the only agency they had approached.'

'Until today, certainly.' Schnabel paused. 'If you indicate your willingness to discuss such a document with your attorneys, then the situation will remain unchanged.'

Carrie drummed a perfect, newly-wrapped deep red fingernail on her desktop. 'I take it there would be no commitment implicit in signing such a document?'

'Of course not, Mrs Arias,' Schnabel assured her. 'It is simply a vehicle for moving forward any possible negotiations – once the document is signed, you will be furnished with all the information available.'

Carrie's mind hummed. Something told her that this might not, after all, turn out to be pure bullshit, and she had learned, through the years, to trust her instincts. *New confidence and renewed mental health to a large sector of the American nation.* Those words inclined her towards moving at least one step closer, since she could hardly have her people dream up the hottest campaign in history until she knew the whole story – and if, by any chance, this did turn out to be a dud or just another one of those sicko live-forever drugs, she could always turn them down flat or sue their asses.

'Mrs Arias?' Schnabel said softly.

'Get the papers to me. I'll have my attorneys check them over.'

'They'll be with you tomorrow, Mrs Arias,' Schnabel said.

Carrie cut the call.

In the one-room office on Schänzlistrasse in Bern that Olivia had rented for the next month complete with telephones and fax machine, Olivia and Annie and Felix Pfäniger stared at one another with a kind of awe.

'She bought it,' Olivia said. 'She really bought it.'

'My goodness, Felix,' Annie said, 'you were sensational.'

Pfäniger shrugged modestly. 'I'm an actor. If I can't manage a few lines in a simple telephone call, then I'm not much credit to my profession.'

Olivia stood up from her chair, came over to where he sat at the desk, and bent to hug him. 'Well, I'm with Annie – you were magnificent, Felix.' She kissed him on his gold-highlighted hair. 'Thank you, *Schätzli*.'

'You're welcome.' Pfäniger looked up at Olivia with undisguised adoration. They had met during her time in Geneva when her friend Diana Brünli had introduced them at a mutual friend's party, and he had fallen head over heels in love with her. They had gone out to dinner a few times, and Olivia had gone to Zurich where Pfäniger was based, to see him perform at the Schauspielhaus, but Felix's lust for her had, to his great chagrin, been unrequited. Still, they had kept in touch, for Olivia always tried to maintain contact with the men she dated and liked, and since Olivia made a point of dating only men whom she did like, she had, over the years, assembled many good friends in many places.

'You do realize that this is just the beginning?' Olivia asked him. 'Now that Carrie's taken the bait.'

'If she signs the papers,' Annie pointed out.

'She'll sign.' Olivia was buoyant with confidence. 'Even you thought they looked terrific, and you're the biggest worry-wart here.'

'What looks terrific to me,' Annie said, 'may not look so convincing to Carrie or her attorneys.'

'Julius thinks they'll pass muster,' Olivia said. She'd had another good friend, Julius Staheli, an ace corporate lawyer resident in Lausanne, draw up the confidentiality document.

Annie looked at her watch. It was a quarter past five. If she'd been home in Stone Bridge, she would have been giving afternoon tea to the children and helping Marie-Louise think ahead to dinner. 'Shouldn't we call FedEx, Livvy? Confirm dispatch?'

'Right away,' Olivia agreed. 'And don't let me forget to turn on the answering machine, just in case Carrie gets it into her head to call back.'

*   *   *

Olivia thought she had it pretty much worked out, as far as it could be at this early stage. She'd talked Maria di Benetto, another freelance translator in Strasbourg, into taking over her engagements for the next few weeks, and had managed to assemble a considerable team of expert friends to join in what she had persuaded them all was a harmless, but hopefully effective exercise in late-twentieth-century monster-slaying. Annie, impressed as hell by Olivia's array of friends and ex-lovers, all ready to play their specialist roles, called them 'Segal's Standbys' and knew that, though she was still apprehensive about what might happen if and when Carrie found out what they were doing, she had never, in her entire life, had more fun.

Thirty-six hours after Carrie signed the confidentiality agreement in the offices of Herbert, Morgan and Bendell, her attorneys, Gerhard Schnabel, aka Felix Pfäniger, arranged for her to be flown First-Class to Zurich.

'Do we have to waste all that money on First-Class?' Annie had asked Olivia. 'Surely Business would be good enough?'

'Carrie Beaumont Arias never flies any class other than First if it's available,' Olivia answered firmly. 'Try downgrading her, and we might easily lose her. Besides, I'd say it's money well spent.'

'I just hate the idea of giving her pleasure.' Annie sighed.

'Just think of it as a means to an end, Annie,' Olivia reminded her. 'A triumphant end.'

A black stretch Mercedes picked Carrie up at Kloten and drove her directly to the Bellevue Palace in Bern, where a friend of Felix Pfäniger, a member of the Stadtheater, was waiting with Felix to play her role in one of the handsome

Louis XV-style suites. Less than three hours later, Carrie was on her way back to Zurich, more galvanized than she had been for many years.

'Why are we meeting here?' Carrie had asked Gerhard Schnabel and Ruth Müller, an elegant, conservatively dressed woman in her mid-thirties, after Müller had introduced herself as a director of Lumitechnik AG, manufacturers of lasers.

'Partly for your convenience,' Müller answered.

'But mostly because of security, Mrs Arias,' Schnabel added. 'Lumitechnik is a subsidiary of a company with a factory near St Gallen, but since some of their laser applications are for the weapons industry, the factory's address is unlisted and, of course, off-limits to visitors.'

'Once the product has been launched,' Müller went on, 'and the full manufacturing process is under way, we will be glad to make arrangements for you to go to the factory.'

'More secrecy,' Carrie said, new irritation compounded by weariness.

'Perhaps, Mrs Arias,' Schnabel suggested, 'you might like to take some lunch with us. There is an excellent grill room here in the hotel—'

'Just coffee, please,' Carrie said, crisply. 'And some facts, if you don't mind.' She paused. 'I take it this product is not a weapon.'

'Certainly not,' Ruth Müller said. 'Quite the opposite, as you will see.'

Carrie settled back in an armchair rather too comfortable for her liking. She preferred a certain, mild level of discomfort during important business meetings. Too much comfort could render one too relaxed, could dull one's critical powers. She had no great objection to having come thus far; First-Class Swissair, and a night to look forward to at the Baur-au-Lac in Zurich, the hotel of her personal choice, was no great penance. Carrie thought she deserved a vacation, had not taken one in some years, and had no intention of doing so, however much Peter tried to persuade her. By the time she got back to Boston and to the office, she would have been away for at least forty-eight hours – to Carrie that *was* a vacation. She had no objection to that, she reflected again, but any more delaying tactics by these people, and they would not see her for dust.

'Galvanized', she decided later that night, over filet mignon in her suite at the Baur-au-Lac, was the right word. Ruth Müller had done an excellent job of selling her the product merely by saying as little as possible and letting her judge the evidence for herself.

The product, as Carrie now knew, would – if it lived up to its promise – be a revelation in the practice of cosmetic surgery; a double-beamed laser developed for aesthetic applications by a Czechoslovakian scientist now working for Lumitechnik, with the power, precision and delicacy to remove wrinkles and to heal the underlying skin so rapidly that, depending on the extent of the surgery, a patient could be returned to everyday life within days of treatment with scars already at a stage of healing normally expected several weeks or even months after more conventional surgery.

'There are a number of laser processes under development,' Müller had explained to Carrie, 'which will – as I'm sure you will discover for yourself when you conduct your research – at first glance, seem to offer the same end result – a resurfacing of the skin with rapid healing. When you examine those processes more closely, however, you will notice that initial improvement is normally promised within a few weeks, and that total recovery will take anything up to three months.'

'But won't the lasers remove wrinkles by burning the skin?' Carrie was sceptical. 'I can't imagine that burned flesh could very well heal in any less time.'

'These lasers will resurface by vaporizing the water content of the surface skin, but so far as healing is concerned you are, of course, absolutely correct, Mrs Arias,' Müller had said. 'Which is precisely what has made Lumitechnik so uniquely placed to revolutionize this whole area of surgery.' She paused. 'Frankly, once the men and women who are willing to endure having their faces literally peeled to appear more youthful, learn about our laser, they will refuse to accept anything less.'

'And the other processes will not reach the public for some years,' Schnabel said with complacency.

'So what exactly is the invention?' Carrie persisted. 'What makes your laser so different from the others?'

'You may have heard,' Müller said, 'of lasers being used to repair retinal tears. They can quite effectively seal small tears, or holes, if you prefer.' She paused. 'What we have done is to combine two separate lasers: one the more conventional, which, in the most simple terms, will remove the wrinkle; the other, called a *Heilunglaser*, which will heal the wound simultaneously.'

'As if,' Carrie said, trying to focus on an image, 'a dentist were drilling and filling a cavity at the same time?'

'An almost perfect analogy,' Müller agreed. 'Removing the decay and drawing the healthy remains of the tooth together in one operation.'

Schnabel smiled at Carrie. 'Perhaps another application for the *Heilunglaser* in the future.'

'I'll expect royalties,' Carrie said.

'I imagine that patent has already been applied for,' Müller said quickly.

'I was joking,' Carrie said.

They took themselves so *seriously*, Carrie thought later. Lord knew she wasn't exactly famous for her humour, but Lumitechnik AG weren't exactly planning on using this thing the Czech scientist had handed them on a plate for brain surgery. On the other hand, they were a thousand per cent right when they said that with the right marketing approach, it would make billions and see off everything else in the same marketplace. This was not perceived as being a treatment available to the masses. This would be a costly retail product, a package of equipment that would be supplied, together with training for its use, on demand to practitioners; and those practitioners would only pay for the product if their patients or clients were clamouring for it.

The marketing and advertising campaign, Ruth Müller had told Carrie, needed to be masterminded by an advertising wizard, someone who understood the pitfalls of hyping something that many might see as exploitative and exclusive, and Carrie, the manufacturers felt, was that wizard. And although Müller had explained that – with licensed testing procedures now officially ended and legal technicalities prohibiting any further use of the *Heilunglaser* until full production was under way – it would not be possible for Carrie to see the laser in action for herself, she was satisfied by the proof that had been lain before her: a folder of evidence, before-and-after photographs of two middle-aged women, dated and certified by a notary public, and, most convincing and reassuring of all, a letter of approval from the American Food and Drug Administration.

*   *   *

That night, as Carrie was climbing into her comfortable bed in Zurich, Annie, sharing a suite at the equally, perhaps even more comfortable, Schweizerhof in Bern, was getting an attack of the jitters.

'I wish you hadn't done that, Livvy.'

'Done what?' Olivia was sitting curled up on the sofa, wearing a bathrobe and eating Lindt *truffes de jour*, content in the knowledge that the actors at the Bellevue Palace had done their job to perfection.

'A lot of things. Registered a dummy corporation, for one.'

'We had to get Lumitechnik listed, Annie. You know Carrie would never do business without checking them out first.' It had cost a small fortune in legal and accountancy fees, and Olivia now owed favours in Bern, Geneva and Zurich, but she'd always known paying Carrie back would not be cheap.

'Mostly, I wish you hadn't faked that FDA letter.'

'Why? It was easy.' Gianni Dressler had got hold of a similar piece of FDA authentication, and Olivia had simply paid a small printing firm she had used in Geneva to use their state of the art equipment to duplicate the letterhead and have their own letter printed in the same style as the original.

'It was forgery.' Annie was pacing, running her right hand repeatedly through her blonde hair.

'Surely not.' Olivia went on calmly eating chocolate. 'Not exactly, anyway. I didn't forge anyone's signature.'

'Have you any idea what the jail sentence is for forgery these days?'

'No.' Olivia looked up. 'Have you?'

*   *   *

Back in Boston, Carrie's appetite began to grow, not only professionally for the marketing coup of a lifetime, but also on another, infinitely more private level. Carrie was still only in her mid-thirties, yet being the perfectionist she was, she had lately, despite all her strenuous, meticulous care and efforts, begun to notice some tell-tale flaws in her previously flawless skin, not noticeable, she was certain, to anyone else – not yet, at least. But they were there, those minute tracings and infinitesimal signs of slackening that promised betrayal, further down the line, of the immaculate beauty that had brought first James and then Peter Arias to their knees.

The temptation of being able to take no more than a handful of days away from the office and from her new husband, and then to return renewed and sublimely confident that all was smooth again, was almost too great to ignore. And if she played her hand well, Carrie realized that she would be uniquely placed to have the treatment before America knew about it, and no one else here would ever need to know, no one would ever suspect.

She called Ruth Müller at Lumitechnik and left an urgent message. Müller called back within the hour.

'What can I do for you, Mrs Arias?'

'I want a consultation.'

'Of course,' Müller said, steadily. 'How may I help you?'

'You don't understand,' Carrie said. 'I want a consultation with a view to having the treatment for myself.'

'For yourself?' Müller did not disguise her surprise. 'To what end?'

'To the same end as all your millions of clients once the product hits the headlines,' Carrie said. 'I have some early lines, nothing major, but this seems an ideal opportunity to kill two birds with one stone – I get rid of my wrinkles, and I get the proof I need that this *Heilunglaser* really works.'

'I thought you were satisfied with our evidence,' Müller said.

'So far as it went,' Carrie said.

Müller paused for thought. 'I'm afraid, Mrs Arias, that even if it were not legally impossible – as I explained to you previously – for the laser to be used again before production has officially begun, it would be both unethical and unwise for you to test it in this way.'

'On the contrary,' Carrie argued, 'it's not only ethical but sound business practice. When an agency's asked to dream up a campaign for, say, a new brand of cookie, everyone concerned is encouraged to munch away on as many of those cookies as they can eat.'

'This is not a cookie,' Müller said, gravely.

'No, it isn't,' Carrie agreed. 'For one thing, it's about twenty-five thousand dollars more expensive than a pack of cookies.' She paused. 'If I'm prepared to come back to Switzerland, and if I'm prepared to put my faith in your product, and if I'm prepared to pay anything for it – and I mean *anything* – then if you people refuse even to try to get over this licence difficulty, I can only translate that into a lack of conviction in your own product.'

Müller went silent for a long moment. 'I will, of course, have to put your proposal to my colleagues,' she said, at last, rather stiffly.

'You do that.' Carrie paused again. 'I presume, Frau Müller, that you came to me because you figured I'd do the best possible job for you, which means, for one thing, that you must have done your homework pretty carefully when it came to checking me out.'

'Naturally we did,' Müller said.

'In which case,' Carrie went on very coolly, 'you must have found out that when I want something I either get it or I kick a lot of ass. That's a rather crude Americanism, Frau Müller, for which I apologize, but I'm sure you get the point.'

'I believe I do.'

'So when you speak to your colleagues at Lumitechnik, I would ask you to warn them that if they refuse to grant me this consultation, not only will I feel unable to allow Beaumont-Arias to proceed with the campaign, but I will also see to it' – she sharpened her tone – 'without in any way infringing the terms of our agreement, that no other agency in the United States will touch you with a ten-foot pole.'

'Holy shit,' Olivia said, in the office on Schänzlistrasse.

There were now two more telephone lines installed in the room, one of them purporting to be Lumitechnik's main number, the other Ruth Müller's direct line, and Olivia had employed a second actress to play the double role of switchboard operator and Müller's secretary.

'We're finished,' Annie said. She had gone home to Edward and the children for a few days, but, as luck would have it, had returned to Bern just in time to listen in on Carrie's challenge.

'No, we're not,' Olivia said.

'Don't be crazy.' Annie had gone pale. 'We have to stop now.'

'No, we don't. There's no way we're going to stop now.'

The actress playing Ruth Müller, wearing blue jeans and a baggy pullover with patches at both elbows, shrugged her shoulders. 'The lady sounded as if she meant business,' she said.

'Carrie always means business,' Annie said. 'Livvy, we have to know when to stop. This is getting out of hand.'

'I agree with you.'

'Thank God.'

'I mean, I agree we have to know when to stop, but we don't have to stop yet. Carrie has no idea that this whole thing isn't kosher, so there isn't any danger.'

'Perhaps Olivia is right,' the actress said to Annie. 'I suppose the worst thing that might happen if you don't agree to her terms is that she pulls out.'

'Since we can't agree to her terms,' Annie pointed out, 'that part of it's obviously inevitable.'

'Who says we can't?'

Annie and the actress stared at Olivia.

'You've flipped,' Annie said flatly.

'Not necessarily,' Olivia said.

Even in her wildest dreams, Olivia had to admit it had not occurred to her that this highly intelligent, street-wise businesswoman would get so suckered in by their invention that she would demand treatment for herself.

'You know,' she said to Annie later over dinner at the Vieux Moulin, 'this is almost enough to make me feel sorry for her – but only almost.'

'It's certainly enough to make me feel incredibly guilty,' Annie said, playing with her soup.

'You're such a softie, Annie Thomas.'

'You're not so tough yourself,' Annie said.

'Oh yes I am,' Olivia said, and meant it. 'I am when someone hurts a person I love.' She looked intently at Annie. 'Carrie's been hurting Jamie for years, and getting away with it, and now she's started lashing out at us, too. And we both know she hasn't finished yet – the moment

Jamie tries to do the smallest thing she disagrees with, Carrie's going to use her ménage à trois invention, and then Jamie won't be the only one she hurts – you'll suffer too, and Edward, and probably the children.'

'I'm not sure she'd go that far.'

'Why wouldn't she?' There was a harsh note in Olivia's voice. 'She left Jamie for his own *brother*, Annie, and she left him without a trace of shame. What kind of a person does something like that?'

Annie said nothing.

'We can't just stop, you know,' Olivia said. 'If we did, and if Carrie found out that we were Lumitechnik before we'd got to the payback, then Jamie's life would be more hellish than before.'

'And we'd be in jail,' Annie said.

'She has to be taught a lesson,' Olivia went on. 'Okay, I have to agree that this looks like getting a little more complicated, and maybe a little riskier than I thought—'

'A little,' Annie said, ironically.

'But it's nothing we can't handle.'

'How, for God's sake?'

'Same way we handled the meeting at the Bellevue. With actors.'

'Jesus.' Annie, who still seldom drank, reached over for Olivia's glass and gulped down some burgundy.

'It's like you said,' Olivia continued. 'It's a question of knowing when to stop, and obviously there have to be limits on how much further we can take this thing.'

'You mean you're not going to take a laser to Carrie yourself?' Annie asked sarcastically.

'Not quite,' Olivia said thoughtfully.

'Not quite? Not *quite*?' Annie reached for Olivia's wine glass again.

'Get a grip,' Olivia said. 'I'm just trying to work this out in my mind, see how we can make sure we get to the perfect climax, the perfect payback.'

'Without going to jail?'

'Certainly.'

'I read somewhere that Swiss jails are terrible places.'

'We're not going to go to jail, Annie.'

'We will if Carrie finds out what we're up to.'

'No, we won't, Annie.'

'You're just making this up as you go along, aren't you, Livvy?'

Olivia looked across the table at Annie, saw that her panic was real.

'Do you want to go home, Annie? Do you want out of this?'

'No.·Yes. I don't know.'

'I'll understand if you do.'

'But you're going on with it anyway.'

'Yes.'

Annie sighed. 'Then I guess it looks like I'm as crazy as you.'

Olivia went into overdrive. The computer and printer they'd had brought to their suite at the Schweizerhof grew hotter, the payments to the phoney switchboard operator at the Schänzlistrasse office and to Federal Express grew larger as a compromise agreement was hammered out between Lumitechnik and Carrie. Olivia rejoiced; from all that Jamie had told them over the years, compromise and Carrie were about as incompatible as Jello and mustard, so that in itself was a small victory. Carrie was – Ruth Müller had persuaded her co-directors to agree – to be granted a consultation without delay, but licensing complexities aside,

Lumitechnik felt that both Carrie and the corporation might be laying themselves open to accusations of corruption if she had exclusive access to the *Heilunglaser* prior to its official launch.

'They will contract, however,' Schnabel told Carrie, 'that you will be the first American citizen to undergo the new treatment, and that this will be paid for by Lumitechnik at whichever location you elect.'

'I don't recall asking for a freebie,' Carrie said brusquely.

'Of course not, Mrs Arias,' Schnabel answered swiftly. 'This is merely a part of Lumitechnik's desire to take care of your concerns. I am authorized to tell you that, if convenient, you could plan your journey now, perhaps in order to prepare your colleagues for your brief absence. The treatment can be carried out anywhere in the United States, wherever you choose, and your confidentiality, of course, would be guaranteed.'

'But you're telling me I can't do this until after the launch.'

'I'm afraid that is so.'

'And if I say that's not good enough?'

'Then, with great regret,' Schnabel said, courteously, 'Lumitechnik will be compelled to take their business to another agency.'

Carrie called Müller direct one hour later.

'I can come back to Switzerland this weekend for the consultation,' she said. 'I trust that would be in order.'

'Perfectly,' Müller agreed. 'Let us know your flight requirements, and everything will be arranged.'

'First Swissair of the day into Zurich,' Carrie said, 'and I want to return to Boston the same day, so I'd prefer to fly from Kloten to Bern.'

'I see no problem with that,' Müller said, calmly. 'The airport is just five or six miles south of the city, and the consultation should take no more than about two hours.'

'I'll expect the tickets,' Carrie said.

'You are unbelievable,' Annie said to Olivia as they walked around the room in the handsome house in Neufeld – a suburb of Bern – that had been made ready for Carrie's consultation. The house belonged to a cousin of Diana Brünli who spent six months of each year in Canada and had agreed to its use in what Diana had called a 'good cause' for one day.

'Why?' Olivia asked absently, checking over the leather-topped desk and steel trolley to see that everything was present and correct.

'All this.' Annie shook her head. 'It all looks so – authentic.'

'I should hope it does.'

'I didn't think you'd pull it off.'

'We,' Olivia corrected her. 'And anyway, we haven't pulled it off yet.'

'Did you have to remind me?' Annie's temporary burst of near-confidence departed.

'Uh-huh.' Olivia went on checking.

'What about him?'

'Who?'

'The actor – Felix's new friend.'

'Professor Pfister, you mean.' Olivia looked up and smiled.

The 'professor' – at that time in the kitchen, perspiring and running his lines and moves for the twentieth time with Felix Pfäniger and the actress who was to play the part of his assistant – was the kind of middle-aged actor who could make a fair living out of playing lawyers, judges, surgeons and politicians. He had, Felix told Olivia, done more than a little television, and was, therefore, less likely to overplay his role as the quiet, confident plastic surgeon than some theatrical actors. He had also been coached for several hours by a surgeon in Geneva, an acquaintance of Gianni Dressler who had been misled into believing that the actor was preparing for a movie audition.

'He'll be fine,' Olivia said.

'But we can't be sure,' Annie said.

'We can't be sure of anything,' Olivia agreed. She finished checking. 'But he's been told to keep it simple. Gianni's friend says it's mostly down to basic logic.'

Annie's eye caught the clock on the mantelpiece over the fireplace.

'Two hours,' she said, starkly. 'She'll be here in two hours.'

'We'll be ready for her,' Olivia said.

'Felix is meant to be meeting her at the airport.'

'He will.'

'But he's here, in the kitchen.'

'Annie, it doesn't take two hours to get to the airport.'

'But he has to get there and back – and he has to change – and the professor has to change, too – and the assistant—'

'Annie,' Olivia said.

'Yes. What?'

'Stop.'

Carrie was impressed by Professor Pfister, by his keen-eyed, gentle-fingered competence and by the thoroughness of his questioning and examination.

'My first question must be,' Pfister had said almost as soon as she had sat down in his office, 'why do you feel you need cosmetic surgery?'

'I have some lines,' Carrie said. 'I know they're minimal, but they're the beginning of bigger things, and I figure if I can get a headstart—'

'You realize they won't be gone forever,' the professor pointed out. 'The *Heilunglaser* will remove your existing wrinkles, but cannot prevent further lines forming in the fullness of time. We are, of course, resurfacing your skin, but the new surface will still be your own human skin.'

'According to the people at Lumitechnik,' Carrie said, 'the effect should be good for a long time. I seem to recall a promise of years.'

'In all likelihood, that should be accurate. I'm merely reminding you that it is not permanent.' He shook his grey head. 'I must tell you, Mrs Arias, that I don't notice any significant wrinkling or even creasing on your face.' He smiled, a gentle, twinkling smile. 'You are, as I'm sure you realize, a very beautiful woman.'

'Who wants to stay that way.' Carrie smiled back at him.

'Very well. Let's take a close look.' He nodded to his assistant who had, until then, stayed in the corner. 'If you could help Mrs Arias to remove all her make-up, please.'

He agreed, after careful examination under a bright light through a magnifying glass, that the Lumitechnik laser would undoubtedly wipe away the tiny traces of ageing that so concerned her. Working methodically alongside his quiet, efficient assistant, he had taken two cold-wax impressions of each section of her face, and then he had taken photographs from a number of angles and in different lights, asking Carrie alternately to smile, to scowl, to speak, to laugh and just to sit in repose. And then he asked questions, more questions than she was able, later, to remember, some of which Carrie had anticipated – relating to her medical history, to general sensitivity, to allergies, to previous serious illnesses and problems with healing – and others relating to her personal life.

'Does your husband find you attractive?' Pfister asked, having established that Carrie was in her second marriage.

'He says he does.'

'Do you notice him looking at other women, perhaps younger than yourself?'

Carrie frowned. 'Is this relevant?'

'To your emotional state, yes.'

'What does my emotional state have to do with the treatment?'

'Insofar as a patient in distress can sometimes take longer to heal, it is relevant, Mrs Arias.' Pfister paused. 'Also, any physician of any integrity should be aware of his patient's needs and should also be certain that her expectations are reasonable.'

'I don't expect you to turn me into a teenager,' Carrie said briskly.

'Who would want to be a teenager again, Mrs Arias?'

And she laughed.

Back home, wholly committed, she set to work, confident that no one, not in Boston, not in New York, not even in California, was better equipped to find the perfect way to sell this product to the ugly, the exquisite and the tens of millions who fell someplace between those two poles and who could afford – barely, she supposed, in the majority of cases – to have it sold to them.

'We need your presentation in one month,' Ruth Müller had told her.

Carrie had considered all her alternatives. She could put her two top creative teams on the Swiss account, remove them for ten days from the work they were currently engaged in and force them to compete, to pit their wits against each other; she could choose just one team and pile all the pressure on them; or she could do what she had always been best at in the good old days, go it alone, at least with the early solo brainstorming.

'Why use two people to do the work of one?' she had once said to James, when he'd been singing the praises of Baum and Carmichael, his pets.

'Two heads,' he'd replied, simply, aggravatingly.

It was funny, in an irritating kind of way, that the only other person Carrie had a curious desire to work with on this account, to share the excitement with and watch it stimulate his remarkable mind, was her ex-husband – though of course James and JAA would hear about this account over Carrie's dead body. Her new husband's world was shipping, the vast iron sea-horses that rode the oceans and brought the Arias family their multi-millions, yet Carrie knew that Peter didn't see even that in the same way that she did. Peter saw only figures, endless reams of computerized numbers, and he saw very clearly what those numbers could buy. It was Michael Arias, Carrie realized, who had the passion for their family's industry which had wholly bypassed James – Peter was simply along for the ride. Carrie thought, sometimes, that maybe twice in a row she had picked the wrong Arias, thought that if she hadn't known that Michael was so irretrievably married to Louise, she might have made a play for him instead of Peter.

*　　*　　*

She decided to trust no one and shut herself into her office at Beaumont-Arias, had Mark Reiss divert all calls except those from Lumitechnik or Gerhard Schnabel to Mitzi Palgrave, her second-in-command, and began work. Part of her brief was to create a brand name under which to market the *Heilunglaser*, but that had hit Carrie after her first visit to Bern. *Light Years* was both perfect and available – all she needed now was the right campaign to sell it. For ten days, she worked slavishly and entirely alone, more consumed by her task than she had been by anything else in as long as she could remember. She delegated the essential research to Mitzi Palgrave but explained nothing and undertook the more detailed work on her own, took no one into her confidence, not even Peter – *least* of all Peter, given her plans for undergoing the laser surgery herself. She had a second private fax line installed in her office, saw that every letter, every memorandum to Lumitechnik was sealed in its envelope before it left her hand, and directed to Switzerland that each item for her continued to be marked strictly for her eyes only.

A kind of fever took her over. She slept little, ate only what she needed to keep going, saw only those people she had to see and attended the minimum of meetings. She worked late into every night, letting her mind roam free, dragging ideas from the ether, some of them wild and foolish and useless except for the fresh thoughts that sprouted in the wake of their rejection.

She was dealing with a scientific invention with a medical application, but in realistic terms Carrie knew that she was dealing with the ultimate beauty product. Yet unlike so many of those miracle pots of night cream and moisturizers, this treatment was for *real*, and despite the fact that it would cost big bucks – what didn't, for goodness sake? – it seemed downright criminal not to get the word through to the masses in the most appealing and effective way so that they could have their whack at going for it.

She couldn't book the ad spaces or billboards or TV prime time slots or editorial feature spaces in *American Health* or *The Physician* or *Woman's Journal* or any of the other trade or consumer magazines or newspapers, not, at least, until she'd made her pitch and won the account; and that was a bitch because they'd be hard-pressed to make it for what they'd alerted Carrie was their ideal launch date, June 1st. But they'd given her a month on top of the almost four weeks it had taken to get to that point, which indicated to Carrie that they believed in her and that she'd have to screw up pretty royally to make them hand it over to another agency.

Over at JAA on Boylston Street, Jamie had got wind that something was up with Carrie. People at Beaumont-Arias still talked to him, much to his ex-wife's chagrin, still let slip the odd morsel, always with a swift glance over their shoulder just in case, for everyone knew that Carrie was paranoid about Jamie and anything more than a passing nod in the street could be grounds for retaliation. But he heard snippets from time to time, and he knew right now that Carrie was locked into her office working on something big, and that Beaumont-Arias was, to all intents and purposes, grinding on almost without its leader. And Jamie had to admit he was curious to know just what could have got her so steamed up, though even if it meant that JAA might have missed out on something important, at least while Carrie was so involved it meant she had no time to make mischief in his life.

He saw her just once during that period, in the offices of Herbert, Morgan and Bendell, her attorneys, for the essential signing of some papers connected with their property settlement.

'I gather you're on to something big,' he said to her afterwards.

'Huge would be a better word,' she said. 'Infinitely more exciting than anything you ever brought in.'

'I'm glad,' Jamie said, 'for the company.'

'You still think of it as your company, don't you, James?'

'It still bears my name.'

'That is the one aspect of my marriage to Peter that I do regret,' Carrie said with a smile filled with malice. 'Still having to be named Arias.'

'I guess you can't have everything,' Jamie said wearily.

'I'm coming close though,' Carrie said.

Everyone Jamie knew seemed to be leading unusually crazed lives right now, come to think of it. He'd called Olivia several times in the past few weeks, but according to her office she was out of town, they didn't know where. He had wondered, with a brief, idiotic stab of jealousy, who she was with, and he'd called Annie, too, thinking they might be together, but she, too, was away, and Jamie missed them both, missed having them at the end of a telephone line to share stuff with, big or small.

Carrie had it worked out before the tenth day. It was simple and perhaps lacking in the uniqueness she had initially dreamed of bringing to the campaign, and yet she knew, in spite of that, that it was the perfect campaign, that it would make its point, reach its target – bottom line, the only line that mattered, it would sell the product wonderfully effectively.

Her artwork was rough and clumsy, the photographs she was using and the subjects contained in them could and would be vastly improved upon, but the concept was right. Three images. The first, a young girl's flawless, innocent face. The second, a teenager just into womanhood, skin still aglow with youth. The third, an older woman's silhouette, the face in shadow, no ageing process to be seen, left to the imagination. And the copy:

> ### You _can_ go back in time
>
> #### (and no one except your physician need ever know)
>
> ### LIGHT YEARS

She brought in Mitzi Palgrave and Joe Moritzio, her art director, swore them both to secrecy on pain of never finding work again at any agency in any city, sold them the concept, brand name and slogan and set them to work.

Two weeks later, three days inside the deadline, armed with a now perfectly formed campaign including the best logotype Moritzio had ever created for Beaumont-Arias or anyone else, Carrie was back in Switzerland, this time in a suite at the Dolder Grand Hotel in Zurich, making her presentation to Müller, Schnabel and a video camera.

'So that we may consult with my co-directors,' Müller told Carrie.

'When may I expect your decision?' Carrie asked.

'Within one week,' Müller said.

*   *   *

'I love it,' Annie said, next day, when Olivia ran the tape for her. 'God forgive me, but I think it's a fantastic campaign.'

'Enough to make anyone look forward to old age,' Olivia said.

'She sold me,' Felix Pfäniger said, wryly fingering the laugh-lines around his eyes. 'I only wish *Light Years* existed – I'd be its first customer.'

'After Carrie,' Olivia reminded him.

'Poor Carrie.' Annie sighed.

'Don't start, Annie,' Olivia said.

'What now?' Felix asked.

'Now you tell her that Lumitechnik loved her pitch and the campaign is hers,' Olivia said.

'And then?' Felix wanted to know. 'You let her create the whole campaign or what?'

'We can't go quite that far, unfortunately,' Olivia replied, 'not because of any compassion for Carrie, but because we have to put a lid on the costs. The price of the print and space alone would run into hundreds of thousands – we'd probably be talking millions for the whole package.'

'So how much further are we taking it?' Annie asked.

'One more stage,' Olivia answered. 'Just one more.'

Felix, back in his role as Schnabel, called Carrie within the week as promised.

'Congratulations, Mrs Arias.'

Carrie felt the old shiver of success-related pleasure run through her. 'Thank you, Herr Schnabel,' she said, staying cool. 'Beaumont-Arias looks forward to taking *Light Years* to the people.'

'The name is perfect,' Felix said. 'Ruth Müller told me she found it almost a masterstroke.'

'There's a great deal to be done,' Carrie said, moving right along.

'Starting,' Felix jumped in, 'with a second presentation, this time for the practitioners – the physicians and surgeons and clinic directors who will be ordering the equipment for their patients and clients after the launch to the public in June.'

'Are Lumitechnik sure that's a wise move?' Carrie was surprised. 'The whole concept has been directed *to* the public; these professionals are bombarded month after month by pharmaceutical and equipment companies promising them new miracles – surely there's a danger in pitching at such a cynical audience?'

'You sound as if you don't believe in *Light Years* yourself, Mrs Arias,' Felix said rather coolly.

'Obviously that's not true, Herr Schnabel,' Carrie countered, 'or else I'd hardly be planning to have the laser used on my own face.' She paused. 'I'm simply doing my job by pointing out the risks.'

'I understand perfectly,' Felix said, his tone more conciliatory. 'And I will, of course, pass your comments on to Lumitechnik. But I believe they are convinced that this approach will, in the worst case scenario, pinpoint any weaknesses in the campaign' – he waited a beat – 'and if, as seems to us far more likely, the opposite applies and they are enthusiastic, then the ordering, manufacturing and delivery processes will be facilitated.'

'So that *Light Years* could be available to patients on demand in their physicians' offices,' Carrie said, warming to the notion.

'Precisely.'

She prepared meticulously, keeping many arrangements in-house that would normally have been farmed out to professional conference organizers. Ruth Müller had informed her that the entire Lumitechnik team of experts would be in Boston for the presentation, scheduled for May 3rd, and that their responses to the medics' questions would, of course, need to be planned as a crucial part of the show. Schnabel would be taking care of Lumitechnik's travel arrangements, but so far as Müller was concerned, the rest of the event was in Carrie's hands.

She chose, of course, the Ritz-Carlton – the backdrop needed to be a class act – had Mitzi Palgrave put together an A+ guest list of relevant medical and surgical movers and shakers across the country, and issued invitations to them and to both mainstream and specialist journalists telling them that one of the most important breakthroughs in aesthetic surgery since the skin graft was about to be announced.

'Carrie told Felix it's going to be a mix of dignity and razzmatazz,' Olivia told Annie on the phone.

Annie had gone back to Stone Bridge, to Banbury Farm House and Edward and the children and a week or two of reflexology study and practice – a sampling of normality, as she'd put it, to keep her sane in the run-up to the grand finale. Annie dreaded the climax of what Olivia called payback time. She had nightmares about it, about Carrie having them arrested, about their lengthy, internationally publicized trial and their exile in some correctional institution. She thought, in her heart, that they probably deserved all the retribution that Carrie was going to sling at them, that even though Carrie was the bitch of the century, practical jokes were – had always been – reprehensible things, and that they had, quite simply, taken this one too far.

'It's a late-afternoon presentation,' Olivia was telling her now, 'with a champagne reception at five, and the presentation to be made at six, with the Lumitechnik team answering questions afterwards.'

'Except that they won't be there,' Annie said, her stomach lurching.

'No, they won't. Just you and me.'

'Quite,' Annie said.

'I've told you before, you don't need to come if you'd rather not.'

'You know I'd rather not,' Annie said, 'but I will be there.'

'How much have you told Edward?' Olivia asked curiously. Edward had gone on being an angel, raising the odd eyebrow but little more when Annie had disappeared for days on end.

'Not as much as I should have.'

'You're feeling horribly guilty, aren't you?' Olivia said sympathetically.

'Horribly,' Annie agreed. 'But I'll still be there.'

Olivia hated to admit it, but she, too, was suffering intermittent, acute pangs of shame, and she, too, was having the occasional nightmare. Not about going to jail, because she was just as confident as she had been all along that if they handled Carrie properly at the end of the affair, there was little risk of the law being brought in. She'd had one truly ghastly dream in which Carrie, presented with the truth, had taken a revolver and shot herself in the head, and another when she'd jumped through a window. But in the light of day, Olivia didn't think there was the remotest possibility that cold-hearted Carrie would ever do such a thing. If she was going to shoot anyone, it would be Olivia.

After all, that was more Carrie's style, and at least then, even if it was the last thing she did, Olivia would have to acknowledge that the woman had guts.

The trouble was, she knew Annie was right when she said they'd gone too far. She'd known it the instant Carrie had exposed her own vulnerability by asking for the treatment herself, and Olivia had seriously considered pulling out then, but she'd known that was impossible, had been aware that if you started playing games with someone as potentially dangerous as Carrie, you had to see it through to the bitter end.

Olivia had created this hoax telling herself that Carrie needed someone imaginative and bold to teach her the lesson she richly deserved, but she had a nasty feeling now that somewhere along the line she had come perilously close to being sadistic. She had always accepted, not altogether happily, that there was an unforgiving streak in her nature; she hoped now, with all her might, that she was not also cruel. The whole Lumitechnik creation had gone so much further than she had dreamed it would; it had become so complicated and so fascinating and so compellingly intricate that Olivia had almost begun to believe in it herself. And Carrie, poor Carrie – Olivia could hardly believe that she could think of her that way – had become utterly deluded, wholly and completely suckered in.

Jamie had once said to Olivia that she was the most honest person he had ever known. She wondered how he would feel about her if he knew what she had been doing, what she had been coercing Annie into helping her do.

She thought perhaps she'd rather not know.

17

Carrie had hoped that Peter would be with her that evening at the Ritz-Carlton, but he was in Athens with Michael on Arias Shipping business, had sent two dozen red roses to the suite she'd taken there for the night, with a card wishing her well, and so Carrie was all alone. She didn't particularly mind being alone, had always considered herself an entirely independent spirit, but she thought it might have been nice to have her husband in the wings while she took her bows. Though Peter was not really that type of husband; Peter didn't cater to her needs the way James had. James had certainly had his faults, and he too had been capable of great obstinacy, but he had unquestionably been a kind, generous and empathic partner, and if anyone in the world would have understood the mix of stage-fright and excitement she was experiencing as she made her last-minute preparations for the biggest presentation of her career, it was James.

Schnabel had reported to Mitzi Palgrave that Lumitechnik's team of four experts were flying in from London with Ruth Müller and were due to arrive in Boston shortly before four, and Carrie had ordered two limousines to meet them at Logan and bring them to the hotel.

When the car company contacted Beaumont-Arias a little after four-thirty to inform them that the party had not arrived, Mark Reiss called the Ritz-Carlton and found Carrie still in her suite.

'I've tried checking with Swissair to see if they missed the flight, Mrs Arias,' Reiss told her, 'but I'm having trouble getting any information out of them. Should I call Lumitechnik?'

'I'll do that myself,' Carrie said. 'But tell the drivers to stay at Logan and check every incoming European flight – they may have changed their minds about London and be flying in from Zurich or Geneva or any damned place, for all we know.'

She called Lumitechnik. The number rang out, unanswered. It was, of course, after nine-thirty their time, but Carrie had spoken to Ruth Müller late in the evening on other occasions and there had always been a night service manning the telephones. She called Schnabel's number. It was unobtainable.

The first prickle of foreboding crept up her spine. She called Mark Reiss at the office.

'Anything?'

'Not yet, Mrs Arias.'

Carrie looked at her watch. It was a quarter to five. The guests would be assembling downstairs and she needed to go down.

'Make sure those drivers stay at the airport, Mark, and if you have any news at all, tell the hotel operator to find me wherever I am.'

She put down the phone, took a few deep breaths. Time was still on her side, she told herself, there was more than an hour until the presentation was due to begin. But she'd designed the show around the Lumitechnik boffins, for Christ's sake, and though she was confident enough about her personal presentation of *Light Years*, there was no way on earth she was qualified to field the technical questions of almost two hundred physicians and surgeons.

'Don't panic,' she said aloud. 'No need to panic.'

Snatching up the receiver again, she redialled Lumitechnik, then, on impulse, tried their facsimile number. Like Schnabel's line, there was just that long, unmistakable whine telling her it was unobtainable. She punched the number for the hotel operator.

'Operator, I need you to run an urgent check for faults on two numbers in Switzerland – and I mean urgent. This is an emergency.'

'Of course, Mrs Arias.'

'Call me right back.'

It seemed an eternity till the operator came back.

'Apparently both those lines have been disconnected, Mrs Arias.'

'They can't have been,' Carrie said. 'They're major business lines. I was talking to them yesterday. There must be a mistake.'

'I don't believe so, ma'am,' the operator said. 'The Swiss supervisor was very definite. She said they'd been disconnected.'

'Was she speaking English?' Carrie knew she was clutching at straws. 'Maybe she told you there was a fault and you didn't understand her.'

'She spoke very good English, Mrs Arias.' The woman paused. 'Would you like me to have the lines checked again, ma'am?'

'Right away.'

Carrie slammed down the receiver and checked her watch again. Two minutes past five. She had no choice but to go downstairs and to pray that the Lumitechnik no-show and the telephone failure were just coincidence, and that maybe the limo drivers had located the experts and were, even now, hustling them into their cars.

Fifty ghastly minutes later, with no word from Lumitechnik, with corroboration from Mark Reiss that the Swiss corporation and G. Schnabel AG both appeared to have suddenly vanished from the face of the earth, and with two hundred physicians, surgeons and clinic directors draining their last drops of champagne and taking their seats for the main event, Carrie, having taken refuge back in her suite – ashen-faced and quivering with humiliation and fury – needed no further confirmation of the catastrophe that had befallen her.

It was her worst nightmare. She had been conned. She was the victim of a most elaborate, gold-plated hoax. She, Caroline Beaumont Arias – who prided herself on being one of the smartest, toughest, most impregnable women in the business – had been taken for a patsy, a sucker, an *imbecile*. Which, as it turned out, she clearly was.

She wanted, right there and then, to kill. She wanted to die.

But she did not know who to kill and she could not die, not just yet anyway, because there was an audience waiting and she had her image to preserve and she had to take care of that. And in almost any other crisis situation she could imagine, Carrie felt she might have been able to handle it herself, but this blow – this stunning betrayal –

was so shocking, so physically and emotionally *painful* for her that she knew she could not walk onto that podium and face all those people.

'You'll have to tell them,' she told Mitzi Palgrave on the house phone.

'Tell them what?' Palgrave sounded alarmed. 'Mrs Arias, what do I tell them?'

'Whatever you goddamned like, Mitzi.' Carrie found she could not speak rationally. 'Tell them Lumitechnik's plane got struck by lightning – tell them there's been an earthquake in Switzerland – tell them someone stole a laser and zapped the whole team of experts before they could get here. Tell them whatever the fuck you can think of.'

'Better keep it simple, I think,' Palgrave said gently, rising to the occasion, aware that for the moment, at least, her hard-ass boss was out of it. 'I'll just tell them they've been unavoidably detained.' She paused. 'I'll say it's just a temporary glitch, but that unfortunately it means we've had to postpone the presentation.'

'Fine.' Carrie was still shaking. 'Thank you, Mitzi.'

Palgrave hesitated. 'Are you okay, Mrs Arias? Can I do something else for you? Call someone?'

'Nothing. Just get rid of those people.'

She sat for a long, long time on the bathroom floor after she'd thrown up. She felt drained and exhausted, yet all the while her mind was racing, searching, seeking out her enemies. James was first up, but swiftly dismissed again – James would never, *could* never dream up anything like this, would not do such a thing to anyone, not even to her. And it wasn't as if she hadn't made a score of enemies on her path to success – who didn't when they were busy getting to the top of their chosen tree?

Whoever it was, Carrie thought bitterly as she rinsed her mouth and mechanically fixed her make-up, had to hate her one hell of a lot to want to put her through this. She looked into the mirror, looked into her angry, defeated eyes and shook her head violently. She had seldom anticipated more from a campaign, but now there would be no fanfares, no *Light Years* to hype from coast to coast. No campaign, no fee, no commission. No magical, mythical instant laser surgery to wipe away her own early wrinkles.

She went into the bedroom and lay down on the bed. There were no words to describe what a fool she'd been. She'd wasted a fortune in time and money, she'd neglected valuable clients – *real* clients, goddamnit – and worst of all, worse than all the rest of it rolled into one, if the truth ever got out, if she failed to find a way to effectively silence Palgrave and Reiss and Moritzio (she thanked God, silently, briefly, that she'd kept the build-up so quiet, that she'd at least been so selective about whom she'd taken into her confidence), she would be laughed out of Boston, out of the whole advertising arena. Out of everything that had ever mattered to her.

Carrie began to weep, great wounding tears of rage and shame and misery, just lay there on the big bed and bawled as she had not done since childhood.

Until she heard, penetrating through the sound of her own raw sobs, the sharp rapping on the outer door of the suite.

'Go away.'

The knocking went on.

'Go *away*.'

It became louder, more insistent. Carrie lay there for another moment, trying to ignore it, but still it went on and she knew it might be Palgrave or someone more important, and at the end of this ghastly fiasco she might still have some kind of image left to preserve.

'Just a minute,' she called and got to her feet, ran back into the bathroom, splashed a little cold water on her face, offered a swift, sharp word of thanks for waterproof mascara, and, taking a deep, steadying breath, went to open the door.

And learned the truth.

Olivia and Annie stood on the threshold of the suite.

'You.' Carrie almost spat the word.

'May we come in?' Olivia asked, softly.

For a long moment, Carrie stared at her, right into Olivia's unwavering green eyes, and then she transferred her gaze to Annie, saw the apprehension and – damn her to hell – the pity on her face.

'By all means,' she said.

They all walked into the sitting room.

'You'd better have a seat,' Carrie said.

Annie looked at her. 'Are you okay?'

'Why wouldn't I be?'

They sat, Annie rather gingerly on the edge of the sofa, Olivia in one of the armchairs, a black calfskin briefcase propped against her left leg. Olivia looked at Carrie's face, saw that she was ashen beneath her make-up and that she'd been weeping, and another brief but sharp pang of guilt stirred her uncomfortably.

'I rather think,' Carrie said, 'that I deserve a drink.'

Slowly, keeping her movements smooth and careful, she went to the bar and fixed herself a vodka and tonic, then sat down in the armchair closest to her and took a long swallow.

'Now then,' she said, 'can you give me one good reason why I should not call the police?'

'As a matter of fact' – Olivia pushed the guilt firmly away again – 'I rather think I can.'

Carrie looked at the briefcase. It was easy to imagine what it contained; if she had been running the scam, she would have done precisely the same as Segal. Her mind raced. Copies of her letters to Lumitechnik and Schnabel, of course, tapes of her phone calls, video recordings of her presentation, perhaps of her meetings, and certainly the photographs and wax impressions taken of her naked face at the 'consultation' with Professor Pfister. The memory of that cold discomfort flooded her with fresh hatred, and sharpened her wits.

'I take it,' she said to Olivia, keeping her eyes on the case for another moment, 'that this represents your graduation from hoaxer to blackmailer?'

'I wouldn't have put it quite like that,' Olivia said.

'Oh, I would,' Carrie said. She took another drink. 'What,' she asked, 'do you plan to do with the evidence of my naïveté?'

'That depends,' Olivia answered.

'Upon what?'

Annie, on the sofa, shifted nervously.

'You look very anxious, Annie, dear,' Carrie said. 'Perhaps you'd like a Valium?'

Some of Annie's shame melted away. 'No, thank you.'

'Maybe you're on something stronger these days?'

'Revenge,' Annie answered, startling herself. 'It's quite fulfilling.'

'Yes,' Carrie said. 'I imagine it is.'

Olivia wanted to get to the point. 'What we do with the evidence, as you call it,' she said, 'depends on you, Carrie. There are a number of ways we could use it, and all of them would have much the same end result.'

'To make me a laughing stock,' Carrie said harshly. 'I assume that was your goal.'

'Not necessarily. Not if you agree to our terms. In which case, Annie and I will be happy to bury it all. All you'll have to worry about then will be your share of the costs and inventing a plausible backdown.'

'My share?' Carrie's eyes darkened. 'Have you the slightest notion of what this evening alone has cost?'

'Probably not quite as much as Annie and I have spent,' Olivia said, good-naturedly. 'Setting up Lumitechnik, all that First-Class travel, the rooms at the Baur-au-Lac and the Dolder Grand. Such good taste, Carrie.' She smiled. 'Not that we'd have expected anything less of you.'

Carrie drained her drink, stood up, still trembling, and went back to the bar and fixed herself another. 'Who were all those people? Müller and Schnabel – the physician, his nurse?'

'Friends,' Olivia said.

'You have interesting friends,' Carrie commented and returned to her chair. 'You're very quiet,' she said to Annie. 'Perhaps you'd care to tell me about these terms of yours?'

'With pleasure.' A curious new calm was flooding Annie now; she was almost beginning to believe that Olivia might be right, that maybe they were going to walk out of the Ritz-Carlton without handcuffs. 'First,' she said, and took a deep, cleansing breath, 'a full retraction, together with an apology to Jamie for the libellous implications of Silas Gilbert's interview—'

'And not just one of those tiny pieces buried on page fifteen of the *Boston Daily News* or in the back of *Advertising Life*,' Olivia came in. 'It has to be substantial and clear in both publications.'

'Together,' Annie went on, warming up nicely, 'with a whole new business deal with Jamie – legally signed and sealed, obviously – allowing him to move all his old accounts to JAA without delay or penalty—'

'Unless, of course,' Olivia added, 'any of them want to stay with you.'

'How considerate of you,' Carrie commented.

'And,' Annie took back the reins, 'you agree to hand over to JAA fifty per cent of any profits that Beaumont-Arias has made from those clients and kept from Jamie since your split.'

Carrie sat for several moments, her face expressionless, watching them both.

'Is that it?' she asked finally.

'Not quite,' Olivia said.

'I thought not.'

'You undertake never to make another poisonous innuendo that might tarnish Annie's good name.'

'What about your name?' Carrie asked.

Olivia smiled again. 'You're welcome to try, Carrie.'

'What else?'

'Last, but most certainly not least,' Olivia said, 'you give your personal guarantee – prepared by our various attorneys and notarized – never to try to bring any action against us for this little charade.'

Carrie's eyes were ice cold now. 'Is that what you call it? Not fraud? Not forgery? Not blackmail?'

Annie's calm disappeared.

'I prefer charade,' Olivia said.

304

Carrie took a long swallow from her glass and then set it down on the table beside her. 'I never did enjoy party games,' she said.

Time passed. The three women sat, silent now, alone with their thoughts.

Carrie asked one more abrupt question. 'Was James involved with this?'

'Jamie doesn't know a thing about it,' Olivia answered.

'I thought not,' Carrie said. 'Not his style.'

They fell silent again. The telephone rang once, and Carrie moved swiftly to pick it up, spoke briefly and tersely and listened to Mitzi Palgrave's report that the proceedings had wound up good-humouredly enough, thanks mostly to the champagne that had preceded the non-event. Carrie asked Mitzi to instruct the switchboard to hold all calls unless otherwise directed and hung up.

'So,' Olivia said, at last. 'What's it to be, Carrie? Do you come after us, or do we lay the whole mess to rest?'

Carrie sat back in her armchair and looked at them both.

'I could almost – *almost* – respect you for your skill,' she said, 'if you hadn't made a fool of me.'

'No one has to know,' Annie said.

'Some people know already.'

'No, they don't,' Olivia said. 'They know that something's gone wrong, but they don't know what. Even the employees who've worked on the campaign don't ever have to know. You just tell them Lumitechnik's suffered a financial collapse and that you're going to sue. Tell them your lawyers are dealing with it and then get them back to work, hard and fast, as only you can, Carrie.'

Another minute ticked by.

'Are you a gambler by nature, Olivia?' Carrie asked.

'Perhaps.'

'Gambling with your own freedom and good name is one thing,' Carrie said. 'But surely you must have realized that Annie has far more to lose than you if I refuse to play the game your way.'

Annie sat very still. 'I took my own risks, Carrie.'

'You're quite a brave woman, Annie. I'm rather surprised by that.'

'Me, too,' Annie said.

'Olivia, of course, knew she was taking a well-calculated risk,' Carrie went on. 'She gambled on the assumption that by bringing a prosecution, I would lay myself open to public ridicule and that, therefore, I would simply cave in to your demands.'

'Was I wrong?' Olivia asked.

Annie held her breath.

Carrie lingered one more moment.

'Of course you were not wrong,' she said.

She saw them to the door.

'Is there room for negotiation on the precise wording of the apology?' she asked. 'I assume, for example, that Mr Gilbert's contrition will suffice.'

'I don't see why not,' Olivia said.

'So long as it looks sincere,' Annie added.

Carrie opened the door. 'James is a fortunate man,' she said.

'Thank you, Carrie,' Olivia said.

Annie hesitated. 'It was,' she said, softly, 'a wonderful campaign.'

A small, grudging, cold smile touched the corners of Carrie's mouth.

'It was an extraordinary product,' she said.

* * *

Silas Gilbert's retraction appeared in both publications in the same week that Jamie learned from Bob Jacobson of Carrie's offer to renegotiate the terms of their business agreement in his favour.

Two days later, he telephoned Olivia in Strasbourg.

'What did you do?'

'Do?' Olivia, in her office, gritted her teeth and waited.

'Don't bother pussyfooting around, Olivia. Carrie told me that you and Annie are responsible for her change of heart.'

'What change of heart?'

'Olivia, cut it out. There's no point – Carrie's told me.'

'What exactly has she told you?' Olivia picked her cordless phone off its base and began to spin her chair, as she often did when she was in good spirits. It was going to be all right, she could tell. At worst, Jamie was going to get on his high horse and say he didn't need help and that she oughtn't to have got involved and she *certainly* shouldn't have dragged Annie into it.

'She hasn't really told me anything,' Jamie said, 'except that if I want to know what's been going on, I should ask you.'

'You can ask,' Olivia said brightly. She spun the chair twice to the right.

'So I'm asking.'

'Doesn't mean I'm going to answer.' Now twice to the left.

'Do you want me to ask Annie?'

'You can try.' Olivia stopped spinning, feeling a little dizzy. She and Annie had come to an agreement that it really was best if Jamie never learned exactly what they had done.

'Olivia, this isn't fair and it isn't right. I didn't ask you to get involved.'

She grinned to herself. 'You know me.'

'And as for Annie – you promised you wouldn't tell her about the Gilbert interview.'

'I crossed my fingers, so my promise didn't count.'

'Olivia, it's not funny.'

'Tell me something, Jamie. Are things better or worse for you now than they were before?'

'Better, goddamnit, but that's not the point.'

'Maybe you should make it the point,' Olivia said, gently.

Jamie paused. 'Are you going to tell me how you did it or not?'

'Not,' Olivia said. 'Never. Nor will Annie. And Edward only knows we were up to something, no more than that.'

'Oh, Olivia,' Jamie said.

'Oh, Jamie, stop.' Some of the brightness went out of her. 'I admit I took a few risks that I probably shouldn't have – with other people too, not just myself, and I don't feel too good about that. But no one got really hurt, thank God – Carrie's pride took quite a tumble, and you may not believe this, but I came close to feeling bad about that, too.' She gripped the phone more tightly. 'But I'm not going to tell you any more than that, Jamie, and it did pay off in the end, so please, please don't spoil a happy ending by worrying too much about how we got to it.'

Jamie was silent for a long moment.

'Tell me just one more thing,' he said at last.

'If I can.'

'Why did you do it?'

'You know why,' Olivia said.

'Tell me anyway. Please, Olivia.'

It was Olivia's turn to be silent. A parade of thoughts and hopes and longings swung through her mind, all of them leading back to those hours in Newport and Boston. Perhaps, after all, Jamie had not forgotten, had not wiped it out. Perhaps he was waiting, hoping for her to say something now, to give him a sign.

No, she told herself. *Not now. Probably not ever*.

'Olivia?' Jamie's voice urged her on. 'Tell me why you did it.'

'You know why we did it,' Olivia said. 'You, me and Annie. Our pact.'

'Was that the only reason?'

She thought she heard a yearning in his voice, but she wasn't sure, could not be sure. 'Of course not,' she answered, softly. 'We both love you, Jamie.'

'Oh,' he said.

18

Olivia's Box

On November 6th, 1938, a young Jew from Hanover studying in Paris named Hirsch Grynszpan, enraged by news he had received concerning the inhumane treatment of his family by the Nazis, went to the German Embassy in Paris and shot an official named Ernst vom Rath.

Two days later, on November 8th, Georg Brauner came to our house for what was to be his final visit. Of the few paintings that still remained in the cellar, he chose just two: a Hodler and a Redon. On most previous occasions, Brauner had conducted what he still euphemistically termed 'business' in a manner so leisurely that I know it had driven my mother almost wild with the effort of having to suppress her outrage. He would go, with Papa, down into the cellars and make his selection; he would refuse every offer of help from me, claiming that only my father could be entrusted with the handling of the precious paintings. Then he would stand back and watch as Papa fetched and climbed a ladder and struggled to bring down the works from the racks in which they – together with the one hundred and thirty other paintings already stolen by Brauner – had previously been so meticulously and lovingly stored; and then he would observe as my father carefully wrapped the works and made them ready for transport.

On this occasion, however, Brauner was plainly in a great hurry, allowing me to assist my father, chivvying us down to the cellar, urging us repeatedly to move faster, to be certain not to damage the two paintings but to work more rapidly nonetheless. As my mother stood, fists clenched, waiting at the top of the cellar steps, listening to Brauner's commands, hearing our breathless efforts to comply, I think we all knew, without being told, that the end of the Georg Brauner episode was near. And though a part of us rejoiced at the prospect of never seeing him again, I think that the greater part was aware that our troubles had barely begun.

'A word before I leave,' Brauner said upstairs in the hall.

'Of course,' Emanuel said, still fighting to catch his breath. Hedi, anxious for his health, had wanted to snatch the Redon out of his arms as he had struggled up the cellar steps in front of Anton, who was carrying the Hodler, but Emanuel had been too proud, too obstinate – things were bad enough, bad enough, without allowing his wife to *schlepp* for a thief.

'In the salon, if you please,' Brauner told them.

Hedi, straight-backed, head held high, refusing to show her apprehension, led the way into the room in which Brauner had so often made an irritating point of taking a drink before leaving, his manner always so damnably cordial, as if he actually believed they might enjoy his presence in their home.

'A schnapps for you?' Emanuel asked wearily.

'No,' Brauner said, as Anton, thin and tall and strikingly like his mother, closed the door. 'No more schnapps.'

They waited. Brauner did not sit, as he always had,

perfectly relaxed, legs elegantly crossed, taking his time. His suit was as exquisitely tailored as ever, his shoes as finely made and highly polished, yet he was, indisputably, ill at ease.

'This is the last time I shall come to this house,' Brauner said. He spoke softly, as if he feared that someone outside the room might be listening to their conversation. 'But I leave you with some important news. Important, at least, for you.' He paused. 'You know, of course, about the shooting in Paris.'

'We do,' Emanuel said, his stomach tightening painfully.

'I have learned from certain of my contacts,' Brauner went on, still speaking quietly, 'that reprisals against Jews all over Germany are imminent.'

'Here, too, in Baden-Baden?' Anton asked quickly.

'Here, too.' Brauner regarded them with his sharp, dark eyes. 'I have managed to obtain assurances that, so long as you all remain here, inside your home, you and your family will be safe.'

There was a brief silence. Emanuel had become very pale.

'Where else could we go, Herr Brauner?' Hedi's question was wry. 'Since our travel documents have still to materialize.'

Brauner gave her a small, curt nod. 'Your papers, Frau Rothenburg, should very soon be with you.'

'Are you sure?' Anton asked.

'Unfortunately,' Hedi added, 'we've heard that many times before.'

'But the situation now is changed,' Brauner told her, 'because our business dealings have come to an end.'

'Have they?' Emanuel asked.

'Alas, yes,' Brauner said, 'since the cupboard, so to

313

speak, is almost bare.' He paused. 'It has been,' he added smoothly, 'I know, a disappointing period for you all, but when times are difficult we must all look after our own. I'm sure you agree.'

Neither Emanuel nor Hedi nor Anton spoke.

'The time has come,' Brauner went on, 'for me to fulfil my side of our bargain, and this I intend to do. You will not hear from me again, but your papers will come, and they will come soon.'

'That's very good news.' A little of Emanuel's tension left him.

'If it's true,' Anton said.

'Anton, please,' Emanuel said.

'I understand your son's scepticism,' Brauner said, 'but I assure you all that what I tell you is, to the best of my knowledge, the truth.'

'And the reprisals?' Emanuel asked, cautiously.

'Imminent, as I said.' Brauner moved closer to the door, preparing to leave. 'Do as I tell you, Herr Rothenburg. Stay here, with your family, in this house, until it's all over, and nothing will happen to you.' He paused. 'They may come, there may be some small trouble – a little damage, perhaps – but I'm promised it will be purely for show.'

'Can you guarantee that?' Hedi asked him.

'I can only tell you what I have been promised, Frau Rothenburg,' Brauner replied. 'I have no reason to doubt it.'

My mother did doubt it, with every fibre of her being. She told us, after Brauner had gone, that she did not believe that their visas and other necessary documents would materialize now any more than they had in the past; neither did she have any real faith in Brauner's assurances of safety. Papa argued with her: Brauner had seemed to him so frank. In stressing that the situation was different now because the cellars were almost empty, Brauner was admitting that he had blocked their departure so long as he had still needed their cooperation. Why should he not admit it, Mama asked ironically, since there was no action they could take against him? She, for one, could not believe in the word of a thief.

'What would you have me do?' my father asked her.

'There is nothing to be done,' she answered flatly. 'We must stay, as he told us, and we must wait, and then—'

'Then?' Papa asked.

'Then we'll learn the truth,' she said.

And I said nothing at all.

We waited all through the rest of that day and night, and on through the next, long day. It was Leo Landau's birthday, and I wanted to go next door to visit him, but Papa would not permit it. I felt restless and irritable. Lili became argumentative; Trude became tearful. Perhaps, Mama suggested gently to our father, we might all go to the Landaus' for a little while, but Papa stood firm. Brauner's instructions had been clear and, given no better alternative, we would all remain in the house. And if my mother's instincts warned her that if there was to be trouble of some kind in the area there might be greater wisdom in dividing the family, she clearly had neither the heart nor the will to argue the point with him.

I know now that as the night of November 9th – *Kristallnacht* – unfolded, Jewish neighbourhoods all across Germany were facing a wave of unprecedented wanton destruction and violence, but for our family it began quietly, with an uneasy calm, our house remaining, as George Brauner had promised, untouched.

Shortly before eleven, after Maria, our housekeeper, had gone to her own home for the night and with Lili and Trude already asleep in their rooms and Mama, too, getting ready for bed, I looked at my father.

'Shall we go to bed, Papa? Try to sleep?'

His smile was so strained, I can still see it now.

'We can try,' he said.

As we had done the previous evening, after Brauner's departure, we took the two Danes and made a last patrol together, checking the locks on every door, going from room to room ensuring that each window was properly closed, that each curtain was securely drawn.

Outside, to the front and sides of the house, all seemed silent, all seemed peaceful.

We, too, went to bed.

Emanuel dreamt that his father was beside him, standing close, his prayer shawl wrapped around his shoulders, a skull cap on his head, and he knew, even in his dream, that it was Yom Kippur, and the more devout amongst them were rocking back and forth, lost in their prayers, but his father was standing quite straight and he was looking down at Emanuel, his son, and his face was filled with pride and his eyes glowed.

'You can leave soon,' he said, very softly, so that no one else would hear. 'You and Hedi and the children, you can come to us now.'

'But we don't have our papers,' Emanuel said to his father.

And his father smiled down at him. 'You don't need papers,' he said, and he put his strong left arm around his son's shoulders. 'Your mother will be so happy to see you again, so happy.'

The cold awoke him. Against his right temple.

He opened his eyes. He was lying on his side and

Hedi was close beside him, her warmth pressing into him, her left arm around his shoulder. For one more infinitesimal instant he thought that the cold had been a part of the dream, and then he became aware that it was still there.

Cold steel.

Emanuel blinked, once. He heard the movement from behind him. And he knew that the steel was a gun.

He began to pray.

Please, dear Lord, don't let her wake.

The man said just two words.

'Die, Jew.'

Emanuel saw Hedi's eyelids flutter, felt her body stir. Quickly, he slid his right arm about her.

Please, God, Creator of the universe, save our children.

I heard nothing. Not any of the sounds that our dogs must have made before they were silenced. Nor the shots. Nor the spilling of the gasoline, or the rasp of the matches being lit.

Lili, Trude and I slept on, right through the murder of our parents, through the burning of our house around us. Gretel Landau, Leo's mother, woke just after one o'clock and went to her window, saw the light from the flames and roused her husband, Samuel, who threw on his dressing gown and ran downstairs and out of the house, feet bare; ran across the lawns and through the gate that linked their land with ours. His voice, as he screamed out our names, over and over again, was my awakening, tore me, choking from the smoke, first to my bedroom door, where the flames forced me back, and then to my window, where I watched, bewildered and terrified, as Landau found a ladder and put it up and helped me safely down.

Next morning, on November 10th, I have heard that all the Jewish men in Baden-Baden were marched through the streets

317

to the synagogue and ordered to read aloud extracts from *Mein Kampf*. Neither Samuel Landau nor I were amongst them, for we were already on our way to the recently opened concentration camp at Buchenwald.

I had seen the fire destroy the house, incinerating the bodies of my parents and my sisters, as well as the pitiful remnants of my father's once great art collection. I am certain there will have been no postmortems, no investigation.

Neither into the shootings, nor the fire.

Nor into the man known as Georg Brauner.

Two months have passed since they brought us here, and I know now that I am very ill. They separated me from Samuel Landau on our arrival, and I can only pray that he has fared better than me. I have eaten nothing at all for more than a week, and I am coughing blood. My lungs have been bad since the beginning – I think that the smoke must have damaged them, made it harder for me to fight.

I found this little notebook on my first afternoon in the camp. I stepped on it in a patch of muddy earth, and almost overlooked it. Paper is like gold dust here. I have written down our story as well as I could manage, and I keep the book carefully hidden. Before the end comes, I hope to pass it on to someone stronger than myself.

I would like someone outside this place to know the truth.

Otherwise, what hope is there?

19

For Olivia

Olivia was the only person either Annie or Jamie knew who liked moving house. Most people – normal people – agreed that moving was hell, not exactly up there, as some statistics claimed, with bereavement and divorce, but certainly something to be endured with gritted teeth and overdraft.

Olivia said that moving was fun. She said that every move she had made – excepting the leaving of her parents' house in 1976 – had seemed to her a joyous leap into unknown territory.

'It's all adventure,' she told Jamie and Annie when they visited her for the last time in Strasbourg in August 1994, as she was preparing to uproot herself again for a spell in Brussels. 'It's finding another set of walls and turning them into home – it's making new friends and working out where to buy great food and which restaurants to go to—'

'And which language to speak on the way to work,' Jamie said, scrubbing potatoes in Olivia's kitchen. They were all wearing T-shirts, jeans and aprons – they'd eaten out for the last six nights, so this evening Annie and Jamie had agreed to stay home, cook *pot au feu* and help Olivia with some of her packing.

'French and Flemish this time.' Olivia lifted the lid of her big casserole to inhale the aroma of beef, chicken, pork and herbs.

'Flemish is almost Dutch, isn't it?' Annie asked.

'Just about,' Olivia answered. 'And Brussels is a bilingual city – every street has a French and a Flemish name.' She spooned out some broth and held out the spoon to Jamie. 'Taste, please.'

Jamie tasted. 'Gorgeous. How soon can we eat?'

'When you've boiled those potatoes.'

'I'd hate it,' Annie said.

'What?' Olivia asked.

'Moving to another country.'

'You did it and survived,' Olivia pointed out.

'Not exactly easily,' Annie said.

'Would you do it again,' Olivia asked, 'if Edward wanted to?'

'I can't imagine Edward ever wanting to leave England,' Jamie said, lighting the gas under the pan of potatoes.

'Thank God,' Annie said.

'What about you, Jamie?' Olivia asked. 'Would you think of relocating again?'

'I might,' Jamie said. 'For a good enough reason.'

'A woman,' Annie said. 'You went to Boston for Carrie.'

'It wasn't exactly alien territory for me,' Jamie said, 'with my family home almost around the corner.'

'Funny,' Olivia said, sitting down at her table, 'but I've never seen the Newport house as your home at all.'

'But it is, in a way,' Jamie said.

'I know,' Olivia said, 'but it still doesn't feel like it to me.'

One of the things Olivia loved about moving house was the excuse it gave her to delve into what she called her family trunk – the vastest of the handsome, solid pieces of dark green leather luggage Arthur Segal had bought from Swaine Adeney & Briggs in Piccadilly soon after the family had moved to London, and into which Olivia had placed many of his and Emily's possessions when she'd closed down the house in Hampstead. Moving house was an appropriate time to rummage through old belongings and clear away some of the detritus, the accumulated nonsenses that she always seemed to hold on to for no good reason, like matchbooks and theatre programmes and Christmas store catalogues.

Every time she moved, Olivia told Jamie and Annie as they sat around her dining table and ate the *pot au feu*, she seemed to find something new in that old trunk. When she'd moved from New York to Geneva, she'd found an old dictaphone of Arthur's with a previously unnoticed tape still inside; Olivia still remembered the excitement of scrabbling around for the right battery to make the old machine work, and the pure joy, when it did still play back, of being able to hear her father's voice again, dictating to his secretary.

'And then, when I left Geneva, it happened again,' she said, pouring more wine for them all. 'I'd often seen this old camera of my mother's, but for some reason I still can't understand, it seems I'd never checked to see if there was film inside – maybe because Mom was always so busy working, I didn't really remember her taking pictures. But there was this film, and I was so upset because I thought it wouldn't develop—'

'Surely it didn't,' Jamie said, 'after so many years?'

'Oh, yes, it did,' Annie said. 'Livvy showed the pictures to me just after she moved here, didn't you?'

'Wonderful, happy pictures,' Olivia said. 'I'll show you later, Jamie – Mom and Dad away together somewhere – it looks like France, but it's all countryside and there were no signposts or other clues, so I could never be quite sure.'

'So what are we going to find this time?' Jamie asked.

Olivia shook her head. 'I'm going to assume there's nothing new left to find – that way I won't be too disappointed.' She stood up, started clearing dishes from the table. 'Not that I mind either way – it's fun just looking at the same old stuff again.'

They dragged the trunk together into the middle of the spare room floor, and began, and there were all the wonderful old familiar items: the report cards, the rolled-up diplomas, the bulky shortwave radio Olivia remembered Arthur tuning into late at night to listen to news reports from distant places; diaries, letters galore of gratitude to Arthur from international charities, photographs – endless piles of black and white and colour snapshots never stuck into albums – and her parents' love letters, tied up with ribbon by Olivia after she'd first found them back in 1976 and never, she'd promised silently, to be read by anyone else again.

'What's in here?' Annie asked.

Olivia looked at the old pigskin briefcase with the broken lock, and remembered, suddenly, sitting on the floor in her father's study in their house in Hampstead picking that lock with the blade of a small kitchen knife. And she remembered, too, what she had found in the case. A strange, starkly worded little note from Carlos Arias to Arthur, written shortly before their deaths. '*Shock and dismay*', that was it, Olivia recalled, seeing the note again in her memory, remembering that it had been handwritten and that it had jarred her, disconcerted her a little. She remembered too, now, that she had mentioned it to Annie and asked if she should show it to Jamie, but that Annie had thought it better she didn't, and so Olivia had put it back in the case.

'Livvy?' Annie was looking at her questioningly.

'What's up?' Jamie asked her.

Olivia took the case from Annie and opened it up.

'I just remembered something that was in here,' she said, looking for it.

It was there, folded up, as she had left it all those years before.

'What is it?' Annie asked.

Olivia unfolded it and read it again.

Dear Arthur,
   Deeply shocked and dismayed to learn that your suspicions are not, after all, unfounded.
   We must meet soon.
      Carlos Arias.

'I'd forgotten this,' she said to Jamie. 'I found it while I was clearing out the London house, and then I put it away and forgot about it.' She held it out to him. 'I didn't understand it then, and I told Annie about it and she thought it might upset you, so I put it away.'

Jamie read it, frowning, then shook his head. 'It doesn't mean anything to me. I wonder what it was about?'

Annie leaned across, read it and remembered. 'It could have been about anything,' she said. 'Something really trivial.'

'The words don't make it sound trivial to me,' Olivia said. 'They didn't to me then either, Jamie. I'm sorry, maybe I should have shown it to you at the time.'

'I can't see that it would have meant more to me then than it does now.' Jamie paused. 'And I think Annie was probably right – it might have upset me.'

'What surprised me most was that I didn't remember our fathers talking to each other that often,' Olivia said. 'I mean, there were the occasional charity affairs, and American School stuff, but I wasn't aware of much more than that, were you?'

'Not really.' Jamie thought for a moment. 'Maybe they were doing some business.'

'What kind of business?' Annie asked. 'Shipping and art don't seem to go hand in hand.'

He shrugged. 'Don't know.'

'Ask Michael,' Olivia suggested.

'What for?' Jamie asked.

'He might know if they were involved in any kind of deal.'

'More than eighteen years ago?' Jamie said.

'I think you should both leave it alone,' Annie said warmly.

'Why?' Olivia asked, surprised.

'Because you're not going to find anything out,' Annie answered. 'And because it seems a very private note. It sounded to me back then – and it still does – as if Jamie's dad was really upset about something.' She paused. 'And whatever it was, neither he nor your father probably got to do too much more about it. So what's the point in dwelling on it?'

'Curiosity,' Olivia said.

'You're way too big on curiosity, Livvy,' Annie told her.

'I know, I know, and it killed the cat,' Olivia said.

'*A man should live if only to satisfy his curiosity*. Yiddish proverb.' Jamie grinned.

'How come you're quoting Yiddish proverbs?' Annie wanted to know.

He shrugged. 'It just popped out.'

'New Jewish girlfriend?' Annie asked.

'Not this month,' Jamie said.

Olivia said nothing.

The day after Olivia's move that September into the Amigo – a luxurious hotel built in the fifties on the site of an old Brussels prison, which she had decided to make her base while she hunted for her new home and office – Jamie phoned from Boston to check on her.

'How're things?'

'The usual at this stage.' Olivia was sitting on the bedroom floor surrounded by suitcases. 'This is where I always discover that I've put the really important stuff that I need right away in the boxes that have gone into storage. So far, I have all my saucepans and no underwear.'

'Good thing it's summer,' Jamie said.

'Good excuse to go shopping, too.'

'Speaking of boxes,' Jamie said, 'I mentioned my father's note to Michael one day last week. It didn't mean any more to him than it did to us.'

'Did he know if they'd ever done any business?' Olivia asked.

'No, he didn't. He thought it sounded a little strange, too – he asked if you'd found any more correspondence. I said I assumed you hadn't.'

'I never came across any more,' Olivia said. 'But then I don't think I really looked.'

'That's what I thought.'

'I have a whole cabinet jammed with my parents' papers. I could take a look if you'd like me to.'

'I don't see the point,' Jamie said. 'Like Annie said, it's all so long ago.'

'Then I think I'll focus on buying underwear instead,' Olivia said. 'I'm dying to go shopping anyway.'

'Olivia,' Jamie said.

'Yes?'

'Stop talking about underwear.'

'What do you have against underwear, Jamie?'

'Nothing at all.'

'So why can't I talk about it?'

'Olivia,' Jamie said again.

'What?'

'Go shopping.'

It was extraordinary, Olivia reflected, after putting down the receiver, how even after so many years, just the merest, tiniest *scrap* of a hint that Jamie might, after all, remember – perhaps even sometimes think about – what had gone on between them that one single night in Boston, was enough to inflame her every nerve-ending. It was more than extraordinary, she decided, still sitting on the floor, it was far worse than that, it was both depressing and pitiful.

Unless, of course, Jamie really did remember. Unless, of course, he, too, still felt something more than friendship for her.

But if that was the case, that would mean they were both fools, outsized idiots for having done nothing about it. And, alas, neither of them was a fool.

'Only one thing to do,' Olivia said aloud, and got to her feet.

Like the man had said.
'Go shopping.'

She met Bernard Martens three weeks later. It was a dull, cool October afternoon when she strolled into Martens Antiques just off the rue des Sablons, partly to take a closer look at the treasures inside, partly to get out of the rain. Within half an hour, she had fallen in love with a Georgian silver tea kettle, and Bernard, the proprietor of the store, had fallen head over heels in love with her. He was fifty-seven years old and a widower with grown-up children and five grandchildren, living in solitary splendour in a great house outside the city near the Foret de Soignes with only his full complement of household staff to keep him company. Bernard was the oldest man Olivia had ever had a relationship with, but he was in such wonderful shape, was such an attractive man, such a great companion with his marvellous blend of intellect and earthy humour, that she could hardly imagine herself ever again being satisfied by a younger man.

Except, perhaps, Jamie. If Olivia was honest with herself, there was no longer any perhaps about it. She had not meant to, certainly hadn't *wanted* to, fall in love with her best male friend, and she knew that she'd done and said all the right – all the *sensible* things – after that night in Boston, about it having been pure friendship and nothing more. But the truth was that she had not really meant a word of what she'd said, had known that right away. Yet she was still sure it had been the right thing to say to Jamie, who'd only just begun to recover after being put through the wringer by Carrie.

'How is Carrie?' Olivia asked him from time to time, trying to be casual, wanting to find out if his ex was still keeping to her side of the bargain more than four years after she and Annie had brought her into line.

'I don't hear much from her,' Jamie usually answered, and Olivia said that was good, wasn't it? And then she would ask – also casually – about other women, and Jamie would mention the occasional name and sometimes tell her a little more but there was never anything serious going on. And Olivia – shame on her – would experience, in spite of herself, an instant of almost overpowering relief, and it was so wrong of her because Jamie deserved someone wonderful, someone loyal and generous who would respect him and be faithful. Someone, she supposed, a little like Annie. Nothing like her.

It was Bernard Martens who helped Olivia find her apartment in rue Charles Hanssens near the corner of rue Ernest Allard and almost a stone's throw from his own store. It was a rare find in the exclusive, artistic, entirely cobbled Sablon area: an exquisitely renovated, beautifully furnished home on the ground floor of a narrow old house belonging to a wealthy diamond merchant from Antwerp. The three apartments above had attractive small balconies, but Olivia's pride and joy was her tiny, private, white-walled backyard which she swiftly turned into a cobbled garden with big earthenware pots planted with flowers from the market in Grand Place and La Palmeraie in rue Ernest Allard.

'And I've found an office in the place du Grand Sablon,' she told Annie on the phone in the second week of November. 'I can hardly believe my luck – it's just one room, and it's really small, so I'll have to keep it tidy—'

'That's impossible,' Annie said.

'I know, I know' – Olivia, as Annie and Jamie both

knew, had inherited Arthur Segal's knack of untidying a room the moment she entered it – 'but in this case I'll just have to try.'

'So you can walk to work?'

'In minutes, Annie – and it's just so gorgeous around here – it really is the nicest part of the city by far.'

'And Bernard's store must be practically next door too, mustn't it?'

'Yes, it is, though he's not there that much.'

There was a smile in Annie's voice. 'He sounds such a nice man, Livvy.'

'Yes, he is,' Olivia said. 'But don't start reading too much into that – I've met a lot of nice men, as you know.'

'Are you happy, Olivia?' Bernard asked her one evening in December as they were finishing dinner at La Maison du Cygne, one of his favourite restaurants. 'Is life in Brussels enough for you?'

She looked at him in surprise, replete as she was with fine food and champagne and the pleasure of overlooking what really had to be, at night, one of the most enchantingly illuminated great squares of Europe. 'Can't you tell that I'm happy, Bernard? Brussels has been so good to me.'

'But is it enough?'

She understood then what it was he meant. 'For now or for always?' she asked.

'You tell me.'

'I seldom think about always,' Olivia said.

'Do you think you could try, just for once?'

Olivia regarded him for a moment. He was a quite wonderful looking man, with his perfectly groomed silvering hair and his merry, kind blue eyes and his firm, straight mouth. He was also extraordinarily good to her, so decent, and gentle and generous. He deserved honesty.

'I think,' she said, 'for now.' She paused. '*Ça va?*'

He gave a tiny shrug, but his smile, if a touch wistful, was all warmth.

'*Pas bien,*' he said, '*mais ça va.*'

He was a clever man, far too intuitive not to be aware that emotionally theirs was an uneven relationship; that although Olivia was immensely fond of him, she was not in love with him. And because he was also a fair-minded man, he had no wish to tie her to him any more tightly than she might be comfortable with. That, Martens knew, would be the swiftest way to lose Olivia Segal, and while he knew, just as surely, that the day would dawn when that would happen, he had every intention of postponing the evil moment for as long as possible.

Which was one of the reasons he had helped her to find her apartment. Martens would have infinitely preferred Olivia to come to live in his house, but even if it had not been much too early in their relationship, he was far too wise not to recognize her need for space and privacy and, most of all, independence. As it was, because she had a home in which she felt more comfortable and at ease than she had felt anywhere since her parents' house in London, and because Bernard Martens was perfectly willing to spoil her with love and affection, yet knew when to stand back and let her breathe, Olivia felt better able to respond to him, both physically and emotionally.

'Which is why,' she told Annie in another of their telephone chats, 'the time we spend together is just so great.'

'I must say,' Annie commented, 'I've seldom heard you sound quite so comfortable with any man.'

'Comfortable?' Olivia hated the sound of that. 'I don't think comfortable is the word at all.'

'Settled then,' Annie suggested.

'Hardly settled either. We're too busy, for one thing.'

'You've always been busy, Livvy,' Annie pointed out, 'always the most active of us. It just sounds different with Bernard – you do different things: all these concerts, the opera, the ballet, the gallery openings – those are settled, comfortable kinds of things, whether you like it or not.'

'Grown-up things, you mean.' Olivia was wry.

'Well, yes.' Annie paused. 'Is that such a bad thing?'

'For a thirty-something-year-old woman?'

'Well, yes,' Annie said again.

'I guess not,' Olivia said, but she was not entirely sure that she meant it.

Life in Brussels did suit her wonderfully well, at least for the time being. Being the restless spirit she was, Olivia did not truthfully imagine for a moment that she would be able to consider settling there for ever, but for now her daily life was pretty close to sublime. As there had been in Geneva and Strasbourg, there were a vast number of translation agencies in Brussels, but because Olivia's preference was to deal with artists, novelists and media people in general, and because she was relaxed about tailoring her fees to her clients' means – often working for several weeks at a heavily cut rate because she liked and respected one of these talented but tight-budgeted individuals – the Segal Translation Agency's books were generally filled with interesting bookings.

With Bernard, Olivia wandered further afield, and when she was in a shopping frame of mind, she visited the chic and seriously expensive boutiques on avenue Louise, but she seldom tired of the Sablon district. She loved to browse through the weekend market stalls in front of the church in Grand Sablon, and she liked wandering along the cobbled lanes near her home, delving into the less traditional of the antique shops and galleries. She delighted in buying delicacies at Confiserie Wittamer and then – on one of those sunny, energizing winter's days that she had always enjoyed – sitting on a bench to eat them near the goldfish pool in the lovely statued garden of the place du Petit Sablon, listening to the pealing bells of Notre-Dame du Sablon. She looked forward to lazing at tiny tables in one of the street cafés when spring and summer came, reading or watching the tourists go by, and in the meantime, on rainy days, she was content to sit inside the cafés and brasseries or at one of the long communal tables at Le Pain Quotidien, eating slices of their wonderful brown bread spread with brie and walnuts.

The year 1995 began auspiciously enough, with Olivia staying for three weeks in Gstaad in a marvellous chalet with Bernard and two other couples, all old friends of his and all entertaining and relaxing to be with; yet she felt almost relieved to be back in her own apartment after the trip because, she supposed, it had been just a little too comfortable, a little too much like being half of a permanent partnership. She bought a small blue Renault a week after their return to Brussels, partly so that she could drive herself when the fancy took her out into the Belgian countryside, but partly, if she was honest – with herself if not with Bernard – because it made her feel more independent, less hemmed in, when it came to staying at his house. She worked hard through February and March, interpreting for and generally helping out an Australian television crew on location in Brussels; and then in early April she went to England for Edward Thomas's fiftieth birthday celebrations, before accompanying Jamie back home to Boston, where they spent five lovely days together, sailing in the *Joie de Vivre* and just hanging out. Jamie wanted Olivia to stay in his apartment, but she preferred, these days, to stay close by at the Boston Harbor Hotel, had done so ever since that night in 1989, though that was so long ago now, and she was almost sure that while she had not and never would forget it, Jamie must have by now.

Bernard flew down to New York to meet her at the end of that trip, and they had a few days shopping and buying at antique auctions, and it was always quite a struggle persuading him not to spend a fortune on her. Olivia was happy enough to let him buy her the occasional gift – they both enjoyed surprising each other and neither was short of a few dollars – but she had to draw the line, otherwise Bernard might have gone wild at Harry Winston or Tiffany's, and that didn't seem right, somehow, given that Olivia had no more intention of moving in with him than she ever had.

They flew back to Brussels on April 22nd. Olivia, who had parked her car at Zaventem Airport, dropped Bernard off at his house and then drove back to rue Charles Hanssens alone.

The cool breeze brushed her face, stopping her in her tracks, as soon as she stepped inside the apartment. Slowly, fully alert, she bent to pick up her two suitcases from the doorstep and set them down on the parquet floor of the entrance hall. She listened for a moment for strange, alien sounds and then, hearing nothing, closed the front door.

'Hello?' she said, her voice low and tentative, not knowing what she would do if someone answered.

No one did.

The breeze was unmistakable. Somewhere, a window was open and Olivia knew she had closed and locked everything before the journey. She was many impractical things – untidy, impulsive, sometimes irresponsible – but when it came to securing her home before a trip abroad, even before going to work, she was pretty methodical.

'Shit,' she said, softly.

The right thing, she supposed – the smart thing – to do would be to go to a neighbour, but she and the people who lived to left and right of her had exchanged little more than a passing nod, usually when she was in a tearing hurry to get somewhere, and she knew that the two upper flats in her own house had not been leased.

Another puff of wind blew her short hair, coming through the narrow hall from the kitchen and garden room. The garden door, Olivia thought, with a chill.

She took a few paces forward. The door to the sitting room was ajar. Taking a deep breath, she opened it fully and stepped inside.

'Oh, shit,' she said again.

They had turned the whole room and its contents upside down. Lamps, tables and chairs lay fractured like so many fatal accident victims on the rug. Books, some of them with their spines broken, were strewn everywhere, as if they had been hurled around. Her lovely mid-Victorian mahogany writing table lay on its side, its drawers several feet away, their contents scattered around. The handsome mahogany dresser that had been included in the apartment's inventory had clearly been rifled, all its doors open and the ornaments that had stood on its exposed shelves smashed. Yet still,

Olivia supposed, standing looking at it, even at that awful, depressing, angering moment, it might have been worse – they might have taken an axe to it or urinated all over the place, and they had done neither.

'The whole place is such a mess,' she told Bernard three hours later on the telephone, while the police were still dusting for prints. 'We figure they must have done it about a week ago, because they got in through the garden door and the carpet close by is pretty wet, and apparently it rained really heavily around then and it's been dry ever since.'

'But you're all right?' He was anxious. 'I wish you'd called me straightaway.'

'There's nothing you could have done, Bernard. I'm fine,' she said. 'Furious, but resigned. I guess it's the price you pay for living in any city these days, especially if you're lucky enough to have a little garden like mine.'

'Maybe you should move to another place.'

'Like yours, I suppose?' Olivia smiled.

'Sounds a good idea to me,' Bernard said, lightly.

'I think, for the moment,' Olivia said, 'I'll get a stronger set of locks.'

'Ah well' – he took the rebuff in his stride – 'at least I can come round now to help you.'

'There's still not much you could do, Bernard. The police need me to compile lists of everything that's missing, and someone's going to call from the insurance company, and the glaziers are coming, and the locksmith, so I'm going to have my hands pretty full.'

'Just for company then,' Bernard said, 'if you refuse actual help.'

'The place is crawling with company, Bernard.' Olivia

paused. 'Tomorrow,' she said. 'Tomorrow I'll accept all the help you're willing to give me.'

'And tonight?'

'Tonight,' she answered ruefully, 'I expect I'll crash.'

'Have you an idea yet what they've taken?'

'The silver tea kettle, for one thing. Remember it?'

'It brought us together,' Bernard said warmly. 'I'm not likely to forget.'

'And my silver menorah.' She paused. 'And my mother's jade horse.'

'The Ming? I'm so sorry, Olivia. I know how much you loved that.'

For the first time since she'd discovered the break-in, Olivia felt angry, tears pricking at her eyes. 'She never cared much for possessions, you know, but she really loved that horse. I remember she used to touch it very lightly with her fingertips, and say it made her feel she was connecting with the past.'

'I can understand that kind of feeling.'

'I expect you can.'

He waited a moment. 'Don't you think you might be nervous alone tonight, *chérie*?'

'I don't think so, Bernard.' Olivia paused. 'But if I am, can I call you?'

'Any time. I mean it, any time at all. I'm always here for you, Olivia.'

'I know you are.'

Cleaning up seemed to take Olivia for ever. Every drawer of every wardrobe, desk and night table had been turned upside down by the thieves. The contents of the three personal filing cabinets in her study had been strewn over the floor. Her own briefcase and a handbag she had left behind before her trip to Britain and the United States had been tipped out, too – even the refrigerator had been ransacked. One of the police officers had told Olivia that the burglars had, more than likely, been searching for cash.

'In the refrigerator?' She raised an eyebrow.

'You would be surprised,' the policeman had told her, 'where some people keep their money.'

'Though in many cases,' his fellow officer had said, 'intruders simply get excitement from rampaging through their victims' homes.'

'I like a mess as much as the next person,' Olivia remarked drily, 'but I can't say it's ever turned me on.'

They had been selective, had taken mostly easily portable antiques like the tea kettle and recumbent jade horse, three lovely silvered bronze Art Deco dancers, a late-eighteenth-century French mantel clock and a pair of Flemish tapestry covered cushions; and they had taken, too, the solid silver Victorian frame that had housed Olivia's favourite picture of her parents, though the photograph itself was thankfully still there, just torn a little at one corner, Arthur and Emily standing, arms entwined, smiling out at her. And that seemed symbolic to Olivia, a reminder, if she needed one, that no one had been hurt and nothing truly irreplaceable had been lost, and so it was simply a case of gritting her teeth and riding out the aggravation.

Three days later, Olivia's office in place du Grand Sablon was broken into. These were, of course, thieves of a different bent, their target her computer, photocopier and fax machine, but once again the greatest source of irritation was the wreckage they left behind, as well as the chaos and inconvenience and the apologies to clients that Olivia had to make while items were replaced and lost work was redone. But still, Olivia said to Bernard at the end of another day's cleaning up, it was just an office, not the place in which you slept or ate breakfast or made love.

'It must be catching,' Jamie said on the phone from Boston a few days later. 'I've just had a break-in at the apartment, along with three of my neighbours.'

'Did they take much?' Olivia asked.

'The usual – TV, video recorder, hi-fi. Nothing I really care about – guess they didn't think much of my taste. Peter and Carrie had a break-in at the Beacon Hill house last month, and I gather they lost a whole lot more.'

'Who told you about it? Michael?'

'Carrie told me herself, actually.' There was a smile in Jamie's voice. 'I saw her at a party last week and she was quite civil. I mean, things have been pretty straight between us for a long time now, but last week I'd almost say she was hovering on the edge of warm.' He paused. 'Maybe it's true what they say about time and old wounds.'

'Maybe it's just because she has different wounds to rub salt in.'

Jamie had told Olivia a while back that Carrie's second Arias union was foundering, but that cousin Michael, his Catholic faith by now grievously offended, was pulling rank within the company and pretty much ordering Peter to fix his marriage or have him to reckon with.

'Is there any more news on that front?' Olivia asked.

'Not that I know of,' Jamie said.

'Are they still living together?'

'Some of the time.'

Olivia detected reluctance in his tone. 'Jamie, tell me you're not still carrying a torch for Carrie.'

Jamie laughed. 'Not even a match. Why do you ask that?'

'Because you manage to sound almost guilty for just discussing her problems, and I know it can't be because you feel bad for Peter.'

'I don't, not really. But just because my marriage didn't work out doesn't mean I don't want it to work out for them either.'

'God, Jamie,' Olivia said with feeling, 'if it were me, I'd be jumping up and down with the *justice* of it. They deserve to be miserable – they deserve each other.'

'I can't disagree with you there,' Jamie said readily. 'That's something, I guess.'

A fortnight later, on a Sunday afternoon, Olivia decided to stay home and try to restore some order. Untidiness was one thing, but the ugliness left by her intruders had been something else entirely, obliging her to set to cleaning up with unprecedented vigour; yet still, pressure of work during the last two weeks meant that the lovely apartment had still not fully recovered.

Filing. Lord, she hated filing more than anything, did just about *everything* before she got around to that – even cleaned her new cat's litter tray in preference. Bernard had given her little Cleo, her gorgeous, independent, free-spirited tortoiseshell kitten, a few days after the burglary.

'I'd prefer to give you a dog,' he'd said. 'A big one to make you feel safe, but I know it's not possible for you.'

'It wouldn't be fair,' she'd agreed, 'leaving it alone so much.'

'But little Cleopatra' – he had handed the little complaining creature over to her in its wicker basket – 'will occupy herself while you are out.'

Many men, Olivia knew, would have sulked after her rejection on the night of the break-in, but Bernard, instead, had managed to turn the aftermath of the burglary into a pleasure, for he did, of course, have a store full of gorgeous antiques as well as a wealth of marvellous contacts. And Olivia had loved the new excuse to spend hours on end in galleries and shops, replacing what she had lost – though nothing she or Bernard bought proved as much sheer fun as Cleo. The kitten had, as he had predicted, certainly learned to occupy herself during Olivia's absences; had studiously ignored the scratch post and basket that Bernard had bought for her and had swiftly taken to exercising her claws on the Persian rugs and armchairs, and to sleeping on Olivia's bed, preferably, when Olivia was not home, on her pillow.

'You're not helping, Cleo,' she told the kitten now as she came flying from the hall into the study, making a riotous dive into a pile of alphabetically sorted letters. 'You're not helping at all.'

The kitten took off again, and the papers flew.

Olivia groaned.

'Chocolate cake,' she said. 'I need chocolate cake.'

She had bought a handsome slice the previous afternoon at Wittamer, and now she settled herself comfortably on the sofa in the sitting room and prepared to enjoy it.

Within a minute of taking her first taste, Cleo bounced onto her lap.

'No way,' Olivia said.

The kitten stared at the cake.

'Cats don't eat cake,' Olivia told her.

Cleo went on staring, her black pupils huge.

They went halves, Olivia eating the cake part, Cleo taking the cream, purring loudly. They had just finished when the telephone rang. It was Bernard.

'I'm bored,' he said. 'Are you finished with your work yet?'

'I've hardly begun.'

'Come out to play,' Bernard said.

'I can't,' Olivia said. 'I'd love to, but I can't.'

'Tonight?'

'Maybe. If I've done enough.'

'Shall I come and help you?'

'I've already had more help than I can cope with,' Olivia told him, 'from your cat.'

'She's not my cat,' Bernard said.

'She is when she's bad,' Olivia said.

'Like children,' Bernard commented.

'I wouldn't know,' Olivia said, and put the phone down.

It rang again.

'How're you doing?' Jamie's voice asked.

'Trying to file papers and tidy up.'

'Oh, God.'

'You said it.'

'I'd say I wish I could be there to help you, but you'd know I was lying.'

'I would,' Olivia said.

'So you don't want to take time out to talk to me,' Jamie said.

'I'd love to,' Olivia said. She thought about the mess of filing that Cleo had made even worse. 'But I can't.'

'Call me when you're through,' Jamie said.

'If I ever get through.'

*　　*　　*

Olivia was back in the study, the door firmly closed against Cleo, re-stacking the papers on the floor, when she thought, for no particular reason, of Carlos Arias's note. It occurred to her suddenly that she couldn't recall noticing the old pigskin case either at the time of the break-in or since.

She went into the spare room and hunted through the wardrobes, and there it was, on the floor at the back of one, probably, she thought, where she'd left it. She took it out and opened it, leafed idly through the small wad of old papers still inside, but the note was not there.

It irked her. She was certain she'd put it back into the case right after she and Jamie and Annie had talked about it. And she had not, she was just as sure, taken it out since. She sat down on the spare bed and tried to remember if, perhaps, the case and its contents had been strewn around the place with the rest of her belongings – she'd cleared away so much, had done much of the work almost automatically. Which meant that Carlos's note could be in any number of places in the apartment.

Olivia knew it was of no real importance and that she ought to leave it, to return to the job she was supposed to be doing, but she'd always been like this when something bothered her, like a dog with a bone, especially when she had lost something.

She went back to the study, opened one of the filing cabinets she had been meaning to sort through, and looked under the section marked A–D. There was one letter from Carlos Arias's secretary in connection with a forthcoming event at the American School, but no note. She put the file back, closed the cabinet and went to her bedroom, where Cleo had gone to sleep on the bed. There was a chest at the foot of it, the kind of box in which most people stored blankets but in which Olivia kept her own personal store of memorabilia, including her great hoard of letters from Annie and Jamie.

She stared distractedly down into the chest.

'Why?' she asked Cleo. 'Why does it matter?'

The kitten went on sleeping.

Olivia considered calling Bernard, telling him to come over and take her away from all this, but the urge to find the note remained strong.

She began to search. She looked for a long, long time, regularly sidetracked by the correspondence with her two friends. She found one letter that Annie had written to her from England about a year before her confession to her drug dependency, another, much older, sent from San Francisco during the late autumn after the helicopter crash, and a third that had been written during a school vacation long before the accident. Annie had sounded so different in that early letter, not just because she'd been so much younger, but mostly, Olivia realized, because she'd still had safety and normality – she'd still had her parents – and reading between the lines of those and some of the other letters, it seemed clearer to Olivia than it ever had before how much more damage the tragedy had done to Annie Aldrich than to either Jamie or herself. Except, she suspected – idle again for a moment, watching Cleo who was now awake and lavishly washing on the bedspread – that Jamie might not have put up with Carrie and all that pain for so long if he had not lost his father so early. If Carlos had lived, Jamie would not have needed to go through life agonizing about whether or not he might be letting down his father. If Carlos had been there, they could have thrashed out their differences as they went along, the way most fathers and sons did.

She went on searching. The kitten came to the edge of the

bed, wiggled her behind intensely and rapidly before diving headlong into the chest, and for a time Olivia played with her, tossed envelopes into the air to watch her bat at them or try to catch them, and then she went on searching for a while longer, but she did not find the note.

'If it wasn't important,' Bernard said to her later over dinner, after Olivia had abandoned both the search and her attempts to tidy up, 'why are you so concerned to find it?'

'I'm not sure,' Olivia said.

Bernard waited for more. 'Some intuition, perhaps?' he asked. He set great store by women's intuition.

'Perhaps.' Olivia paused. 'That note always got to me, even when I first found it. Its tone was – disturbing, I guess. Or maybe it was just a symbol of so much unfinished business.' She stopped again. 'But I think what's bugging me now, more than anything, is that I can't seem to think of anything else that's gone missing that wasn't valuable.'

'But would you know?' Bernard asked. 'How could you tell?'

Olivia smiled at him. 'Are you referring to my untidiness?'

'I love your untidiness, Olivia,' he said. 'It's a part of you.'

'You're right, of course.' She went straight on, avoiding, as she always did, any allusion by Bernard to his love for her. 'There's no way I can be sure of what's missing or not, but what I do know is that every single item I have looked for – my bank books, old cheque stubs, my birth certificate, other old letters that I particularly remembered – you name them, I've found them.'

'But not this note.'

'No.' Olivia shook her head. 'And I know I should just

drop it, forget about it, but what's happening instead is that I'm back to where I was when I first found it nineteen years ago – I am disturbed by what Carlos wrote, and I'm still really curious to know what it was about.'

'Your father's foundation is based in London, isn't it?' Bernard asked, referring to the Arthur Segal Foundation, which owned and administered her father's art collection, as well as continuing to look after Arthur's favourite charities in the manner he had wished. 'Perhaps they have kept his personal correspondence on file? After all, he and Arias might have exchanged a number of letters.'

'I never thought of the Foundation,' Olivia said.

'It's a possibility, surely?'

Olivia nodded slowly. 'But isn't it a little over the top to go bothering people in London?'

'A little,' Bernard agreed.

'I should drop it, shouldn't I?'

'Perhaps,' Bernard said. 'Perhaps not.'

'You're a big help.'

'You don't need my help, Olivia.'

'I'll drop it,' she said.

'Whatever you think,' he said.

She waited until seven o'clock the next day to make the call. She had gone to bed the previous night, at her apartment, intending not to do this, meaning to forget the note, to bury the foolish, annoying niggle that had drawn her back, again and again, to wondering why that insignificant piece of paper had vanished when everything else seemed to be present and correct, and why it mattered to her. Olivia seldom lost anything. She mislaid things all the time because of her dreadful untidiness, but she rarely lost them for long because what she lacked in method she made up for in instinct and accuracy in memory. If, in a moment of absent-mindedness, for example, she had placed an invoice in her dressing-table drawer instead of on her desk, Olivia had only to command herself to think things through for a few moments, to retrace her steps or actions, and she would go to the dressing table. This, she realized, was one of the things bothering her about Carlos Arias's lost note. She knew that she had last seen it during Jamie's and Annie's last visit to Strasbourg; she knew that she had replaced it in the pigskin case; and she knew, just as certainly, that because the burglars' mess had offended her in an entirely different way to her own personal disorder, she had taken considerable care when she had tidied up after the break-in. She would, she was almost positive, have been conscious of finding that note in the wreckage, and she would, consequently, remember where she had put it if she had found it.

She had determined, nevertheless, before going to sleep, not to telephone the Arthur Segal Foundation. Olivia thought that perhaps she quite thrived on real drama, but the intuition to which Bernard had alluded smacked of melodrama, which she despised, and so she had decided not to indulge it in herself. On waking, however, Carlos's note had been the first thing to come into her mind, and drinking her first cup of coffee it had come again, and strolling over to the office it had drifted in and out, and then, sitting behind her desk, sorting out administrative tasks, it had gone away, quite satisfactorily, for two whole hours.

And then, there it was again.

She asked to speak to Jerry Rosenkrantz, a New Yorker and one of the Foundation's older directors, a man who had known Arthur personally and with whom Olivia had

had a few dealings in the past. Rosenkrantz was in Israel, his English secretary said, then asked if there was anything she could do to help. Only, Olivia said, if she could gain access to her father's old personal correspondence files.

'Goodness,' the secretary said.

'It's probably an impossible thing to ask, isn't it?' Olivia said.

'Well, no, not really – not ordinarily, anyhow,' the other woman answered. 'But we're still in such a frightful mess after the burglary.'

Olivia sat up straighter. The tiny hairs on the back of her neck prickled.

'You've had a burglary? At the Foundation?'

'Goodness, yes,' the secretary answered. 'It was a couple of weeks ago now, but I can't begin to tell you what a shambles they left us in – papers absolutely everywhere.'

'What did they steal?' Olivia asked.

'Office equipment, mostly – computers, you know the kind of thing.'

'I do,' Olivia said. 'The same thing happened to me just around the same time.'

'Then you'll understand – the mess, honestly. I can't imagine why they have to do all that, throw stuff all over the place, instead of just unplugging the computers and walking out with them.'

'They did exactly the same to me,' Olivia said sympathetically. 'The police say they do it for kicks.'

'Charming,' the secretary said. 'But that's why if you were going to ask me if I could find something in Mr Segal's old files, it really would be easier said than done.'

Olivia's neck prickled again. 'Did they wreck those too?'

'Oh, yes; goodness, yes.'

'Was anything taken from the files?'

'I wouldn't know,' the secretary answered. 'I don't suppose so, but then again, I don't suppose we'd be able to tell. No one would, apart from—'

'Apart from my father,' Olivia said.

'Well, yes. Quite. I'm sorry.'

Olivia replaced the receiver in its cradle. Her home, then her office, then Jamie's home too. And now the Foundation. The coincidences were becoming bizarre.

She picked up the telephone again and called Banbury Farm House, longing suddenly to speak to Annie, but she was out, according to Sally Breecher, the Thomases housekeeper, an amiable, attractive local woman who had taken them on when Marie-Louise had married her cattle farmer.

'Is everything all right?' Olivia asked Sally.

'Everything's fine, thank you,' Sally answered, solidly.

'No problems at all? I haven't talked to Annie for a bit.'

'Nothing,' Sally said, 'touch wood. Not since the burglary.'

Olivia's blood temperature dropped a few degrees.

'You've had burglars?'

'Afraid so,' Sally said. 'Awful mess, but not too much taken – nothing too sentimental, anyway – and no one hurt, which is all that matters, when all's said and done, isn't it?'

'Of course,' Olivia said.

'I'll tell Annie you've telephoned. I'm sure she'll phone you back later.'

'If she has time,' Olivia said.

She was glad, on reflection, that Annie had been out, for she might not have been able to conceal her reaction from

348

her and then she'd have had to explain what had been going on and she wasn't ready to do that. Annie was okay these days – better than okay – but all Olivia's instincts were warning her that something seriously weird and possibly sinister was going on, and Annie didn't need to know that, not yet, anyway. But what? *What?*

She worked on a script translation through the morning, ate a sandwich at her desk, then ploughed on, glad to be focusing her concentration, as she needed to, on ensuring that her translation was accurate in words, nuance and spirit. At seven, she walked home, fed Cleo, changed into one of her little black dresses and drove herself to place de Brouckère where she was needed to interpret at a lavish cocktail reception and dinner at the Metropole Hotel for a Texan film producer who spent much of the evening enthusing about her long silk stockinged legs instead of paying attention to her translations.

It was after one when she got home again. Her message light was flashing, showing three calls. Bernard, telling her she could ring back even if it was very late; Annie, sorry to have missed her and she'd call again tomorrow; and Jamie, saying nothing in particular but sending his love.

Olivia kicked off her high heels, unzipped her dress, poured herself a large glass of fresh squeezed orange juice and sank onto the couch in the living room. Cleo, snoozing in an armchair, twitched her ears but didn't otherwise acknowledge her homecoming.

'Hi, Cleo,' Olivia said. 'Don't bother getting up.'

She drank some juice and switched on the television, watched the headlines on Sky News and turned it off again.

She'd switched off the other thing for almost thirteen hours, but tired as she was, there was no way she was going to be able to drop into bed and sleep if she hadn't at least tried to confront her thoughts first.

She reassembled the facts. Not much. Five burglaries inside the space of a week or two. Her home, her office. Jamie's apartment. The Arthur Segal Foundation's offices. And Annie's house.

She remembered Jamie saying there'd been a rash of robberies in Boston, so it was crazy to discount the possibility that his break-in was mere coincidence. That they were *all* coincidences.

'But I don't really believe that, do I?' she asked Cleo, still out for the count, her soft kitten stomach moving rapidly with her swift kitten breathing. 'No, I don't.'

She drank the rest of her orange juice and rested the glass on her left, silk stockinged knee.

If this was not a coincidence, that meant that she and Jamie and Annie had all been targeted. But by whom? Carrie Arias came to mind first as the only common enemy Olivia had ever been aware they shared.

She shook her head. 'No way, Cleo.' No motive, not any more, and anyway, Jamie said Carrie's and Peter's house had been burglarized, too, as part of the Boston rash. Or were they targets, too, along with the three friends? That made no sense at all that she could think of, and besides, Jamie had said their robbery had happened a month before.

So where was the sense in thinking that Annie and Jamie and she were linked in this thing? Setting her glass down on the rug, Olivia stood up and walked restlessly over to the window, pulled one curtain a little way to the right and peeked through the curtains into the street.

If all three of them were somehow unwittingly involved in something – whatever the hell it might be – then the connection had either to be through their special friendship or, perhaps, through their parents. And what did their parents have in common? Not much really, aside from the fact that they had all been United States citizens who had gone to live in London and their kids had all gone to the American School. Nothing much else, except for a few school events and spin-off parties and maybe the odd business connection and a number of charitable events organized by Arthur. And a single, discomfitingly worded note from Carlo Arias, now vanished.

And, of course, their final, fatal helicopter ride.

Olivia let the curtain drop back as a sharp, almost jagged shiver passed through her.

'Don't be silly,' she said, out loud, briskly.

It was impossible. It had been an accident. Everyone had said so. There had been a full investigation; the pilot had been exonerated. Mechanical failure.

'Don't get crazy,' she said, and went to bed.

20

'What's wrong with you, Olivia?' Bernard asked a few evenings later as they dined on turbot and langoustines at L'Ecailler.

'Nothing's wrong with me.'

'You're not yourself.'

'I'm sorry.'

'I don't need an apology,' Bernard said gently. 'I would simply like to share your problem.'

'Who says I have a problem?'

'Your eyes. Your mouth. Your demeanour.'

Olivia smiled. 'What kind of a problem does my demeanour say I have?'

'Apparently a secret kind.'

'It's misleading you,' Olivia said lightheartedly.

'So you have no problem?'

'None,' she answered, firmly. 'My turbot's delicious, my companion's delightful, if a little paranoid about my demeanour.' She looked into Bernard's face, saw that his concern was real. 'I'm sorry,' she said again. 'I know I may have seemed a little preoccupied for the last few days, but actually I think I'm just a bit tired.'

'You're very seldom tired, Olivia,' Bernard commented.

Her chin went up. 'It can happen, even to me.'

'And that's all it is? Fatigue.'

'That's all.'

'Nothing to do with the note you lost.'

'No,' she said. 'Nothing to do with that. I've decided to forget that it ever existed.'

'So you didn't call your father's Foundation.'

'No,' Olivia said.

It troubled her long into that night. She had lied to Bernard for the first time, and she wasn't even quite certain why. Olivia prided herself on her honesty, had more often, through most of her life, been guilty of being too honest, too blunt. She could fib with the best of them, had, of course, created the most enormous lie when she'd invented the *Light Years* laser, but she thought she could still truthfully say that in general she abhorred dishonesty.

'So why,' she asked Cleo, who lay snugly on the duvet close to her feet, 'did I tell Bernard that I hadn't made that call? And why haven't I told him about all the other burglaries? Why am I shutting him out?'

Because if she couldn't talk to Jamie or Annie about it, came the answer, then she could hardly talk to an outsider.

Outsider. She gave a small shudder of shame, for she knew there had to be something badly wrong with their relationship if, after all these months and all that they'd shared, she was still thinking of her lover as an outsider.

'Which is probably why I'm sleeping here alone

354

with a cat,' she said, and added quickly: 'No offence meant.'

Unable to sleep two nights later, she called Jamie in Boston.

'What's up?' he asked.

'Why should anything be up?'

'Because it's four o'clock in the morning in Brussels.'

'I couldn't sleep.'

'You always sleep,' Jamie said.

'No, I don't.'

'Yes, you do, you've told me enough times.'

'Well, I can't sleep tonight,' Olivia said.

'And that's why you're calling me.'

'Do you mind?'

'Of course I don't mind.' Jamie paused. 'What's wrong?'

Olivia sat up in her bed and held the phone more tightly. 'I'm worried about something, Jamie.'

'What?' Anxiety sharpened his voice. 'What's the matter? Are you sick?'

'No, nothing like that.'

'So what is it?'

She told him about the five burglaries and his father's missing note.

'You didn't take it with you after Strasbourg, did you?' she asked him as an afterthought.

'No, I didn't.'

'I didn't think you did.'

'Anyway, you said you knew you'd put it away,' Jamie said.

'I did. I just thought maybe – I'm not infallible.' She paused. 'So what do you think? Am I overreacting, or what?'

'I'd say so.'

'You think it's all a great big coincidence,' Olivia said.

Jamie thought about it. 'What I think is that I'd take a bet that if you ran a survey of the homes in Annie's kind of neighbourhood, as well as your own, at least a third – maybe a fifth – of them would have been robbed in the past few months. It's normal to be burgled these days – heck, it's almost insulting to be left out.'

'Don't tell me it's normal for three best friends living in three different countries all to be burgled in the same couple of weeks.'

'No, that's not normal,' Jamie said. 'That's coincidence.'

'What about the note?'

'What *about* the note?'

'That's a coincidence too?' Olivia asked ironically.

'I can't see the slightest connection with the burglaries,' Jamie said. 'It's just a little piece of paper that's gone missing.'

'That's all.'

'I think so, yes.'

'Okay,' Olivia said.

'You're really rattled, aren't you?' Jamie was surprised. Olivia was hardly ever, almost never, rattled.

'Yes, I am.'

'Will it make you feel any easier if I ask Michael to check through my dad's personal files for a copy? I think they're all at the New York office.'

'Would Michael be willing to spare the time?'

'I don't imagine he'll do it himself.' Jamie paused. 'I guess it's reasonable to assume that if my father wrote to yours, there might be a copy on file.'

'It was handwritten,' Olivia said. 'He might not have made a copy.'

'Then there might still be something from your dad. It'd

be worth checking anyway, if it's going to help put your mind at rest.'

'I think it might.'

Michael Arias called Jamie back just over a week later.

'I had my secretary check the files herself.'

'And?'

'Nothing at all. She told me she looked through every conceivable section, but the only thing she found relating to Olivia's father were a few letters connected either with Segal's charities or your old school.'

'Nothing more personal?'

'Absolutely not.' Michael paused. 'Why's Olivia getting herself so steamed up about this, do you know?'

Jamie told him about the burglaries.

'So what do they have to do with your father's note?' Michael asked.

'Not a thing, so far as I'm concerned, but Olivia's got some kind of gut feeling about it.'

'I've never had the impression she was the fanciful type.'

'She isn't,' Jamie said.

'Maybe the break-in at her place freaked her out a little?'

'She's never been easily freaked out either,' Jamie said.

'Oh, well,' Michael said. 'Tell her from me I think she's working herself up over nothing.'

'Michael says he thinks you're working yourself up over nothing,' Jamie reported back to Olivia.

'And is that what you think, too?'

'I think,' Jamie said, 'that it's too unlike you to do something like that, for me to say I think it. If you follow me.'

'Not easily, but yes,' Olivia said.

'So that's that,' Jamie said.

'I guess.'

'But you're still not certain.'

'No.' She paused. 'I don't suppose you asked Michael if they'd had a break-in at Arias Shipping.'

'I did, as a matter of fact, and the answer is no. No burglaries at head office, or at Newport.' He waited a moment. 'So really that does have to be that, doesn't it?'

'I guess,' Olivia said again.

'Are you okay?' Jamie asked. 'Should I fly over, maybe spend some time with you?'

'I'd love nothing more,' Olivia answered. 'But not if it's because you think I'm flipping out.'

'I don't think that, Olivia.'

'Good,' she said. 'Then feel free to fly over any time.'

'I can't, not for a couple of weeks anyhow. Too much work.'

'That's great.'

'Yes.'

'How's Carrie's agency doing?'

'Doing fine.'

'No bad stuff happening between you?'

'Not for a long, long time.'

'That's good,' Olivia said.

'Are you sure you're okay?' Jamie asked.

'Peachy,' Olivia said.

There was one avenue left to explore. If there was any validity to the creeping paranoia – as much as she disliked it, there was no other word for it – that had begun to plague Olivia after the burglaries; if there was any truth to her uneasy theory that all their parents might be linked in the affair, then, having had Carlos Arias's old files checked, and having attempted to do the same at the Arthur Segal Foundation, it followed that she should pay Franklin Aldrich's archives the same attention.

The Aldriches hailed from California, but Franklin's still flourishing law firm had three offices: one in London, one in San Francisco and its head office in New York. Olivia made some calls and managed to locate Richard Tyson, one of Franklin's partners and the man who had helped Annie after the accident by removing her father's papers from their mews house to the London office.

She came directly to the point. She was aware, she told Tyson, that Franklin had, during their time in Britain, handled some aspects of her own father's legal work, but she was uncertain if he had ever taken care of Carlos Arias's affairs.

Remembering Arthur Segal quite well and knowing Olivia to be a close friend of Annie, Tyson was courteous, though brisk.

'I can tell you,' he said, 'with reasonable certainty, that Mr Arias was never a client of Mr Aldrich's, and that I personally can't recall any particular connection between the two gentlemen. But as to Mr Aldrich's private papers, they were moved, years ago, to the archives in our New York office.'

'I see,' Olivia said.

'I'm sure you won't need me to point out to you, Ms Segal, that such private papers are precisely that, private, and for family's eyes only.' Tyson paused. 'If Mr Aldrich's daughter needs access to her father's archives, that could, of course, be arranged.'

'I'll pass that on,' Olivia said, knowing that she would not do that.

She knew, too, when she ended the call, that that was that. There was no place left to look. Jamie and Michael were probably right. She had been working herself up over nothing. It was time to curb her too-vivid imagination, time to forget the note.

Coincidences, clearly, did happen.

One week later, on Friday, June 2nd, Bernard took Olivia to a concert at the Conservatoire Royal and then to Vincent for dinner. They walked together, as they had several times before, through the kitchens to their table, admired the old tiled murals, and then Olivia ordered T-bone steak and Bernard ordered fish; but when the food arrived, Olivia noticed that he was picking at his.

'Are you sick?' she enquired, concerned.

'No,' he answered. 'I'm well.'

'Then what's the matter?'

Bernard smiled.

'What's funny?'

'Our role reversal,' he said. 'For some weeks, it seemed I was always asking you to explain what was wrong.'

'Yes,' she said. 'I know. I'm sorry.'

Bernard laid down his knife and fork. 'I'm not hungry, I'm afraid.'

'But you're always hungry.' Olivia grew more anxious.

'Not when I'm upset.'

She said nothing, waited for him to go on.

'I'm going to take a trip,' he said. 'To the Far East.'

'When?'

'Soon. A week or two.'

'Sounds exciting.' Her own appetite a little diminished, Olivia cut another slice of steak, ate it and laid down her own knife and fork. 'Where exactly?'

'Tokyo, T'ai-pei, Hong Kong, perhaps Bangkok.'

Olivia's eyes brightened. 'That's wonderful – you never mentioned you were planning it. Will you be buying or selling or both?'

'Both, I imagine. But mostly looking, experiencing.' Bernard paused. 'I had hoped that when I made such a trip you might travel with me, share it with me.' He looked at her for a long moment, his blue eyes searching, almost piercing. 'I've hoped for other things, too, Olivia, as you know.'

'I do,' she said softly.

'I've tried very hard to stay inside the parameters you laid down for us,' Bernard went on. 'To play what you call our "relationship" your way.'

'I know you have.' Olivia knew now, thought she knew, what was coming, steeled herself for it.

'I thought I didn't mind too much, but I realize now that I was lying to myself.' Bernard drank a little of his Sancerre. 'I told myself how fortunate I was to have this young, beautiful, vibrant woman in my life; this woman who enriched me so, yet was so anxious never to crowd me, who was content to be my friend and my lover, without wishing for any more commitment.' He drank a little more. 'Whenever I found myself thinking of more, wishing that we were living together, longing for us to be married, I told myself to stop. No, Bernard, I told myself – you're a fool. Every man you know would leap at the chance to have such a woman, yet to keep his freedom.'

'But you didn't want your freedom,' Olivia said.

'No, I did not. I do not.' Bernard paused. 'But still, I think, I believe, I could have gone on that way, even with those differences between us. If you had just been willing to commit your heart a little further.'

'I care for you a great deal, Bernard.'

'I know you do,' he said. 'But not enough to share your troubles with me.'

'Oh,' Olivia said. She didn't know what else to say.

'You've lately been so distracted, Olivia, and I've never complained, or not too much—'

'You've been wonderful.'

'I have not been wonderful at all, but I longed for you – more than you can imagine – to come to me, to confide in me, to depend on me. To *use* me.'

'But there hasn't been anything to confide in you about,' Olivia tried to explain. 'Or nothing real anyway.'

'Real enough for you to be distracted,' Bernard said.

'Yes. That's true.'

'Real enough, I imagine, for you to confide in Jamie or Annie.'

Olivia felt her cheeks grow warm. 'I haven't talked to Annie about it.'

'But Jamie.'

'Briefly, yes.' She felt defensive. 'But he thought there was no problem, and that was the end of it.' She paused. 'There really was nothing for me *to* share with you, Bernard.'

'Olivia.' Bernard reached out across the table and took her hand lightly. 'You are an honest woman.'

'I hope so. On the whole.'

'Then be honest now, for both our sakes.'

'All right.'

'You are fond of me, I know that.' He went straight on, giving her no chance to speak. 'But I love you. And that, for me, means that I want – that I need – to share my life with you. My small doubts and anxieties as well as my bigger fears or troubles. *Tu comprends?*'

'Of course.'

'In order for us to go on, in whichever way we choose – you choose – you would need to feel the same way about that. About sharing.' He paused. 'Can you do that, Olivia?'

She waited a moment or two before answering.

'I don't know,' she said.

Bernard nodded. '*Voilà.*' He took his hand away and returned it to the stem of his wine glass. His eyes were deeply sad.

'What do you want to do?' Olivia asked, gently.

'What I think I must do,' he answered carefully, 'is to travel to the Far East alone. Don't you agree?'

'I suppose I do,' she said. 'With regret.'

'I believe that,' Bernard said.

'How long will you be gone?'

'A month, maybe a little longer. The business here is perfectly run without me – better, I think, sometimes.'

'And afterwards?' Olivia asked.

'Afterwards,' Bernard said, quietly, 'I will come home to Brussels, to my large, too empty house, to my business, to my friends. To my life.'

'Will you—?' Olivia took a sip of her red wine to moisten her lips. 'Will you be willing to count me amongst your friends, do you think?'

'After a time,' Bernard said. 'If you wish it.'

'I value your friendship, more than I can say.'

Bernard's smile was wan.

'You have a great many friends, Olivia.'

The weeks passed. Bernard left Brussels for Tokyo. Annie and Jamie came for a long weekend. Olivia caught a cold, which she passed on to several of a troupe of visiting dancers from Toronto for whom she had been interpreting. Cleo graduated from catnip-impregnated toy mice to the real thing, when a small grey mouse found its way from the cellar beneath the house into Olivia's apartment. At least Olivia assumed it had come from the cellar, which she had never seen. There was a door, solid, locked and keyless, in the wood-panelled hall which the real estate broker who had first shown the apartment to Olivia and Bernard had dismissed as of no relevance, since the disused cellar that lay beyond the door did not form part of the property Olivia was planning to lease.

'Good kitten,' Olivia, who did not care for mice, told Cleo as she crouched, purring loudly, over her prey. 'Excellent almost-cat.'

She got over her cold and launched herself into her next assignment, which was to help a Welsh crime novelist named Ian Jones with his researches in Brussels and Antwerp. Jones was middle-aged, craggy, lively, intelligent and amusing, but he drank too much Belgian beer and made no bones about his latest ambition, which was to get Olivia into bed. Olivia, who was well practised in the art of diplomatic rejection, spent almost as much time avoiding Jones's whisky kisses and smacking his wandering hands as she did translating old editions of *Le Soir* and helping him track down and comprehend the books he needed in FNAC and other book shops, and by the time he returned to Cardiff she was glad to see the back of him.

Olivia missed Bernard. That was, she missed his companionship, their conversations and intimate dinners; but asking herself if she felt bereft without him, she had to answer honestly that she did not. There was a gap in her life into which Bernard had slotted rather comfortably – she remembered Annie, some months ago, using that same word when describing their relationship, and she remembered thinking then that 'comfortable' was for armchairs or beds or big, old sloppy sweaters, not for relationships, certainly not for lovers – but it was a gap that would be, for her at least, all too easily refilled once Bernard returned from the Far East and became – she hoped – resigned to being no more than her friend. They would see each other once in a while, would attend the occasional gallery opening together, would have lunch, would value each other's friendship greatly, but feel no need for anything more profound.

July came, the city grew warm – Bernard, back home, made brief contact but alas nothing more – and with the summer weather came a slackening of Brussels' pace as some offices, restaurants and stores began to close for their summer vacation. Olivia, who had feared that by August, like Paris, the city might seem almost entirely dead, found, to her pleasure, that she enjoyed this slowing down, liked the softer, sleepier atmosphere. Her own business calendar was filling up for the autumn, and she brought home piles of brochures and maps and travel books in order to contemplate a real holiday for herself. Something adventurous, she thought, something decidedly *un*comfortable – white water canoeing, maybe, or an African safari – or maybe just something rare and fascinating like a visit to Russia or China or to India where she longed to go.

She had almost forgotten the note and the burglaries when she came in to her apartment on July 19th and listened to the message on her machine asking her to call Jerry Rosenkrantz at the Arthur Segal Foundation in London.

She telephoned first chance next morning from her office.

'Olivia, how are you?' Rosenkrantz always sounded breathless. He smoked two packs of cigarettes a day and every head cold he ever had turned into bronchitis, but nothing and no one had ever persuaded him to give up.

'Fine, thank you, Jerry. How about you?'

'Pretty good, can't complain.' Rosenkrantz paused. 'Heard you called a few weeks back when I was in Israel. My secretary said you were hunting for something in your dad's old files.'

'That's right,' Olivia said. 'But you'd just had your robbery—'

'And the place was pretty much a shambles,' Rosenkrantz finished for her. 'Thing is, we've gotten it all back together now, which was one reason for calling you.'

'That's kind of you—'

'But the main reason is that I've just come across something that might interest you. Seems your father rented a safe-deposit box in London a while before his death, but because he rented it through the Foundation it never came up when his estate was being prepared for probate.' Rosenkrantz coughed twice, then cleared his throat. 'Seems we've been paying for the box ever since by direct debit, and no one thought to ask me about it.'

'It's been nearly twenty years, Jerry.' Olivia was disbelieving.

'Tell me about it.' He coughed again, and wheezed. 'Thing is, no one at the Foundation seems to have a key to the box, and I wondered if you either knew about it, or if you'd maybe ever come across some keys you hadn't been able to account for.'

'I don't know.' Olivia's mind flew to the big leather trunk in her spare room at home. Keys. She had seen a bunch somewhere, some time. 'Listen, Jerry, I didn't know anything about the box—'

'I presumed you didn't.'

'But I'd certainly like to take a look around for the key.'

'You think there's a chance you might find it?'

'I have a zillion things of my parents' – it's a good excuse for another rummage through.'

'You sound like your dad,' Rosenkrantz said warmly. 'He was always a hoarder, I seem to remember.'

'Like father, like daughter,' Olivia said.

She picked up a container of fresh pasta and ready-made sauce on her way home, together with a carton of cans of the only brand of cat food that Cleo seemed willing to eat and a pack of microwavable french fried potatoes – Cleo was predictable in that she'd virtually kill for fresh fish, but Olivia had learned over the past few months that her little cat also had a passion for french fries.

'Hi, Cleo,' she called as she came through the front door.

There was no response.

'Come and greet me,' Olivia threatened, 'or I'll get a dog.'

The tortoiseshell was curled up beside the fruit bowl on the kitchen table. Olivia swept her off onto the floor, chastised her, then, feeling guilty, tried to pet her, but the cat stalked off into the hall.

'You'll be back,' Olivia said, 'if I make you fries.'

Olivia fed Cleo, cooked her own pasta, heated the clam sauce she'd bought and opened a half bottle of wine, and then she sat at the kitchen table and ate her dinner reading *Le Soir*.

She was perfectly conscious of putting off the moment when she would finally drag out the trunk and start searching for the key. It was her reason – or her reasons – for all the delaying tactics that she wasn't quite clear about. She would, she supposed, be disappointed if she failed to find the key; but rather more than that, she found herself reluctant to open herself up again to all that edginess and confusion if she did find it. And then there was something else besides, a curious feeling connected, she imagined, to what might be inside that safe-deposit box. A feeling no more logical than any of the others she had experienced since the coincidences had begun. Olivia thought, perhaps, that it was fear, but it was hard to be certain because she so seldom knew real fear, was one of those people who just happened to be blessed with a natural absence of the commonplace, everyday kinds of fear that others appeared to suffer from. Some people seemed afraid of so many things, most of them outside their control and mostly starting out with 'What would happen if . . . ?' What would happen if they had left the gas turned on and the house blew up? What would happen if they came down with flu the week they'd booked their vacation? What if they went to New York and got mugged? What if they went to San Francisco and got caught in an earthquake?

Olivia remembered how many of Annie's problems had been hypothetical, mostly groundless fears concerning Edward's reaction if he found out that she, like most people, had feet of clay. And how Jamie had always fretted – still did, perhaps – over what Carlos might have felt about him had he lived. Olivia knew how to be scared of real things, had experienced, many times, the adrenalin-pounding chill of taking one too many risks on a ski slope, or hang-gliding too close to a mountain, or taking a corner too fast on the road and going into a skid. But she'd never been prey to those pointless anxieties; there were enough real things in the world to be afraid of, she thought, *real* diseases and wars and famines and accidents.

Which was why she couldn't understand, and did not like, what she was thinking now. That if she found the key and went to London and opened her father's old safe-deposit box, she might, somehow, live to regret it.

The bunch of keys was there, in the green leather trunk. Four keys on a tarnished silver ring. Three of them perfectly ordinary: one made to open a British front door, one smaller, probably the key to a filing cabinet, one the kind of key made to fit a padlock. And the fourth, silver-coloured, flat and slim, with a number engraved on it.

That feeling struck Olivia again. Like a small, hard fist against her stomach. Part excitement. Part apprehension.

Cleo was sitting in the doorway watching her intently. Olivia took a deep breath, detached the flat key from the ring, tossed the other keys back into the trunk, shut the lid and stood up.

'Looks like I'm going to London,' she said.

She went five days later on July 25th, a Tuesday, travelling on the breakfast Eurostar, the best way now, she felt, to get quickly into the heart of London. She parked her Renault in the underground car park at the SNCB building, walked over to the check-in and strolled on board with nothing but the huge Hermès shoulder bag that Bernard had bought her for Christmas – into which she had tossed her passport, credit cards, some sterling currency, a tiny bottle of First perfume and the latest John Grisham – and sat in a state of suspended calm comfort while the train carried her smoothly through the pretty, undulating Belgian countryside towards England.

At least, she thought, leaning back between chapters, she hadn't had to decide whether to see Annie or not, or to tell her what was going on, for she and Edward had left for New York three days earlier and would not be back for a fortnight. It was more years than Olivia could remember since she had come to Britain without seeing, or even talking to, Annie.

'Is something up with you?' Annie had asked her the previous week.

'Nothing,' Olivia had answered, knowing she could get away with that, because Annie was so unlike her, was too discreet by nature and upbringing to pry or push. Annie would always be there for Olivia, just as Jamie would, but unlike Olivia, she would never thrust herself forward, would wait to be asked and would then do anything, *anything*, for her.

'Are you sure you're okay?' Annie had persisted that time, because though she was discreet, she was also too intuitive not to know when Olivia was keeping something from her.

I'll have to tell her, Olivia thought now, as the announcement was made that the train was about to enter the Channel Tunnel, and some of the passengers turned their faces to the windows to watch the sunlight of France funnel down with breathtaking speed to the size of a penlight and then disappear into darkness. *If, that is, there's anything to tell*.

She had arranged to meet Jerry Rosenkrantz – who had ascertained that as a Foundation director he would need to sign if Olivia was to be allowed access to her father's box – at the Britannia Safe Deposit in Leadenhall Street in the City shortly after eleven o'clock. She had not seen Jerry for years, was a little startled at how old he looked, still as immaculately dressed as she remembered him, and with a fine head of white hair, but his increased frailty made Olivia realize, with a mix of emotions, how old Arthur would now have been had he lived.

'Mind if I smoke?' Jerry asked while they waited in the general seating area for papers to be brought out to them.

'If I smoked,' Olivia said, her Eurostar tranquillity long since gone, 'I'd want one too.'

'Why?' Jerry glanced at her, surprised.

She shrugged. 'Just wondering what I'm going to find.'

'I shouldn't expect too much,' Jerry cautioned her. 'Probably just some fusty old legal papers. Or maybe nothing at all – some people hold on to these things for just the odd eventuality.'

'I know they do,' Olivia said, trying to settle down.

'You okay?'

'Fine, Jerry.'

She went alone, with a uniformed man, past a great, heavy vault door into a cavernous room with wall upon wall of locked steel safes of varying sizes. Her father's safe was large, much larger than Olivia had anticipated, about the size of a small suitcase.

'You put your key into the left-hand lock, madam,' the man told her, 'and I put the master key into the other lock.' They turned their keys simultaneously and the hinged grey door opened.

There was a box inside. Quite large, made of heavy cream-coloured card, its lid sealed down with brown sticky tape.

'Would you like one of our rooms, madam?' the uniformed man asked.

'Please.'

He walked ahead of her, carrying the box carefully in his arms, took her to a small room, not much bigger than a cubicle, with a wooden table and a plastic chair. He set the box down on the table and stepped out of the room.

'The door will be locked, madam. You just press that buzzer when you've finished.'

'I will,' Olivia said. 'Thank you.'

The door closed.

She looked down at the lid. There was nothing written on it, nor on the sides of the box, no identification, no hints as to what lay within.

Olivia sat down on the plastic chair. It was uncomfortable, and there was a slight smell of damp in the room. She folded her hands in her lap and stared at the box for a moment longer. She knew, without opening it, that this was it; that she had found what she had been, half unknowingly, seeking ever since the first burglary at her apartment almost three months before.

The fear came back, the same sickly, unfamiliar chill.

She unfolded her hands.

'Okay, Dad,' she said, softly, almost on a sigh. 'Here goes nothing.'

And leaning forward, she peeled off the old, half-perished tape.

And opened the box.

21

Olivia's Box

The box contained a foolscap-sized, stoutly filled manila envelope and two packages wrapped in brown paper and tied with string. The first package, when Olivia opened it, appeared, at first glance, to contain copies of correspondence: letters and notes between her father and Carlos Arias, and a third man named Paul Walter Osterman. The second contained documents, sworn statements and photographs, several old monochrome pictures, of a man, woman and three children, all of them attractive, finely dressed and happy-looking, a family of strangers. And two of another man, black-haired, dark-eyed, elegant and – though Olivia was certain she had never laid eyes on him before – disturbingly familiar.

She turned the photographs over. The family shots all bore the same words on the back, written in blue ink by hand. *The Family Rothenburg: Emanuel, Hedi, Anton, Lili and Trude*. She turned over one of the pictures of the other man. *Georg Brauner*, the handwriting identified him. *Also known as Juan Luis Arias*.

The chill passed through Olivia again, gripped her briefly,

seemed almost to paralyse her. There it was. The final proof
that the crazy instincts and events that had driven her to
this point had been neither coincidental nor symptoms of
paranoia. She didn't know what she had expected. Some
long-buried sin, perhaps. An explanation. But this was going
to be bad for Jamie, she was certain of that now. Whatever
she was about to face was likely to affect him deeply in some
dark, dangerous way, and the thought of bringing pain to
Jamie, of all people, was almost unbearable.

She thought of stopping, felt a great desire to do so, to go
no further, simply to stuff the papers back into the box and
leave. But the manila envelope lay on the table, still sealed.
By her father. Olivia knew she could not ignore it.

She opened it. There was a typewritten letter inside,
and a small, badly stained, very old brownish-coloured
notebook, its covers worn down and frayed, the handwriting
within tidy but urgent on the early pages, growing wilder,
perhaps weaker, as it went on, changing from faded ink to
pencil and then back again to another shade of ink. The
letter, addressed to Arthur Segal from Paul Osterman of
Philadelphia, Pennsylvania, and dated April 13th, 1976,
fell into two clearly separated sections, with directions for
the first part to be read prior to reading the notebook and
the second, much longer, section to follow.

Olivia began to read.

You will wonder, my dear, unfortunate Mr Segal, why I have
chosen you, of all men, to share Anton Rothenburg's story with.
It is a dark, evil, sickening tale, and it concerns you not at all,
not directly at least. Yet I do choose you, for a number of reasons.
Partly because of your acknowledged love of fine art. Partly because
of your well-documented contributions to the Wiesenthal Centre
in Vienna. Partly because of your dealings with the late Max

Wildenbruch of New York City. But most of all, because of your acquaintance with Carlos Miguel Arias.

I have borne the weight of this tale alone since 1952, and in almost a quarter of a century I have gathered a fair amount of evidence. Enough, yet not enough. And all of it, too late. Too late to help. But I believe, with all my heart, that the story of the Family Rothenburg of Baden-Baden must live on, no matter what. I am a sick man now, nearing the end of my life, and so, as young Anton did so many years ago, it's time for me to pass my burden to another man.

It's your misfortune, Mr Segal, that I have chosen you.

Olivia turned her attention, as directed, to the notebook. She had no idea how long she read for. Time seemed simply to cease to exist as she read the tale of Emanuel and Hedi Rothenburg and their three children, from the day in 1932 when the man calling himself Georg Brauner had first come to call on them, to the night of November 9th, 1938, *Kristallnacht*, when all the Rothenburgs, except for Anton, had been murdered.

She paused for a few moments then, composed herself sufficiently to press the buzzer and summon the uniformed man, and to ask him to tell Jerry Rosenkrantz to leave, not to wait for her. And then she returned to the second part of Paul Osterman's letter.

It is true that none of the family survived, that Anton Rothenburg died, just over two months after the others, in Buchenwald. But he did, as he had hoped to, live just long enough to tell their tale and pass the notebook to a fellow inmate in the concentration camp. And it was that Holocaust survivor who passed it all on to me in the autumn of 1952 during one long, rather drunken night in the bar of an Amsterdam hotel.

We were two strangers, both businessmen travelling alone, both lovers of art, both Jews. As I said before, at the beginning of my letter, I had heard – we had all heard – so many terrible stories of those nightmare years, and yet this particular one seized my imagination, my heart, so profoundly, so savagely, that I knew immediately that it would remain with me until my dying moment.

I was consumed that night by a curiously wild compulsion to discover the true identity of Georg Brauner, and by an equally passionate yearning for justice. The first, at least, was not so difficult to achieve. Brauner believed that by arranging the deaths of the Rothenburgs, the chief witnesses to his crimes in Baden-Baden, he had eradicated every significant shred of evidence. No one, after all, in Nazi Germany of 1938 was going to query the end of another handful of Jews.

But the disappearance of a great painting by a famous artist is harder to conceal for ever. Emanuel Rothenburg's collection of Symbolist art was recorded and reported by the Nazis as having burned to ashes in the *Kristallnacht* fire. Georg Brauner was a man of property, a man – not, in that at least, unlike Rothenburg – who took great pride in the art he owned and stole.

I guessed, from all I had learned, that if I waited long enough, at least one of those paintings would emerge into the light. I employed scouts to cover all the major art centres in the world. (Not such a vast undertaking and certainly no penance for a lover of paintings to scour catalogues in museums and galleries and auction houses, waiting for one work from the Rothenburg list to emerge.)

I thought, once, in early 1956, that I was on the right trail, when I received word that one of Emanuel's Hodlers had recently been donated to the Kunsthaus in Zurich. But it turned out to be one of the nine paintings that Georg Brauner, covering his tracks perfectly, had allowed to reach Max Wildenbruch in New York.

One of the paintings, Mr Segal, which Wildenbruch had sold to you after the war.

Nothing else, not a trace, not a whisper, came to light for another five years. Until I read for myself a report in the *Herald Tribune* that a work by Paul Gauguin, long buried in a private collection, had been loaned to the Museum of Fine Arts in Boston. I had a hunch (more than a hunch, really) even before I read the painting's title, *La Rêveuse* – The Dreamer – that, at last, I was on my way.

I flew to Boston less than a week later, went directly to the museum, wanting, needing quite passionately – as if foolishly, egotistically, perhaps, I might in some way be keeping faith with Emanuel Rothenburg by just standing before the painting, *his* painting – to see it for myself. I had expected that this would be only a beginning, that the plaque beside the Gauguin might tell me, enigmatically, that the work was on loan from an unnamed source, but the small, polished plaque told me all I wanted to know.

Paul Gauguin – 'La Rêveuse'
On loan from the Juan Luis Arias Private Collection.

It was a wonderful painting, a thing of great beauty. I understood, standing before it, how a person might ache for the privilege of owning such a work of art. But nothing, no part of me, thank God – not even the tiniest, darkest fragment of my mind – was, or is to this day, able to comprehend how a man might have conspired to destroy not just one person, but an entire family, for that privilege.

In the small locked room in the depths of the Britannia Safe Deposit, Olivia leaned back against the small hard plastic chair and closed her eyes.

She was thinking about the painting, about the Gauguin.

She was seeing it again in her mind, as she had seen it the last time, in the drawing room of the Arias mansion in Newport when Jamie had brought her back there after her fall, back in that strange, briefly remarkable spring of 1989. She remembered looking up at *La Rêveuse* while Louise and Daisy Arias fussed about her, remembered its sinuous beauty, remembered registering, even in the midst of that abruptly, crazily awakened desire – no, lust – for Jamie, how much Arthur would have loved the work.

And she was thinking about the painting now partly because she wanted, desperately, not to think about Jamie, because thinking about Jamie, right now, in the depths of this ugly, monstrous tale, was unbearable.

Go on, she told herself. *Get to the end. The sooner you reach the end, the sooner you can get up off this chair and leave this room and get back up into the light and air.*

She opened her eyes, leaned forward again, and went on reading.

I remained in Boston for a time, gathering what information I could about the Arias family of Newport, Rhode Island. In general terms, it was not difficult, listed as they were, still are, in *Who's Who* and various other registers.

Juan Luis Arias and his younger brother, Carlos Miguel, were the second generation of the Arias family of Bilbao to be citizens of the United States, Juan Luis the First having immigrated during the period of unrest and anarchy that had swept much of Spain after the First World War. The Ariases were an old family of shipbuilders, high-born, wealthy and proud, both of their ancestry and their considerable achievements in America. It was Juan Luis the First, a man with a liberal heart and conscience that blended intriguingly with his vast ambition, who determined to gain the most solid foothold possible in his new country, who fell in love with and, against great odds, bought the Newport mansion; who must have used every ounce of his innate good breeding and charm to gain acceptance for himself and his family in this old-moneyed enclave of giants with names like Vanderbilt and Astor.

I considered, at this point, employing a private detective to investigate the second Juan Luis Arias and, more particularly, his art collection, but I chose instead to employ a local researcher. The facts she gleaned for me were sparse, but devastatingly clear evidence – clear enough, at least, to me – of his guilt. Like many proud, arrogant men, Arias – a widower with one son – simply could not bear to conceal his trophies for the whole of his life. He had striven too hard, too ruthlessly, to accumulate his treasures; now, presumably, he ached to show them off. Until 1960, there was no public record to be found of the Juan Luis Arias Private Collection, and then suddenly mentions of it began to creep into specialist journals, catalogues and newspapers. Though my researcher found no comprehensive documented list of the works forming the collection, she did find details of twenty-seven of the Symbolist paintings that had once been owned by Emanuel Rothenburg.

I left Boston for a while, returned to my home in Philadelphia, trying to prepare myself, to steel myself to confront the man I was by now certain had been Georg Brauner. I spent many restless, feverish nights tossing and turning, finding myself suddenly afraid of the prospect. I was a businessman, an ordinary, run-of-the-mill American Jew with a small company, a wife and one son; how, in God's name, I asked myself over and over again, was I to confront a man of vast wealth and influence and to accuse him of conspiring with the Nazis to steal and to commit murder?

I thought, for a while, as I had thought many times before during the preceding eight or so years, that perhaps I should hand the case over to Simon Wiesenthal or one of the experienced Israeli

Nazi hunters, but I found that even after so much time I still could not let go. Emanuel Rothenburg and his loved ones had become, in some illogical, ghostly fashion, my family, *my* responsibility. To a man like Wiesenthal, the Rothenburg story might have been just one more horror, one more crime, to add to the list, but it had become everything to me. I was, I suppose, obsessed.

I lived my own life, going about my business, trying to feign normality with my wife (who knew something, of course, of my quandary, though not, for which I am grateful, the full extent of my absorption) and our child, for three months.

And then I returned to Boston, where I learned, within twenty-four hours of my arrival, that I had come back too late.

Juan Luis Arias the Second had died.

Olivia paused, aware suddenly that she had, in her suspense, been digging the fingernails of her left hand so deeply into her palm that one of the nails, a little sharper than the others, had drawn a tiny crescent of blood.

She stood up, pushed the chair back, almost knocked it over and reached out to steady it. Her breathing was rapid and shallow, her pulse rate felt as fast as if she'd been running, and she was both warm and cold at the same time. Jamie came into her mind again, and forcibly she ejected him. And then, in his place, was Arthur. Her gentle, philanthropic, beauty-loving father. If she felt this way now, so many years later, two generations past the evil, if she felt this degree of horror and revulsion and rage and outrage, how must Arthur – always, she remembered, so contented with his lot, so grateful that his own father had escaped in time from Nazism – have felt receiving this out of a clear blue sky? This burden, as Paul Osterman had so accurately described it, this challenge from a long-dead family.

Olivia drew the chair back to the table and sat down

again. The letter, she saw, was nearing its end, most of the pages stacked to the left of the table, only a few more remaining to be read.

I was at a loss. It might have been one thing to try to tackle the man himself, but I still had no more than circumstantial evidence and intuition. For all I knew, Arias could have come by those twenty-seven Symbolist paintings legitimately, perhaps from the real Georg Brauner. How could I approach the man's grieving relatives, not knowing whether one, or more, or perhaps all of them had been guilty of complicity? I had evidence but, as yet, I had no absolute proof, which meant that yet again I had to wait, had to find a way to get that proof.

I had to wait much longer than I had anticipated. Back in Philadelphia, my son was sick, my wife distraught, her emotional state not helped by my repeated absences from home. Priorities were brought home to me, and there could be no question that the needs of my own family – my own, thank God, *living* family – had to come before the memory and honour of people I had never known. It was more than a year before my son's health had improved sufficiently for me to consider the Rothenburgs again, and then, alas, I realized, too late, that my marriage was in deep trouble.

It was 1964 before I felt free to turn back to Georg Brauner. Juan Luis Arias had been dead for three years. There was, at least, no question that I might be intruding on fresh grief. I took a gamble. I instructed an art dealer in Boston to approach the Arias family, saying that he had a buyer for one of the paintings in their collection. I named a work from Emanuel's list by Gustave Moreau, *Nymphe Dansante*, which had not appeared on the list compiled by my researcher of exhibited paintings from the Juan Luis Arias Private Collection. The dealer, I directed, was to ascertain that *Nymphe Dansante* was in the possession of the Ariases, and was then to make an attempt both to authenticate the painting and to establish provenance. It took time, of course. Everything connected with Brauner and the Rothenburgs took time, I had long since become resigned to that. But in all respects my gamble, or rather my hunch, paid off. The Moreau painting was in the Arias collection, and my dealer was as satisfied of its authenticity as he could reasonably be, but with regard to provenance, he had not even managed to ascertain the work's previous owner, let alone its origins.

Every lingering doubt dispelled, I tried to make an appointment to see Juan Luis's younger brother, Carlos Miguel Arias, now the head of the family and shipping company, but was given no choice but to make do with Juan Luis's son Michael. The Newport mansion was not, I was politely informed, open to visitors, and so we met in the Manhattan offices of Arias Shipping on a Monday morning in May. Michael Arias was only twenty-one years old, but I found him a smooth, articulate, mature man for his age. His uncle, he explained, with immaculate courtesy, was away in Europe, but had empowered his nephew to speak for him on the subject of the Moreau, which, Michael told me immediately, the family was not eager to part with.

Deeply disappointed by Carlos Arias's absence and uncomfortable having to speak to Juan Luis's own son, knowing in any case that it was immensely unlikely that the young man might know anything of use to me, I set about my business regardless, asking about the painting's history. Michael told me that he knew only that his late father, in common with many private collectors, had accumulated his collection over a great many years. I asked if there was a record of when and where and from whom his uncle had obtained any of the other works – *La Rêveuse*, for example, the Gauguin that had, for a time, been lent to the Boston Museum of Fine Arts. Michael paused for a moment and then replied that the family's admiration had always been for the paintings themselves, and for his father's remarkable overall achievement in gathering them under one umbrella. Whether *Nymphe Dansante*, for example, had previously been owned by an old lady in Marseilles or by a museum in Guatemala, had never been of the slightest interest to any of them.

That was when I posed the question I most wanted to ask. It was an unwise question, clumsily put, and yet I found that I had to ask it.

'I don't suppose you happen to know,' I asked the young man, 'whether your father spent much time in Germany between 1932 and 1938?'

Michael Arias frowned, a small furrowing of his smooth, handsome young brow. 'How could I know?' he asked me in return. 'Given that I hadn't even been born.'

'Your uncle would probably know,' I said.

'He might,' the young man said. The frown grew a little deeper. 'Why is that of interest to you?'

'I think,' I said, carefully, 'your father may have had some dealings with an old friend of mine who lived in Germany at that time.'

'Who was that?'

I took a breath. 'A man named Emanuel Rothenburg,' I said.

Arias shook his head. 'The name means nothing to me, I'm afraid.'

'He was an art collector, too,' I said. 'He lived in Baden-Baden.'

Again the young man shook his head. 'I'm sorry,' he said.

'Perhaps you could ask your uncle?'

'I could.' Michael Arias paused. 'It seems important to you.'

'It is,' I said.

'More important, apparently,' Arias said slowly, 'than buying the Moreau.'

'But didn't you imply,' I answered with a small shrug, 'that your family doesn't want to sell the painting?'

'Yes,' the young man said. 'I did imply that.'

That was the end of the meeting. He had remained courteous throughout and he was, of course, as I've already said, far too young for me to have expected him to know much about his father's pre-war activities. I can't even claim to have sensed that he knew more than he was saying. Yet a wall had gone up from the instant I had begun asking questions about Juan Luis Arias, and I had a picture in my mind of that dark young man telephoning his uncle in Europe as soon as I'd left his office, reporting my curious questions. Whether or not Juan Luis's son or other relatives knew about his crimes, it was obvious to me that this was the kind of family that protected its own, and that a stranger asking personal questions about any family member was decidedly unwelcome.

I found out exactly *how* unwelcome less than a month later when, back home, I received a letter from a Boston firm of lawyers warning me that any further intrusion into the private affairs of the family of Juan Luis Arias would be responded to by legal means. It was the clearest evidence I'd had to date that I was right about Georg Brauner, but it still left me no closer to proving it.

While taking care to steer clear of the family, I have assembled more through the years. Photographs of the Rothenburgs, found in a Jewish library in Baden-Württemberg, and of Juan Luis Arias, alias Georg Brauner, retrieved from the picture library of the *Boston Daily News*. Signed documents attesting to Emanuel's pre-war ownership of many of the works now in Juan Luis's private collection. Character 'references' obtained by a private investigator from men and women who knew both men during that wartime period, demonstrating the substantial differences between Juan

Luis and his younger brother, Carlos. It's clear from the descriptions that Juan Luis was the more powerful man, invariably charming but also vain and prideful, while Carlos was strong but gentle and more liberal in his opinions, like their father, Juan Luis the First. There's an account from a female acquaintance, a lady from New York who prefers to be unnamed, detailing an encounter she had experienced with both brothers at a party in Manhattan in 1936. The lady says that at that party Juan Luis Arias drank a great deal and disclosed to her not only his sympathy with but also his immense admiration for Adolf Hitler. She also says that his younger brother, Carlos, displayed both shock and the most intense embarrassment at Juan Luis's statements.

I send you all these things, Mr Segal: the photographs and statements and the information about the paintings that once belonged, without doubt, to Emanuel Rothenburg, and then came into the hands of Juan Luis Arias. I send them to you because where I have failed, perhaps you, who are personally acquainted with Carlos Arias – who can unquestionably reach the man I was never permitted to speak to – may find a way to make use of them. And I say to you now, in the hope that it may ease your mind at least a little, that in spite of the family's strenuous efforts to keep me from peering more closely into their private history, in all these many years I have found no trace of evidence of any direct involvement by Carlos Miguel Arias in his brother's crimes.

I have asked myself so often since that chance encounter in 1952 why the fate of the Rothenburgs gripped my heart so fiercely, so relentlessly. I have no profound answer to pass on. Perhaps it was because the stranger's descriptions of Emanuel Rothenburg reminded me so much of my own father. Or perhaps it was simply because the evil perpetrated by Georg Brauner or Juan Luis Arias – a man in no possible way compelled by his environment or his masters to do as he did, a man who could so easily just have stayed away, could have left the Jews alone, could have gone on with his own comfortable, successful life in his own world – seemed in its way so much more evil than anything I had ever come across before.

I asked the stranger in the Amsterdam bar why he had not gone forward to the authorities after Buchenwald to give evidence against Brauner, and he explained that he had been too physically and emotionally scarred by his own wartime experiences, too afraid, too weary to face another ordeal. Yet Anton Rothenburg's story, and the young dying man's longing for the truth to reach a world beyond Buchenwald, had affected him deeply, and he suggested to me that perhaps if I had the strength and the will, I might try to accomplish what he was too weak to do.

I remember thinking when I fell into bed that night, that the sudden, violent urge for justice, created perhaps by a surfeit of whisky, would probably have left me by next morning. But it did not leave me. To this day, it is still with me.

And now, perhaps, Arthur Segal, it is with you.

For a long while, after she had finished reading Paul Osterman's letter, Olivia sat in the little room and stared at the pages and at Anton Rothenburg's notebook and at the photographs that Osterman had so painstakingly gleaned of the Jewish art collector and some of his priceless treasures; and at all the other signed declarations and documents that still, in spite of Osterman's conviction, added up to insufficient evidence of Juan Luis's guilt.

A rapping on the door jolted her.

'Are you all right in there, madam?' It was the courteous voice of the Britannia Safe Deposit's manager.

Olivia looked at her watch and saw, startled, that she had been in the cubicle for more than three hours.

'I'm fine, thank you,' she answered.

'Could I get you something? Some coffee, perhaps?'

'No, thank you,' she said. 'No coffee.'

'Sorry to have disturbed you then,' he said.

'I'm sorry to be taking so long,' Olivia said.

'Take as long as you like, madam.'

Olivia heard him walk away, and then she turned her attention to the package of correspondence, and here, at last, were copies of every letter that her father had sent to Carlos Arias between April and June 1976, and the replies he had received. And there was a small cassette tape, too, and Olivia guessed that it might be a recording of a conversation between the two men. And the tone of all Carlos's letters and notes was the same as in the first one Olivia had found in the pigskin case, the one that had disappeared after the break-in: Jamie's father had been, as Osterman had believed, innocent of any complicity.

I knew nothing [Carlos wrote in one letter] of the existence of Georg Brauner. But I did know that my brother often travelled to Europe, and in particular to Germany, during those pre-war years, and that he returned after many of these trips with magnificent additions for his art collection. Including, alas, the Symbolist paintings that you have listed. Juan Luis explained to me, when I asked how he had obtained them, that because of the ever-growing atmosphere of fear and uncertainty in Europe, works were becoming widely available that otherwise would have remained forever out of reach. People, Juan told me – Jews especially – needed funds more than they needed paintings, and when I suggested to him that this sounded to me like exploitation, his response seemed frank enough. He was, perhaps, he agreed, taking some advantage of a bad situation, but I ought to understand how infinitely preferable it was for the Jews to sell their treasures to a family like ours in a free country, rather than to see them ultimately confiscated without compensation.

I did not, in all honesty, either understand or agree with my brother, but Juan Luis was the head of our family, and it was not my place to question him. Respect and family loyalty were everything to us, you know. But I tell you now, that if I had had even the smallest inkling of the evil that my brother was perpetrating, all the family loyalty in the world could not have kept me either silent or quiescent.

I am, my dear Arthur, horrified, and deeply ashamed. There are matters that must be dealt with and addressed. I wish with all my heart to make such amends as may be possible, though nothing, I realize only too painfully, can ever make up for the loss of an entire family.

We must, as you suggest, meet soon.

And there, Olivia realized, in her hand, was the final proof that Paul Osterman had sought for so many years. He had chosen her father for all the reasons he had given: his love of art and his dealings with Max Wildenbruch and the Hodler which had once belonged to Emanuel Rothenburg and which now hung in the Zurich Kunsthaus; his established wish to help – albeit previously only in financial terms – anti-Nazi causes; but chiefly, because Arthur Segal would be able to reach the ear of Carlos Arias.

Osterman had tried, but had been restrained by law from doing so. Olivia's father had got through to Carlos, and it seemed clear to her from his letters that Carlos had been thinking of ways to make restitution of sorts, but then both men had died in the crash.

Too drained to think further, Olivia packed the contents of the box into her big Hermès bag, apologized to the Britannia manager for having taken so much time and made a swift telephone call to Jerry Rosenkrantz to thank him for his help, to tell him that the papers in the safe-deposit had been of a private nature, and to explain that she would not now have time to come to the Foundation's offices for a drink as he had suggested, because she would be returning directly to Brussels.

She emerged into Leadenhall Street, momentarily confused by the City of London hubbub, found an empty taxi and headed for Waterloo Station. Perhaps, she considered, she ought to have abandoned her train reservation and gone to a hotel to rest for the night, but she was too shaken by what she had read, so hugely weighed down by the burden she suddenly realized she had now taken from her father's shoulders that she could hardly seem to think straight, found she did not really want to think at all. She just wanted, needed, to be back in her own home, where she could be by herself until she was ready to think again, to plan the next step of this dreadful voyage back into the past, to be rational again, *normal* again.

She boarded the Eurostar at five o'clock, allowed herself just one glass of white wine before the dinner she knew she would be unable to eat. She wished now that she had not parked her car at the Gare du Midi, wished she could have simply fallen into the back of a cab, preferably too drunk to remember Anton Rothenburg's notebook or Paul Osterman's letter. But the Hermès bag on the empty First Class seat opposite her was a tangible reminder, if she needed one, that she had a duty now to her father and to Carlos Arias, and to the long dead art collector and his family—

And, she was beginning to realize – though it was, of course, too bizarre, too *hideous* to contemplate – to Emily, her mother, and to Grace and Franklin Aldrich and to the pilot of the helicopter whose name, God forgive her, she could not at that second recall.

For Osterman had been prevented from getting too close, after his single meeting with Michael Arias. And Arthur had deemed it prudent to lock the box into a vault. And Carlos had written that there were 'matters to be dealt with and addressed.' And he and her father must have been making plans, must have been working out what step to take next.

Before death had stopped them.

She didn't notice the dark-haired man in the black leather jacket in the next compartment who sat, with tinted glasses covering his eyes, reading the *Daily Express*. She had not noticed him earlier that morning, either, on the journey from Brussels to London, or, later – a lifetime later – when she had come out from the safe-deposit into Leadenhall Street and he had followed her, had watched her climb into her cab and had hailed another behind her.

And she did not notice him when she left the train shortly before ten o'clock and headed, still wearily, still half-numbed, towards the SNCB building and the underground car park.

It happened too fast, much too fast for her to have time to react, to do anything, even to see anything. There was only the sound of a car abruptly, aggressively picking up speed, and then a blinding glare of headlights, forcing her free hand up to shield her eyes, and then a screeching of tyres.

And the awful, ugly noise that was the wing of the car hitting her.

And after that, nothing at all.

22

For Olivia

She came to in the emergency room of the Saint-Pierre Hospital. They were kind to her, gave her something to ease the pain and told her that she'd had a quite miraculous escape, that her left arm was fractured but otherwise her injuries were minor, mostly small cuts and bruises.

'First,' one of the doctors, young and harried and tired looking, said to her, 'we'll get your arm set in plaster, and then we'll get you to a room for one night's observation, and then, if all's well, you can probably go home in the morning.'

Olivia looked dizzily up at him. 'The car didn't stop, did it?'

'No, mademoiselle,' he said. 'The police will speak with you soon.'

'Good,' she said.

He touched her right arm gently, and shook his head. '*Vraiment*, mademoiselle, you have been very, very lucky.'

Olivia believed him, just as she'd almost believed the nurse who'd mentioned miracles, for there was not a single, solitary doubt left in her mind that whoever had been driving that car had intended to kill her.

She knew, too, even before she asked, that the Hermès bag was gone.

'It was a deliberate hit-and-run,' she told the two officers from the *Gendarmerie* who came to see her while she waited for her arm to be set.

'The driver failed to stop,' one of them said. 'Probably he panicked.'

'Or she,' the other officer said.

'You say you didn't see the driver, mademoiselle?'

'I didn't see anything,' Olivia said, 'except the headlights. I couldn't even tell you what kind of car it was.'

'They may report the accident later,' the first man said. 'It sometimes happens that way.'

'It won't this time,' Olivia said, fuzzily. 'And it wasn't an accident.'

'Why do you say that, Miss Segal?' he asked, frowning.

She closed her eyes for a moment. 'It's a very long story.'

'Perhaps you should rest, mademoiselle.'

She opened them again. 'What are you doing to find the car?'

'There's not too much we can do,' the second officer said with a hint of a shrug, 'without any description.'

'You're sure there's nothing you can remember?' the first man asked.

'It was dark,' Olivia said, very softly. 'It happened too fast.' She paused. 'No one else saw it happen?'

'No one has come forward, alas,' he answered. 'Not yet, at least.'

'Maybe later,' the second man said.

They began to turn away.

'I need to tell you,' Olivia said, 'about the bag.'

'You told us, Miss Segal,' the first officer said, patiently. 'It's missing.'

'Stolen,' she said.

'It's possible,' he said. 'An opportunist, passing by after the accident—'

'It was stolen by the driver,' Olivia said. 'Or by an accomplice.'

The two policemen glanced at each other quickly.

'You should rest, mademoiselle,' the first man said again.

'But I need to tell you,' she said. 'I have to explain.'

'Not tonight,' he said, soothingly.

'*Ecoutez, mademoiselle*,' the other man said, more firmly. 'You told us yourself that you've made two long journeys today, and you admit that you were very tired and perhaps a little careless, and you drank some wine on the journey from London—'

'One glass,' Olivia said, as firmly as she could, but the drugs and the pain were making her feel sick, making it hard for her to be assertive, to be herself. 'And it wasn't an accident.'

'You may be right, Miss Segal,' the second man said. 'But we still won't achieve anything more tonight, so we're going to leave you now and let you get some rest.'

'How can I rest,' Olivia asked him, 'when someone's trying to kill me?'

'You'll rest when they operate on your arm,' the first man said, smiling.

The second officer looked down at her seriously for an instant. 'Why are you so sure that it was deliberate?'

'I told you, it's a long, long, awful story,' she said, wearily.

'And it's pretty wild – and maybe I wouldn't believe me either if I were you – but it goes all the way back to war crimes in Germany, and if I'm right, then whoever tried to have me killed did the same thing to another six people nearly twenty years ago.'

She knew, as soon as the words were out, that she'd made a mistake. She'd had their attention – sceptical, but on the job nevertheless – until she'd said those two things – 'war crimes' and 'another six people' – but now she'd lost them, and she knew they'd written her off as suffering from shock or concussion or having an over-active imagination or maybe having her period. Or perhaps, looking at their faces, they thought that she was just downright crazy.

In a private room for the night, she slept for a little over two hours, then woke again at around four o'clock, still groggy but with the sudden, urgent realization that what she needed now, more than anything, was to speak to Jamie. He would listen to her, he would believe her – she would *make* him believe her – but more important than that, she needed to make him understand that once he, too, knew the truth about Juan Luis, he might be in just as much danger as she was. It occurred to her, briefly, while she was struggling with her freshly plastered, startlingly heavy left arm and fumbling with the telephone, telling the operator that she needed to call overseas and she needed to do it now, whatever the time was – that Jamie might be better off being left in the dark, but that thought was swiftly dismissed. He had to know; Carlos would want him to know. It was his right to know.

He wasn't at home, his machine was picking up, and suddenly Olivia remembered Jamie telling her that he was going to be spending a few days at the Arias house in

Newport because Louise was throwing a birthday party for Michael.

She put the phone down and, struggling not to fall asleep, started to hunt around for her address book, but it had, of course, been in the Hermès bag and so she had to start all over again and ask the hospital switchboard to get her the international directory enquiries operator.

It took forever to get through, and when she did, the woman who answered the phone – not Louise or Daisy, probably a housekeeper – said that Jamie wasn't home right now.

'When will he be there?' Olivia asked.

'I'm sorry, miss, I can't hear you very well,' the voice in Newport said.

'When will Jamie be back?' Olivia said more loudly.

The door opened, and a nurse stuck her head around and raised a finger to her lips to hush her, and Olivia nodded, still waiting for an answer, but the woman on the phone had gone away and left her on hold, and she wanted, suddenly, to cry, which was not at all like her, but she couldn't help it.

'Hello, Olivia.' Michael Arias was at the other end. 'What's up?'

'I need to talk to Jamie,' she said. 'It's very important.'

'Jamie's not here right now.'

'I know, but I just want to know when he'll be back.'

'Are you okay, Olivia? You don't sound quite yourself.'

'I'm not,' Olivia said.

'Are you sick? Has something happened? Can I do something for you, Olivia?'

Michael sounded so warm and friendly and concerned, and Olivia was about to tell him that she was in hospital – and then, suddenly, something stopped her; something in that pleasant voice, in the extra attentive way he was speaking to her, scared her.

'No, thank you, Michael,' she said. 'Just tell Jamie I called, and ask him to get back to me as soon as he can.'

Except, she was perfectly aware as she put down the receiver, that he wouldn't be able to reach her, not tonight at least, because he didn't know where she was. And Olivia tried to think what exactly it was that had stopped her giving Michael the hospital's telephone number, but she couldn't think properly, because all the dope in her bloodstream was weighing her down, fuzzing her brain, and she had to lie down again and close her eyes, and she was so *tired*, and she had to sleep.

She dreamt about Michael wearing the British panama hat and sunglasses she'd seen him in at the Newport house that May afternoon all those years ago. In the dream he was smiling at her, a warm, charming smile, but his eyes were completely obscured behind the glasses and then he walked towards her, and he took off first the hat and then the sunglasses, and his eyes were black as coal, hard as iron, and he was holding out both his arms towards her as if he was going to embrace her. And suddenly he looked so like Jamie that she felt overwhelmed by an enormous sense of relief, and she ran straight into those welcome arms, and Jamie was holding her tightly. Except that it wasn't Jamie, it was Michael, and he was gripping her too tightly, encircling her arms and body so hard that she cried out in pain, but he kept on hugging her more and more tightly, and her left arm was agony, and he was squeezing the breath out of her, and she tried to kick him, but it only hurt her more, and she cried out again—

'Miss Segal—'

She kicked out again.

'Olivia—'

She heard the voice, and opened her eyes, and saw the nurse bending over her, a small flashlight in her hand.

'*Qu'est-ce qui se passe?*' the nurse asked, softly.

Olivia tried to struggle up, but her plastered arm made it hard to move, so she lay back again, and forced herself to breathe normally.

'Was it a bad dream?'

'Yes.'

'Can I get something for you? A warm drink, perhaps?'

'No, thank you.' Olivia shook her head. 'It was just a nightmare. I'm okay now.'

'It's the anaesthetic,' the nurse said. 'It gives some people bad dreams.'

'Yes,' Olivia said. 'Was I making a noise?'

'Just a little.'

'I'm sorry.'

'*Ne vous en faites pas, mademoiselle.*' The nurse patted her good arm. 'Don't worry about it, just try to sleep again.'

She left the room and softly closed the door. Olivia lay in the semi-darkness, eyes wide open. She tended to dream a good deal, often had wild, action-packed dreams, believed they were her subconscious encouraging her to get out and do more, but she rarely suffered nightmares.

This one was staying with her. Keeping her awake.

Michael Arias. Jamie's older cousin. Michael Arias, head of the family, as his father Juan Luis, too, had once been.

Olivia had seldom seen Michael, just at the occasional family gathering over the years when she and Annie had happened to be included. He was a man, she thought suddenly, of many faces: proud, wealthy, third-generation American businessman; Newport-style good husband with just that gentle, amusing hint of elegant, old-world British-style spy; protective, Spanish-style older relative with a whiff of Mafia-style don. All of those faces so unlike Jamie, considering they shared almost the same blood and upbringing. There was no dark side to Jamie – there were shades, of course – but not even a soupçon of sinister; nor was there, Olivia had to admit, to Peter Arias, much as she loathed him for what he'd done to his younger brother. Peter was a swine and she felt contempt for him, but she could not imagine ever being afraid of him.

She thought again about that last letter from Carlos Arias to her father. *There are matters to be dealt with and addressed.* Had those matters included speaking to his nephew, Juan Luis's son, whose meeting with Paul Osterman back in 1964, when Michael had been just twenty-one, Carlos might only then have learned about? The meeting after which Osterman had been warned off in no uncertain terms?

Olivia sat up, careful of her arm. There was that chill again, that stinging, previously unfamiliar sensation that she'd been experiencing more and more often since the burglaries. Fear. It cleared away the last remnants of the nightmare, swept away the wish, if not the need, to sleep.

During the years in which Georg Brauner had been ransacking Emanuel Rothenburg's collection, Michael Arias had not yet been born. It made no sense to try to harness Michael to crimes committed by his father. But Carlos had written about loyalty and respect in a Spanish family. He had also written, shortly before his death, that had he had even the smallest inkling of what Juan Luis had done, all the family loyalty in the world would not have kept him silent. Perhaps Michael's sense of loyalty to his late father had been stronger than Carlos's family pride –

or maybe it had been just his horror of what might come to pass if the truth came out.

For if the world had discovered what Juan Luis had done, not only would the Arias name have been tarnished for ever, but their remarkable – and, by the mid-seventies, almost priceless – art collection would have had to have been broken up, perhaps surrendered completely. Pride and a fortune lost, all for the sake of honour and inherited shame.

If Olivia was right, then Michael Arias had found a legitimate way to keep Paul Osterman at bay back in 1964. But faced, twelve years later, with his Uncle Carlos's shock, moral outrage, guilt and determination to make whatever restitution possible, Michael might have felt compelled to find a more permanent way to silence him. Together with her father. The only other person who knew the truth.

He couldn't. Olivia felt a terrible, deep shudder pass through her. *He could not, surely, have done that to his own uncle.*

Let alone to five more innocent people.

She thought about Emily, her mother, about the loss to all those sick children. She thought about Grace and Franklin Aldrich, about all that their deaths had done to Annie. She thought about Jamie, and what, if she was right, this would do to him.

'No,' she said aloud, softly, into the dark.

It was too monstrous to contemplate.

Yet, of course, she did contemplate it, and it sharpened her own, now intensely personal fear with a finely hewn, technicolor clarity. For whether it had been done for the sake of a dead father's honour or for personal greed and pride, what had been priceless enough to kill for nineteen years ago, was certainly worth killing for again now. And a man who could bring about the death of the uncle who had, Jamie had often told Olivia, become almost a surrogate father to his nephew, would scarcely blink at the prospect of having an outsider murdered.

The steady, throbbing ache in her left arm grew more intense. Olivia thought of ringing for a nurse and asking for a tablet for the pain, but she knew that would send her back off to sleep and she wasn't ready for that, not yet, not until she had worked it all out. She was planning, after all, to break this to Jamie as soon as she could get hold of him, to tell him that his uncle had been a blackmailer, a thief and a murderer, and that his own cousin had somehow engineered the helicopter crash that had killed Carlos and the others.

I have to get it clear in my own mind, she told herself, gritting her teeth against the pain, *because if I'm wrong, I could lose Jamie for ever*.

She went over it again and again. She'd first found Carlos's note to Arthur back in 1976 while clearing out her parents' house, but she had mentioned it to no one at that time except Annie, who'd talked her into putting it away and forgetting about it. Which she had done, until she'd moved from Strasbourg to Brussels and shown the note to Jamie – and asked him to mention it to Michael, which he had. She tried to remember what Jamie had told her Michael had said about it. She couldn't remember exactly – something about Michael having agreed that the note sounded strange, and asking if Olivia had found any more, similar, correspondence, and she'd said, of course, that she hadn't.

And then, after her trip to America in April, she'd come home to find the break-in. And after that the note had vanished. And the other burglaries had followed: at her office, at Jamie's apartment, at the Arthur Segal Foundation and at Annie's house.

And Olivia had talked to Jamie about her growing suspicions, and she'd encouraged him to speak to Michael again about them, and Michael had told Jamie he'd had Carlos's personal files checked. And she remembered rather clearly what Michael had said about a week after that: that Olivia was either fanciful, or that the robbery at her apartment had freaked her out, and that she was working herself up over nothing.

But since then, there'd been nothing, no contact, even indirectly, with Michael Arias, and Olivia had ceased mentioning the note to Jamie. May, June and more than half of July had gone by. Her relationship with Bernard had ended, and she'd got on with living in the present. Until she'd had the message from Jerry Rosenkrantz at the Foundation about the safe-deposit box.

She had told no one that she was going to London, not even Jamie. So how could they have known? Unless Michael was having her watched, was maybe even bugging her apartment. Which was, of course, absurd.

Or not absurd at all, not for a man she thought might be responsible for killing six people.

The night nurse came back then, said the doctor had written her up for pain relief if she needed it, and Olivia was ready to give in at last, because she'd got it pretty much all worked out – she wished she hadn't, but she had, and now, more than anything on earth, she wanted to blot it all out, at least for a few hours.

There was nothing else to be done this long night. She could hardly try Jamie again, not after midnight, Rhode Island time. And the pain, in her arm and all over her poor, bruised body, was really bad now, was making her feel nauseous again.

The nurse gave her a pill. Olivia swallowed it. The pain began, slowly, blissfully, to recede.

She slept.

They released her next morning, and Olivia was so eager to be dressed and out of the hospital that she lied about having someone at home to help her. But the moment she got outside fear kicked in again, making her glance over her shoulder as she climbed into the cab the hospital had called for her because her own car was still at the Gare du Midi, and even if it hadn't been she could not have safely driven it home. Arriving at the apartment, she was almost too scared to open the front door, and she found herself wishing that Bernard was there, living with her, or better yet, that she'd agreed to go and live with him in his big, beautiful, safe mansion. But then she saw that everything in the apartment was just as she had left it, and there were no bogeymen hiding behind doors, and she grew angry with herself for even contemplating using Bernard just because she was afraid.

She fed Cleo and consoled her poor little cat who seemed disturbed by having been left for so long without food, fresh water or love – and then she made herself a pot of coffee. Everything took twice as long without her left arm – it would probably drive her crazy, she realized, before she got used to it, if she did get used to it before it was time for the plaster to be cut off. But the coffee tasted wonderful, and it was so good to be back in her own place, surrounded by her own things, able to lean back against her own sofa.

At one o'clock, unable to wait any longer, she reached

for the telephone, then remembered there was a chance that her calls were being tapped. Which hardly mattered, since she was going to call Jamie inside Michael's own house.

She dialled the number.

'Arias residence.' It was the housekeeper again.

'This is Olivia Segal calling again.' She tried to sound normal, as if she made a habit of calling at seven in the morning. 'I'd like to speak to James Arias, please.'

'Just a moment, please, Miss Segal,' the woman said.

A minute ticked by.

'Good morning, Olivia. This is Michael again.'

She took a quick breath. 'Hello, Michael. Sorry to call so early. Is Jamie up yet?'

'Not early enough, as it happens,' Michael said, amiably. 'He's gone horseback riding with Louise – she enjoys this time of day.'

'When do you expect them back?'

'I'm not sure exactly.' Michael paused. 'Are you sure there's nothing I can do for you, Olivia?'

'No, thank you, Michael.'

'Are you at home? So I can ask Jamie to call you back.'

'Yes,' Olivia said. 'Thank you.'

'You're quite welcome.'

She tried to gather her scattered wits together. At times like this – when had there ever *been* a time like this? – it was surely sensible to do practical, useful things. She called a local taxi firm to organize the return of her own car from Midi, took two of the painkillers the hospital pharmacy had dispensed to her, and emerged from the apartment, shortly after two o'clock, to do some one-armed grocery shopping.

She walked slowly and not at all comfortably up to rue Ernest Allard and turned into rue Watteeu, and she was doing well enough, was steadier now, back on home turf, more like herself again. She bought fresh bread, cat food, more coffee, eggs, milk, a bottle of wine and the midday edition of *Le Soir*, and began to head home.

She knew, about halfway back, that someone was following her. A man, dark-haired, stocky, wearing a black leather jacket. She had noticed him fleetingly for the first time as she had paused to glance in the window of a shop specializing in antique mirrors and had seen him stop a little way up the street. Then again, a few minutes later when she set down her bags for a moment, trying to get to grips with being without her left hand, it had happened again. Olivia could not, dared not, look at him more closely, could not see his face, except that when she turned the final corner back into rue Charles Hanssens, her heart beating too rapidly, she saw that he was wearing dark glasses and that he was clean-shaven.

She walked faster along the street to her house, glanced back, saw that he had stopped at the corner of Ernest Allard, and even as she was putting her key into the lock on her front door – and her hand was shaking, damn it – she felt – no, she *knew* – that he was watching her, and worse, much worse, was making no pretence of not watching her.

Safely inside, she closed and double-locked the door, checked all the windows and the garden doors, and then rang the *Gendarmerie*.

They sent two officers, one a woman, within ten minutes.

'Where is the man?' the male officer asked.

'He was practically right outside,' Olivia said. 'On the corner of rue Ernest Allard.'

'You say he was following you?' the woman said.

'Definitely.'

They went back out, returning five minutes later.

'No one there now,' the policeman told her.

They checked around the apartment, went out into the garden, looked over the walls, found not a sign of the man. Aware that Olivia had been hit by a car just the previous evening, they helped her make a fresh pot of coffee and sat with her for a while.

'He was there,' Olivia said, calmer again now, more assertive, 'and there's no question that he was following me.'

'It happens, regrettably,' the man said. 'Some men get a kick out of intimidating women.'

'This was more than that,' Olivia said. 'I tried to tell your colleagues that last night.'

'We know,' the policewoman said.

Olivia looked up at her sharply. 'Did they tell you they thought I was crazy?'

'Of course not,' the woman said swiftly. 'They said you were very upset – who wouldn't be after a hit-and-run?'

'But they still think it was someone panicking after an accident.'

'They're following up all possibilities,' the man told her. 'We always do, mademoiselle.'

'How?' Olivia asked. 'When there were no witnesses.'

'It makes it hard,' the woman said, frankly.

'So no one's doing anything at all.' Olivia was blunt and angry.

'You must be very frightened,' the man said.

'Yes, I am – and if you knew me even a little, you'd know that that's not a normal state of mind for me.' Olivia put down her coffee cup because she could feel her right hand starting to tremble again. 'What nobody seems to want to understand – and I guess I shouldn't blame you all for that, because it's such an incredible story – but I do, I'm sorry, but I *do* blame you, because this is real, and it's happening now, and it's happening to *me*—'

She stopped, knew with a thud of sick resignation, just as she had last night, that it was pointless going on. Without evidence, no one was going to believe her. And all that evidence, every last trace of it, had vanished along with the Hermès bag.

'Do you have someone who could stay here with you?' the policeman asked.

'No.' Again, Olivia considered contacting Bernard, realized she could not bring herself to do that. 'Not really.'

'Maybe,' the policewoman suggested gently, 'you could go somewhere else – a hotel, perhaps. Just till you're feeling stronger.'

'I can't do that either.' She looked at their perplexed faces and accepted that none of this was their fault. 'I'm expecting a call from the United States, from a friend. It's very important.'

The two officers looked at each other, appeared, without words, to reach an agreement.

'We'll try to arrange a patrol,' the policeman said.

'Try?' Olivia couldn't help looking sceptical.

'We'll manage it,' he said, more positively. 'You have cause, after all, mademoiselle, to be afraid after your experience at Midi.'

'The man was there,' Olivia said again.

'We believe you,' the woman said.

The gendarmes made another circuit of the block, returned once more, checked around the apartment, made sure all the locks were secure, and assured Olivia that arrangements had been made for a car to patrol rue Charles Hanssens once each hour. If anything further happened, they told her, she should not hesitate to contact the local station. They would see to it, they said, that she was safe, and in the meantime they suggested that she had a rest, took care of herself.

Olivia thanked them both, locked the front door behind them, picked up Cleo with her good right arm, and went back into the sitting room. They were well-meaning enough; she doubted they'd lied to her. A car on routine patrol would doubtless take a short detour once an hour to take a cursory look at her house. But she knew that, like their colleagues the previous night at the hospital, these two officers did not believe that anyone was out to kill her.

She knew, too, that if the man in the black leather jacket wanted to get to her, there would be ample time between patrol circuits for him to do so.

The rest of Wednesday afternoon passed slowly. Olivia tried, alternately, to read, to watch television, to do some work and to sleep. Nothing lasted for long. Now and again, she stood up and went to the window in the living room, looking out into the street. Twice, she saw a police car, saw it slow right down outside her house and felt, briefly, comforted.

She thought from time to time about what she was going to do. It was so hard today, with the pain from her arm and bruises still blooming like black roses over her rib cage and legs, with the shock and fear still too fresh, still distorting her logic, to know what was right. But one thing was becoming clear enough. With Osterman's papers stolen and Jamie stuck unknowingly in the heart of what she was now almost certain was the enemy camp, there was only one person left who might be able to help.

Nothing in either Carlos's or Arthur's letters had indicated that they might have taken Franklin Aldrich into their confidence, yet Annie's home had been broken into, and Annie's father had been one of Arthur's lawyers, and Richard Tyson, Franklin's partner, had told Olivia that all Franklin's old papers had been shipped after his death to the archives in their New York office.

'If Mr Aldrich's daughter needs access,' Tyson had said to her, stuffily, 'that could, of course, be arranged.'

And Annie was there now, on the spot, in New York.

Except that if – and it was a big if – Arthur had passed copies of Anton Rothenburg's notebook and Paul Osterman's documents and his correspondence with Carlos Arias to Franklin Aldrich, and if Annie was able to locate the proof, then if Michael Arias found that out, Annie, too, might be in danger.

It was seeing the man again that made up her mind.

Olivia wandered over to the window at ten to five, and he was there, standing directly across the road, and she gasped and dropped instinctively down to the floor, her right hand over her mouth. And when she was sufficiently recovered, when she felt able to breathe again and to risk taking another look, he was gone, and she knew there was no point calling the police because he'd vanished again and there was no evidence that he'd been there. And she thought of getting her camera, of keeping it at her side ready to shoot if he came back, and then at least she'd have *something* to show them, but she had no film in the camera or anywhere in the apartment, and she certainly couldn't go out to buy some. And she was afraid again now – truly, intensely scared – she wished, really wished, for the first time since the burglary that she'd compromised her desire for light and atmosphere and appearance and had had bars fitted over all her windows – and even little Cleo seemed to be getting antsy, skittering around all the time yet staying close, following her around like a dog.

And there really was nothing left to be done but to call Annie.

23

She sat, with Cleo on her lap, in the centre of the sitting-room floor, on the faded Kashan silk prayer rug she'd found with Bernard at an auction back in January, and used her tiny black Ericsson cellular phone to call the St Regis Hotel. It was eight minutes past five, Brussels time, just past eleven in the morning in New York. Edward was almost certainly out and about by this time, and there was every likelihood that Annie would be with him.

'Mr and Mrs Edward Thomas, please,' she told the hotel operator, and held her breath.

It rang three times.

'Hello?'

'Annie, thank God you're there.'

'Livvy? How lovely. I'm just getting ready to meet Edward for lunch.' Annie paused. 'Livvy, what's the matter?'

On Olivia's lap, Cleo kneaded her claws, hurting her. Olivia shut her eyes for a moment, then opened them again.

'A great deal, Annie.' She waited another instant. 'I wish I didn't have to tell you any of it. But I can't seem to find

Jamie, and there is no one else I can trust, and I can't go on alone.'

'It's all right,' Annie said, alarmed. 'You don't have to.'

And Olivia told her.

It was hard for Annie to absorb the enormity of Olivia's story, and had it been anyone else but Olivia Segal telling it to her, she thought she might not have believed a word of it. But Olivia was one of the most honest people in Annie's world, and Olivia was not given to flights of fancy. And Olivia was not easily frightened – in fact, Annie could not remember Olivia *ever* being frightened.

She had told Annie everything, as swiftly, concisely and calmly as she could manage, and then she had asked her to do two things. First, to get hold of Jamie in Newport and to make sure, if she could manage it, that no one else overheard their conversation. Second, to try and get access, as quickly and discreetly as possible, to her late father's private files.

Annie had put down the telephone and had gone on, mechanically, getting ready to go out. She considered, briefly, finding Edward and telling him everything, but then she decided against it, for she realized that Edward would not let her take any risks, and getting hold of her father's files was something he could not do for her, so she would simply leave a message for him cancelling lunch, telling him that something had come up and she'd see him later.

Still numb, still functioning on a strange, calming kind of auto-pilot, she telephoned the Arias house in Newport, was told that Jamie was out, and put down the phone before Michael or any of the others could speak to her.

Annie sat on the edge of the big hotel bed.

This could not be happening.

She forced herself to go over it again, her mind going in a wild, unwilling, non-chronological zigzag. The story about Jamie's uncle's crimes. The attempt on Olivia's life. The burglaries. And the helicopter crash that it now seemed had not, after all, been accidental.

She thought about the possible risk to herself if she got involved, made herself consider Sophie and William and Liza, not to mention Edward, and she knew that it probably was dreadfully irresponsible to think of taking a chance like this – and she wasn't the *type* to take risks ordinarily—

But then she thought about her mother and father, and how dreadfully she had missed them all these years, and if Olivia was right, then they had been murdered, for the love of God, *murdered*.

And if she could help, if her father's archives did contain the proof they needed, then she was damned if she was going to let Olivia bear the brunt of this alone, or Jamie, come to that.

Annie was trembling a little as she strode – Annie had never been a woman who strode anywhere – into the Aldrich law offices on Fifty-seventh Street, her passport in her purse in case there was no one at the office who remembered or recognized her.

'My name is Ann Aldrich Thomas,' she told the receptionist, 'and I need urgent access to my father's personal archives.' She swept straight on before the younger woman could answer. 'I'd appreciate it if you would arrange for someone to telephone Richard Tyson in London, so that he can vouch for me and make the archives available.'

The receptionist opened her mouth to speak.

'When I say urgent,' Annie said swiftly, 'I mean urgent.'

It was all there. Olivia's hunch had been accurate, Franklin had been holding copies. By four o'clock, Annie had located and skimmed through a complete set of her father's privately filed copies of Arthur Segal's correspondence with Carlos Arias, alias Georg Brauner, and a xeroxed copy of the pages in Anton Rothenburg's notebook. Annie was profoundly shaken, yet she knew at the same time that she had never been so dramatically galvanized by or focused upon anything.

She emerged back into the wood-panelled reception area, arms laden with papers, and found Eleanor Cohen, one of the partners, waiting for her.

'Mrs Thomas, I'm so sorry I wasn't here when you arrived.'

'That's perfectly all right.' Annie smiled at the receptionist. 'I was well looked after.'

'Do you have everything you need?' Eleanor Cohen asked.

'Almost.' Annie smiled again, apologetically. 'I need to use your photocopier.'

'I'll have someone take care of that for you.'

'No,' Annie said. 'Thank you, but I'd rather do it myself.'

She made two sets, returned the originals to the archive room, packaged one set to take away and asked Eleanor Cohen to deposit the final set in the company vault.

'To be passed, with this letter, to my husband, in case—' Annie stopped.

'In case of what, Mrs Thomas?' Eleanor Cohen asked.

'In the extremely unlikely event that I either disappear

from the face of the earth or meet with an accident.' She saw the concern on the attorney's face and tried to smile again. 'It's just a precaution,' she said. 'Both those eventualities really are very unlikely.'

'I should hope they are,' Eleanor Cohen said.

'One more favour?' Annie asked, tentatively.

'Of course.'

'I have some calls to make. I have a charge card.'

'That's not necessary,' Eleanor Cohen told her.

'All the same,' Annie said. 'The calls are long-distance.'

Olivia snatched up the cellular telephone. It was ten-fifteen in Brussels.

'Livvy, it's me. I have it all.'

Briefly, Olivia closed her eyes. 'Thank God for that. You've read it?'

'Most of it – as much as I had time to.'

'So you don't think I'm crazy?'

'I never did.' Annie paused. 'Livvy, it's all too hideous to think about.'

'Have you talked to Jamie?'

'Not yet. I've tried twice, and they say he's not there, but I think you're right – I do get the feeling someone doesn't want us to talk to him.'

'Michael,' Olivia said. 'You think it's Michael too.'

'Unless it's Peter.'

'It's not Peter's style, Annie. And he was still at school when Osterman had his meeting with Michael in '64.'

'And Jamie always refers to Michael as head of the family.'

'It's Michael, I'm sure of it,' Olivia said. 'But what now?'

'I've had an idea,' Annie said. 'There is someone who might help us get past the others to Jamie.'

'Who?'

'I don't have time to tell you any more, Livvy – I've got a plane to catch.'

'Where are you going?' Olivia grew alarmed. 'Annie, what are you planning? You can't do anything on your own.'

'I'm not going to.' Annie sounded very calm. 'I'll call you later, Livvy, as soon as I know more.'

'Annie, wait—'

Olivia heard the call cut out, stared at the small black phone in her hand.

'Damn it,' she said. '*Damn* it.'

At the Arias family compound in Newport, final preparations were under way for Michael's birthday party. Louise Arias adored throwing parties, had always entertained as often and as lavishly as possible no matter where she'd lived, even when she'd shared a small Cambridge home in her college days. But from the first moment she'd laid eyes on her husband's lovely cliff-top mansion, she had vowed that no birthday, anniversary or other cause for celebration would pass unmarked so long as she lived in that house, and it was a tribute to Louise's skills that even in Newport – even during the festive season – her invitations were received with pleasure and anticipation.

Jamie was not in the mood for a party. In the first place, he'd only recently landed the Korda Shoe Corporation account, worth at least ten million dollars a year, and he hadn't liked abandoning Maggie and David at JAA just when they were on the edge of being ready to burst their latest campaign ideas on him. In the second place, he had a lousy head cold, and would infinitely sooner have been in his own home, drinking hot toddies, watching old movies and maybe having a gossip with Olivia on the phone – Olivia was the best at taking his mind off a trivial complaint like a common cold, Olivia was the best at taking his mind off most things, when he let himself think about it, which he seldom did these days. And in the third place, both he and Michael were furious with Peter for insisting on bringing Angie Rogos, his new mistress, for the whole two-day run-up to the party which had clearly been meant for family only.

'Peter really is the prick of the universe,' Daisy had said to Jamie on day one, a little drunkenly, after an interminable luncheon on the lawn during which Angie, dressed in an ankle-length but almost entirely see-through voile shift, had fawned all over her lover, heedless of his and Daisy's two young sons.

'I'm afraid he really is,' Jamie agreed.

'Though it's easier for me than you, of course,' Daisy had gone on. 'Michael and Louise were always decent to me about Peter's infidelities, though I felt they were almost too embarrassed to bear to *look* at me after he stole Carrie from you. But now, the worse Peter's behaviour gets, the more Louise seems to consider me more family than him.'

'What makes you think it's harder for me?' Jamie had asked.

'Because it's easier to cope, long-term, isn't it, when you think they've left you for real love?' Daisy had paused for breath. 'And because now, knowing what a dear man you are, Jamie – not even a bit like your brother – some little piece of you is bound to think you should feel sorry for Carrie – which, of course, you should not.'

'I don't,' Jamie had said.

'Even though you know she knows leaving you for Peter was the biggest mistake she ever made,' Daisy said, and smiled ruefully. 'Even bigger than Peter leaving me.'

'Carrie doesn't think that.'

'Oh, yes, she does. She told me, or at least she told me she knew you were the better brother.' Daisy grinned again. 'Mind you, she did add that she hadn't tried cousin Michael yet.'

'I'd like to see her dare,' Jamie said, thinking about Louise.

'Louise wanted to invite Carrie, you know, but Michael told her it was asking for trouble.'

'Thank heaven for Michael,' Jamie said, and meant it.

Yet still, Michael's birthday aside, he was not in the mood for a party.

Annie had left a message for Edward at the St Regis telling him not to worry about her, had caught the shuttle from La Guardia to Logan and, taking the Boston rush hour into account, had jumped on a ferry across the harbour, bringing her a short cab ride from her destination.

At twenty-two minutes past six, she was rapping on the exterior glass door of the offices of Beaumont-Arias on Newbury Street, praying silently that Carrie Arias was still inside. Jamie had always said that Carrie liked to work late, claimed she got more done when the paid help – as she had called their employees, not always behind their backs – had left for the day.

She had completed eight series of raps, each series growing louder and more resonant, and was just about giving up, when Carrie's blonde hair – blonder than the last time she'd seen it, Annie couldn't help noting – and her Jean Muir-clad body came stalking around the corner.

'Who the hell can't read?' Her wide blue irritated eyes grew even wider when she recognized Annie. 'And what the fuck are you doing here?' She made no move to unlock the door, just stood there glowering through the glass.

'I need to talk to you,' Annie said.

'Why should that be of the slightest interest to me?' Carrie asked.

'Please,' Annie said. 'Open the door, Carrie.'

'We're closed,' Carrie said. 'If you want to make an appointment, call my assistant.'

'Carrie, it's an emergency.' Annie let the full weight of her anxiety swell that last word. 'I mean it, a real emergency. Life or death.'

Carrie moved an inch or so closer. 'Whose life or death?'

Annie had thought about her answer to that question all the way from New York, and had decided that total, stark, if dangerous, honesty was her best and only way of tackling Carrie Arias.

'Olivia's,' she said.

Carrie's eyes widened still further and she opened her mouth to laugh, then shut it again. She stepped right up against the glass. 'Which option am I supposed to be backing, Annie? I have to tell you I'm considerably more inclined towards death.'

Annie managed a half smile. 'I guess I can't blame you for that.' She paused. 'Please open the door.' Her smile was gone. 'Please.'

Carrie turned around, went over to the receptionist's desk, opened a drawer, took out a key and held it up.

'Do I get to help?' she asked loudly, so that Annie could hear her through the thick glass.

'You do,' Annie replied wryly. 'But maybe not in the way you might have in mind.'

With deliberate slowness, Carrie opened the door.

*   *   *

At half-past midnight on Thursday morning in Brussels, Olivia – with Cleo burrowed in beside her – was in bed, drowsy from painkillers, but too tense to sleep and unwilling to knock herself out completely with one of the pills the hospital had given her.

She had seen the police patrol car from her window several more times during the evening, and once, an officer had rung her bell to check on her, and she had felt more reassured then, had seen no further sign of the man in the black leather jacket. Perhaps, she was beginning to think, that had, after all, been coincidental; maybe he had just been a city sleaze picking on a vulnerable-looking woman – which of course she was right now with her arm in the sling – and maybe she *had* been overreacting.

And her tension now was stemming more from what Annie might be doing than from fear, and soon, soon, surely she would *have* to fall asleep from sheer, unutterable exhaustion.

'You must,' Carrie said to Annie a few minutes later in her own office – a monument to Beacon Hill-bred taste and refinement in spite of the awards and photographs displayed in a cabinet on one wall – 'be crazy.'

'I understand your feeling that,' Annie said steadily. 'But I think you may feel differently when you hear everything I have to tell you.'

Carrie leaned back in her chair, her body language perfectly relaxed. She remembered their last encounter only too well, knew she would never forget, and certainly never forgive, her defeat and humiliation at the end of the *Light Years* fiasco. But then again, she had always known that it had been Olivia Segal's scheme, not Annie Thomas's, and now the mere knowledge that Olivia was in trouble and that Annie was here begging for her help was purest music to her ears.

'If you think,' she said, 'that anything you could ever tell me could possibly persuade me to lift a finger to help Olivia Segal, then you're not only crazy and incredibly brazen, but plain stupid into the bargain.'

Annie sat very straight. 'I gather that you and Peter are finished.'

'We most decidedly are, if it's any of your business.' Her voice was even more cool, clipped Bostonian than usual.

'It's not my business at all,' Annie admitted. 'But I imagine you'll be looking for a good settlement.'

Carrie's eyes narrowed coldly. 'That really is none of your business.'

'I imagine' – Annie ignored what she'd said – 'you'll be hoping to squeeze him dry. Lord knows he deserves it.'

'Surely what you really mean is that I deserve it, Annie.'

'At this precise moment,' Annie said, 'I'm not in the least interested in what you do or don't deserve.'

'I'm surprised,' Carrie said. 'I mean, I'm surprised by you. I thought you were such a mouse, Annie Aldrich Thomas, Jamie's gentle, trank-gulping little friend. Even when you came to the Ritz-Carlton that day with Olivia, even when you had your say, I knew you were just hanging on to Olivia's coattails, still a mouse. What are you on these days, Annie, to make you so bold?'

Annie felt strangely calm. 'Even a mouse has to stand up and be counted sometimes.' She paused. 'I have ammunition for you, Carrie, to use against Peter. All the ammunition you could ever dream of, and more.'

'I don't think I need much more than I have,' Carrie said confidently. 'Given that my husband's been flaunting his mistress over half of New England and Manhattan.'

'Twelve mistresses would be nothing compared with what I have for you, Carrie,' Annie told her, 'nor would a half-dozen of their children.'

For the first time, Carrie permitted herself a flicker of interest.

'Go on,' she said.

At a quarter to seven, already dressed in his damned tuxedo – Louise always insisted on black tie for her major parties; if she could really have her way, Michael said that she'd have every Arias man, preferably every male guest, wearing white tie and tails – Jamie blew his cold-blocked nose, looked at his watch and wondered if he had time to call Olivia. They hadn't spoken for several days, and there was a fault on the phone extension in his room, and he missed her, and suddenly it seemed to him that the long, long evening ahead for which he still was no more in the mood than he had been, might be made more bearable if he could just snatch a few minutes of conversation with her first.

He wandered down the handsome winged staircase, past the haunting painting by Puvis de Chavannes which Michael had once told him his late father, Juan Luis, had personally helped to hang about a year prior to his death. Louise had placed a huge bowl of lilies on the stand beneath it, and as Jamie glanced down to the grand entrance hall below he thought for an instant that, for his personal taste, the house was looking just a touch too wedding-like for a man's birthday party; but then he remembered Louise telling him at a previous celebration that she regarded all parties, no matter what their *raison d'être*, as the province of females. 'Women,' she had told Jamie, 'understand how to make people feel welcome and comfortable and light-hearted far better than men, except, I suppose, gay men, and their parties – their *top* parties – are the best of all.'

He went into the library to use the telephone, sat down in the cool, dark peace and quiet, finding it just what his poor banging head needed, savoured it for just a moment, picked up the phone and began to dial.

The door opened and Michael came in.

'Jamie, just the man.' He looked apologetically at his cousin. 'Is that urgent or can it wait?'

Jamie put down the receiver. 'It's not urgent.'

'Not calling the office?'

Jamie shook his head. 'Olivia.'

'Pretty late for her, isn't it?'

'Not really – we often speak around this time.' Jamie looked up at Michael. 'What can I do?'

'I need a second opinion on the champagne,' Michael said. 'Louise just brought me a glass for a private toast and I'm not certain if it's quite right.'

'I'm not sure if I'm the man for the job this evening,' Jamie said. 'This damn cold's playing havoc with my taste buds.'

'I'm afraid you're the only man,' Michael said firmly. 'Since Peter's locked in his bedroom with Miss Rogos. Besides, champagne's an excellent cure-all.'

Jamie stood up. 'I guess it can't hurt.'

Michael opened the door. 'You're sure you don't mind leaving that call for now? I really could use your opinion.'

Jamie shook his head.

'It's nothing that can't wait till tomorrow,' he said.

*   *   *

'I don't believe it,' Carrie said, about a half-hour later. 'I really don't believe it.'

'I think perhaps you should,' Annie said. She indicated the package resting on the desk in front of her. 'It's all there, after all. All the proof you could ask for.'

She felt suddenly drained. She had given Carrie an edited version of the long, dreadful tale, had told her and shown her just enough and no more, but she had observed its ever-growing impact on the other woman's now taut and paler face.

'I've shocked you,' she said.

'Of course you've damn well shocked me,' Carrie said, sharply. 'What do you take me for? I'm not soft, God knows, and I have no wish to be, but even I draw the line at murder.' She shook her head. 'Jesus, I can't *believe* it – Michael? Solid as a Spanish rock, pillar of the community Michael Arias, a *murderer*?'

'You do realize, don't you,' Annie said, slowly, 'that whether or not you decide to use this to get what you want from Peter, you're very much better off knowing about this ahead of its getting out.' She paused. 'Which it will, Carrie, one way or another. After which being a member of the Arias family may not be quite the bonus it's been in the past.'

'It's reasonably common knowledge,' Carrie said, 'that I'm finished with the Arias family.'

'You're still married to Peter.'

'Meaning what exactly?' Carrie spoke slowly, still allowing Annie's story to sink in.

'That you might be wise to distance yourself from them more completely,' Annie said. 'Before it's too late.'

'I think that's a little melodramatic, from my standpoint,' Carrie said. 'After all, no one's going to believe that I knew about any of this. We don't even know for sure yet if Peter knows about it.'

Annie trod as carefully as she could, fully conscious that it was only Carrie's shock that was allowing her to remain there, and that, knowing Carrie, the situation could alter at any moment. 'Let's just say,' she went on, 'that Peter's going to have to prove his ignorance.' She paused. 'And we both know that a lot of wives have been found guilty by association.'

Carrie was silent.

'Of course, Olivia and I could help you out,' Annie went on, 'by speaking for you. We could make it absolutely clear – we could even testify, if that became necessary – that you knew nothing about either the Rothenburgs or the helicopter crash until we told you.'

Carrie's eyes grew chillier again. 'I take it this is where my help comes in.' She paused. 'The implication being that if I don't help you get Olivia out of trouble, you might suggest that I did know something.'

'I didn't say that,' Annie said, far more calmly than she felt.

'You're getting rather good at this, Annie,' Carrie said. 'Blackmail becomes you.'

Annie couldn't help flushing.

'So what do you want me to do?'

'Come with me to Newport and help me get to Jamie. I know he's there, at the house, but I haven't been allowed to speak to him.'

'And you expect me to persuade them to let you in?'

'Yes.'

'When?'

'Now.'

'Now?' Carrie looked startled. 'It's after half-past seven.'

'So we could be there by nine-thirty or ten.'

'It's out of the question,' Carrie said crisply. 'I have two engagements this evening, and I have no intention of cancelling them.'

Annie looked at her, saw the familiar coldness back in her blue eyes, and knew she still had work to do if she was going to talk Carrie round.

'Someone has to warn Jamie,' she said quietly. 'I understand your not caring about Olivia, but I can't imagine you'd want to see Jamie in actual danger.'

'I can't imagine that James is in any danger,' Carrie said.

'Can't you?' Annie asked, pointedly.

Carrie glanced at her antique Cartier watch, then shook her head impatiently. 'There's no purpose in even considering going to Newport tonight, not with Louise giving a birthday party for Michael.'

'We could join the party,' Annie said.

'Even you must have heard of security, Annie,' Carrie said. 'These parties are scrupulously guarded. No invitation, no entrance.'

'But you're still Mrs Peter Arias.' Annie paused. 'You're still Caroline Beaumont Arias. Are you going to tell me you'd let some security guard stop you from walking into an Arias family party?'

'Certainly not,' Carrie said.

Annie held her breath.

'I don't like being bulldozed, Annie.'

'And I don't like my two best friends being in danger.'

'Do you honestly believe,' Carrie asked, 'that Michael would go so far as to harm his own cousin?'

'I don't know,' Annie answered. 'I'd like to think he wouldn't.'

'But if Michael had his own uncle killed . . .' Carrie's voice trailed off.

'Quite.' Annie sat in an agony of suspense.

Carrie was silent for several seconds.

'Wait outside,' she said at last. 'I have some calls to make.'

Annie picked up her bag and the package and stood up.

'Are you going to come with me, Carrie?'

Carrie looked at her. 'I think, perhaps, this is one confrontation I would like to witness first hand.'

Annie felt weak with relief. 'So you're coming?'

'Not if you don't get out and let me make my calls.'

Olivia answered the telephone just after two. She was still so groggy with sleep that she thought she heard Annie telling her that she was on the way from Boston to Newport with Carrie, and that she was using Carrie's car-phone, and that one way or another they'd have Jamie out of there within a few hours; and Olivia was to go back to sleep now, she was no longer in this on her own, she could get some rest and Annie would be back on to her as soon as there was any news to pass on.

'Did you say Carrie?' Olivia asked fuzzily.

'That's right,' Annie answered.

Olivia put the receiver down again, and lay back, and half smiled into the dark on her way back down into the luxurious escape of sleep. She knew now, was comfortable in the knowledge that, she was in the middle of the strangest dream. Which only went to prove how crazy dreams could be. Because the very notion of Carrie Beaumont Arias coming to Annie's and Olivia's aid was one of the wildest, craziest things that anyone's subconscious could possibly dredge up.

Annie and Carrie encountered their first obstacle at the outer entrance of the Arias compound where the gateman asked for their invitations or, failing that, their names, so that he could check them off on his list, and two armed security guards hovered in the background as if Al Capone were going to leap from the trunk of Carrie's car any second.

'You're not on my list, ma'am,' the gateman said, leaning down to Carrie's window. The sound of distant music filtered through the warm summer night air.

'I didn't say I was,' Carrie said.

'It's invitation only, ma'am. I'm sorry.'

Carrie nodded towards the gate house. 'Why don't you call the main house and ask permission to let us in?'

'No point, ma'am. As I said, it's strictly invitation only.'

Carrie stuck her head a little further out of the window. 'What are the names of the hosts of this party?'

'Mr and Mrs Michael Arias, ma'am.' The man managed to blend courtesy and snobbishness into his tone.

'And what did I say my name was?' Carrie's acidity was soft, gentle.

'Mrs Peter Arias, ma'am.'

'Do you know who Peter Arias is?'

'Mr Michael Arias's cousin.'

'Whose wife I am,' Carrie said.

'Yes, ma'am.' There was a hint of a sigh behind the words.

'So don't you think you could, after all, make an exception and let us in?'

'No, ma'am, I don't think I could.' The man observed the slow, dangerous narrowing of Carrie's eyes. 'But I will call the house and check with them.'

'Well, thank you,' Carrie said, sweetly.

'You're welcome, ma'am.'

In less than four minutes, the time it had taken to get Louise Arias to give the okay, they were heading up the long driveway towards the house, the music growing louder, sounding, Annie thought, like Duke Ellington – though of course it couldn't be Ellington because he was dead, and from what she'd heard about Louise's parties, she'd rather be dead than play recorded music.

'You were great back there,' Annie said, weakly. She was still scarcely able to believe that she'd talked Carrie into coming all that way with her, and now, watching and listening to her in fighting form and – on the face of it, at least – on her side, was almost too much to take in. 'I'd never have got this far without you,' she added.

'No, you wouldn't,' Carrie agreed.

'I owe you already.'

Carrie shrugged, driving on. 'Nothing to it, not for a hard-nosed bitch like me. Though you're right. You do most certainly owe me.'

'Oh, God,' Annie said, her throat tightening as they slowed down again. 'There's Louise.'

Mrs Michael Arias stood in the doorway in slender, immaculate, cream silk glory, her silhouette almost entirely merged with the dazzle of chandeliered brilliance in the entrance hall behind them.

'When in doubt,' Carrie told Annie, 'leave it to me.'

She got out of the car, handed the keys to the waiting attendant and walked up the stone steps, followed by Annie.

'Carrie, what an unexpected surprise,' Louise said, and leaned forward to give her a careful air-kiss on both cheeks. 'And with Annie Thomas, of all people. How lovely.'

'I hope you don't mind too much, Louise.' Annie held out her right hand. 'I was in Boston and bumped into Carrie, who said she was coming up for the party.'

'Jamie didn't mention that you were in Boston,' Louise said.

'He didn't know.'

Michael appeared behind his wife. 'Good Lord,' he said. 'It's true.'

'Happy birthday, Michael,' Carrie said. 'May we come in?'

'Of course you may.' Louise stepped back graciously. 'Isn't this a lovely surprise, Michael.'

Michael closed the door, his face impassive. There were no guests to be seen in the hall – just two waitresses hurrying past – but the sounds and scents of a large party, still distant, a heady combination of music, conversation and laughter, of food and a score of predictable perfumes and smoke, lapped around Annie and Carrie, enveloping them.

'Everyone's having dinner, I'm afraid,' Louise said.

'So what can we do for you?' Michael asked, a little brusquely.

'Michael.' Louise sounded reproving. 'That's not very hospitable.'

'We're in the middle of a party,' Michael said reasonably. 'For which they're hardly dressed.'

'I can take care of that,' Louise said, and smiled at Carrie. 'If you wouldn't object too violently to borrowing something of mine.'

'Not at all,' Carrie said, 'but I won't, thanks just the

same, Louise. I've always believed Jean Muir can take me just about anywhere.'

'I'm quite happy as I am, too,' Annie said, not remotely happy in the daytime Escada suit she'd put on that morning – an eternity ago – to meet Edward for lunch, though her unease, of course, had little to do with her clothing. 'I've only come to see Jamie.'

'We've really come,' Carrie said, quickly, 'for a family talk.'

'Tonight?' For the first time, Louise looked disconcerted. 'You can't be serious.'

'Not tonight,' Michael said firmly.

'Definitely tonight,' Carrie said.

Louise lowered her voice. 'I know you have good cause to feel hostile towards Peter, but surely Michael's birthday is not the right time.'

'It's the perfect time,' Carrie said, softly. 'But it has nothing to do with my hostility towards my husband.' She paused. 'Where is Peter, by the way? Tête à tête somewhere with his mistress, I suppose?'

'I'm not sure.' Louise was growing flustered. 'In the gardens, having dinner, I imagine.'

'If you've come here with the idea of creating some kind of spectacle, Carrie,' Michael said, 'then we'll have to insist you leave.'

'No spectacle, Michael.' Annie answered instead of Carrie. 'Just a small family gathering.'

'You're not family,' Michael said, dislike showing. 'What does this have to do with you?'

'I thought you said you'd come along to see Jamie,' Louise said.

'I have,' Annie agreed. 'Do you know where he is, Louise?'

'Jamie has a bad cold,' Michael said abruptly. 'I think I saw him going up to bed a while back.'

'Did you, darling?' Louise was surprised. 'I'm sure I just saw him dancing.'

'Perhaps, Louise, you could find him for Annie?' Carrie asked, sweetly.

'I'd rather go myself, if you don't mind,' Annie said.

'Then perhaps you could go rustle up Peter,' Carrie suggested to Michael. 'We really do need to have this little talk as quickly as possible.'

'It's completely out of the question,' Michael said, tightly.

Louise was growing more baffled than annoyed. 'We can hardly disappear from our own party to have a meeting, Carrie – surely even you must see that.'

'Not really,' Carrie said. 'I heard you say once, Louise, that if a party's properly organized, it should be able to run perfectly all on its own.' She paused to listen to the sounds coming from beyond the house. 'They all seem to be getting on with things rather well without you right now.'

'All right.' Michael's anger became more open. 'That's enough. You'll have to leave.'

'I don't think so,' Carrie said.

'Don't make me throw you out, Carrie.'

'Michael, please,' Louise protested. 'Let's not have a scene.'

'Don't worry, Louise,' Carrie said confidently. 'He won't throw us out. Unless he wants us to bring in the police.'

'Oh, stop, Carrie,' Louise said, upset and vehement. 'This is getting out of hand. You know, I wanted to invite you tonight, but Michael said it would just create embarrassment – I do hope you're not going to prove him right.'

'I'm rather afraid I am,' Carrie said. 'Though not in the way you mean.'

Annie, having kept silent for a time, letting Carrie, as she'd suggested, take the lead, knew it was time to speak up.

'You haven't asked after Olivia, Michael,' she said.

His dark eyes hardened. 'Why should I have done that?'

'Is something wrong with Olivia?' Louise asked, growing ever more confused.

'She's not very well,' Annie answered. 'After her accident.'

'Oh, dear,' Louise said. 'Nothing too serious, I hope.'

'Not as serious as it might have been,' Annie said, and took a breath. 'She was hit by a car.' She looked directly at Michael. 'Do you think we can have that talk now?'

'I suggest the library,' Carrie said.

'And I suggest,' Michael said, 'for the last time, that you leave.'

Louise tossed her perfect auburn hair. 'Oh, for heaven's sake, darling, let's talk to them and get it over with.' She looked at Carrie. 'How long is this going to take? I really do have to get back to our guests.'

'Why don't you get back to them right now?' Michael said. 'I can take care of this meeting without you.'

'No, Michael, you can't,' Carrie said.

Annie reached out, unexpectedly, and touched Louise's left arm gently. The older woman was cold, and Annie, feeling suddenly quite certain of her innocence, felt intensely sorry for her. 'I really do think that you should stay, Louise,' she said.

'For goodness sake, let me throw them out,' Michael said to his wife. 'Carrie's trouble, she's always been trouble.'

'And glad of it,' Carrie said coldly, 'knowing what I do now.'

'I'm going to find Jamie,' Annie said, abruptly.

Jamie was dancing with Daisy, the worst of his cold chased away temporarily, at least, by champagne and atmosphere. Louise had drawn her white lily theme like a lovely, pure, luxuriant chain throughout the house and gardens, so that everywhere guests wandered, from the hallways to the pool house to the bathrooms, the chaste, yet oddly seductive flowers nestled around them, never intrusive, just promoting a sense of having stepped into some nameless, exotic land where beauty and pleasure ruled and outside concerns had no place.

'I want to go swimming,' Daisy said.

'Really?' Jamie looked down at her in surprise. 'And risk ruining your lovely hair? That's not like you.'

'I think I'm a bit drunk.'

'You've been drunk quite a lot the last few days, Daisy Arias.'

'It must be the company.'

'Thank you,' Jamie said.

'Not you, Jamie. Certainly not you.'

'I thought you enjoyed being around the family,' he said, affectionately. Daisy sometimes tended towards prissiness, yet Jamie found, as time went by, that he liked Peter's first wife more and more.

'I do, usually,' Daisy said, clinging to him a little more tightly, as if she might fall down otherwise. 'But I haven't this time, not much, and it really isn't because of Peter and Angie.'

'What then?'

'Michael's been in such a grouchy mood.'

'Has he?' Jamie hadn't noticed.

'You've not been yourself either,' Daisy said, 'but that's probably just your cold.'

'I'm sorry,' Jamie said.

'Not your fault,' Daisy told him politely.

The music stopped.

'Hello, Jamie.'

Jamie let go of Daisy and turned around.

'Annie!' A smile of pleasure and surprise lit up his face, then vanished when he saw the expression in her eyes. 'Annie, what's happened?'

For the first time since she and Carrie had arrived in Newport, Annie felt herself go weak at the knees.

'Oh, Jamie,' she said. 'Thank God I've found you.'

The sound of breaking glass woke Olivia just after four-fifteen. Instantly, icily awake, without a hint of grogginess now, she turned on the bedside light.

The cat was wide awake too, standing by the door, her tortoiseshell fur standing on end, her tail erect and the green of her eyes almost completely swallowed up by huge, black, fully dilated pupils.

'It's okay, Cleo,' Olivia whispered.

She heard another sound.

Olivia reached for the phone, dialled 100 for the police, heard nothing. Quickly, tucking the receiver between her ear and her chin, she pressed her finger on the cut-off button and released it again. There was no tone.

'Oh, God,' she said, then remembered the cellular phone. It was there, where she'd left it after Annie's call, on the other night-table. Swift as she could, hampered by her arm, she snatched it up. The battery was drained and the spare, she knew, was in her study.

'Oh, God,' she said again.

And the light went out.

Peter Arias was half drunk. Jamie, knowing only that Olivia was in some kind of trouble, was distraught and confused. Louise was having a hard time keeping her outrage, dismay and embarrassment under control. Michael was tight-lipped and patently furious. They were all sitting in the library on dark leather chairs, and they were waiting.

'Well,' Carrie said, closing the door. 'Since the gang's all here, Annie, you may as well begin.'

'What the fuck,' Peter asked, 'has she got to do with us?'

'If by us,' Carrie answered, 'you mean you and me, nothing at all.'

'Annie?' Jamie was pale. 'What is going on?'

Annie stood up. If anyone had asked her how she felt at that moment, she could only have answered that she felt entirely outside herself, like an observer. If Olivia had been there with her, she knew she would have been glad to melt into the background, to let Olivia take over. But Livvy wasn't there – Livvy was in Brussels with her arm broken and lucky to be alive. Because of one of these people.

'I'll keep it short,' she began, 'which is not easy, when you're telling people about more than fifty years of evil.'

Michael got to his feet. 'What is this nonsense?'

'Sit down, Michael,' Carrie said, from her chair near the door.

'Don't tell me what to do in my own home.'

'Please, Michael,' Annie said, 'sit down.'

Louise reached out for her husband's hand to draw him back down. 'It's all right, dear. The sooner we let her have her say, the sooner we can get back to the party.'

'I'm not sure,' Annie said, gently, 'that you'll be feeling much like a party when I've finished.'

Peter swivelled around in his chair, trying to get comfortable. 'I must say, your friends have a weird sense of timing,' he said to Jamie. 'This one's the junkie, isn't she?'

'Ex-junkie,' Carrie said, uncharacteristically fair.

'Shall I get on with it?' Annie asked them all.

'No,' Michael said, flatly.

'Oh, for pity's sake, please do,' Louise said, desperately, and drew her husband down beside her again.

Annie looked down at Jamie, into his soft, dark eyes. 'I'm so sorry to have to tell you this, in this awful, cold way. To be honest, I didn't think I had it in me.' She paused. 'Carrie says she's always thought I was a mouse, and I tend to agree with her.' She paused again. 'But I suppose that discovering that your parents have been murdered to cover up a war crime tends to toughen up even the most timid mouse.'

'What,' Jamie asked, 'are you talking about, Annie?'

'What *is* she talking about?' Peter asked.

'I think she's hallucinating,' Michael said.

'What are you *talking* about, Annie, dear?' Louise asked.

'She's talking about your husband,' Carrie answered for Annie. 'She's telling you all that Michael arranged the deaths of six people nineteen years ago – including his own Uncle Carlos—'

'Dear God.' Michael shook his head and stared at Annie as if she were entirely mad.

'Don't be such a fucking idiot, Carrie,' Peter said loudly.

Louise's hazel eyes were huge with horror. 'I never heard anything so *disgusting* in my entire life! Such *lies*!'

Michael patted her arm. 'Don't worry, sweetheart. The woman's obviously deranged.'

'I'm afraid not, Louise,' Annie said, quietly.

Jamie was ashen-faced. 'Annie, I don't know what's going on – I don't know what's wrong with you—'

'There's nothing much wrong with Annie,' Carrie said. 'Though it does pain me a little to admit that, as you can imagine, James.' She looked at Annie. 'Go on. No point stopping now.'

'No,' Annie said. 'I know there isn't.'

She told it briefly and starkly, told her stricken, appalled audience what she was now more certain than ever Michael already knew. That Juan Luis Arias had been a thieving, opportunistic, blackmailing murderer. And that when Arthur Segal had told Carlos Arias what his brother had done, and when Carlos had gone to Michael, to his trusted, beloved nephew, to tell him what he had learned and what he planned to do about it, Michael, acting either in defence of his father's honour, or simply because he was unwilling to lose everything because of his uncle's crisis of conscience, had arranged the helicopter crash.

'And no one else would ever have been any the wiser,' Annie told them, nearing the end of her story, 'if Olivia hadn't happened on a note that Carlos had sent to her father.' She looked straight at Michael, now sitting rigid with anger. 'It was only after Jamie asked you if you knew what the note meant, that her apartment was broken into and the note was stolen.'

At last Michael moved. He stood up and stared down at her and his eyes were black with anger.

'And that,' he said, 'is just about enough, Mrs Thomas.' His hands, down by his sides, were tightly clenched. 'I've listened quietly and patiently to your ramblings about Nazis and Jews and paintings. I've sat still while you accused me of murdering my own uncle – my own *uncle* and five other people, for the love of God—'

'Michael—' Louise was standing too, reaching for her husband's left hand. 'Don't upset yourself. You were right, the woman's obviously deranged. She's probably not even responsible for what—'

'She's a goddamned drug addict, for fuck's sake,' Peter said.

Annie stood her ground, went on as if no one else had spoken. 'And then Olivia found out about the other break-ins, and she began to realize that someone was trying to make sure that there were no more notes or proof—'

'So now I'm a burglar, too, am I?' Michael asked drily.

'Not personally, of course not.' Annie felt her legs beginning to buckle, knew that she was almost finished, and she hadn't really figured beyond this; she didn't know, did not have the faintest notion what was going to happen next. 'Just as you didn't personally run Olivia down at the Gare du Midi in Brussels yesterday, or steal her bag—'

'For God's sake,' Louise burst out, still clutching Michael's hand for dear life. 'Have you no shame, Annie? Is there to be no *end* to this lunacy?'

'The bag,' Annie went on, 'that contained all the evidence of everything I've just told you.'

'Which has gone, I take it,' Michael said. 'How inconvenient for you.'

'Not really,' Annie said. 'Not any more. Not once I found that my own father had copies of everything.' She paused. 'I have one set here with me, Michael.' She bent down to pick up the package she'd brought from the New York office. 'Proof. Absolute proof.' She paused again. 'And there are paintings, Olivia tells me, all over this house, that once belonged to Emanuel Rothenburg.'

'The Gauguin, for one,' Carrie said softly, with gentle malice. 'The one in your drawing room, Louise.'

Louise sat down again. Everyone in the room went completely silent. From outside, the sounds of music and partying continued.

'It is true,' Carrie said. 'Hard as it is to swallow, it really does seem to be quite true.'

'Michael,' Louise said faintly, 'tell them they're wrong.'

'Of course they're wrong.' Michael's voice was stiff.

'No,' Carrie said. 'We're not. Are we, Michael?'

Annie had that odd feeling again, as if she were watching everyone in the room from a distance. Jamie, lost in his nightmare, engulfed by disbelief, struggling to comprehend the total annihilation of all his foundations, not knowing whether to be more aghast by what had happened to Olivia or what had gone on so many years ago. Louise, her face, her whole immaculate cream silk body seeming to crumple, as she sat slumped in her chair, staring at her husband as if he were a stranger. Peter, his face on the edge of green, plainly as appalled as the rest of them, wishing he were more drunk than he was.

Michael was still standing. Annie made herself look at him again, and fancied for a moment that she saw it all behind those black eyes, the fury consuming him, his mind racing, calculating, planning what to do to her.

'I don't think there's anything you can do now, Michael,' she said softly. 'The truth's going to come out, whichever way you turn.'

'Unless, of course,' Carrie said, 'you're planning to kill everyone who knows.'

'But even that wouldn't be enough,' Annie said, holding

firmly to the package of her father's papers, 'because this is not the only set of copies, and I have, of course, made arrangements for the information to be passed on if anything should happen to me.'

She sat down at last, finished, and simply, suddenly, quite unable to go on. She stared down at the package of papers on her lap and felt her mouth quivering. She found that she could not, any longer, look at anyone else in the room. She could not, more than anything, bear to see Jamie's face.

Michael looked down, for a moment, at his wife, but Louise was just gazing now, unseeing, into the distance, and so he turned to Peter, but Peter only shook his head. He looked past Annie, towards the door, where Carrie still sat like a sentry, perfectly composed in her Jean Muir dress.

'Thinking of leaving, Michael?' she said.

Peter's eyes were suddenly quizzical. 'How in hell,' he asked Carrie, 'did you get in on this act?'

'Annie figured I might help' – his estranged wife's smile was cool and unruffled – 'because I might want to use this against you. Which, of course, I might.'

'Christ.' Peter shook his head again. 'Oh, Christ.'

Louise began to weep, and Jamie, automatically, pulled out a crisp white handkerchief and passed it over to her.

The door opened.

'Am I family enough,' Daisy Arias enquired, scathingly, 'to be allowed to join this little private party?'

'Only,' Carrie answered, 'if you've brought a stiff drink with you.'

Olivia, fear-chilled in her sleeveless nightdress, knew that she had to leave her bedroom. She couldn't just wait there like some pathetic sacrificial lamb for him to come to get her. She had to at least *try* to get either to her study for the telephone battery or to the kitchen for a knife or – best of all – to the front door for freedom, whichever was easiest, whichever was *possible*.

It had been a good half-hour since she'd heard the breaking glass, and maybe, just maybe, it had come from somewhere outside, maybe from a neighbouring house or a car.

But the lights had gone out. And the telephone was dead.

She opened the door slowly, stood very still on the threshold, and listened. Nothing. Uncertain whether nothing was better than something – for at least if she could hear him, she might know where the son-of-a-bitch was—

Unless nothing meant that he'd come for something rather than her, and that he'd already gone. But she didn't really believe that. Her broken, plaster-weighted, painful arm told her otherwise. The man in the black leather jacket had tried to kill her once and had failed. He had, presumably, been ordered to come back and finish the job.

Something brushed her ankle and Olivia gasped, couldn't help gasping, even when she realized it was only Cleo moving on past her. Cleo, her little feline advance guard, all stealth and claws and speed when she needed it.

Olivia listened for another, long minute, and went after her.

Halfway along the corridor, with her first choice to make – *study to right, kitchen to left, front door straight ahead* – she stopped.

She could hear something.

Her eyes, wide and terrified, stared into the darkness, her ears strained to identify the sound.

Breathing? Not breathing.

It was hissing. It was Cleo, only Olivia had never

heard a sound like it coming from her cat, part hiss, part growl.

She felt him coming too late, felt the movement of air from the left – *he's been waiting in the kitchen* – and then he was on her, one strong leather arm around her throat, one glove over her mouth, stopping her from screaming.

She heard the cat again, heard a yowling, felt the man kicking, heard a small thud, and Olivia wanted to kill him then, felt all the rage she'd been suppressing for the past thirty-six hours or so against Juan Luis and Michael Arias, and summoning all her strength she twisted around and kicked her attacker, Cleo's attacker, as hard as she could.

'*Pute!*'

He punched her, twice, once in the face, once on her left shoulder, and Olivia saw light then, dazzling, whirling light, but all the pain was in her broken arm. Jesus, it hurt, she'd never, *never* felt such pain before in her entire life.

'Please,' she gasped, sobbing. '*Please.*'

'Shut up,' he said, in English.

'Please don't kill me,' she said.

He did not kill her. He gripped her hard with one arm, gripped her bad side so that she shrieked with the pain – 'Shut *up!*' he said again – and turned on a torch with his other hand, and then he dragged her along the corridor to the wood-panelled hall. And Olivia thought he must be going to take her out into the street, that he was going to kidnap her, and hope kindled inside her for a moment because maybe, just *maybe*, the police patrol car might come along at the right moment – it was only a chance, but it was better than nothing—

But then he stopped, right in the middle of the hall. He

bent down, dragging Olivia down as he went, and the pain shot through her again—

'God!' she cried out.

'*Ferme ta gueule!*'

He set down the torch, and took a key from his pocket, and through her tears of pain, Olivia saw that he was unlocking the door to the cellar that she had never seen, the door that had never been opened in all the time she'd lived there. And it wasn't as good as the front door would have been, but maybe if he was just going to lock her into the cellar she stood a chance, because it had to be only a matter of time before Annie and Jamie found out she was in trouble, and—

'*Viens.*'

He went ahead of her, sideways, keeping his grip on her, went down the steps, shining the torch as he went so that he didn't fall. Olivia struggled to keep her footing, stumbled once, yelped again as he dragged at her poor arm, and then they were down in the cellar.

It smelled of damp and disuse and something else, rats, perhaps, but then Olivia remembered the mouse that Cleo had caught a couple of months back, and she'd once heard that mice and rats never lived together, and she thought she could handle mice if she had to, could handle anything so long as he gave her some time.

'*Voilà,*' he said.

He raised the torch and shone it straight ahead.

Olivia looked. There was a safe in the middle of the floor. A big, open, walk-in safe with a heavy, solid steel door that reminded her of the vault door at the Britannia Safe Deposit in London. She remembered that the real estate broker had told her that the owner of the house was an Antwerp diamond merchant; this, presumably, was where he had kept his jewels on the premises.

She looked again, saw that there was something inside the safe. She tried to focus, and recognized the pair of Georgian silver candlesticks she had bought with Bernard after the robbery – and there, too, was the lovely Victorian silver biscuit box he'd bought her as a gift.

'*Un p'tit accident*,' the man said. 'While you were putting them away.'

She stared at him, and suddenly understood.

'No,' she said, shaking her head violently. 'I never had a key – no one will believe it.'

'Maybe they will, maybe they won't,' he said. '*Allez*.'

He pushed her hard from behind, and then, when she struggled to stand firm, seized her by her plaster cast and hauled her, screaming with agony, into the safe.

'Best to try and sleep,' he said.

And closed the door.

24

At midnight, they were all still in the library, with the exception of Louise – who had dragged herself sufficiently together to return to their guests and try to wind down the party without too much fuss.

'I shall tell everyone,' Louise had said to the room in general before leaving, 'that Michael has a bad migraine.' She had not looked at her husband. 'Please will someone lock the door behind me so that no one else can wander in.' She had glanced down at Peter, half-sitting, half-lying in his leather armchair, his eyes glazed over with drink, fatigue and shock. 'If Miss Rogos asks, what would you like me to tell her?'

'To go home,' Peter had answered. 'That would be best, don't you think, Louise?'

'I wouldn't like to say what I think about anything any more, Peter,' Louise had said.

The library was one of the smallest rooms in the Arias mansion, but it was still large enough for the six people who remained to have split into three camps. In one, Jamie and Annie sat on either side of the mahogany desk as Annie tried, for the third time in ten minutes, to telephone Olivia. In the second, Peter sat over by the shelves housing Carlos Arias's old collection of Spanish literature, one ex-wife on either side of him: Daisy – briefly but succinctly filled in by Carrie – sat bolt upright with a glass of champagne in her hand, her fascinated, horrified eyes roaming around the room; Carrie, bored for the moment but with no intention of leaving, leafed idly through a leather-bound edition of Ramón José Sender and waited for things to heat up again.

Michael's camp was a solitary affair. He was still strangely immaculate, superficially at least, untouched by all that had gone on, a handsome middle-aged man in a tuxedo. He had confessed to nothing, was for the moment displaying no emotion at all, yet already he seemed isolated by the crimes of which he had been accused. He might still, Daisy thought, watching him, be boiling with rage inside, or maybe he was being consumed by the hellfires of guilt, or maybe he was just calculating like mad how to get out of the god-awful mess he seemed to have got himself into. But if he was doing any of those things, they did not show.

'There's still no answer,' Annie, her eyes afraid, said to Jamie at ten past midnight.

'Maybe she's really sleeping,' Jamie said.

Annie shook her head vehemently. 'She was pretty much asleep when I spoke to her last time, but she still managed to answer the phone.'

'Perhaps she's taken a pill,' Carrie suggested from across the room. 'They can knock you out – you should know that, Annie.'

'Olivia hates sleeping pills,' Annie said, ignoring the jibe.

'Did you try her mobile?' Jamie asked.

'No answer. Just that damned voice that takes messages when the phone's out of range or whatever.'

'Did you leave a message?' Daisy asked.

'I left two messages,' Annie said tersely.

'Sorry,' Daisy said. 'Stupid question.'

'No, I'm sorry,' Annie said. 'It isn't your fault.'

'You're really worried about her, aren't you?' Jamie asked.

'Aren't you?' Annie said.

'Yes,' Jamie said. 'Of course I am.'

Annie stood up. 'Something must be wrong. It's six o'clock in the morning in Belgium, and Olivia wasn't in any condition to get up and go anywhere, and she was incredibly anxious to hear from you or me.' Her fear, now that she had accepted it, given voice to it, grew rapidly, gathered force. 'Something's really wrong, Jamie, I know it is.'

'Okay,' he said, his own alarm growing with hers. 'Okay, let's call the Brussels police.'

'Just a minute.' Carrie put down the Sender novel. 'I have a question for Michael.'

Michael did not acknowledge her.

'Is the person who tried to kill Olivia still after her?'

Michael did not move.

Jamie stood up. 'Michael?'

Slowly, Michael looked up at his cousin, and for the first time there was a flicker of uncertainty in his eyes.

'Michael?' Jamie's voice was disbelieving. 'Is Carrie right?'

'How should I know?' Michael said, quietly.

With a roar Jamie was on him, dragging him out of his chair, and he realized that though he'd experienced rage, he had never in his whole life known what it felt like to want to kill another human being, but he felt it now, he wanted to kill Michael – he wanted nothing more. His right fist smashed into his stomach, his left into his face, and he heard Michael groaning with pain, but pain just wasn't *enough*, so Jamie, maddened, out of control, went for his throat, fastened both his hands around his neck and started to squeeze—

'Jamie, *stop* it!' Annie was trying to pull him off, but he wasn't listening, wasn't coherent, wasn't really Jamie. 'Somebody stop him before he *kills* him!'

'Peter!' Daisy shrieked, still holding on to her champagne for dear life. 'Peter, do something, for God's sake!'

'I should let him carry on, if I were you,' Carrie said calmly.

'Jamie, *no*!' Annie tried to get between the two men. 'Jamie, think of Olivia – what about *Olivia*?'

He stopped instantly, just stopped dead and let go and Michael fell back onto the floor, gasping for air, slumped against the bookshelves behind him. No one helped him. No one went near him. Annie put her arms around Jamie, held him, felt him shaking violently.

Peter stood up.

'What can you do, Michael?' His voice was very hard. 'What are you going to do to stop this?'

'Nothing,' Michael said hoarsely, and for the first time since Louise had left the room, he looked really afraid. 'How can I do anything to stop something I know nothing about?'

'Of course you know something,' Peter said.

'Even if I did,' Michael said, 'I probably couldn't do anything.'

'Why not?' Peter asked. 'Why *not*?'

'Because if any of this were true,' Michael answered, picking his words carefully, 'I imagine that a man would have been paid to do a job. In which case, there might be no way of contacting him.'

Jamie pulled away from Annie. 'What do you mean, no way?' The worst of the physical rage was spent now, but the hate was still there simmering in his dark eyes. 'There must be a way.'

Michael still sat on the floor with his back to the bookshelves. His black tie hung loose, the top two buttons of his shirt were undone and there was blood on his lower lip and around his left nostril.

He shook his head slowly, looking straight up at his cousin.

'I doubt it,' he said.

The crisp, hard quality of Carrie's voice was almost a welcome breath of sanity in the wild atmosphere in the room.

'I must say, Annie,' she said, 'that if you don't need a Valium or three after this little show, then I really do have to hand it to you.'

Annie made a small sound, half laughter, half despair.

And Jamie turned back to the desk and picked up the telephone.

It was a little after seven o'clock in Brussels. Four or five feet above Olivia's head, above the roof of the safe, above the cellar, the man in the black leather jacket had completed his work a while back. He had closed, but not locked, the cellar door (since it was intended that the woman's death should be regarded as accidental), pocketing the key, and then he had flipped the lever at the main fuse box back to ON. He had reconnected the telephone, had fixed the pane of glass he'd smashed to gain entry, and he had made her bed and generally tidied up the place to look normal. And all the while, Cleo, still in pain from where he had kicked her, crouched in a corner of the entrance hall, behind the coat stand, and quivered with fear and loathing until he had gone.

The safe, Olivia had long since figured out, was made the way refrigerators had been in the past, had the kind of door that, even unlocked, was impossible to open from the inside once closed. Inside it was pitch black. The air was still cool enough but musty, and although the fingertips of her right hand had located two tiny holes on the back wall – too tiny and dust-caked to allow any significant air through – Olivia had long since concluded that, if no one came in time, she would die of suffocation. There was, she thought, some mathematical formula for calculating how long a person could survive on a limited supply of oxygen, but she didn't know what the formula was, which was probably just as well. She knew there was no point in screaming for help because there was no one to hear, and screaming would, almost certainly, use up more oxygen than just sitting still and waiting. But Olivia had never been much good at sitting and waiting for anything in life. Olivia liked – she *needed* – to get out and do things for herself, to make things happen.

The way she had gone to London and opened the box. And made this happen.

She wondered how Annie was doing, wondered if Jamie had by now learned the truth about Michael and Juan Luis. She thought that they had, in all probability, been trying to reach her, and she thought it was not unduly optimistic to believe that they would, in time, become concerned about her and send someone to check on her. And she tried, very hard, not to dwell on the likelihood that even if someone did come, and even if they came into the apartment, they were not terribly likely to think of opening an old, never used door to a cellar that did not even belong to her property.

Olivia sat down in the black, cold, claustrophobic safe and allowed a huge, all-enveloping wave of panic to engulf her. And then, several minutes later, after the last of it had ebbed away, she tried valiantly to persuade herself that the worst of the fear was over now, that she could go on now, could survive without losing her mind; because the idea of that – of growing so demented with terror that she got hysterical and went crazy – seemed almost worse than dying. But if she was honest with herself – and stupid, *stupid* Olivia Segal was always so fucking honest with herself and everyone else, wasn't she? – she knew that the fear was anything *but* over.

And she had no way of knowing how much time she had left.

An inspector with the Police de Bruxelles told Jamie that they had been patrolling rue Charles Hanssens all through the night, and no problems had been reported.

'I can send a car to check the place again,' the inspector said. 'If there is any indication of a problem—'

'But there may not *be* any indication,' Jamie yelled, trying but failing to keep his temper for Olivia's sake. 'For Christ's sake, I've told you that someone is trying to kill her – I've told you that there's every likelihood that they may try again – for all we know they already have!'

There was a soft knocking at the door as he slammed the phone down, and Daisy got up to open it. Louise came in looking pale and drawn.

'The party's finally over,' she said. 'There's no one left.

It's not easy throwing people out and staying tactful.' She paused. 'They all seemed to have a good time.'

'So no one missed the birthday boy,' Carrie commented. 'I told you, Louise, it's a tribute to the way you organize your parties.'

Louise looked over at Michael, saw the smear of blood still on his face and on his shirt, but did not remark on it.

'Any more developments here?' she asked no one in particular.

'What's happening here' – Peter got to his feet again, walked over to where Michael was now sitting in a chair, and kicked him hard on the sole of his left Bennis and Edwards shoe – 'is that this skunk is going to wake up our fucking company pilot and tell him to get his ass over to Newport State Airport and get our plane ready to fly these people to Boston in time for the first damned connection to Brussels.'

'Why?' Louise asked.

'Because your husband says that if there is a hit man after Olivia, there's probably no way of stopping him.'

'Then of course they must go.' Louise was exhausted but superficially calm now and in command. 'But Peter, why not raise the pilot yourself?' She looked down at Michael briefly, with something approaching disdain. 'After all,' she added, 'you are in charge now, surely.'

Olivia had lost all track of time. She had, for a while, sat in a kind of cramped half-lotus position trying to do some basic yoga relaxation in an attempt to stave off the terror, but then it had struck her that she was breathing too deeply, was probably using up too much precious air, and she was neither skilled enough nor calm enough to drill herself into taking shallow breaths. And the thought that she had been wasting oxygen had pushed her into new panic, had sent her adrenalin pumping crazily. She had given in to that for a few minutes, had let herself pound on the steel walls and roof of her prison, had wept and railed and yelled for someone to help her, for anyone to come. And then she had settled down again, numbed and dulled by the exertion and the pointlessness of it all, and for quite a good long time she stayed that way, and it was easier, far easier. And maybe it might be better to do what the man had told her to. Just go to sleep, give in and go easy.

She slept then – maybe for minutes, maybe hours – but she woke up with the sudden realization that she had been missing something, had been sitting there just waiting to be rescued or to die when she could, instead, have been doing something to help herself.

The candlesticks. She fumbled around, found one of them and clambered awkwardly to her feet.

The two tiny holes on the back wall. She'd had a tool all along and she hadn't thought to use it. *For crying out loud, Olivia, what's* wrong *with you?*

She felt over the candlestick searching for sharp edges, but it had an ornate foliage decoration, and it was all too rounded, too smooth, and the only remotely useful part was at the candle-holder end. *So use that then, damn you, woman—*

There was no contest. The silver was too soft, the steel wall too rigid and thick, and Olivia found that she was weeping again as she fought and failed to enlarge those two little holes, and of course it was useless, because it was a *safe*, for fuck's sake, a reinforced box built to withstand the custom-made tools of professional thieves, and all she was doing was wasting more air, and all that would happen was that she would die sooner.

The Brussels police reported that since the officers who'd rung Olivia's doorbell just after 8 a.m. had received no reply, they were assuming that Olivia had taken their earlier advice and left the apartment, perhaps for a hotel.

'Bernard Martens,' Annie said, shortly before she and Jamie were due to take off from Newport State Airport in the Arias jet. 'Bernard will want to help.'

They located him at his home, and Annie was right; they didn't need to tell him too much, little more than that they believed Olivia might be in danger, because although Bernard had kept communications with her to a minimum since his return from the Far East, he still cared for Olivia and always would.

'I'll go straightaway,' he had told Jamie.

'Tell the police,' Jamie had said. 'Maybe you can persuade them to help you break in.'

'That won't be necessary,' Bernard said. 'I still have her key on my ring, so I can let myself in, if need be.'

'That's great, Bernard.' The relief was immense. 'Thank you.'

'Don't thank me.' Bernard was already reaching for his jacket. 'Call me when you reach Boston, if you can – I'll hope to have good news.'

'She's not there,' he told them when they called from Logan at five-thirty local time. 'I've been inside, and I've looked everywhere, and the police are perfectly right – there's no sign of any problem. As a matter of fact,' Bernard added, 'I have never seen the apartment looking so immaculate.'

'Maybe the police are right,' Annie said to Jamie after he'd hung up. 'Maybe she has gone to a hotel.'

'Maybe,' Jamie said.

It was not until they were airborne en route to Paris that he sat up with a violent jolt of fresh alarm.

'Annie.'

Annie, who had been dozing fitfully, opened her eyes. 'What?'

'Can you remember ever – I mean *ever* – seeing any home of Olivia's looking immaculate? That's the word Bernard used.'

Annie sat up straighter. 'No. You're right. Livvy likes chaos – or at least controlled chaos.'

'And even if she did feel like tidying up to take her mind off things—'

'She couldn't have done that much because of her arm,' Annie finished for him.

'Which means' – Jamie swallowed hard, feeling sick at the thought – 'that if the place really is as immaculate as Martens said it was—'

'Then someone else must have cleaned it up.'

It was hardly a conclusion they could ask the Air France pilot to radio through to the Brussels police.

Olivia, dozing uncomfortably on the floor of the safe, thought she had heard a noise, faintly, from somewhere above her head. She had sat up quickly, feeling dizzy, had listened hard, then heard it again.

Footsteps, maybe?

She had climbed to her feet and shouted for help, but she was so weak now, and though her voice had echoed inside the safe, there was no real power left in it. Yet she had gone on calling, over and over again, pausing to listen some more, hearing nothing and trying again. She had gone on calling through the tiny, inadequate holes, and then she had remembered the candlesticks, had picked one up and banged it on the steel roof, but the sound had almost deafened her, had made her cringe with the reverberations, and the movements had sent new pain shooting through her broken arm. Yet still she had gone on screaming, using up her ebbing reserves of strength and oxygen.

But Bernard Martens, checking meticulously over every inch of the apartment, had heard nothing at all, and he had not given a thought to the cellar, because he, like Olivia, knew that it had never been used, knew that the door had always been locked and that there had not even been a key.

And it was not until after he was long gone that Cleo, too shocked to risk confronting any man, emerged from her hiding place behind the coat stand in the hall, and padded slowly and cautiously, her tail swishing from side to side, to the cellar door.

Where she lay down, curled neatly in the most comfortable, comforting position she could find, to wait for her mistress to come upstairs again.

While down below, in the dark, Olivia slept, waiting to die.

25

It was almost eight in the evening when their connecting flight from Paris finally touched down at Zaventem Airport. Jamie and Annie had long since stopped talking about what might have happened to Olivia. Their imaginations, already so horribly inflamed by all they had learned over the past twenty-four hours, were running too painfully wild and they were both, by now, superstitiously afraid that voicing their worst fears might somehow make them more real than bottling them up.

'Shouldn't we call the police again?' Annie asked at Passport Control, breathless from running, as Jamie seethed beside her in the queue. 'Or what about Bernard Martens?'

'No more delays,' Jamie said, through gritted teeth. 'Let's just *go*.'

With no luggage to claim and no hold-ups by customs officials, they ran for the exit. Annie had never seen Jamie like this before, pushing luggage trolleys out of his way, almost sending strangers flying, cutting through the line of passengers waiting for taxis and giving the driver of the first car in the line a wad of dollar bills to get them to

Olivia's street fast, whatever the traffic. And the wildness in his eyes and the increasingly desperate set of his jaw sent shivers through Annie, because she realized it meant that Jamie had a powerful sense that time was running out, and that terrified her almost more than anything else.

It was almost dark before they got to rue Charles Hanssens.

'How will we get in?' Annie asked, standing on the cobbled pavement outside Olivia's house as the taxi drew away and disappeared into rue des Minimes. 'I knew we should have called Bernard.'

'I'll smash a window.' Jamie was already taking off his jacket and winding it around his right hand to protect it.

'You really think Bernard missed something, don't you?' Annie stared wide-eyed around the empty street as Jamie marched straight up to the sitting-room window and punched through the glass. 'You really think she's in there.'

'I don't know.' Jamie tried to reach the catch.

'Let me – my arm's thinner.'

'It's okay,' he said, his voice strained with the effort of stretching. 'I've got it.' It was a sash window, it pushed up easily enough, and in another moment he was inside and letting Annie in at the front door.

'Get the lights,' Jamie said and headed for the sitting room.

'Bernard was right.' Annie was right behind him. 'It is immaculate.'

Everything was in its place, every cushion plumped, every newspaper neatly folded, not a coffee cup in sight.

'Olivia didn't do this,' Jamie said. 'Not in a thousand years.'

Annie stopped in her tracks. 'Cleo. Did Bernard say anything to you about the cat?'

'No.'

Jamie was out of the room and on his way to the bedroom, but Annie found she could not bring herself to follow him there. In all her waking nightmares on the plane, the bedroom was where she had pictured Olivia. She knew it was impossible – she knew Livvy couldn't be there because Bernard had looked, and yet still Annie had gone on imagining her there, hurt and frightened or worse, much worse . . .

'Cleo!' she called, tersely.

'No sign,' Jamie said, coming back from the bedroom.

Annie breathed again, called the cat again.

'Maybe Olivia took her,' Jamie said.

'So you think maybe she has gone somewhere, after all?' Annie asked hopefully.

'No.' Jamie shook his head in confusion. 'Yes. I wish to God I knew.'

'I'll check the kitchen,' Annie said.

That, too, was uncharacteristically tidy, but the little cat was in the corner, cowering under the table, black-eyed with fear.

'Cleo's in here,' Annie called to Jamie.

The cat hissed at her.

'Sweetie, what's wrong?' Annie crouched down, and the tortoiseshell arched her back and hissed again, her tail erect and warning.

Jamie came in behind her.

'Be careful,' Annie said, softly, still crouching. 'Something's upset her. She's always been such a friendly little thing.'

Slowly, gently, she held out her hand. Very tentatively,

Cleo sniffed at it and jumped a little, but Annie just stayed quite still and waited patiently, making soothing, comforting sounds, and after a few moments, the cat stood up and came out from under the table.

'That's a good puss,' Jamie said softly.

Cleo rubbed her head against Annie's hand.

'Maybe she's just hungry,' Annie said.

'She can eat when we've found Olivia,' Jamie said.

The cat walked past Annie, gave Jamie a wider, more suspicious, berth, and skirted out of the kitchen into the hall, stopping beside the cellar door.

She miaowed.

'Okay, sweetie,' Annie said, looking down at her. 'I know you're starved, but Jamie's right, you'll have to wait.'

Cleo miaowed again, and crouched low.

'What do we do now?' Jamie asked, emerging from the kitchen.

'Call Bernard – see if he's heard anything.' Annie paused. 'And check in case Livvy's been back and turned on her answering machine.'

Jamie headed back to the sitting room.

Cleo extended her right paw and scratched at the cellar door.

Annie looked at the door.

'There's no access to the basement, is there?' she called out to Jamie.

'No,' he called back. 'Olivia said the door was always locked.'

Cleo stood up, hunched low and started scraping with both paws.

'Jamie,' Annie said, still quietly but with urgency. 'Come out here.'

He came back out into the hall and looked down at the cat. All the tension was back in him.

'Try the handle,' he said.

It turned in Annie's hand. She pulled, but nothing happened.

'It's locked,' she said.

Jamie licked his dry lips. 'Try pushing,' he said.

She pushed hard. The door opened with a groan. Cleo jumped, hissed and ran for the kitchen. Annie's heart began to race.

'Oh, God,' she said, softly.

Jamie stepped past her, looking for a light switch. He found one, just inside the door, and flicked it. Nothing.

'We need a flashlight,' Annie said.

'Kitchen,' Jamie said.

They opened cupboards, banging the doors. Cleo raced out, back to the cover of the coatstand in the hall, just as Annie opened the last one. 'Got it,' she said, and tossed a flashlight at Jamie.

They ran back out into the hall and for one more instant they looked into each other's eyes, sharing their thoughts and fears, and then Jamie switched on the beam and started down the steps.

'Olivia!'

'Jamie, be careful,' Annie cautioned, right behind him.

'Olivia?' he called again. He reached the bottom, turned to help Annie down, then shone the beam slowly around from left to right and then back again. It was a large cellar, with a lot of empty racks – probably once used for wine – along all its walls. There were four – no, five – wooden crates piled up in front of one of the racks, but otherwise, apart from an ancient safe to the left of centre, the cellar had been entirely cleared. It was empty, and there was nowhere to look.

'There's nothing here.' Annie's voice echoed Jamie's feelings: half relief, half disappointment.

Jamie walked around for a few moments, shining the flashlight up to the ceiling, then, once again, into each corner.

'Nothing,' he said, flatly.

'I really thought—' Annie stopped.

'I know. Me, too.'

Jamie turned around. 'We'd better get back upstairs, call Bernard, check a few hotels.'

'Maybe Livvy's been in touch with the police.'

'Let's hope.'

Annie started up the steps first, then stopped.

'What?' Jamie asked.

'I thought I heard Cleo.'

'Dumb cat,' Jamie said. 'For a moment back there, I really thought she knew something.'

The sound came from behind them. Jamie, on the third step up, turned around and shone the flashlight back down into the cellar.

'There she is,' Annie said, pointing. 'She must have come down with us.'

Cleo was beside the old safe, crouched low again, tail swishing, nose sniffing at the dusty black steel.

'Oh, God,' Annie said. 'You don't—' Terror closed her throat, made it impossible to speak.

Jamie said nothing, went back down slowly, walked over to the safe. He registered dimly that his heart seemed to have stopped; his thoughts were coming at him vaguely, as if they hardly belonged to him, were going on without him.

They both stared at the safe. There was no combination, just a lock and no key, and they both knew, looking at it, that there was no way on earth even a far stronger man than Jamie could get it open without help.

'Try the door, Jamie,' Annie said, her voice hoarse with fear.

He did not, could not seem to move.

'Jamie, try it.'

He shook his head. If Olivia was in there—

'*Try* it,' Annie said again.

Jamie, ice cold with dread, put out his right hand and gripped the handle. It turned, and clicked. Cleo gave one of her little startled jumps and backed off. *Hail Mary, full of grace*, his mind prayed silently, unexpectedly.

'Open it, Jamie.' Annie's voice was suddenly hard.

He pulled the door open.

Olivia lay curled up on the floor, her face cushioned by her right arm and hidden from view by the fractured left arm, still in its grimy sling. She wore a flimsy, sleeveless nightdress and her legs and feet were bare, and she was not moving.

She did not, from where Jamie and Annie stood, seem to be breathing.

Neither of them said a word.

Jamie passed Annie the flashlight and stooped to get inside. Numbly, tenderly, he put his arms around Olivia, and she was so cold, so lifeless, and he knew, suddenly, as he lifted her out of the safe, what people meant when they talked about hearts breaking.

Annie shone the light on Olivia's face and touched the side of her neck.

'Put her down,' she said tersely.

Jamie cradled Olivia closer, bent his head so that his face touched her hair. Somewhere inside him anguish was waiting to be let out, but there was too much rage ahead of it, building and building—

'Put her down, Jamie,' Annie said more sharply. 'Quickly.'

He looked up at her, startled.

'Jamie, for God's sake, do as I say.'

He laid Olivia gently down, and Annie pushed him firmly away, and Jamie had seen so many new sides to Annie in the past day and night, and she was being so strong again, so self-possessed, so *competent*, and he saw that she was feeling for Olivia's pulse—

'She's alive,' Annie said, hope blazing. 'We need help, Jamie. Call an ambulance.' She looked up at him, saw that he was in shock and hardened her voice still more. 'Jamie, *move*. Call an ambulance and tell them suffocation and hypothermia and maybe more.'

He raced up the steps.

'And bring down a blanket!' Annie called after him.

She was vaguely aware of the cat over by the wall, too nervy to approach, but Annie was no longer thinking about Cleo or Jamie or about anything except Olivia. She knew what she was doing, she only needed to *remember*, because she'd learned about first-aid and CPR when Sophie and William had been little, and she just had to keep calm and remember what she was supposed to do and then it would come back—

She saw a flutter then, saw that Olivia was definitely breathing and there was no need for CPR, and Annie gave a quick, loud, involuntary sob of relief, and then quickly, deftly she got her into the recovery position. And there was nothing more to do now than stroke Livvy's hair and speak to her softly and gently, and try to keep her warm and wait for the ambulance to come.

* * *

It really was mostly hypothermia, they said at Saint-Jean Hospital, trying to answer Jamie's still wild-eyed questions gently and calmingly – and exhaustion, and, of course, shock, but the young lady seemed to be a most resilient person. And no, Jamie could not see her again just yet – he and Madame Thomas had spent enough time with her already – but it might be possible a little later, so long as he promised not to stay too long.

When they finally let him into the room again, Olivia was lying back, her eyes closed, her plastered left arm in a fresh, clean sling propped on a pillow.

Very quietly, anxious not to wake her, Jamie sat down on a chair.

'Don't sit so far away,' she said, her eyes still shut. 'Come sit on the bed – just mind the arm.'

'I thought you were asleep.' He sat down carefully on her good side.

Olivia opened her eyes. 'Where's Annie?'

'She's talking to the police again.'

'Have they caught the man?'

'I don't think so. Not yet. But they will.'

'The doctors said there's a guard outside.'

Jamie nodded. 'There is. There will be until it's over.'

Olivia looked into his face. 'And how are you doing?'

'Better now that I know you're okay.'

'What about the rest of it?'

'Michael, you mean?'

'And your uncle.' She paused. 'It must have been a terrible shock.'

'You could say that,' Jamie said, softly, his eyes very dark. 'I'm so sorry, Olivia. So desperately sorry.'

She was startled. 'What do you have to be sorry for?'

'They're my family. Michael killed your parents, and Annie's.'

Olivia tried to sit up then, but found she could hardly manage it. 'Jamie, stop that. You're not responsible for any of it. Your father died too.'

'Yes.'

'Then stop it, do you hear me? No guilt. No collective family shame.'

Jamie gave a small, bleak smile. 'Easier said than done.'

Olivia reached for his hand. 'I love you, Jamie,' she said.

'I know. I love you, too.' He paused. 'Bernard's here, you know.'

'Is he? Poor Bernard.'

'He feels terrible,' Jamie said. 'Because he didn't think to try the cellar door.'

'No reason he should have,' Olivia said. 'I hope you told him.'

'I think he needs to hear it from you.'

Olivia nodded. 'Later, maybe.'

The door opened, and Annie came in, treading carefully.

'You're allowed to breathe,' Olivia said, warmly.

Annie embraced her, mindful of the arm, then stood back to look at her. 'You look okay – I can't believe it.'

'You look like hell,' Olivia said, and squeezed Annie's hand. 'Come to think of it,' she added, looking at Jamie, 'you both do.'

Annie sat on a chair. 'We're not supposed to stay long.'

'What did the police say?' Olivia asked.

'Not much. I told them the whole story. It took a while.'

'What are they doing?' Jamie was grim-faced again. 'Have they contacted the Rhode Island police yet?'

'Not yet,' Annie said. 'They say it's too early.'

'Too early for what?' Olivia asked.

Annie looked uncomfortable. 'I think we should leave this till morning. You have to sleep, Livvy, and we could both use some rest, too.'

'What's going on, Annie?' Olivia asked.

'You may as well tell us,' Jamie said. 'You know she's not going to rest till you do.'

Annie waited another moment. 'They say they don't have enough proof to take action against Michael.'

'Not enough *proof*?' Fresh anger and disbelief revived Jamie. 'How much more do they need?'

'All the papers we have accuse Juan Luis of war crimes, but there isn't any solid evidence of what Michael's done.' Annie paused. 'Not until they get the man in the leather jacket.'

'But Michael as good as admitted that he'd set it up,' Jamie said.

' "As good as" may not be enough.' Annie paused. 'Especially if the rest of the family decide not to back us up.'

'There wasn't any doubt in that room, Annie,' Jamie said tautly. 'We all knew. Even Louise believed it.'

'I know,' Annie said softly. 'But Michael didn't actually confess.'

'And even if he had' – Olivia spoke up – 'the others might decide to rally round Michael.'

Neither Annie nor Jamie spoke.

'They all have a lot to lose, Jamie,' Olivia said, feeling his anguish.

'Look,' Annie said. 'Let's not get too upset too soon. The police haven't said they don't believe us – just that they can't ask the Rhode Island police to arrest Michael without something positive to go on.' She paused. 'The helicopter crashed nineteen years ago. The investigation decided it was mechanical failure.'

'We'll get the case reopened,' Olivia said.

'It won't be easy,' Annie pointed out.

'None of this has been easy,' Olivia said.

'It might get easier,' Jamie said, 'if they catch the man.'

'Or if Michael confesses,' Olivia said.

26

The Pact 1995

One week passed. Olivia was released from hospital and went home to rue Charles Hanssens with Jamie, while Annie agreed to fly back to England where Edward, shocked almost beyond words, wanted her safe and sound with him and the children.

A second week went by. The man in the black leather jacket had not been caught by the Brussels police, and with no other force involved, either in Europe or in the United States, no one thought there was a realistic likelihood of his capture unless he tried again – which Olivia, Jamie and Annie were now all pretty much agreed he would not. The hit, they reasoned, must by now have been called off, and with so many more people now in possession of the facts – not to mention the file on Juan Luis Arias – there was simply no more purpose to be served by killing Olivia.

Jamie, still in Brussels, made numerous calls to Peter and Louise, but whether he called them in Newport, Boston or New York, and whether he called Arias Shipping or their respective homes, neither was ever available to speak to him. The same applied to Daisy, and though Carrie was quick to return his call when Jamie tried her, she was equally swift to point out that her version of what they all knew had gone on in the library that night, would mean fuck-all if the others had all decided to lie their heads off.

'They've closed ranks,' Olivia told Annie on the phone on August 10th, with Jamie on the bedroom extension. 'I knew they would.'

'I don't see how they can.' Annie was appalled all over again.

'Simple,' Olivia said. 'Michael will have told them how he did it all for the whole family. For their future, for their children. For the Arias name. He'll have reminded them how much they enjoy their wealth – how much they'd hate losing their standing in the community – how awful it would be for them all if he went to prison.'

'What about Peter?' Jamie said bitterly. 'Michael killed *our* father, for God's sake.'

'Peter has his children to consider, I guess,' Annie said quietly.

'And Peter has no backbone,' Olivia pointed out. 'That's no surprise.'

'I can't bear it,' Jamie said. 'It's intolerable.'

'I know,' Olivia said.

It was not the only thing that both Olivia and Jamie found intolerable. Left alone together, with so much residual tension still humming inside them and with the rawness of their trauma-heightened emotions still vivid in their minds, both Olivia and Jamie had become abruptly, almost unbearably, aware of the other, silent agitation between them: the sexual energy that had been quieted but never wholly laid to rest. Love was not the issue now. There had never been any doubting the intensity of their feelings for one another. They loved each other, as they loved Annie, more, they supposed, than they had ever been able to love any outsider. Love, pure and simple, had never been the problem. But the memories of that one night in Boston had never ceased to simmer in the back of both their minds, and somehow, the hell they had been through in the past two weeks had turned the heat back on high.

Olivia's body was still sore and her arm in its cast, and Jamie was still drained and shocked, still yearning for disbelief. And yet suddenly – after having coped more than adequately with spending platonic, affectionate but sexless time together for over six years – neither she nor Jamie seemed capable of being in the same room as each other for more than a few minutes without feeling weak with lust.

It blew up, finally, at breakfast one morning.

'I think I might go back to bed,' Olivia said as Jamie filled the electric kettle with water and switched it on.

'Why?' Jamie looked at her sharply.

She shrugged. 'I just feel like it.'

'Is the arm hurting?'

'Not much.' She smiled at him. 'I'm fine, Jamie. I just feel like indulging myself.'

He nodded. 'Good idea. You head on back, and I'll bring you a tray.'

'I can manage.' She wandered over to the cupboard where her two big pine trays were kept.

'No, you can't,' Jamie said.

'Sure I can.'

'How are you going to carry a tray?'

'Easy.' She took out the tray and put it on the table. 'I take one thing at a time – first the tray, then the coffee, then the toast.'

'I'll bring it all to you. Go back to bed, Olivia.'

She looked at him. He was wearing grey shorts and a grey Calvin Klein T-shirt and his forearms and face were a little more tanned than his legs, and his feet were bare – such nice, neat, strong feet – and his dark hair was rumpled. Olivia felt desire kick her again, more violently even than it had the previous evening and afternoon and morning, and she knew that she'd never longed for any man as she longed for Jamie now, at this instant – that even the hunger she remembered during that long-ago afternoon and evening with him had been a weak and trifling hunger compared to this.

'For God's sake,' she said, suddenly, fiercely.

'What?' He looked startled.

'What's *wrong* with us?'

Jamie granted himself permission to look at her. She was wearing a man-sized white shirt with one sleeve hanging useless, and her hair was still wet from the shower, and the beauty of her high cheekbones and slender neck was even more pronounced than usual because she'd lost weight since the hit-and-run, and there was an area just over her left collar bone that seemed to be crying out to be kissed.

'What's stopping us now, Jamie?' Olivia's voice was husky with yearning. 'Carrie's a hundred years ago – *everything* that stopped us is a hundred years ago—'

'I know.'

She walked over to him. And without the slightest hesitation, looking straight into his eyes, she laid her right hand on his erection. He thought he would explode, but not even a groan left his lips. She took her hand away.

'Why are we still fighting this, Jamie?' Her green, slanting eyes blinked. 'I can hardly breathe for wanting you, and you have a big enough hard-on to take on

Sharon Stone, and yet you still just stand there and look at me.'

'I don't want Sharon Stone,' Jamie said.

'But you do want me.'

'I've never stopped wanting you.'

Her eyes softened, seemed to melt. 'Then for God's sake, kiss me.'

The kettle boiled and turned itself off.

'No,' Jamie said, softly.

'Why not?' Olivia stared at him. 'Why the fuck *not*, Jamie?'

For one long moment, Jamie closed his eyes. And then he opened them again, turned away, and switched the kettle back on.

'Go back to bed, Olivia.'

'No, I won't go back to bed.' Her cheeks were hot, as if she had a fever. 'Not until I know what is *wrong* with you.' Her voice was tight, strangling in her throat. 'You just said you've never stopped wanting me, and you know how much I want you – and we both know we love each other just about every way there *is* to love someone.'

'If you won't go to bed,' Jamie said, still softly, 'then at least sit down at the table, and I'll pour us both a cup of coffee and I'll tell you what's wrong.'

'Okay.' She nodded her head, fighting a sudden urge to cry.

'Sit.'

Olivia felt a warm, furry body against her legs. She swallowed hard. 'Cleo needs breakfast.'

'I'll feed Cleo.'

'Thank you.'

'You're welcome.'

Olivia drew back one of the chairs and sat down. 'Shit, Jamie.'

Jamie smiled wryly. 'I agree.'

'Then I don't understand.'

He spooned cat food into Cleo's bowl in the corner, poured fresh water into her second bowl, then got their coffee and sat down opposite Olivia.

'I'm not going to kiss you,' he tried to explain, 'because I couldn't stop. I wouldn't want to stop.'

'I wouldn't want you to.'

His dark eyes were filled with pain. 'I can't take another one-night-stand with you, Olivia.'

'It's morning,' she said.

'I mean it.'

'I know,' she said, unsmilingly. 'I couldn't take it either. I think it would just about kill me.' She paused. 'I don't understand how you can even think that could happen, Jamie. When we both love each other, when we both know that and accept it.'

'Unfinished business,' Jamie said.

'What kind?' Olivia took her first sip of coffee.

'You know what kind.'

She put down her cup. 'So are you going to let Michael destroy us too?' The tightness that had been in her throat was in her chest now. 'Hasn't he done enough to us already?'

'It isn't just Michael,' Jamie said. 'It's me. And you, too.'

'I don't have a problem.'

'You're post-traumatic.'

'No, I'm not.'

'Sure you are.'

'Even if I am,' Olivia said, 'I know how I feel about you. In every way.'

'Maybe you do, maybe you don't,' Jamie said. 'Either way, what harm can it do to wait a little longer?'

She drank some more coffee. 'Is that what you're proposing? That we wait?'

'Yes.'

'How long?'

'I'm not sure.'

Cleo jumped up onto Olivia's lap, and began to knead her claws against her bare thighs.

'Doesn't that hurt?' Jamie asked.

'Yes.'

'Want me to take her?'

'No, thank you. It takes my mind off wanting you.'

Jamie reached over and picked Cleo up. Unphased, the cat continued where she'd left off, content enough with his soft grey shorts.

'I guess I'm post-traumatic, too,' he said, 'in a way.'

'You're still feeling guilty for being an Arias,' Olivia said flatly. They'd had a few conversations in the past week about Jamie's guilt and shame, and she had tried repeatedly to put him straight, but she knew she had not succeeded.

'There's still so much to be resolved,' Jamie said. 'I know you feel it too.'

'Of course I feel it.' She shook her head slowly. 'I just don't connect any of that with our feelings for each other.'

'I'm not denying our feelings,' Jamie said. 'I know what we have. I think I always did, deep down—'

'Not so deep,' Olivia said.

'No,' he admitted.

'But now, surely, it's out in the open – at least between us—'

Jamie laid his right hand on the table, as if he were reaching for her, then changed his mind and took it away again.

'I want it to be perfect, Olivia.'

'It will be.'

He shook his head. 'Not yet.' He grimaced as Cleo dug her claws into his left leg. 'I want to be able to come to you when I can face myself in the mirror in the mornings without remembering what my family has done.'

'Michael is your cousin, not your brother. You barely remember Juan Luis – and your father didn't do anything, except try to help.'

'That doesn't help me now,' Jamie said.

She looked at him accusingly. 'This is crap, Jamie.'

'Maybe.'

The tears came back, stinging, hot behind her eyes, but the thought of crying now, in front of him, made her angry. 'I mean, this is *really* crap. We should be getting each other through this, not turning each other away.'

'We are getting each other through it,' Jamie said.

'I'd get through it better with your arms around me.'

'I wouldn't.'

'Then you'd better go home,' Olivia said abruptly.

Jamie flinched. 'I don't want to leave you.'

'Are you going to change your mind?'

'No. I can't.'

'Then I mean it.' Olivia stood up, and Cleo, her good mood disturbed, jumped off Jamie's lap. 'You'd better go back to Boston, because I don't think I can stand having you around.'

'That isn't what I want,' Jamie said softly.

'Right now,' Olivia answered, 'I don't think I care what you want.'

Her mood was gentler by the time he left the next day, August 14th, though right until the last moment before check-in Jamie pleaded to stay to take care of her and she remained adamant that she would not be alone with him until he was ready to act on his feelings for her.

'I love you,' he said, for the dozenth time that day, before he went through to Passport Control.

'I know you do,' Olivia said. 'Our love isn't in question.'

'Maybe now I'm going back, I'll be able to get through to Michael or the others.'

'I doubt you'll even get close.'

'They'll have to talk to me sooner or later,' Jamie said.

'Maybe.'

Olivia knew that she had not the slightest intention of accepting the Ariases' new and outrageous status quo, but when Jamie, who was still hoping against hope that decency would ultimately prevail, called from Boston to ask for more time, she saw no good reason not to agree.

'After all,' Olivia said to Annie later on the phone, 'what's another four weeks, after nineteen years?'

'Does Jamie really believe Michael may still confess?' Annie asked.

'No, not really. I think his hopes are hinging on Peter developing some kind of a conscience. Or maybe Louise.'

'What do you think, Livvy?'

'I think there's not a hope in hell. Not unless they're pushed.'

'I think you're right,' Annie agreed. 'But you're still willing to wait?'

'I think it's as good an idea as any other,' Olivia said. 'Let them think we've given up.'

'Lull them into a false sense of security, you mean,' Annie said.

'It can't hurt,' Olivia said.

'And then what?'

'Then we'll see.'

Annie's antennae went up. 'Whatever we do decide, ultimately,' she said, firmly, 'promise me we'll act together.'

'Of course,' Olivia said.

'Promise me, Livvy,' Annie persisted. 'No more solo stunts.'

'Definitely not.'

'Promise me.'

Olivia smiled into the phone.

'I promise,' she said.

The month passed, and apart from the cast being removed from Olivia's arm, nothing altered.

'We can't wait any longer,' Olivia told Jamie on the telephone.

'I know,' he said.

'Annie wants us to come to her place to talk over our plans.'

'Do we have any plans?' Jamie asked.

'I have a kind of a plan,' Olivia said.

'I thought you might,' Jamie said.

'Is that all right with you?' Olivia asked.

'Is what all right with me?'

'Putting your life on hold again.'

'It's what you're doing, isn't it?'

'It's different for me,' Olivia said. 'You have JAA to consider – all I have to do is find a stand-in, which isn't too hard in Brussels – and Bernard's already agreed to take Cleo for as long as it takes.'

'You're talking about arrangements, not life,' Jamie said.

'All our lives are on hold, as you put it, until this is over: yours, mine and Annie's.'

'See you in Stone Bridge, then,' Olivia said.

'When?'

'I can leave tomorrow.'

'I'll need two days,' Jamie said.

They were both acutely, painfully aware that the other subject closest to their hearts had not even been mentioned.

They started out with a gentle, English country weekend with Edward and the children. The hot summer was holding, and much of Stone Bridge life seemed to be happening outdoors, with Banbury Farm House being used more for cooling-off purposes than anything else. They picnicked and barbecued and swam and cycled and went horse riding, and Annie gave everyone reflexology sessions – though in Olivia's case it was impossible because Olivia was ticklish and shrieked with laughter every time Annie touched her feet – and the slaughter of the Rothenburgs, the murder of their parents and the attempts on Olivia's own life seemed, just for those few happy days, a million years away.

And then, on the evening of Sunday, September 17th, Edward returned to London. And it was time to talk.

'I have a kind of a plan,' Olivia said. 'It's not much, but it's better than trying – and probably failing – to get the crash investigation reopened—'

'And even if we do get them to look at it all again,' Annie said, 'it'll take forever.'

'So what is this plan?' Jamie asked.

They were sitting around the table in Annie's kitchen, and it reminded Olivia and Annie of another time, back

in the winter of early 1990, when they had sat, without
Jamie, plotting their revenge against Carrie. Then, Olivia
remembered, Leo and Boots, the two cats, had slept beside
the Aga for heat, and Bella, the retriever, too, had snoozed in
the toasty warmth, but this September evening, the kitchen
seemed the coolest, least heatwave-draining place to be.

'First,' Olivia began, 'we need to be sure that we all want
the same end result.'

'Which is?' Jamie asked.

She looked at him very directly. 'I want to see Michael
pay for what he's done. I don't care how, exactly – I'm not
baying for blood, and the thought of a trial makes me sick
to my stomach—'

'Me, too,' Annie said, softly.

'But I just can't bear the thought of him getting off
scot-free,' Olivia went on. 'I mean, he's gone unpunished
for nineteen years, for Christ's sake, but at least none of
us knew the truth.' She paused. 'But we know now.'

No one spoke.

'Okay.' Olivia gave a small smile. 'Here's my plan, for
what it's worth, which may not be a damn.' She paused.
'I want us to sit on them – all of them, except Michael. I
want us to be wherever they are, all the time. I want us to
fly to Boston and hire investigators to do the legwork, so
that we can just move in at all the right moments. I want
them to see us wherever they go. I want to bug them, to
haunt them, to goad them. I want us to drive them nuts.'
Her face was very serious now. 'I want them to know that
we haven't gone away. That we're never going to go away.
That they can't just bury what you told them on Michael's
birthday and forget it ever happened.'

'Why not Michael?' Jamie asked. 'You said all of them
except Michael.'

'Because sitting on Michael would be a waste of time and effort,' Olivia answered. 'Because Michael has no conscience – he might even have enough nerve to stick a lawyer, or even the police, onto us. But Louise and Peter and Daisy are different – you both told me how shocked they were that night in the library.'

'They managed to forget quickly enough,' Jamie said, bitter again.

'They haven't forgotten,' Annie said. 'They're just weak and unprincipled and afraid—'

'And greedy,' Jamie added.

'And probably very confused,' Olivia said, surprisingly gently. 'I've had a lot of time to think about it from their side, Jamie, and I think I can almost understand the temptation to try to forget it.'

'I can't,' Jamie said.

'I said almost – and of course you can't understand,' Olivia said. 'You're so different from them – you're as different from Peter as Carlos was from Juan Luis. Peter is unprincipled, and he's a bastard, but I think he's more of a fool than actively wicked. There may just be hope for Peter.'

Annie was warming to the plan. 'Thinking back to that night, and the way she reacted, I don't think it would take too much to sway Louise.'

'Or Daisy,' Jamie added. 'Daisy's fundamentally decent.'

'Provoke them all enough, make them all uneasy enough – *panic* them enough,' Olivia said, 'and who knows, they may just turn on Michael.'

Less than six days later, on Saturday, September 23rd, when Peter emerged from Angie Rogos's apartment on Park Avenue where he'd spent the night, Olivia, waiting outside on the sidewalk, looked right through them. And when, two and a half hours later, Daisy Arias stepped blithely out of B. Loren where she'd just had her nails wrapped, Annie was standing out on Newbury Street doing the same thing. And when, an hour or so after that, Louise came away from her homeless charity luncheon at the Ritz-Carlton, she saw Jamie leaning against a lamppost directly opposite where her chauffeur was waiting with her grey Bentley.

Each of them looked disturbed.

'It's Peter's birthday on Monday,' Jamie told Olivia at the end of the first day, 'and Carrie says she knows they're all going to be in New York having dinner at Le Bernardin.'

'You told Carrie about our plan?' Olivia was startled.

'She called me about some Beaumont-Arias business,' Jamie explained, 'and I made a snap decision. She's on our side in this, Olivia – I think she proved that back in Newport – and she thinks it would really freak them all out if the three of us got a table close by.'

'She's right,' Olivia admitted.

'But don't you have to book weeks in advance to get reservations at Le Bernardin?' Annie said.

'I'll get us a table,' Olivia said, 'even if I have to buy the place.'

They all agreed, late on Monday night in the suite they were sharing at the Plaza, that the collective discomfort of the Ariases had indeed been wondrous to behold. Which was not, they decided, all that surprising when they considered that during the course of that same day – many hours before Annie, Olivia and Jamie had been shown to the next table at Le Bernardin – Louise had been startled and openly upset to see Olivia at La Guardia getting off the same Boston–New York shuttle she'd just flown in on; Peter had looked jolted when he'd spied Annie buying the *Times* in the lobby of the Arias Shipping Building on Third Avenue; and Daisy, pink-faced with embarrassment and unease, had spotted Jamie watching her paying for three brassieres and matching panties in Bloomingdale's lingerie department.

'It's working,' Olivia said. 'I really think it's working.'

'What's really getting to them all,' Jamie said, 'is that we haven't made a single attempt to speak to any of them.'

'Did you see Michael's face when we sat down tonight?' Annie said with satisfaction.

'Talk about *wrath*,' Olivia said.

'I thought he looked a little sick,' Jamie disagreed.

'I was talking about Louise,' Olivia said, with pleasure. 'Daisy's just mortified by the whole thing and Peter's obviously feeling like hell. But I still think it's Louise who holds the most power when it comes to Michael – and Louise is most definitely getting mad.'

'With us or with Michael?' Annie asked.

'With us, obviously, but she has to be starting to ask herself if staying with Michael is quite the decision she thought it was.'

'How did you think Michael looked?' Jamie asked Olivia.

'I don't know.' The pleasure went out of her eyes. 'I don't think I can judge anything too well when it comes to Michael. He's too sly – he has too many faces.'

It seemed to go on and on, the three of them darting back and forth between Boston, Newport and Manhattan, constantly alerted by the electronic pagers issued to them by the investigation agency to their subjects' whereabouts.

'How much longer?' Annie, losing confidence, asked Olivia over breakfast on the terrace at the Stanhope on Friday morning. 'How much longer before we give this up and take the long haul approach?'

'Not much longer,' Olivia said, refilling her coffee cup and starting on her scrambled eggs.

'You still think there's hope?' Jamie, too, was growing pessimistic and increasingly depressed about his family. 'Nothing's happening.'

'We don't know that for sure,' Olivia said. 'A lot may be happening behind closed doors.' She looked at them. 'Am I the only one eating here?'

'I'm not really hungry.' Annie pushed her plate to one side.

'They may be fighting,' Jamie said. 'Louise and Peter probably are giving Michael a hard time, and Daisy's probably on the phone every day wanting to know what they're going to do. But I'll bet you Michael's probably telling them right back that all they have to do is hold on and we'll go away.'

'Which we will,' Annie said, 'sooner or later.'

'I won't,' Olivia said, quietly.

'You'll have to, ultimately,' Jamie said.

'No,' Olivia said. 'I won't give up.'

'What do you mean?' Annie asked.

'What I say.' Olivia bit off a piece of bagel and cream cheese. 'Don't look like that, Annie – I'm not going to do anything crazy – I'm not going to buy a gun or buy my own hitman, tempting as the thought is—'

'Not just to you,' Jamie said.

'I don't see the joke,' Annie said. 'And what do you mean when you say you won't give up or go away?'

'I don't know,' Olivia answered frankly.

'You don't have some other plan then?'

Olivia smiled. 'No, Annie, I don't. Just this one.'

'But don't you think we may have to change our tactics soon?' Jamie asked. 'If we don't achieve anything this way.' He paused. 'I mean, maybe it's time to stop trying to psych them out from a distance – maybe we need to start attacking close up.'

'Maybe,' Olivia said. 'Except that once we actively harass them, we'll be giving Michael grounds to take out an injunction against us.'

Annie sighed. 'So we keep on as we are.'

'I guess,' Jamie said, 'for the time being.'

'So we're all agreed?' Olivia asked.

'I guess,' Jamie said again.

Olivia glanced at him again, surreptitiously, anxiously. 'Are you okay?' she asked him, quietly.

'Just about.' Jamie looked into her eyes, then swiftly looked away again. 'How about you?'

'Hanging in,' Olivia said.

Annie looked from one to the other, and longed, abruptly, to kick them both. But she said nothing at all.

That Saturday night, while Annie stayed at the Plaza so that she could dog Peter's movements over the weekend and while Jamie stayed home so he could go on giving Daisy the jitters, Olivia chose to overnight at the Inn at Castle Hill in Newport. Ostensibly, she was there to spend a restful morning and early afternoon and still be on hand for when Louise and Michael left the house to return to New York as they often did on Sunday evening. But her real intention – which she had shared neither with Jamie nor Annie – was to attend the eleven o'clock Sunday morning Mass at St Mary's Roman Catholic Church, because she remembered Daisy telling her – an hour or so before she'd fallen off Cliff Walk all those years ago – that when Louise and Michael weekended in Rhode Island, they generally made a point of going to the mid-morning Mass at the old Catholic church where Jacqueline Bouvier had married John F. Kennedy.

Olivia sensed, even before she left the Inn, that if this too-vague, too-imprecise plan of hers was ultimately to succeed, this encounter might be the most telling, perhaps the most crucial of all. She gathered from Jamie that even more than her husband, Louise Arias was a devout Catholic, and Olivia was not particularly proud of using religion to her own ends. But on the other hand – given that she was dealing with a man who had, in all probability, been receiving absolution for all of the nineteen years since he had killed Arthur and Emily, Grace and Franklin, Carlos Arias and the pilot of their helicopter – she found that she was not particularly ashamed either.

She watched their arrival, watched the chauffeur open the rear doors of Michael's limousine, watched Louise straighten her black skirt with one gloved hand, watched Michael place a supportive hand beneath his wife's elbow, and knew the instant when they both, simultaneously, saw her, observed the look of true desperation on Louise's face and the flash of hot rage on Michael's, and relished it all.

Olivia stood perfectly still, waiting, her eyes cool and remote, and she realized, as the Ariases recovered and turned their backs and walked slowly and decorously up the steps into the church, that they believed they would be safe from her once they were inside.

Oh, no, she thought, *you don't get off that easily*.

She waited five minutes more and then, just before the

service was due to begin, she took a Hermès headscarf from her shoulder bag, unfolded it and tied it, fittingly Jackie Kennedy style, over her dark hair, and then she, too, walked into St Mary's.

It was cool and peaceful and three-quarters filled. Ahead of her, men, women and children were dipping their fingers into holy water, were making the sign of the cross and then genuflecting before taking their seats, and Olivia felt out of place, felt almost tempted to go through the motions, but she refrained, looking around instead for Michael and Louise. And they were pretty much where she had expected them to be – almost at the front, in the second pew over to the right of the altar – and pretty much as she had pictured them, on their knees, beneath one of the stained-glass windows, the picture of piety.

Olivia looked for a seat – the right seat – and it was there, and it was even more perfect than she'd hoped for, right behind Michael in the third pew. Slowly, smoothly, she made her way down the centre aisle and slid into the seat just as both Ariases rose from their knees.

'Good morning,' she said.

They turned. Louise's face was white, her lips tightly compressed. Michael's was unreadable, except for the hate in his dark, almost black eyes.

I wish you dead, those eyes said.

Olivia smiled.

'What time's confession?' she asked.

Louise looked as if she had been slapped.

The Mass began.

Olivia went out ahead of them when it was over, and her stomach was churning a little, but she felt, on the whole, quite calm.. She waited on Memorial Boulevard, close, but not too close, to where the limousine was waiting, several cars away from the church; watched them emerge, exchanging swift, tight-lipped greetings and smiles with acquaintances and friends, watched them walk towards her slowly, arms linked – not, Olivia felt, for closeness, more, she thought, because Louise required the support.

'Have you no shame?' Michael asked, softly, menacingly, when they were about a foot away.

'Hello, Michael,' Olivia said. 'Hello, Louise. No time for confession this morning?' She almost felt the other woman's tremor, but felt no compassion. 'Maybe you can come back later, or doesn't it work like that?'

'I'm surprised at you,' Michael said. 'I was sure you'd have learned your lesson by now.'

'Which lesson is that?' Olivia looked at Louise. 'Does he mean having my arm broken, do you think? Or being locked in a safe to suffocate?'

'Michael, I want to go,' Louise said, still holding onto his arm.

'What if Peter's children had been with us?' Michael asked Olivia.

'Michael—' Louise was whiter than ever.

'What *about* the children, Louise?' Again, Olivia ignored Michael. 'What will they think when Michael's put on trial for murder? When the whole truth comes out?'

'Please,' Louise said. '*Please*.'

'Please what, Louise?' Olivia asked quietly. 'Please leave you alone, so that you can protect your murderer husband?' She looked around, saw that there were still a growing number of people standing around, and it was a lovely morning, and no one seemed in any rush to go home. 'Shall I say it more loudly, Louise?'

'Do that,' Michael said, violently, 'and you'll regret it.'

'Will I? I don't think so.'

'Get in the car, Louise.' Michael removed his arm from his wife's.

'I will start saying it more loudly soon, Louise,' Olivia said. 'We all will. Jamie, and Annie and her family, and I – and there are just too many of us for Michael to silence now.'

'Louise, get in the car,' Michael said again.

Louise started moving towards the car, but Olivia moved with her. 'Surely you must realize, Louise,' she kept on at her, 'that it can only be a matter of time before all this shit hits—'

Still sidling along the sidewalk, Louise began to cry and Michael put out his right hand and pushed Olivia hard—

'Go on, Michael.' She almost fell, recovered, kept on moving with Louise. 'I dare you, I *dare* you – and you, too, Louise – I warn you, for your own sake, do something about this man soon, before it's too late—'

'Michael!' Louise tried to grab at his sleeve. '*Do* something!'

'Get away from my wife,' Michael spat at Olivia.

'Dump him, Louise.' Olivia was getting breathless now, but she wasn't through yet. She knew this was it, this was her one big chance, sensed that she had all but penetrated this poor woman's remaining defences, that she was almost there. 'Distance yourself before he destroys you all. Do it whichever way you like – I don't care, I really don't care how you do it, but stop protecting him before it's too late.'

They were almost at the limo, and the chauffeur had the back kerbside door open, and Olivia saw from his face that he'd heard what she'd been saying.

'See him, Louise – he's heard us, and he's wondering what's going on, and he won't be alone—'

Louise scrambled and half fell into the back of the limousine.

'Think of your reputation, Louise. Don't let him drag you down. You didn't know my father, did you? But you knew Carlos – of course you knew Carlos – he was a good Catholic, like you—'

'You go to *hell*,' Michael said.

He pushed her again as he passed her to get into the car after his wife, and Olivia felt the weight of his body against her shoulder, and again she staggered a little and almost fell, and again she felt the force of his loathing, his unspoken wish for her death.

But bending down, looking into the dim car, past his livid, furious, bitter face, and seeing Louise Arias's eyes for the last time – staring, weeping, horrified eyes – Olivia felt nothing but triumph.

It was Monday evening, back at Jamie's apartment, before Carrie telephoned to give them the news.

That Louise and Michael had stayed over in Newport on Sunday night, and that Louise had woken up later than usual that morning, and that when she had realized that her husband had not yet come back from the early swim he took most mornings in an inlet near the house, she had raised the alarm.

Michael's body had been found late that afternoon. It was clear that death had been by drowning. There were, according to the Newport police, no suspicious circumstances, and when questioned about her husband's state of mind, Louise said that Michael had been in an excellent mood following a peaceful weekend – so peaceful that they had made their decision to stay at the house for one more night.

*   *   *

'Seems we did it,' Annie said, very quietly.

'I guess so,' Jamie said.

'Are you okay?' she asked him.

'I don't really know,' he answered.

They both looked over at Olivia. She was standing in the glass-enclosed alcove in Jamie's sitting room, staring out over Boston Harbour. She had hardly spoken since the call.

'Livvy?' Annie said. 'Are you all right?'

She didn't answer.

Jamie stood up, went over to her, laid a hand on her right shoulder.

'What are you thinking?'

Olivia didn't turn around, didn't trust herself to look at him.

'That I killed a man,' she said.

'No.' Jamie's voice was clear and firm. 'No, you didn't.'

'As good as.'

She had told them about St Mary's, had told them what she had said and done, and neither of them had blamed her for going as far as she had, for both Jamie and Annie had shared the same sense of relief because that part of this awful time was over now.

'None of us thought Michael would kill himself,' Annie said from the middle of the room.

'You couldn't have known what was going to happen,' Jamie said.

'Couldn't I?'

At last, Olivia turned around.

'I don't think either of you understands.' Her eyes seemed darker with the intensity of her self-examination. 'It isn't the knowledge that I pushed Louise to the point where she must have told Michael he had little choice. It isn't even the fact that I as good as dragged him into the ocean for that last swim—'

'Livvy, don't,' Annie said, distressed.

'It's the fact' – Olivia wasn't finished yet – 'that I can't pretend to feel a scrap of remorse for it. Oh, sure, I feel bad for Louise and for the family – that's easy enough to do. But the fact is – the cold, hard truth – is that I'm glad, really *glad*, that Michael Arias is dead.'

'And do you think I'm not?' Jamie asked, gently.

'Do you think we don't both feel that way about it?' Annie moved closer.

Olivia shook her head. 'It isn't the same.'

'Why not?' Annie asked.

'Because you didn't do it,' Olivia said, simply. 'I did.'

The coroner's verdict was death by misadventure. At the funeral, one week after the inquest, Jamie, back in England with Olivia and Annie, was the only member of the Arias family who did not attend. The eulogies, Carrie reported to them afterwards, were glowingly panegyric.

The man in the black leather jacket was never found.

27

Dukesfield Fell: July 4th, 1996

'Do you think,' Olivia asked the others, nearly ten months later, as they stood on the familiar, windswept, rugged hillside, 'we've done the right things since then, made the right decisions?'

'Don't you?' asked Annie.

'I asked you first,' Olivia said.

Annie waited a moment. 'Yes,' she said. 'Under the circumstances, yes, I do.'

'Jamie?' Olivia asked.

'You know what I think.'

'I'd like to hear it again. Here, in this place.'

Jamie nodded. 'Then no, I don't think anything we've done has been exactly right. None of it's been fitting, or proper. Justice has not been served.' He paused, felt the cool summer wind ruffle his hair. 'But I think we did the best we could.'

'Livvy?' Annie looked at her. 'What about you?'

Olivia's green eyes were very distant, her wide mouth a hard, straight line. 'I hate it all so much,' she said. 'I still hate it so much that it hurts me, physically, to think about it. To think that Juan Luis got away with it, and then Michael—'

'Michael didn't exactly get away with it,' Annie said.

'Oh yes, he did,' Olivia said. 'That's exactly what he did. And I hate it. And I hate, almost more than that, that Jamie still feels responsible for what those two men did – even if you say you don't, Jamie, I see it in your eyes. And I hate it.' She shook her head. 'And yet—'

'And yet?' Jamie nudged her gently.

'And yet I know we did do the best we could.' Olivia looked down at the ground, at the place where their parents had died. 'And that it has to be enough.'

They had done what they could. They had, for the sake of Peter's children, gone along with Louise's pleas for silence, and, in exchange, Louise had agreed that part of Juan Luis's collection should be auctioned for the most fitting of the charities sponsored by the Arthur Segal Foundation, and the remainder donated, in Emanuel Rothenburg's name, to museums in New York, Berlin, Paris, Tel Aviv and Zurich.

They had done what they could, yet in the months that had followed Michael Arias's death, as the three friends had come to see – if not to wholly accept – that it was too late for true justice to be done, Jamie had suffered more than the others, living as he had to with the knowledge of his family's crimes. Olivia and Annie reminded him, over and over again, how much they loved him, told him that it was insane for him to feel even the remotest shred of guilt, yet still he could not seem to shed the shame. He felt, he tried to explain to them, as if he needed to give up everything he owned, to scrub away every trace of the blood money that had helped make him the man he was.

'For heaven's sake,' Olivia told him impatiently on

the phone one day before Thanksgiving, 'you're not a goddamned monk – stop whipping yourself and get on with your life.'

'That's almost exactly what Carrie told me last week,' Jamie said.

'You're in touch quite a lot these days,' Olivia said, jealousy rising as it always did now, had, against her better nature, ever since Carrie had redeemed herself by coming to their aid.

'We have lunch,' Jamie said, 'every now and again. It's easier now that her divorce from Peter's been finalized.'

'Anyway,' Olivia said, grudgingly, 'Carrie's right. You should listen to her and stop giving yourself such a hard time.'

'Maybe,' Jamie said, but they both knew he didn't really believe it.

'Isn't it time,' Annie said when she called Olivia a few days later, 'you shook him out of this?'

'How can I? We've both tried often enough.'

'You know how.'

'What do you mean?'

'Be honest with him,' Annie said. 'About your feelings for him.' She paused. 'Don't you think it's time you both opened up about the fact that you're in love with each other?'

Olivia was startled. 'How did you know?'

'Don't be absurd, Livvy,' Annie answered. 'I've known for years.'

Olivia thought about it for a few moments. 'It won't work, you know, Annie. Even if he does still feel the way I do, Jamie doesn't think he deserves anything good to happen to him any more.'

'You'll find a way,' Annie said, positively.

*　　*　　*

Olivia had found it by courtesy of Paul Osterman. She had been trying, for a few months, to trace his family in Philadelphia, and early that December she learned that his wife had died some years back, but that his son now lived in Florida with his own family. She wrote to Simon Osterman at the end of the month and received, in response, the warmest of letters, inviting her to bring Jamie and Annie to his home in Fort Lauderdale.

They all went together in March – Annie accompanied by Edward and their children – but Jamie, Annie and Olivia went alone to their first meeting with Osterman, and they talked, at great length, about the burden that his father had carried to his grave, and they talked, too, about culpability and restitution and guilt. And Simon Osterman advised Jamie to focus his mind on the goodness of his father rather than on the evil of his other relatives, for it was transparently clear to him that Jamie was his father's son; and by the time they were ready to go home, Jamie had begun to feel a little easier in his mind, had begun to look towards the future.

'So what about you two?' Osterman's wife, a warm, easy-going woman, had asked Jamie and Olivia in their back garden on their last evening. 'Any plans to get married?'

'Not yet,' Olivia answered, and the look that Jamie threw at her was so filled with surprise and confusion and, underscoring it all, with purest love, that she had to suppress her own sudden urge to crow with delight.

And Jamie had reached for her hand.

'But soon,' he had said.

They made love that night, at long last, in Jamie's room at their hotel, and it was not the way it had been all those years before in Boston, nor was it as either of them had pictured it during those hot, frustrating days and nights they'd spent denying themselves in Brussels. There was passion, and there was desire, and, ultimately, there was the most glorious staving of the hunger they had both experienced for so long, but it was less wild, less driven than they had anticipated, and there was a peacefulness about it, a sweetness and rightness that spoke volumes about what they could expect in the years to come.

They had been married less than two months later, in May, after Olivia had given up her apartment in Brussels and moved, with Cleo, into Jamie's place in Boston, and they were making plans to move JAA to New York, where Olivia knew there would never be a shortage of clients for the Segal Translation Agency.

And on July 4th they all went together, as they had ten years earlier, and almost ten years before that, up to Dukesfield Fell, where the helicopter had plunged back to earth and scattered their parents' remains over the hillside, and they held each other in the chill but sweet-smelling summer wind, and remembered.

'I find myself wishing sometimes,' Olivia said, 'that I'd never found Carlos's note, and that I'd never opened my father's box.'

'But if you hadn't,' Annie said, 'we would never have known any of it.'

'But are we better off for knowing?' Olivia asked. 'Is anyone?'

'I think so,' Jamie said. 'I think Anton Rothenburg would think so.'

'I'd like to believe that,' Olivia said.